PENGUIN  CLA

MARY/MARIA/MATILDA

MARY WOLLSTONECRAFT (1759–97) was an educational, political and feminist writer who early in her life worked as a companion, teacher and governess. In 1788 she settled in London as a translator and reader for the publisher Joseph Johnson, becoming part of the radical set that included Paine, Blake, Godwin and the painter Fuseli. Her great work, *A Vindication of the Rights of Woman*, was published in 1792. She lived in Paris during the French Revolution and had a child by the American Gilbert Imlay, who deserted her. She returned to London in 1795 and, following her attempted suicide, became involved with Godwin, whom she married in 1797, shortly before the birth (which proved fatal) of her daughter, the future Mary Shelley. She left several unfinished works, including *Maria*.

MARY SHELLEY was born in London in 1797, daughter of William Godwin and Mary Wollstonecraft. After her mother's death in childbirth, Mary experienced an intellectually stimulating though emotionally difficult childhood. In 1814 she met and soon fell in love with the poet Percy Bysshe Shelley; in July they eloped to the continent. In 1816, after Shelley's first wife Harriet committed suicide, Mary and Percy married. Of the four children she bore Shelley, only Percy Florence survived. The couple lived in Italy from 1818 until 1822, when Shelley drowned in a boating accident. Mary returned with her son to London, where she continued to live as a professional writer until her death in 1851. She is best known for her work *Frankenstein*, but among her other novels are *The Last Man*, a dystopic story set in the twenty-first century (1826), *Perkin Warbeck* (1830), *Lodore* (1835) and *Falkner* (1837).

JANET TODD has been a pioneer in the recovery of early women writers. She has worked in universities in Africa, the United States and Britain, and is currently the Francis Hutcheson Professor of English at the University of Glasgow and an Honorary Fellow of Lucy Cavendish College, Cambridge. She is the author of more than fifteen works of non-fiction, including most recently biographies of Aphra Behn (1996) and Mary Wollstonecraft (2000).

MARY WOLLSTONECRAFT

Mary · Maria

MARY SHELLEY

Matilda

Edited by JANET TODD

PENGUIN BOOKS

PENGUIN BOOKS

Published by the Penguin Group
Penguin Books Ltd, 80 Strand, London WC2R 0RL, England
Penguin Group (USA), Inc., 375 Hudson Street, New York, New York 10014, USA
Penguin Books Australia Ltd, 250 Camberwell Road, Camberwell, Victoria 3124, Australia
Penguin Books Canada Ltd, 10 Alcorn Avenue, Toronto, Ontario, Canada M4V 3B2
Penguin Books India (P) Ltd, 11 Community Centre, Panchsheel Park, New Delhi – 110 017, India
Penguin Books (NZ) Ltd, Cnr Rosedale and Airborne Roads, Albany, Auckland, New Zealand
Penguin Books (South Africa) (Pty) Ltd, 24 Sturdee Avenue, Rosebank 2196, South Africa

Penguin Books Ltd, Registered Offices: 80 Strand, London WC2R 0RL, England

www.penguin.com

This edition first published by Pickering & Chatto (Publishers) 1991
Published in Penguin Classics 1992
Reprinted with a new Chronology and revised Bibliography 2004

035

Editorial material copyright © Janet Todd, 1991, 2004
Text of *Matilda* copyright © North Carolina University Press, 1959
All rights reserved

The moral right of the editor has been asserted

Printed and bound in Great Britain by Clays Ltd, Elcograf S.p.A.

ISBN-13: 978-0-140-43371-5

CONTENTS

Introduction   vii
Note on the Text   xxviii
Bibliography   xxix

Mary Wollstonecraft

Mary   1
Maria   55

Mary Shelley

Matilda   149

Chronology   219

INTRODUCTION

In the Preface to her first novel *Mary, a Fiction* (1788), Mary Wollstonecraft wrote that no work would last that did not show the soul of the author. In the Advertisement to the last book published in her lifetime, *Letters from Sweden* (1796), she declared that she 'could not avoid being continually the first person – "the little hero of each tale"'; she had tried to correct the fault 'if it be one', but, having failed, had finally concluded that 'A person has a right ... to talk of himself when he can win on our attention by acquiring our affection'. After years of publishing such fictional works as *Frankenstein*, which critics have insistently interpreted through biography, Mary Shelley wrote, 'I am a great enemy to the prevailing custom of dragging private life before the world.'[1]

For the first time this book brings together three extraordinary fictions of the 'extraordinary ... pair' of mother and daughter, Mary Wollstonecraft Godwin and Mary Wollstonecraft Godwin Shelley.[2] The works, *Mary, a Fiction*, *The Wrongs of Woman: or, Maria* and *Matilda*, are not the highest aesthetic achievement of either author but, interacting as they do across the grave of Mary Wollstonecraft who died of complications following her daughter's birth in 1797, they gain psychological and allusive resonance through association with each other and with the experiences of their authors.[3] Biographical criticism is not currently fashionable but it is hard to avoid noting the linkages of life and literature in two writers called Mary, who named their fictional heroines Mary, Maria and Matilda, who in a way wrote parts of the same novel – for Mary Shelley's *Matilda* in its original version, 'The Fields of Fancy', was a reworking of her mother's unfinished tale, 'The Cave of Fancy' – and whose lives are tangled with those of two men: the philosopher and novelist William Godwin, who published his wife's *Maria* but refused to publish his daughter's *Matilda*, and the poet Percy Bysshe Shelley, whose love for his future wife Mary developed by the grave of the mother whom he so much admired. *Mary* and *Matilda* are both passionate introverted works, bound up in the intense relationships of their authors and demanding sympathy for these authors beyond the narrative; while falling into this mode at times in its depiction of the middle-class heroine, *Maria* is a more socially conscious, less self-indulgent novel, remarkable for the way it moves from the author's immediate experience to show the complicated miseries of women of many classes. All three novels have at their centres the exploration of the identity and subjectivity of women caught within the 'magic circle' of constructed femininity and the claustrophobic nuclear family unit.

MARY WOLLSTONECRAFT

Mary Wollstonecraft was born in 1759, the eldest daughter in a family of seven children. She soon came to resent her father, who, during her childhood, sank from would-be gentleman farmer to impecunious drunkard and, in his descent, often treated her mother with contempt. Equally she resented her mother for her meekness under the treatment and, even more, for her socially sanctioned preference for the eldest son over the eldest daughter. The despotic parenting of this mismatched pair is, according to Godwin's *Memoirs*[4] of his wife, depicted in *Maria* in the heroine's unsatisfactory childhood, and it forms a model for the opening pages of *Mary*. The young girl sought comfort from her blighting home life in intense friendships with other girls in which she insisted that she have 'first place' or none. The most important of these friendships was with Fanny Blood, a genteel but poor girl whom, from the age of sixteen, Wollstonecraft loved 'better than all the world beside'. Immediately on meeting the 'slender and elegant' Fanny who was ministering to her family in their shabby house, she took, 'in her heart, the vows of an eternal friendship'.[5]

It was a bookish age and, according to Godwin's *Memoirs*, the encounter of the two girls was like the fictional meeting of the chief characters in Goethe's *Young Werther*,[6] in which the narcissistic and passionate hero loves the domestic and pretty Charlotte. By the age of eighteen Wollstonecraft was dreaming of a life with Fanny Blood and, in a bid for independence, she left her family and took a place as a lady's companion in Bath. In this fashionable resort she saw herself as a 'spectator' of society, refusing to 'dress violently' like other girls and declaring herself averse to marriage.[7] She still, however, felt the pull of feminine duty and, when after two years she heard of her mother's illness, she left her place to tend her.

After her mother's death she moved in with Fanny Blood's impoverished family and helped them earn a living through sewing. The Bloods were in a lower social position than Wollstonecraft had been used to and Fanny's sister possibly became a prostitute and certainly entered the workhouse. Some of Wollstonecraft's experiences during this time might well have informed her depiction of lower-class suffering in *Maria*. But again she was interrupted by her family's needs. Her younger married sister Eliza had borne a child and was suffering a postpartum breakdown; Wollstonecraft saw her as a victim of matrimony and boldly rescued her from both husband and baby, recognising however, the unconventional nature of her act: 'I knew I should be ... the *shameful incendiary* in this shocking affair of a woman's leaving her bedfellow,' she wrote to her other sister Everina.[8] When she used this episode of the runagate wife in her last novel, she sent the wife into hiding with her baby, only to have it snatched away later by the husband; in the real-life situation the baby remained with the husband and soon died.

With Fanny and her two sisters, Eliza and Everina, Wollstonecraft now planned to start a school in which they could all work and support themselves. Fanny Blood, the most experienced in poverty, was sceptical of the plan and was, in addition, eager to marry a young merchant now working in Portugal. After several false starts, a successful school was established in Newington Green where Wollstonecraft enjoyed the company of radical Dissenters such as Richard Price and became exposed to libertarian political and social ideas. By this time the power relationship between the two friends, Fanny and Mary, had clearly shifted, for, as Godwin wrote in the *Memoirs*:

> The first feeling with which Mary had contemplated her friend, was a sentiment of inferiority and reverence; but that, from the operation of a ten years' acquaintance was considerably changed. Fanny had originally been far before her in literary attainments; this disparity no longer existed. In whatever degree Mary might endeavour to free herself from the delusions of self-esteem, this period of observation upon her own mind and that of her friend, could not pass, without her perceiving that there were some essential characteristics of genius, which she possessed, and in which her friend was deficient. The principal of these was a firmness of mind, an unconquerable greatness of soul, by which, after a short internal struggle, she was accustomed to rise above difficulties and suffering. Whatever Mary undertook, she perhaps in all instances accomplished; and, to her lofty spirit, scarcely any thing she desired, appeared hard to perform. Fanny, on the contrary, was a woman of a timid and irresolute nature, accustomed to yield to difficulties, and probably priding herself in this morbid softness of her temper.[9]

The work at Newington Green was interrupted at the end of 1785 when Fanny Blood, now consumptive, went to Portugal to marry; ten months later Wollstonecraft set sail for Lisbon to help her ailing friend through childbirth. She arrived there in time to see Fanny die. It was the end of her longest attachment. In death Fanny seems to have recaptured some of her earlier charm for her friend and, many years later, when Wollstonecraft wrote *Letters from Sweden*, she was experiencing her as a valued presence: 'The grave has closed over a dear friend, the friend of my youth; still she is present with me, and I hear her soft voice warbling as I stray over the heath'.[10]

Back in London Wollstonecraft found her school in shambles, wrote a book on how to bring up daughters, and used the money to help establish Fanny Blood's parents in Ireland. With little chance of rescuing her school and no longer wanting 'cohabitation with her sisters', who, according to Godwin, did not share her 'activity and ardent spirit of adventure', she took the final ladylike option of employment and became a governess on Lord and Lady Kingsborough's estate in Ireland.

It was not a derisory post for a barely educated young woman but it was deeply unsuited to Wollstonecraft's dominating and independent character.

Almost at once she clashed with Lady Kingsborough, regarded rather like the eldest Wollstonecraft brother as the holder of improper and corrupting privilege. The governess's literary response was a stream of letters alternating abjectness and arrogance and complaining of headaches and nameless fevers. Despite her contempt for women's romantic fiction, which she saw as self-indulgent and weakly wish-fulfilling, she herself began a novel at this time. She entitled the work *Mary, a Fiction*; Godwin wrote of it, 'A considerable part of this story consists, with certain modifications, of the incidents of her own friendship with Fanny'.[11]

Along with her friendship with Fanny Blood, *Mary* also reflected Wollstonecraft's past life at home and her present life at work. In the novel, the heroine Mary is given Lady Kingsborough's land and rank, but she keeps her creator's sensibility and self-conscious virtue. The fictional Mary's mother receives Lady Kingsborough's hated lapdogs and Wollstonecraft's own mother's marriage to a bestial man, while Mary like her creator finds comfort in friendship with a refined but ultimately inadequate girl whom she watches die in Portugal as Wollstonecraft had watched Fanny die. In the last year of her life Wollstonecraft mentioned *Mary, a Fiction* as 'a crude production' of her earlier years, one that she would 'not very willingly put ... in the way of people whose good opinion, as a writer, I wish for'. But Godwin thought otherwise:

> This little work, if Mary had never produced any thing else, would serve, with persons of true taste and sensibility, to establish the eminence of her genius. The story is nothing. He that looks into the book only for incident, will probably lay it down with disgust. But the feelings are of the truest and most exquisite class; every circumstance is adorned with that species of imagination, which enlists itself under the banners of delicacy and sentiment. A work of sentiment, as it is called, is too often another name for a work of affectation. He that should imagine that the sentiments of this book are affected, would indeed be entitled to our profoundest commiseration.[12]

Mary has considerable interest as a late work of sensibility and indeed some of the heroine's sentimental effusions were excerpted in an anthology illustrating the literary beauties of sensibility. In addition, it has value as an early effort at the creation of an alienated intellectual woman, the beginning of a line that would include the more substantial heroines of *Jane Eyre* and *Villette*, women who tried to make their own way in the world and who expressed a complex misery at their situation and at the feminine images available to them. Inevitably the book also interests as self-representation for, although fictional, it suggests something of Wollstonecraft's vision of herself as a young woman and her sense of impasse in her claustrophobic feminine world. It is ironic that the novel was written just before momentous changes in her life.

After just one year of employment the governess was dismissed by Lady

Kingsborough. As an alternative to the usual middle-class female roles of companion, teacher and governess which she had now experienced, Wollstonecraft left for London to take up a post with the publisher Joseph Johnson, a contact gained during her Newington Green period. Soon she became one of his 'Menagerie of Live Authors' and the assistant on his new magazine, the liberal *Analytical Review*. She exaggerated when she wrote that she was going to be 'the first of a new genus', but it was an unusual role for a woman, one that it is hard to imagine open to her sentimental heroine in *Mary, a Fiction*, the work Wollstonecraft brought with her for publication. She also brought the beginnings of a tale entitled 'The Cave of Fancy', which 'she thought proper afterwards to lay aside unfinished'.

Over the next months Wollstonecraft reviewed copiously, especially novels and educational works, began a book of stories for children, and translated from languages she barely knew. At Johnson's dinner table she met many literary men and women, such as William Blake, Thomas Paine, and Anna Laetitia Barbauld and, briefly and inauspiciously, William Godwin. Her melancholy moods continued but she was beginning to doubt the value of that painful and self-admiring sensibility so extolled in *Mary, a Fiction* as 'the foundation of all our happiness'. She worried over the association of women with acute feeling, seeing it as a trap which encouraged them to indulge themselves with romantic and comforting visions which blotted out a reality of political subordination.

The chance to express her new doubts came with events in England following the French Revolution. In 1790 with the writing of *A Vindication of the Rights of Men* she entered the public controversy over the general political and social significance of the Revolution, begun by her old friend Richard Price from Newington Green; a year later she was extending her libertarian social principles to her own sex in *A Vindication of the Rights of Woman*. In both books she blamed women for accepting belittling images of themselves, for taking pleasure in the momentary gallantry of courtship, and for relying on sensibility and romantic hopes of men instead of battling for rational improvement in themselves which alone would allow society as a whole to progress: 'I love man as my fellow; but his sceptre, real, or usurped, extends not to me', she declared.[13]

Unfortunately, even while she was writing the rational *Rights of Woman* she found herself inspired by the first documented 'irrational' passion of her life: with a fellow reviewer on the *Analytical*, the recently married bisexual painter and philosopher Henry Fuseli for whom she felt, in Godwin's words, 'a Platonic affection': 'The delight she enjoyed in his society, she transferred by association to his person'.[14] By now she was apparently enacting Rousseau's *La Nouvelle Héloise*[15] rather than Goethe's *Young Werther* and she contemplated a real-life version of the book's heady trio of lovers, Saint-Preux, Julie and the passionate female friend Claire. To the Fuselis she suggested a *ménage à trois* with herself as intellectual friend, but her offer was rejected by the wife marked out for the fleshly part.

After the rebuff, Wollstonecraft set off for Paris alone, arriving there at the end of the period of political moderation in late 1792. She saw the king going to the trial that would end in his death, and the pathos of the event and her isolation made her vulnerable to doubt; for a short time she questioned her convictions about the desirability of the Revolution and her belief in the perfectibility of society through political action and right reason. Her isolation also made her vulnerable on a personal level and she soon found a successor to Fuseli: Gilbert Imlay, an expatriate entrepreneur from New Jersey with romantic revolutionary views.

Wollstonecraft saw in Imlay a dashing Saint-Preux, the lover of the Rousseauian heroine. Unusually describing the affair from the man's side, Virginia Woolf wrote, 'Tickling minnows he had hooked a dolphin'; Godwin, however, using another animal image, concentrated on the woman: he saw a moment of sexual awakening and made a comparison later appropriated by Shelley to express a political one: she was 'a serpent upon a rock, that casts its slough, and appears again with the brilliancy, the sleekness, and the elastic activity of its happiest age'.[16] A short idyll followed during which Wollstonecraft, as an Englishwoman, was forced out of Paris to Neuilly; from there she came to meet Imlay at the barrier, a tollgate in the Paris city wall. The child conceived at this time would be named Fanny after her dead friend.

The affair of Wollstonecraft and Imlay soon degenerated into dependence and criticism. Despite her ringing assertion of female independence in *The Rights of Woman*, she described herself as throwing out 'some tendrils, to cling to the elm by which she wished to be supported' while insisting that she was no 'parasite-plant'.[17] At the same time she was critical of Imlay's trade and trading friends. Soon his absences became frequent and long. The course of the turbulent and painful affair is charted in letters published by Godwin after her death, but something of the heady excitement of a love in social isolation such as she must have experienced in revolutionary France is caught in *Maria* which describes a passion feeding on the prisonlike atmosphere of a madhouse.

Back in London in April 1795, intermittently aware of Imlay's indifference, Wollstonecraft tried suicide, probably with an overdose of laudanum, a method later used by the heroine of *Maria*. In her misery in these months she alienated her struggling sisters with her tactlessness when she denied that they could ever expect a future together now that she was in a marital state. The breach with the sisters was never entirely bridged and may possibly have affected their relationship with her eldest daughter twenty years later. Meanwhile, Imlay's response to the suicide attempt was the proposal, quickly accepted, to send mother and baby to Scandinavia on his legal and mercantile business. In *Letters from Sweden* the hope of a reconciliation with Imlay on her return informs the romantic vision of herself which Wollstonecraft created against a backdrop of wild Scandinavian scenery; although there is much about economics and politics in this book published months after her return, it was the image of the melancholy and lonely female that especially moved her daughter Mary Shelley, a frequent reader of this work.

On her return to London, she was not met by Imlay and she soon discovered him living with another woman. Her response was a more serious suicide attempt in October 1795 when she soaked her clothes in the rain and jumped off Putney Bridge. She was rescued unconscious from the river.

In time Wollstonecraft conquered her despair over her lover's defection, resumed her reviewing and remet William Godwin, famous by now as a critic of marriage and other repressive social institutions. The love affair that followed was equal, neither being 'agent or the patient, the toil-spreader or the prey', and Godwin, like the hero of *Mary, a Fiction*, being disposed to love in reaction to the romantic sensibility he saw revealed, in his case in the recently published *Letters from Sweden*.[18] The sexual initiative seems to have been Wollstonecraft's, but perhaps the unsatisfactory contraceptive method was Godwin's; soon she conceived again and, not wishing another illegitimate birth, suggested marriage despite his public views.[19] The pair were married in St Pancras on 29 March, 1797, but kept separate social lives.

Wollstonecraft was already at work on *Maria*, in some ways an answer to the sentimental but sexually frightened *Mary* and in other ways a continuation of *A Vindication of the Rights of Woman*, which sought to generalize and ameliorate the state and status of the female sex. *Mary* (like *Matilda* later) was swiftly written under the influence of strong emotions, but *Maria*, which presented the stories of several women in different walks of life, all suffering social discrimination under patriarchal institutions, was, according to Godwin, slowly composed and often rewritten, so that she was working on it 'for more than twelve months before her decease'.[20] Despite efforts at generalization, the main heroine of the novel has an emotional childhood very similar to her creator's and loves an Imlay figure, here mediated through the literary Saint-Preux of Rousseau about whom the heroine is reading in the asylum cell. Since Maria is already married, her sexually fulfilled love for the hero becomes a plea for greater sexual freedom for women and greater control over their own lives. Although in the suicidal end the romance follows the course of the Imlay affair, some passages may well have been inspired by the new relationship with Godwin which he himself described in his *Memoirs*:

> Mary rested her head upon the shoulder of her lover, hoping to find a heart with which she might safely treasure her world of affection – fearing to commit a mistake, yet, in spite of her melancholy experience, fraught with that generous confidence, which in a great soul, is never extinguished.[21]

Unfortunately public opinion was moving against experimental styles of life and frank expressions of female desire. The book, aided by revelations of

Wollstonecraft's own unconventional life in the *Memoirs*, which also came out in 1798, became something of a cautionary tale for other women. A former admirer of the rational *Rights of Woman*, Amelia Opie wrote *Adeline Mowbray* (1804) to reveal the dangers of the libertarian notions of female sexual freedom such as Wollstonecraft proposed; in 1811 the young Harriet Westbrook sent Opie's book to Shelley, known as an admirer of Mary Wollstonecraft, possibly as part of her strategy to tame his sexual ardour into marriage.

Mary Wollstonecraft died in September 1797 following childbirth, one of her many critics declaring that her death was an argument against the doctrines of her works since it 'strongly marked the distinction of the sexes, by pointing out the destiny of women, and the diseases to which they were peculiarly liable.'[22] She was buried in St Pancras where she had been married five months before. Godwin assuaged his grief by writing the *Memoirs* of his wife, which scandalized the nation with its robust acceptance of her irregular life, and by editing her *Posthumous Works*, including the unfinished *Maria* and 'The Cave of Fancy'. For the former he made the same demand of the readers that he had made in his *Memoirs* on behalf of his wife's first novel, *Mary*: that they bring to the work warm-hearted sensitivity rather than 'fastidious' criticism.

MARY SHELLEY

The daughter, under two weeks old when her mother died, was named after Mary Wollstonecraft; Godwin was left with two motherless children to support, Fanny and Mary, for both of whom he felt a mixture of anxiety and affection. Initially the baby was cared for by Maria Reveley, a married friend of both himself and Wollstonecraft.

Although benevolently disposed, Godwin soon found that the reality of writing with interruptions strained his patience with the children: 'When Fanny interrupts my reading with a request to hold her on my knee and tell her a fanciful tale, I confess I must curb my temper', he admitted to the poet Coleridge, and 'When the wild cries of baby Mary fill the house, threatening to shatter the glass in the windows, I succumb to unreasoning panic'.[23] Despite, then, his devotion to Mary Wollstonecraft whose portrait hung in his study, and despite the fact that he regarded marriage with well-grounded 'apprehension', seeing it as 'property – and the worst of properties', he was soon looking for a new wife to lighten the 'tyranny imposed upon me by these infants'. After being refused by several suitable ladies, including the now widowed Maria Reveley, he was discovered by a 'widow' with two illegitimate children, Charles and Claire; one child, William, was later born to the couple. Mary was four when the new ménage assembled.

Fanny Imlay was accepted as part of the household, although she seems soon to have been told of her true parentage. Godwin appreciated her domestic help as she grew up and praised her 'faculty of memory' and affectionate temper. But he was clear about the respective merits of the two girls in his charge: 'my own daughter is considerably superior in capacity to the one her mother had before', he wrote, and '[she] is, I believe, very pretty'.[24]

Godwin and Mary were famously close and Mary later confessed her 'excessive attachment' to her father in childhood. Inevitably there were strains however: 'If [a father] has other objects and avocations to fill up the greater part of his time, the ordinary resource is for him to proclaim his wishes and commands in a way somewhat sententious and authoritative ...'.[25] But it was not a repressive household, and Mary was exposed to intellectual ideas and people from an early age; although she was not given the formal education accorded to the boys and no one had the time to follow Mary Wollstonecraft's system of rational female education, she was encouraged to read copiously and indeed to write for publication.

The second Mrs Godwin was never favoured by Mary, who intemperately described her as 'odious' and 'filthy', or indeed by many of Godwin's friends, one of whom called her 'that damn'd infernal bitch'. Mary retreated to St Pancras churchyard to read by the grave of her mother. So quarrelsome became the two that when Mary was fourteen Godwin dispatched her to Scotland for five months to stay with a friend's family. There she became deeply influenced by the Scottish landscape, later described in *Matilda* as 'the wild scenery of this lovely country'.

In the Godwin household money remained extremely tight despite hard work in writing and selling books. It was thus a considerable stroke of luck when the young Percy Bysshe Shelley, heir to a fortune which he seemed disposed to mortgage for others, arrived at the house full of admiration for the radical Godwin of the 1790s and his first wife Mary Wollstonecraft; Shelley himself already had a wife, Harriet, and a child. On his first visit to the Godwins he met only Fanny Imlay, Mary being still in Scotland, but in time he encountered the three girls, all of whom, according to Mrs Godwin, became equally infatuated with him. In 1814 while Fanny was on a visit in Wales with her Wollstonecraft aunts and Harriet was away with her baby, a particular intimacy grew between Shelley and the sixteen-year-old Mary. The pair visited Mary Wollstonecraft's tomb where Shelley clothed the daughter in the 'radiance undefiled' of her mother's 'departing glory', as the dedicatory stanzas of *The Revolt of Islam* later expressed it. Soon the absent Harriet had become a dead body weighing down his living soul.

When Shelley informed Godwin of his new passion, he found the father rather than the radical philosopher who had once declared, 'the sentiments of the heart cannot submit to be directed by the rule and square'. In response to Godwin's outrage, Shelley offered suicide pacts and hysteria; shortly afterwards the young couple eloped to the Continent, taking Claire along with them. The public was gleeful at the scandal, reporting that the old radical had sold his two daughters to a baronet's heir. Godwin's disapproval would shadow Mary's next years, although she tried frequently to appease him with letters, a dedication, and the naming of her first son.

By the time the trio returned to England a few months later without money, Mary, like Harriet, was pregnant. A baby girl was born and died, but a son William, born in January 1816 lived. Later in the year, Shelley, Mary and Claire, with the baby, left for Switzerland where they would encounter Lord Byron with whom Claire had become involved. It was a famous summer for English Romanticism, but, abandoned with the Godwins, Fanny Imlay found it intolerable. She was now over twenty-one and feeling herself a burden on a struggling household on which she and Mrs Godwin must have considered she had little claim. Meanwhile the Godwin scandal, so reminiscent of the earlier scandals of their sister in the 1790s, seems to have persuaded the Wollstonecraft aunts to rescind their earlier and welcomed invitation to Fanny to join their school in Ireland. Following the various rebuffs, Fanny in October left the Godwin house and travelled to Swansea where she took an overdose of laudanum. She left a suicide note with the name torn off, possibly by Fanny herself, possibly by the inn servants to avoid a scandal or possibly by Shelley, now returned from Switzerland, or an emissary of Godwin who had been alerted to the suicide by a newspaper account. Worried about further scandal, Godwin ordered Shelley not to claim the body (which was confined in stays marked MW) and he himself saw to it that 'not one person in our house has the smallest apprehension of the truth'.[26]

Following the death of her half-sister, Mary had a 'miserable day' but continued writing *Frankenstein*, while Shelley responded with poetry in which he seems to have accepted that Fanny had died of love for him. A few weeks later Harriet Shelley followed Fanny Imlay to suicide, choosing like Mary Wollstonecraft a London drowning. Mary and Percy Shelley were free to marry, to the satisfaction of the Godwins. In September of 1817 baby Clara was born and by March of the following year the Shelleys and Claire were eager to quit England again. The party set off for Italy. There they travelled incessantly until in September 1818 Shelley demanded that Mary and the baby Clara, now ill, make a rushed and ill-judged journey to Venice. On arrival, the little girl died of convulsions in her mother's arms. Less than twelve months later, in June 1819, in an unhealthy Rome where they were delaying to have their portraits painted, the last child, William, died.

Already pregnant again, Mary responded to all these deaths by sexual and psychological withdrawal, in which the many suicides she had recently contemplated must have preyed on her mind. She thought of her own tomb and declared that 'Everything on earth has lost its interest to me'.[27] Percy Shelley blamed her for her coldness during this period: 'thou art fled, gone down the dreary road, / That leads to Sorrow's most obscure abode' only to sit alone 'on the hearth of pale despair'; later in 'Epipsychidion' (1821) he would describe her as 'the cold chaste Moon' putting him into 'a chaste cold bed'.[28] Mary Shelley responded with bitterness and guilt. In a letter she wrote, 'We came to Italy thinking to do Shelley's health good – but the Climate is not any means warm enough to be of benefit to him and yet it is that that has destroyed my two children'.[29] By August she had begun the work that became *Matilda*, the first version opening, 'It was in Rome ... that I suffered a misfortune that reduced me to misery and despair'.[30]

In *Matilda*, the selfish hero-lover-father plunges suicidally into the sea and the heroine, despite the advent of a charming and sensitive poet, lives a withdrawn life of longing for death, rather like Mary at the end of *Mary, a Fiction* when, left behind by beloved friends, she is faced with the physical demands of an unwanted husband. Initially it seems that Mary Shelley, traumatized by deaths, had turned her sexual withdrawal into an allegory in which the cause was her obsessive love for her father. Certainly Godwin was freshly in her mind since both Mary and Percy Shelley considered that his insensitive letters at this time, declaring that her relatives would 'cease to love her' if she continued self-indulgently to grieve for her children, had intensified her misery. In fact, however, the work is more psychologically complex than this simple identification of Godwin and Matilda's father would suggest, and the trio of poet, father and heroine reflects many aspects of the shifting relationships of the Godwins and Shelleys. Suitably, she sent the work back to England for publication in May 1820 through her close friend Maria Gisborne, formerly Maria Reveley, the woman whom her father had earlier wished to take her mother's place.

When he received the work, it was not its complexity which primarily struck Godwin but its overt subject of imagined incest. According to Maria Gisborne, he found the theme of father-daughter passion 'disgusting and detestable' and he declared that the book could not have been published without a preface stating that Matilda had not committed incest, though 'one cannot exactly trust to what an author of the modern school may deem guilt'.[31] He did not send the work for publication, although he had been quick to send her mother's equally shocking work about adultery, *Maria*, and he did not return the manuscript to his daughter despite repeated requests. The novel was published for the first time in 1959.

As Mary Wollstonecraft's life failed to follow the course mapped out at the end of the autobiographical *Mary, a Fiction*, so Mary Shelley's life did not deteriorate in the way her heroine's had done in *Matilda*. Later she agreed that its writing had quelled her 'wretchedness' for a time. While revising it in November she gave birth to her last child, Percy Florence, the only one to live into adulthood, and named for her husband rather than her father. Less than three years later, on July 8, 1822, Percy Shelley drowned off the Italian coast. Mary was quick to notice her anticipation of the event in the father-lover's drowning in *Matilda*: she describes herself 'driving (like Matilda) towards the sea to learn if we were to be for ever doomed to misery' while to Maria Gisborne she wrote, 'Matilda fortells even many small circumstances most truly – and the whole of it is a monument of what now is –'.[32]

CONNECTIONS

The first version of *Matilda* continues one of Mary Wollstonecraft's unfinished works, the fantastic 'Cave of Fancy' from the period of *Mary*'s creation when Wollstonecraft was dominated by a belief in the importance of feminine sensibility. In this fragment a small girl, daughter of a trivial mother, is orphaned through a shipwreck on a wild shore. She is educated by an ageing and reclusive sage who uses visions for lessons, conjuring up pliant ghosts from purgatory to tell their edifying and moral tales. Only one tale is written, and it tells of a benevolent young woman who, like the fictional and actual Marys, is much endowed with sensibility; her lofty 'imagination ... over-looked the common pleasures of life' and she yearned to 'rise superior' to her contemporaries 'in wisdom and virtue'.[33] Like the Mary Wollstonecraft of Godwin's *Memoirs*, the heroine sacrifices herself for her downtrodden mother, brought to ruin by a weak, extravagant husband; later, unlike the heroine of *Maria*, but like that of *Mary*, she resists an adulterous passion. In her 'Fields of Fancy' Mary Shelley took the outlines of her mother's 'Cave of Fancy' and created Matilda, now in the Elysian Fields after a death by suicide; she tells the narrator her experience of adolescent yearning and unwise passion.

The name Matilda is a common one in literature. Closest in time was the use in the gothic novels of Horace Walpole (in the *Castle of Otranto* [1765]) of Shelley himself (in *Zastrozzi* [1810]), and of Matthew Lewis (in *The Monk* [1796]), another visitor to Byron in the summer of 1816. In *The Monk*, Matilda is a seductress who in the end proves to be a devil, but, before this is known, she appears as a rejected woman whose pain relates her to some slight extent to Walpole's melancholy heroine, mistakenly killed by her father while he is incestuously in pursuit of her friend, his intended daughter-in-law. Within Mary Shelley's novel the heroine herself mentions an earlier Matilda, from the final pages of Dante's *Purgatorio* which Shelley was possibly translating at the time; this beautiful woman, seemingly signifying original justice and innocence, acts as Dante's guide through the Terrestrial Paradise when Virgil is no longer guiding him. She directs him to the waters of forgetting ill and remembering good and helps him to become 'pure and fit to mount up to the stars'; then she hands him on to the divine Beatrice in Paradise. Mary Shelley was herself reading the *Purgatorio* in February and August of 1819 on either side of her son's death; in the novel Matilda quotes from it just before she dies, and expects to be translated to 'some sweet Paradise', reminiscent in its loving freedom from sexual love of Mary Wollstonecraft's realm where there was '*neither marrying*, nor giving in marriage' at the end of *Mary, a Fiction*.

In her *Letters from Sweden* Wollstonecraft had provided yet another Matilda. This work, which both Shelleys often reread, must have helped inspire Mary Shelley's romantic treatment of desolate Scottish nature and its

echoing of psychological desolation in *Matilda*. The tragic story of Wollstonecraft's Matilda had gripped the author on her Scandinavian journey.
This Matilda, sister of George III, had been married off at the age of fifteen
to the unbalanced and sadistic Christian VII, king of Denmark; she became
involved with the royal doctor with whom she largely ruled Denmark and
helped bring in liberal reforms; after her lover was beheaded she escaped,
only to die by the age of 24. With her melancholy and short life, her liberal
views and her superiority to those around her, Matilda became a sort of
alter ego for the depressed and right-thinking Wollstonecraft in benighted
Scandinavia.

In *Matilda* the echoes of Mary Wollstonecraft are not confined to names
or to form and fable. Matilda's mother who died in childbirth is presented as
a very idealized portrait of Mary Wollstonecraft, given an 'amiable' and
'angelically gentle' disposition. She was also endowed with a 'clear and
strong' understanding, which was called 'masculine' in 'The Fields of Fancy',
an epithet frequently applied to Wollstonecraft. In 'The Fields of Fancy', the
guide to truth Diotima provides another portrait of the dead mother: 'a
woman about forty years of age, her eyes burned with a deep fire and every
line of her face expressed enthusiasm and wisdom'. Most significantly Mary
Shelley's Matilda uses the fatal words that Wollstonecraft herself had used
in her fiction. These words echoed strangely through the lives of three
generations of women as they tried in fiction and life to link suffering and
death with patience and acceptance.

In the *Memoirs* Godwin records the dying words of Mary Wollstonecraft's
mother as 'A little patience, and all will be over!' He notes that 'these words
were repeatedly referred to by Mary in the course of her writings'.[34] In
Maria when the heroine's mother dies she uses almost the same words, 'A
little more patience, and I too shall be at rest!' and her phrases continue to
ring 'mournfully' in her daughter's ears.[35] At the end of Wollstonecraft's
own life when she was in labour, she wrote that the midwife had declared
her in the most natural state and added, 'But that I must have a little
patience'.[36] So it is with considerable resonance that Matilda, who is
pushing a glass of laudanum towards the poet with whom she wishes to
enter a suicide pact, speaks the words which the author underlines, '*A little
patience, and all will be over*'.

It was not the first time that Mary Shelley had made a character try to
face death with 'patience', and the other occurrence suggests a further echo
from the life of the Godwin-Wollstonecraft family. The word is used in
Frankenstein, spoken by Justine, a kind and grateful girl hated by her mother
and taken into the Frankenstein household where she is treated as half
servant, half daughter. Justine is blamed for the Monster's murder of the
child William, and before she herself is judicially murdered she says to the
more favoured daughter, 'Learn from me, dear lady, to submit in patience to
the will of Heaven!' The story of Justine comes into Chapter 5 of *Frankenstein*, revised just after Fanny Imlay committed suicide and, in the unjustified

blame that Justine received despite her goodness, there are inevitable echoes of the blame the second Mrs Godwin seems to have given the orphaned Fanny during the disgrace of Mary and Claire. The suicidal Matilda is in her early twenties, as was Mary Shelley when she was writing her novel, and as Fanny had been when she killed herself. Given Fanny Imlay's close association with both Godwin and Shelley, it does not appear fanciful to see some shadow of her pathetic life and death in her half-sister's fiction.

Mary Shelley's own powerfully unresolved relationship with her living father and dead mother may be illuminated by a psychoanalytical account of the oedipal conflict of Marie Bonaparte whose mother also died giving birth to her:

In a dream, I saw myself descending toward my father, intending to join him in the library. But along the way, the little skeleton always snatched me from behind with its outstretched hand. And I continued to live with my nightmares, and would never dare, when night had fallen – and now even in the day – to go down alone to the library.

This phobia was a too marvelous compromise between two powerful tendencies in my unconscious: to *be* my mother, in dying like her, which satisfied the most positive part of my oedipal complex: the love for my father; and to be *punished* with death by my mother, in reprisal for the death that I had caused her, which satisfied, in the other part of my oedipal complex, the unconscious sentiment of culpability attached to it.[37]

Like her creator, the heroine of *Matilda* is the result of her father's first deadly desire, and the book becomes an even more autobiographical birth-myth than *Frankenstein*. As in the earlier novel too, there is some gender transformation and displacement. Wollstonecraft and Godwin had thought of the unborn Mary as a boy 'William'; in *Matilda* the heroine imagines herself dressed as a boy seeking her lost father. When the father does return, he finds the idealized wife's lineaments reproduced in her daughter who then becomes a possible but improper object of his desire.

At the moment of revelation, Matilda feels a female phantom with fangs in her heart, a sort of material maternal presence; she describes herself as 'stung by a serpent', a conventional image but one which must have gained some resonance for Mary Shelley through Godwin's use of the rejuvenating serpent as an image for Mary Wollstonecraft. The result of Matilda's apprehension of the phantom is horror, the death of the father and in time of herself. As Marie Bonaparte wrote: 'To be dead, for me, was to be identified with the mother, was to be in the place of the wife of my father, was, like my mother, to die – a kind of strange delight – by his agency'.[38] Matilda's response to her father's death is to pretend that she too has died and then to enact death through her withdrawal from life. The lack of mention of the mother in the final pages – the quartet she imagines seems to be of herself, her father, the poet, and his beloved – suggests that Matilda's death is a kind of union of mother and daughter, after which the now non-sexual union with the dead father becomes legitimate. At the end of her tale Matilda admits, in the manner of Wollstonecraft's *Mary*, 'In truth I am in love with death'.

If *Matilda* can be seen to echo Mary Shelley's half-sister and her mother, it is more in open dialogue and even contest with the men in her life, Godwin and Shelley. Godwin had believed that evils could be alleviated by right reason, education and changed environment. Percy Shelley was much attracted to this utopian vision, to part of which Mary Wollstonecraft had herself adhered in her progressive *Rights of Woman*, where it seemed that society could be improved by the national education of women. By the time she wrote *Maria*, however, she held a more complicated vision of social ills and she seems to have doubted the supreme power of reason and education. She also seems to have accepted the melancholy implication of the progressive environmental view: that if environment is supreme in influence, then some people are irreparably damaged. Certainly Maria chooses one feckless and faithless man after another as if imprinted by early yearnings.

As Matilda refuses the rational utopianism of Godwin, so she rejects the utopianism of Shelleyan love. In *Queen Mab* Shelley had insisted on bringing together hope and love. In the fourth act of *Prometheus Unbound* he urged humanity 'To love and bear; to hope till Hope creates / From its own wreck the thing it contemplates'. Matilda however comes to a more pessimistic conclusion: 'I had no idea that misery could arise from love'. She believes in the imprinting of heredity and experience and insists, like the later Wollstonecraft, on the reality of misery.

She also insists on the reality of guilt. In her more robust moments Mary Wollstonecraft did not appreciate the religious concept of guilt (as the story of Jemima in *Maria* suggests) and she declared in the *Moral and Historical View ... of the French Revolution* (1794) that not much could be learnt from the history of Oedipus. But Mary Shelley makes the heroine of *Matilda* associate herself at the outset of her story with the tale of Oedipus, another victim of the incestuous idea, whose lover-parent commits suicide, leaving the child with guilt. Matilda takes on herself all the guilt for the imagined act of incest, forgetful of her father's initiating part and of his blighting act of desertion: 'I believed myself to be polluted by the unnatural love I have inspired'. In a later short story, 'The Mourner' (1829), published in *The Keepsake for 1830*, Mary Shelley again returned to the subject of filial guilt. The suicidal heroine, having clung to her father in a burning boat, is thrown to safety only to watch him drown. She convinces herself that she is a parricide and becomes suicidal like Matilda, sitting at her table with 'the mortal beverages' before her. Again like Matilda, she is prevented from the act by a wished-for sickness and death.

INCEST AND SUICIDE

The theme of incest was a common one in Romanticism and it is probable that Shelley's own interest helped inspire his wife. In both Byron and Shelley's works, sibling incest can suggest an escape from stifling social conventions. In Byron's *Manfred* which Mary Shelley was copying in the summer of 1816, the hero feels a forbidden passion for his sister; the passion is condemned but it does not detract from the heroic stature of Manfred himself. In the first version of *The Revolt of Islam* entitled 'Laon and Cythna' (1817) Percy Shelley presented his utopian vision of political harmony in terms of a sexual and intellectual relationship between a brother and an heroic sister with some of the characteristics of Mary Wollstonecraft.

But father-daughter incest appears the reverse of the sibling sort and is described in the play *The Cenci*, which Percy Shelley had just completed, with Mary's encouragement, at about the time of *Matilda*'s composition. This sort of incest is far more threatening and disturbing than the sibling kind as it suggests patriarchal oppression through both class and gender on a personal and political plane. It is therefore appropriate that the sexual act in the play is not a seduction but a rape, standing for all that is rotten in inequality of power, and that the death of the father is not from suicide but from murder by his raped daughter. In *Matilda*, sibling and parental forms of incest are mixed since father and daughter are in some way enamoured of each other, but the father as in *The Cenci* holds the social and familial power.

While himself writing *The Cenci* in September of 1818 Percy Shelley was urging Mary to translate some of Alfieri's *Myrrha* which may well have served as a source of part of *Matilda*. In the play there is a scene of revelation between father and daughter, in which the father inadvertently forces his daughter to confess an incestuous love for him in the way Matilda had forced her father. After the confession she stabs herself. In *Matilda* the heroine mentions *Myrrha* to her father and provokes a violent and confused reaction from the incestuously desiring man.

Maria and *Matilda* both concern suicide, while *Mary* at the end leaves its heroine yearning for death. Although much is clearly autobiographical when set against a family background sadly marked by successful and unsuccessful attempts, suicide was also a frequently discussed public topic in the late eighteenth and early nineteenth centuries. In fact England was thought to be the suicide's special home, the preeminence being blamed by the pious on religious infidelity and by the impious on social malaise, constitutional melancholy and the miserable climate.

Christianity had made suicide a sin by calling it self-murder. The corpse of a suicide was supposed to be buried with a stake on the public highway. The state in its turn had made the act criminal and sought to confiscate the criminal-victim's property and money. In England suicide remained both sin and crime throughout the eighteenth century – staking and burying on the highway were officially stopped in 1823, forfeiture only in 1870 – but the attitudes were modified long before. By the last decades of the eighteenth century, penalties were almost always avoided, even in the clearest of cases. Fanny Imlay's death was obviously suicide and yet a verdict of unsound mind was brought in.

Although suicide still excited horror and demanded burial in unconsecrated ground, a secular attitude was gaining strength. Along the Thames and by the Serpentine, humanitarian groups set up suicide stations to resuscitate the living or identify the dead. Perhaps one client of such groups was Mary Wollstonecraft, but Harriet Shelley clearly escaped their ministrations.

For the literary classes two new attitudes were available, the rational and the romantic. The philosopher David Hume regarded suicide as a native liberty, and asked why we think that a 'man who tired of life, and hunted by pain and misery, bravely overcomes all the natural terrors of death ... has incurred the indignation of his Creator'.[39] When pain and sickness, shame and poverty in any combination are overwhelming, when a person has weighed up the benefits of the future against the misery of the present, then he has a right to proceed to end his being and not consider either God or society since he is not obliged to do a small good to others at the expense of a great harm to himself.

Godwin sought to refine Hume. In the first version of *Political Justice* he saw suicide as neither criminal nor sinful, but he distrusted the Humean motives for escape from life – pain and shame – for pain, he claimed, was momentary and disgrace imaginary. In a later edition he became more utilitarian, insisting that the would-be suicide consider the net pain caused by life or suicide, including in the latter case the misery to remaining relatives. In *Matilda* the poet's attitude is close to Godwin's utilitarian one: he will not drink the heroine's poison, arguing that suicide is improper where a person may still be useful to society: being young and talented, he should live.

In 1783 an editor bound Hume's essay on suicide with sections of Rousseau's *La Nouvelle Héloïse* in which the passionate Saint-Preux, using the Humean argument, contemplates suicide from thwarted love. But he is easily dissuaded by Godwinian arguments since he is in an improper passion, is young and healthy and still able to do good. Yet, despite this resolution, Rousseau's yearning for suicide emerges from the novel so convincingly that he himself was thought by many to have committed it, and his grave became the site of others' romantic deaths. Wollstonecraft's Maria who tries suicide may then have taken more than her romantic yearnings from her prison reading of Rousseau's book.

The greatest of the romantic suicides was of course Werther, who made suicide into the act of a great soul insisting in dying for love and an indescribable 'inner raging'. He had no Humean justification of poverty or shame, nor did he stop to consider his relatives, as Godwin suggested, being 'lost ... in the happy thought of burying all my sufferings, all my torments,' in the abyss.[40] Rather like Mary Shelley's Matilda and like Mary Wollstonecraft in her suicide note to Imlay, he imagined his dead body or tomb contemplated by his beloved. Mindful of the national problem, the English editor prefaced Goethe's work with cautions against readers following the hero. Nonetheless Godwin saw Mary Wollstonecraft as Werther when he wrote of her melancholy love letters to Imlay, and the young Shelley, worrying about his too avid desire for disintegration, saw himself in the image of Werther. At the height of the uproar that greeted his announcement of love for Mary Godwin, he followed her mother and fictional Maria by catching up a bottle of laudanum and crying, 'I never part from this'.[41]

Socio-historical studies always consider gender in suicide. While men chose to hang or shoot themselves, women overwhelmingly chose drowning or poison, a slower method leaving the body intact. The satiric James Tilson in the eighteenth century noted the same choice when in a piece in *The World* in 1756 he claimed to have provided pistols and nooses for men and 'a commodious bath' for disappointed ladies. Emile Durkheim makes much of the inferior numbers of female suicides, but in fiction they are perhaps preeminent, from the Dido of Ovid's *Heroides* to Flaubert's Madame Bovary. In her suicide note to Imlay, Wollstonecraft put herself in the tradition of fictional female suicides, blaming the man and imagining the effect of her death on him. In *Matilda* the whole story is a kind of lengthy suicide note, addressed to the absent poet who will be left to contemplate her suffering and her grave.

Before she went to France, Wollstonecraft seems to have accepted that suicide was wrong. In *Mary, a Fiction* she drove her miserable sensitive heroine to an emotional impasse, waiting to be rescued by the involuntary ending, and finding suicide no option. But, by the time of writing *Maria*, she had modified her notions and come to admire, if not a weak surrender to life's difficulties, then a noble grasping of death by an heroic spirit. When she returned from a suicide undertaken, in Godwin's words, 'with cool and deliberate firmness', she wrote:

> I have only to lament, that, when the bitterness of death was past, I was inhumanly brought back to life and misery. But a fixed determination is not to be baffled by disappointment; nor will I allow that to be a frantic attempt, which was one of the calmest acts of reason. In this respect, I am only accountable to myself.[42]

Although she admitted that she would not try drowning again because of the pain, she did not state that she would avoid all other 'species of voluntary death'.[43] In *Maria* an abandoned girl jumps into a pond and freezes to death, while in the fragments at the end of the book Maria tries suicide by her creator's first method of laudanum. In *Matilda* Mary Wollstonecraft's attempted heroic death of choice is presented in the father, while the suicidal withdrawing of the heroine of *Mary* recurs in the daughter.

FANTASY, FICTION AND NATURE

The fear expressed by the editor of Rousseau and Goethe that men and women would be encouraged to suicide through reading corrupting and seductive books suggests the power ascribed to literature in the late eighteenth and early nineteenth centuries. Because of their assumed superiority in sensitivity or sensibility, so much denigrated by Wollstonecraft in *A Vindication of the Rights of Woman* but so headily exemplified in *Mary*, women were supposed to be supremely susceptible to fiction and the fantasy world it offered. Sometimes the fear was that they would live in the fictional world and be ruined for reality, foolishly expecting the fictive romantic treatment from a husband within a real-life marriage. At other times it was feared that poetry and fiction would refine the female sensibility to the excessive point that women would become hampered for living. Both Mary Wollstonecraft and Mary Shelley felt the power of fictional and poetic worlds and were attracted to them; both in different ways understood and warned of the danger of substituting enriching and comforting fantasy for painful or dull reality.

In *Maria*, the heroine wrote to her daughter:

> Gain experience – ah! gain it – while experience is worth having, and acquire sufficient fortitude to pursue your own happiness; it includes your utility, by a direct path. What is wisdom too often, but the owl of the goddess, who sits moping in a desolated heart.

Part of this experience seems to have been sexual, since Maria gives her body where she has given her heart. Yet her positive sexuality belongs more to the realm of fantasy and projection than to that of experience; the asylum love affair is fed from the marginalia of *La Nouvelle Héloïse* and Darnford becomes interesting through his literary annotations and his association with Saint-Preux. In *Mary, a Fiction* the heroine's trivial mother displaces her sexuality through the reading of silly romantic novels, while her more serious daughter mediates her adolescence and awakening sexuality through the poetry of male sensibility. In *Matilda*, sexuality is primarily expressed in romantic desire. The girl dreams of the absent father's return and makes the first meeting a deeply romantic one.

Although it seems that no sexual activity has occurred between father and daughter in *Matilda* (as it also fails to occur between fatherly lover and Mary in *Mary*), the guilt suggests that the heroine is so used to living in a world of language and signs that she believes them tantamount to things and experience. She can confuse reality and fantasy so thoroughly that she believes she has enjoyed 'unnatural pleasures' through 'dreams and not realities'. Only in *Maria* is physical sexual activity clearly presented without artistic mediation, and there it is predominantly disgusting as when Maria has to suffer with her drunken husband and Jemima through her raping master.

In each of the novels a literary apprehension is implicated in the swerve from reality to excess and fantasy. Mary nurtures her acute and disabling sensibility in contemplation of a nature which always inspires a literary quotation, while Maria learns to forget the reality of her oppression in her madhouse cell by making an artificial elysian nature. Matilda sees nature as a reflection of her moods and her literary imagination clothes it with associations. In each case there seems hardly any contact with the real physical world which comes as a shock when it touches the heroine. This is especially clear in *Matilda* in which, towards the end, the heroine actually feels real rain and wet grass and comes to realize that her dreams have 'often strangely deformed' the world. If it is the fantasy world that predisposes her to death, it is the wet grass of the real one that brings it about.

The psychological yearning and depression caught in *Mary*, *Maria* and *Matilda* are inevitably involved in the culture of the period and associated with the status of women, although this association is made explicit only in the political *Maria*, which alone allows any exit from the impasse of romantic, subordinate and familial relationships. In *Matilda* no female friend is allowed to mitigate the harm of the confining family for the heroine, who simply embodies the notion that a girl has no other role but as loving daughter and desiring wife. *Mary* ends with a longing for two friends, male and female, while *Maria* in one fragment concludes with an all-female trio of mother, daughter and female friend looking towards a future together.

In Jane Austen's *Persuasion*, the heroine noted that women love longest because they live enclosed and claustrophobic lives where their feelings must prey on them. Wollstonecraft clearly opposed the psychological imprisonment of women through the ideology of passive femininity and urged women to think rightly and act robustly and rationally. Although sympathetic to many of her mother's radical opinions, Mary Shelley sometimes seems to have found her activist legacy oppressive. 'I beleive that we are sent here to educate ourselves and that self denial & disappointment & self control are a part of our education ... though many things need *great* amendment – I can by no means go so far as my *friends* would have me'.[44] The difference is well caught in their stated aims of writing: in *Maria*, Wollstonecraft claimed that she wrote to exhibit 'the misery and oppression, peculiar to women, that arise out of the partial laws and customs of society'; Mary Shelley however declared, 'I shall be happy if any thing I ever produce may exalt and soften sorrow'.[45]

NOTES

[1] *Letters Written during a short residence in Sweden, Norway and Denmark, The Works of Mary Wollstonecraft*, ed. Janet Todd and Marilyn Butler (London, 1989), VI, 241.

[2] The phrase was used by Thomas Holcroft and referred to Godwin and Wollstonecraft on their marriage in 1797. It also seems applicable to Mary Wollstonecraft and Mary Shelley.

[3] In her letters Mary Shelley referred to her work as 'Matilda' and in her draft as 'Mathilda'. For information on the textual problems of *Matilda*, see Elizabeth Nitchie's notes to her edition (Chapel Hill, 1959) and *The Bodleian Shelley Manuscripts*, IV, ed. E. B. Murray (New York, 1988). Mary Wollstonecraft in her letters refers to her last novel simply as her 'M.S.'; Godwin who edited it for the press entitled the work *The Wrongs of Woman: or, Maria. A Fragment*.

[4] William Godwin, *Memoirs of the Author of 'The Rights of Woman'*, ed. Richard Holmes (Harmondsworth, 1987).

[5] *Memoirs*, p. 210.

[6] Johann Wolfgang von Goethe, *The Sorrows of Werter* [sic]: *A German Story*, trans. attrib. David Malthus, 3rd edn (London, 1782).

[7] *The Collected Letters of Mary Wollstonecraft*, ed. Ralph M. Wardle (Ithaca, 1979), p. 74.

[8] *Collected Letters of Mary Wollstonecraft*, p. 86.

[9] *Memoirs*, pp. 216–17.

[10] *Letters from Sweden*, pp. 271–2.

[11] *Memoirs*, p. 223.

[12] *Collected Letters of Mary Wollstonecraft*, p. 385; *Memoirs*, pp. 223–4.

[13] *A Vindication of the Rights of Woman, The Works of Mary Wollstonecraft*, V, 105.

[14] *Memoirs*, p. 234.

[15] Jean-Jacques Rousseau, *Lettres de deux Amants: Julie, ou la Nouvelle Héloïse* (1761).

[16] Virginia Woolf, *The Common Reader, 2nd Series* (London, 1932), p. 160; *Memoirs*, p. 242.

[17] *Memoirs*, p. 242.

[18] *Memoirs*, p. 257.

[19] See William St Clair, *The Godwins and the Shelleys: the Biography of a Family* (London, 1989), for a description of the relationship.

[20] *Memoirs*, p. 264.

[21] *Memoirs*, p. 258.

[22] Richard Polwhele, *The Unsex'd Females* (London, 1798).

[23] Charles Kegan Paul, *William Godwin: His Friends and Contemporaries* (London, 1876).

[24] Kegan Paul, II. p. 214.

[25] Kegan Paul, II, 213–14.

[26] Quoted in St Clair, p. 412.

[27] *Letters of Mary Shelley* ed. Betty Bennett (Baltimore, 1980), I, 100.

[28] 'To Mary Shelley' (1819) and 'Epipsychidion' (1821), *The Poetical Works of Percy Bysshe Shelley*, ed. Mary Shelley (London, 1839), 2nd edition.

[29] *Letters*, I, 101.

[30] *Mathilda*, ed. Elizabeth Nitchie (Chapel Hill, 1959), p. 90.

[31] *Maria Gisborne & Edward E. Williams, Shelley's Friends, Their Journals and Letters*, ed. Frederick L. Jones (Norman, 1951), p. 44.

[32] *Letters*, I, 247 and 336.

[33] *Works*, VI, 201.

[34] *Memoirs*, p. 213.

[35] *Works*, I, 132.

[36] *Collected Letters of Mary Wollstonecraft*, p. 411.

[37] The translation is by Terence Harpold from *Revue française de Psychanalyse* 2.3 (1928). Harpold has drawn attention to the relationship of this quotation to *Mathilda* in 'Did you get Mathilda from Papa?: Seduction Fantasy and the Circulation of Mary Shelley's *Mathilda*', *Studies in Romanticism*, 28 (Spring, 1989), 49–64.

[38] Harpold, p. 57, n.18.

[39] *Essays on Suicide, and the Immortality of the Soul, ascribed to the late David Hume, Esq.* (London, 1783), p. 9.

[40] *Werter* II, 104–5.

[41] For a description of Shelley's suicidal behaviour, see Mrs Godwin's letter of 20 August, 1814, in Edward Dowden, *The Life of Percy Bysshe Shelley* (London, 1866), Appendix A, II, 544.

[42] *Memoirs*, p. 251; *Collected Letters of Mary Wollstonecraft*, p. 317.

[43] *Memoirs*, p. 250.

[44] *The Journals of Mary Shelley, 1814–1844*, ed. Paula R. Feldman and Diana Scott-Kilvert (London, 1987), II, 552–3.

[45] *Letters*, I, 254.

NOTE ON THE TEXT

The texts of *Mary* and *Maria* are those prepared by Janet Todd and Marilyn Butler, with the assistance of Emma Craigie for the *Complete Works of Mary Wollstonecraft* (London, Pickering and Chatto, 1989). Other modern editions have been published by Gary Kelly, Moira Ferguson and Janet Todd. The text of *Matilda* is taken from Elizabeth Nitchie's *Mathilda* in *Studies in Philology* (Chapel Hill, University of North Carolina Press, 1959) reprinted by permission of the University of North Carolina Press with modernization of spelling from *The Mary Shelley Reader* ed. Betty T. Bennett and Charles E. Robinson (New York, Oxford University Press, 1990) and the present editors substantive changes from Nitchie are noted in the end notes.

BIBLIOGRAPHY

Allen, Graham. 'Beyond Biographism: Mary Shelley's *Mathilda* Intertextuality, and the Wandering Subject', *Romanticism: The Journal of Romantic Culture and Criticism* 3:3 (1997), 170–84.

Cameron, Kenneth Neil and Donald H. Reiman, eds. *Shelley and his Circle 1773–1822*. Cambridge: Harvard University Press, 1961–7.

Clemit, Pamela. 'From *The Fields of Fancy* to *Mathilda*' in Betty T. Bennett and Stuart Curran (eds.), *Mary Shelley in Her Times*. Baltimore: Johns Hopkins University Press, 2000.

Flexner, Eleanor. *Mary Wollstonecraft*. New York: Coward, McCann & Geohagen, 1972.

Garrett, Margaret Davenport. 'Writing and Re-Writing Incest in Mary Shelley's *Mathilda*', *Keats–Shelley Journal* 45 (1996), 44–60.

Himes, Audra Dibert. '"Knew Shame, and Knew Desire": Ambivalence as Structure in Mary Shelley's *Mathilda* in Syndy M. Conger, Frederick S. Frank, Gregory O'Dea (eds.), *Iconoclastic Departures: Mary Shelley after Frankenstein. Essays in Honor of the Bicentenary of Mary Shelley's Birth*. Madison: Fairleigh Dickinson University Press, 1997.

Holmes, Richard. *Shelley: the Pursuit*. London: Weidenfeld and Nicolson, 1974.

Johnson, Claudia L. 'Mary Wollstonecraft's Novels' in *The Cambridge Companion to Mary Wollstonecraft*. Cambridge: Cambridge University Press, 2002.

Jones, Vivien. 'Placing Jemima: Women Writers of the 1790s and the Eighteenth-Century Prostitution Narrative', *Women's Writing* 4:2 (1997), 201–20.

McKeever, Kerry. 'Naming the Daughter's Suffering: Melancholia in Mary Shelley's Mathilda', *Essays in Literature* 23:2 (1996), 190–205.

Medwin, Thomas. *The Life of Percy Bysshe Shelley*, ed. H. Buxton Forman. London: Oxford University Press, 1913.

Mellor, Anne K. 'Righting the Wrongs of Woman: Mary Wollstonecraft's *Maria*', *Nineteenth-Century Contexts* 19:4 (1996), 413–24.

Nitchie, Elizabeth. *Mary Shelley*. New Brunswick: Rutgers University Press, 1953.

Paul, Charles Kegan. *William Godwin, his Friends and Contemporaries*. London: Henry S. King & Co., 1876.

Poovey, Mary. *The Proper Lady and the Woman Writer: Ideology as Style in the*

Works of Mary Wollstonecraft, Mary Shelley and Jane Austen. Chicago: University of Chicago Press, 1984.

Robinson, Charles E. 'Mathilda as Dramatic Actress' in Betty T. Bennett and Stuart Curran (eds.), *Mary Shelley in Her Times*. Baltimore: Johns Hopkins University Press, 2000.

Seymour, Miranda. *Mary Shelley*. London: John Murray, 2000.

Shelley, Mary. *The Journals 1814–1844*, ed. Paula Feldman and Diana Scott-Kilvert. Oxford: Clarendon Press, 1987.

　　　The Letters, ed. Betty Bennett. Baltimore: Johns Hopkins University Press, 1980.

Shelley, Percy Bysshe. *The Complete Poetical Works of Percy Bysshe Shelley*, ed. Thomas Hutchinson, collected by G. M. Matthews. Oxford: Oxford University Press, 1970.

Sunstein, Emily. *Mary Shelley: Romance and Reality*. Boston: Little, Brown and Co., 1989.

Taylor, Barbara. *Mary Wollstonecraft and the Feminist Imagination*. Cambridge: Cambridge University Press, 2003.

Todd, Janet. *Mary Wollstonecraft: A Revolutionary Life*. London: Weidenfeld and Nicolson, 2000.

　　　The Sign of Angellica: Women, Writing and Fiction 1660–1800. London: Virago, 1989.

　　　Women's Friendship in Literature. New York: Columbia University Press, 1980.

Tomalin, Claire. *The Life and Death of Mary Wollstonecraft*. New York and London: Harcourt Brace Jovanovich, 1974.

Wollstonecraft, Mary. *Collected Letters of Mary Wollstonecraft*, ed. Janet Todd. London: Allen Lane, 2003.

Wollstonecraft, Mary, *The Works*, eds. Janet Todd and Marilyn Butler. London: Pickering and Chatto, 1989.

Wollstonecraft, Mary and Godwin, William. *A Short Residence in Sweden* and *Memoirs of the Author of The Rights of Woman*, ed. Richard Holmes. Harmondsworth: Penguin, 1987.

Young-Edelman, Diana. '"Kingdom of Shadows": Intimations of desire in Mary Shelley's *Mathilda*', *Keats–Shelley Journal* 51 (2002), 115–44.

Mary

ADVERTISEMENT

In delineating the Heroine of this Fiction, the Author attempts to develop a character different from those generally portrayed. This woman is neither a Clarissa, a Lady G——, nor a* Sophie.[1] – It would be vain to mention the various modifications of these models, as it would to remark, how widely artists wander from nature, when they copy the originals of great masters. They catch the gross parts; but the subtile spirit evaporates; and not having the just ties, affectation disgusts, when grace was expected to charm.

Those compositions only have power to delight, and carry us willing captives, where the soul of the author is exhibited, and animates the hidden springs. Lost in a pleasing enthusiasm, they live in the scenes they represent; and do not measure their steps in a beaten track, solicitous to gather expected flowers, and bind them in a wreath, according to the prescribed rules of art.

These chosen few, wish to speak for themselves, and not to be an echo – even of the sweetest sounds – or the reflector of the most sublime beams. The† paradise they ramble in, must be of their own creating – or the prospect soon grows insipid, and not varied by a vivifying principle, fades and dies.

In an artless tale, without episodes, the mind of a woman, who has thinking powers is displayed. The female organs have been thought too weak for this arduous employment; and experience seems to justify the assertion. Without arguing physically about *possibilities* – in a fiction, such a being may be allowed to exist; whose grandeur is derived from the operations of its own faculties, not subjugated to opinion; but drawn by the individual from the original source.

---

* Rousseau.

† I here give the Reviewers an opportunity of being very witty about the Paradise of Fools, etc.[2]

MARY[3]

CHAPTER I

Mary, the heroine of this fiction, was the daughter of Edward, who married Eliza, a gentle, fashionable girl, with a kind of indolence in her temper, which might be termed negative good-nature: her virtues, indeed, were all of that stamp. She carefully attended to the *shews* of things, and her opinions, I should have said prejudices, were such as the generality approved of. She was educated with the expectation of a large fortune, of course became a mere machine: the homage of her attendants made a great part of her puerile amusements, and she never imagined there were any relative duties for her to fulfil: notions of her own consequence, by these means, were interwoven in her mind, and the years of youth spent in acquiring a few superficial accomplishments, without having any taste for them. When she was first introduced into the polite circle, she danced with an officer, whom the faintly wished to be united to; but her father soon after recommending another in a more distinguished rank of life, she readily submitted to his will, and promised to love, honour, and obey, (a vicious fool,) as in duty bound.

While they resided in London, they lived in the usual fashionable style, and seldom saw each other; nor were they much more sociable when they wooed rural felicity for more than half the year, in a delightful country, where Nature, with lavish hand, had scattered beauties around; for the master, with brute, unconscious gaze, passed them by unobserved, and sought amusement in country sports. He hunted in the morning, and after eating an immoderate dinner, generally fell asleep: this reasonable rest enabled him to digest the cumbrous load; he would then visit some of his pretty tenants; and when he compared their ruddy glow of health with his wife's countenance, which even rouge could not enliven, it is not necessary to say which a *gourmand* would give the preference to. Their vulgar dance of spirits were infinitely more agreeable to his fancy than her sickly, die-away languor. Her voice was but the shadow of a sound, and she had, to complete her delicacy, so relaxed her nerves, that she became a mere nothing.

Many such noughts are there in the female world! yet she had a good opinion of her own merit, – truly, she said long prayers, – and sometimes read her Week's Preparation:[4] she dreaded that horrid place vulgarly called *hell*, the regions below; but whether her's was a mounting spirit, I cannot pretend to determine; or what sort of a planet would have been proper for her, when she left her *material* part in this world, let metaphysicians settle; I have nothing to say to her unclothed spirit.

As she was sometimes obliged to be alone, or only with her French waiting-maid, she sent to the metropolis for all the new publications, and while she was dressing her hair, and she could turn her eyes from the glass, she ran over those most delightful substitutes for bodily dissipation, novels. I say bodily, or the animal soul, for a rational one can find no employment in polite circles. The glare of lights, the studied inelegancies of dress, and the compliments offered up at the shrine of false beauty, are all equally addressed to the senses.

When she could not any longer indulge the caprices of fancy one way, she tried another. The Platonic Marriage, Eliza Warwick,[5] and some other interesting tales were perused with eagerness. Nothing could be more natural than the developement of the passions, nor more striking than the views of the human heart. What delicate struggles! and uncommonly pretty turns of thought! The picture that was found on a bramble-bush, the new sensitive-plant, or tree, which caught the swain by the upper-garment, and presented to his ravished eyes a portrait. − Fatal image! − It planted a thorn in a till then insensible heart, and sent a new kind of a knight-errant into the world. But even this was nothing to the catastrophe, and the circumstance on which it hung, the hornet settling on the sleeping lover's face. What a *heart-rending* accident! She planted, in imitation of those susceptible souls, a rose bush; but there was not a lover to weep in concert with her, when she watered it with her tears. − Alas! Alas!

If my readers would excuse the sportiveness of fancy, and give me credit for genius, I would go on and tell them such tales as would force the sweet tears of sensibility to flow in copious showers down beautiful cheeks, to the discomposure of rouge, etc. etc. Nay, I would make it so interesting, that the fair peruser should beg the hair-dresser to settle the curls himself, and not interrupt her.

She had besides another resource, two most beautiful dogs, who shared her bed, and reclined on cushions near her all the day. These she watched with the most assiduous care, and bestowed on them the warmest caresses. This fondness for animals was not that kind of *attendrissement* which makes a person take pleasure in providing for the subsistence and comfort of a living creature; but it proceeded from vanity, it gave her an opportunity of lisping out the prettiest French expressions of ecstatic fondness, in accents that had never been attuned by tenderness.

She was so chaste, according to the vulgar acceptation of the word, that is, she did not make any actual *faux pas*; she feared the world, and was indolent; but then, to make amends for this seeming self-denial, she read all the sentimental novels, dwelt on the love-scenes, and, had she thought while she read, her mind would have been contaminated; as she accompanied the lovers to the lonely arbors, and would walk with them by the clear

light of the moon. She wondered her husband did not stay at home. She was
jealous – why did he not love her, sit by her side, squeeze her hand, and look
unutterable things? Gentle reader, I will tell thee; they neither of them felt
what they could not utter. I will not pretend to say that they always
annexed an idea to a word; but they had none of those feelings which are
not easily analyzed.

CHAPTER II

In due time she brought forth a son, a feeble babe; and the following year a
daughter. After the mother's throes she felt very few sentiments of maternal
tenderness; the children were given to nurses, and she played with her dogs.
Want of exercise prevented the least chance of her recovering strength; and
two or three milk-fevers brought on a consumption, to which her constitution tended. Her children all died in their infancy, except the two first, and
she began to grow fond of the son, as he was remarkably handsome. For
years she divided her time between the sofa, and the card-table. She thought
not of death, though on the borders of the grave; nor did any of the duties
of her station occur to her as necessary. Her children were left in the
nursery; and when Mary, the little blushing girl, appeared, she would send
the awkward thing away. To own the truth, she was awkward enough, in a
house without any play-mates; for her brother had been sent to school, and
she scarcely knew how to employ herself; she would ramble about the
garden, admire the flowers, and play with the dogs. An old house-keeper
told her stories, read to her, and, at last, taught her to read. Her mother
talked of enquiring for a governess when her health would permit; and, in
the interim desired her own maid to teach her French. As she had learned to
read, she perused with avidity every book that came in her way. Neglected
in every respect, and left to the operations of her own mind, she considered
every thing that came under her inspection, and learned to think. She had
heard of a separate state, and that angels sometimes visited this earth. She
would sit in a thick wood in the park, and talk to them; make little songs
addressed to them, and sing them to tunes of her own composing; and her
native wood notes wild[6] were sweet and touching.

Her father always exclaimed against female acquirements, and was glad
that his wife's indolence and ill health made her not trouble herself about
them. She had besides another reason, she did not wish to have a fine tall
girl brought forward into notice as her daughter; she still expected to
recover, and figure away in the gay world. Her husband was very tyrannical
and passionate; indeed so very easily irritated when inebriated, that Mary

was continually in dread lest he should frighten her mother to death; her sickness called forth all Mary's tenderness, and exercised her compassion so continually, that it became more than a match for self-love, and was the governing propensity of her heart through life. She was violent in her temper; but she saw her father's faults, and would weep when obliged to compare his temper with her own. – She did more; artless prayers rose to Heaven for pardon, when she was conscious of having erred; and her contrition was so exceedingly painful, that she watched diligently the first movements of anger and impatience, to save herself this cruel remorse.

Sublime ideas filled her young mind – always connected with devotional sentiments; extemporary effusions of gratitude, and rhapsodies of praise would burst often from her, when she listened to the birds, or pursued the deer. She would gaze on the moon, and ramble through the gloomy path, observing the various shapes the clouds assumed, and listen to the sea that was not far distant. The wandering spirits, which she imagined inhabited every part of nature, were her constant friends and confidants. She began to consider the Great First Cause, formed just notions of his attributes, and, in particular, dwelt on his wisdom and goodness. Could she have loved her father or mother, had they returned her affection, she would not so soon, perhaps, have sought out a new world.

Her sensibility prompted her to search for an object to love; on earth it was not to be found: her mother had often disappointed her, and the apparent partiality she shewed to her brother gave her exquisite pain – produced a kind of habitual melancholy, led her into a fondness for reading tales of woe, and made her almost realize the fictitious distress.

She had not any notion of death till a little chicken expired at her feet; and her father had a dog hung in a passion. She then concluded animals had souls, or they would not have been subjected to the caprice of man; but what was the soul of man or beast? In this style year after year rolled on, her mother still vegetating.

A little girl who attended in the nursery fell sick. Mary paid her great attention; contrary to her wish, she was sent out of the house to her mother, a poor woman, whom necessity obliged to leave her sick child while she earned her daily bread. The poor wretch, in a fit of delirium stabbed herself, and Mary saw her dead body, and heard the dismal account; and so strongly did it impress her imagination, that every night of her life the bleeding corpse presented itself to her when she first began to slumber. Tortured by it, she at last made a vow, that if she was ever mistress of a family she would herself watch over every part of it. The impression that this accident made was indelible.

As her mother grew imperceptibly worse and worse, her father, who did not understand such a lingering complaint, imagined his wife was only grown still more whimsical, and that if she could be prevailed on to exert herself, her health would soon be re-established. In general he treated her with indifference; but when her illness at all interfered with his pleasures, he expostulated in the most cruel manner, and visibly harassed the invalid. Mary would then assiduously try to turn his attention to something else; and when sent out of the room, would watch at the door, until the storm was over, for unless it was, she could not rest. Other causes also contributed to disturb her repose: her mother's lukewarm manner of performing her religious duties, filled her with anguish; and when she observed her father's vices, the unbidden tears would flow. She was miserable when beggars were driven from the gate without being relieved; if she could do it unperceived, she would give them her own breakfast, and feel gratified, when, in consequence of it, she was pinched by hunger.

She had once, or twice, told her little secrets to her mother; they were laughed at, and she determined never to do it again. In this manner was she left to reflect on her own feelings; and so strengthened were they by being meditated on, that her character early became singular and permanent. Her understanding was strong and clear, when not clouded by her feelings; but she was too much the creature of impulse, and the slave of compassion.

CHAPTER III

Near her father's house lived a poor widow, who had been brought up in affluence, but reduced to great distress by the extravagance of her husband; he had destroyed his constitution while he spent his fortune; and dying, left his wife, and five small children, to live on a very scanty pittance. The eldest daughter was for some years educated by a distant relation, a Clergyman. While she was with him a young gentleman, son to a man of property in the neighbourhood, took particular notice of her. It is true, he never talked of love; but then they played and sung in concert; drew landscapes together, and while she worked he read to her, cultivated her taste, and stole imperceptibly her heart. Just at this juncture, when smiling, unanalyzed hope made every prospect bright, and gay expectation danced in her eyes, her benefactor died. She returned to her mother – the companion of her youth forgot her, they took no more sweet counsel together. This disappointment spread a sadness over her countenance, and made it interesting. She grew fond of solitude, and her character appeared similar to Mary's, though her natural disposition was very different.

She was several years older than Mary, yet her refinement, her taste, caught her eye, and she eagerly sought her friendship: before her return she had assisted the family, which was almost reduced to the last ebb; and now she had another motive to actuate her.

As she had often occasion to send messages to Ann, her new friend, mistakes were frequently made; Ann proposed that in future they should be written ones, to obviate this difficulty, and render their intercourse more agreeable. Young people are mostly fond of scribbling; Mary had very little instruction; but by copying her friend's letters, whose hand she admired, she soon became a proficient; a little practice made her write with tolerable correctness, and her genius gave force to it. In conversation, and in writing, when she felt, she was pathetic, tender and persuasive; and she expressed contempt with such energy, that few could stand the flash of her eyes.

As she grew more intimate with Ann, her manners were softened, and she acquired a degree of equality in her behaviour: yet still her spirits were fluctuating, and her movements rapid. She felt less pain on account of her mother's partiality to her brother, as she hoped now to experience the pleasure of being beloved; but this hope led her into new sorrows, and, as usual, paved the way for disappointment. Ann only felt gratitude; her heart was entirely engrossed by one object, and friendship could not serve as a substitute; memory officiously retraced past scenes, and unavailing wishes made time loiter.

Mary was often hurt by the involuntary indifference which these consequences produced. When her friend was all the world to her, she found she was not as necessary to her happiness; and her delicate mind could not bear to obtrude her affection, or receive love as an alms, the offspring of pity. Very frequently has she ran to her with delight, and not perceiving any thing of the same kind in Ann's countenance, she has shrunk back; and, falling from one extreme into the other, instead of a warm greeting that was just slipping from her tongue, her expressions seemed to be dictated by the most chilling insensibility.

She would then imagine that she looked sickly or unhappy, and then all her tenderness would return like a torrent, and bear away all reflection. In this manner was her sensibility called forth, and exercised, by her mother's illness, her friend's misfortunes, and her own unsettled mind.

CHAPTER IV

Near to hear father's house was a range of mountains; some of them were, literally speaking, cloud-capt, for on them clouds continually rested, and gave grandeur to the prospect; and down many of their sides the little bubbling cascades ran till they swelled a beautiful river. Through the straggling trees and bushes the wind whistled, and on them the birds sung, particularly the robins; they also found shelter in the ivy of an old castle, a haunted one, as the story went; it was situated on the brow of one of the mountains, and commanded a view of the sea. This castle had been inhabited by some of her ancestors; and many tales had the old house-keeper told her of the worthies who had resided there.

When her mother frowned, and her friend looked cool, she would steal to this retirement, where human foot seldom trod – gaze on the sea, observe the grey clouds, or listen to the wind which struggled to free itself from the only thing that impeded its course. When more cheerful, she admired the various dispositions of light and shade, the beautiful tints the gleams of sunshine gave to the distant hills; then she rejoiced in existence, and darted into futurity.

One way home was through the cavity of a rock covered with a thin layer of earth, just sufficient to afford nourishment to a few stunted shrubs and wild plants, which grew on its sides, and nodded over the summit. A clear stream broke out of it, and ran amongst the pieces of rocks fallen into it. Here twilight always reigned – it seemed the Temple of Solitude; yet, paradoxical as the assertion may appear, when the foot sounded on the rock, it terrified the intruder, and inspired a strange feeling, as if the rightful sovereign was dislodged. In this retreat she read Thomson's Seasons, Young's Night-Thoughts, and Paradise Lost.[7]

At a little distance from it were the huts of a few poor fishermen, who supported their numerous children by their precarious labour. In these little huts she frequently rested, and denied herself every childish gratification, in order to relieve the necessities of the inhabitants. Her heart yearned for them, and would dance with joy when she had relieved their wants, or afforded them pleasure.

In these pursuits she learned the luxury of doing good; and the sweet tears of benevolence frequently moistened her eyes, and gave them a sparkle which, exclusive of that, they had not; on the contrary, they were rather fixed, and would never have been observed if her soul had not animated them. They were not at all like those brilliant ones which look like polished diamonds, and dart from every superfice, giving more light to the beholders than they receive themselves.

Her benevolence, indeed, knew no bounds; the distress of others carried her out of herself; and she rested not till she had relieved or comforted them. The warmth of her compassion often made her so diligent, that many things occurred to her, which might have escaped a less interested observer.

In like manner, she entered with such spirit into whatever she read, and the emotions thereby raised were so strong, that it soon became a part of her mind.

Enthusiastic sentiments of devotion at this period actuated her; her Creator was almost apparent to her senses in his works; but they were mostly the grand or solemn features of Nature which she delighted to contemplate. She would stand and behold the waves rolling, and think of the voice that could still the tumultuous deep.

These propensities gave the colour to her mind, before the passions began to exercise their tyrannic sway, and particularly pointed out those which the soil would have a tendency to nurse.

Years after, when wandering through the same scenes, her imagination has strayed back, to trace the first placid sentiments they inspired, and she would earnestly desire to regain the same peaceful tranquillity.

Many nights she sat up, if I may be allowed the expression, *conversing* with the Author of Nature, making verses, and singing hymns of her own composing. She considered also, and tried to discern what end her various faculties were destined to pursue; and had a glimpse of a truth, which afterwards more fully unfolded itself.

She thought that only an infinite being could fill the human soul, and that when other objects were followed as a means of happiness, the delusion led to misery, the consequence of disappointment. Under the influence of ardent affections, how often has she forgot this conviction, and as often returned to it again, when it struck her with redoubled force. Often did she taste unmixed delight; her joys, her ecstacies arose from genius.

She was now fifteen, and she wished to receive the holy sacrament; and perusing the scriptures, and discussing some points of doctrine which puzzled her, she would sit up half the night, her favourite time for employing her mind; she too plainly perceived that she saw though a glass darkly;[8] and that the bounds set to stop our intellectual researches, is one of the trials of a probationary state.

But her affections were roused by the display of divine mercy; and she eagerly desired to commemorate the dying love of her great benefactor. The night before the important day, when she was to take on herself her baptismal vow, she could not go to bed; the sun broke in on her meditations, and found her not exhausted by her watching.

The orient pearls were strewed around – she hailed the morn, and sung with wild delight, Glory to God on high, good will towards men.[9] She was indeed so much affected when she joined in the prayer for her eternal preservation, that she could hardly conceal her violent emotions; and the recollection never failed to wake her dormant piety when earthly passions made it grow languid.

These various movements of her mind were not commented on, nor were the luxuriant shoots restrained by culture. The servants and the poor adored her.

In order to be enabled to gratify herself in the highest degree, she practised the most rigid oeconomy, and had such power over her appetites and whims, that without any great effort she conquered them so entirely, that when her understanding or affections had an object, she almost forgot she had a body which required nourishment.

This habit of thinking, this kind of absorption, gave strength to the passions.

We will now enter on the more active field of life.

CHAPTER V

A few months after Mary was turned of seventeen, her brother was attacked by a violent fever, and died before his father could reach the school.

She was now an heiress, and her mother began to think her of consequence, and did not call her *the child*. Proper masters were sent for; she was taught to dance, and an extraordinary master procured to perfect her in that most necessary of all accomplishments.

A part of the estate she was to inherit had been litigated, and the heir of the person who still carried on a Chancery suit,[10] was only two years younger than our heroine. The fathers, spite of the dispute, frequently met, and, in order to settle it amicably, they one day, over a bottle, determined to quash it by a marriage, and, by uniting the two estates, to preclude all farther enquiries into the merits of their different claims.

While this important matter was settling, Mary was otherwise employed. Ann's mother's resources were failing; and the ghastly phantom, poverty, made hasty strides to catch them in his clutches. Ann had not fortitude enough to brave such accumulated misery; and besides, the canker-worm was lodged in her heart, and preyed on her health. She denied herself every little comfort; things that would be no sacrifice when a person is well, are absolutely necessary to alleviate bodily pain, and support the animal functions.

There were many elegant amusements, that she had acquired a relish for, which might have taken her mind off from its most destructive bent; but these her indigence would not allow her to enjoy: forced then, by way of relaxation, to play the tunes her lover admired, and handle the pencil he taught her to hold, no wonder his image floated on her imagination, and that taste invigorated love.

Poverty, and all its inelegant attendants, were in her mother's abode; and she, though a good sort of a woman, was not calculated to banish, by her trivial, uninteresting chat, the delirium in which her daughter was lost.

This ill-fated love had given a bewitching softness to her manners, a delicacy so truly feminine, that a man of any feeling could not behold her without wishing to chase her sorrows away. She was timid and irresolute, and rather fond of dissipation; grief only had power to make her reflect.

In every thing it was not the great, but the beautiful, or the pretty, that caught her attention. And in composition, the polish of style, and harmony of numbers, interested her much more than the flights of genius, or abstracted speculations.

She often wondered at the books Mary chose, who, though she had a lively imagination, would frequently study authors whose works were addressed to the understanding. This liking taught her to arrange her thoughts, and argue with herself, even when under the influence of the most violent passions.

Ann's misfortunes and ill health were strong ties to bind Mary to her; she wished so continually to have a home to receive her in, that it drove every other desire out of her mind; and, dwelling on the tender schemes which compassion and friendship dictated, she longed most ardently to put them in practice.

Fondly as she loved her friend, she did not forget her mother, whose decline was so imperceptible, that they were not aware of her approaching dissolution. The physician, however, observing the most alarming symptoms; her husband was apprised of her immediate danger; and then first mentioned to her his designs with respect to his daughter.

She approved of them; Mary was sent for; she was not at home; she had rambled to visit Ann, and found her in an hysteric fit. The landlord of her little farm had sent his agent for the rent, which had long been due to him; and he threatened to seize the stock that still remained, and turn them out, if they did not very shortly discharge the arrears.

As this man made a private fortune by harassing the tenants of the person to whom he was deputy, little was to be expected from his forbearance.

All this was told to Mary – and the mother added, she had many other creditors who would, in all probability, take the alarm, and snatch from them all that had been saved out of the wreck. 'I could bear all,' she cried; 'but what will become of my children? Of this child,' pointing to the fainting Ann, 'whose constitution is already undermined by care and grief – where will she go?' – Mary's heart ceased to beat while she asked the question – She attempted to speak; but the inarticulate sounds died away. Before she had recovered herself, her father called himself to enquire for her; and desired her instantly to accompany him home.

Engrossed by the scene of misery she had been witness to, she walked silently by his side, when he roused her out of her reverie by telling her that in all likelihood her mother had not many hours to live; and before she could return him any answer, informed her that they had both determined to marry her to Charles, his friend's son; he added, the ceremony was to be performed directly, that her mother might be witness of it; for such a desire she had expressed with childish eagerness.

Overwhelmed by this intelligence, Mary rolled her eyes about, then, with a vacant stare, fixed them on her father's face; but they were no longer a sense; they conveyed no ideas to the brain. As she drew near the house, her wonted presence of mind returned: after this suspension of thought, a thousand darted into her mind, – her dying mother, – her friend's miserable situation, – and an extreme horror at taking – at being forced to take, such a hasty step; but she did not feel the disgust, the reluctance, which arises from a prior attachment.

She loved Ann better than any one in the world – to snatch her from the very jaws of destruction – she would have encountered a lion. To have this friend constantly with her; to make her mind easy with respect to her family, would it not be superlative bliss?

Full of these thoughts she entered her mother's chamber, but they then fled at the sight of a dying parent. She went to her, took her hand; it feebly pressed her's. 'My child,' said the languid mother: the words reached her heart; she had seldom heard them pronounced with accents denoting affection; 'My child, I have not always treated you with kindness – God forgive me! do you?' – Mary's tears strayed in a disregarded stream; on her bosom the big drops fell, but did not relieve the fluttering tenant. 'I forgive you!' said she, in a tone of astonishment.

The clergyman came in to read the service for the sick, and afterwards the marriage ceremony was performed. Mary stood like a statue of Despair, and pronounced the awful vow without thinking of it; and then ran to support her mother, who expired the same night in her arms.

Her husband set off for the continent the same day, with a tutor, to finish his studies at one of the foreign universities.

Ann went sent for to console her, not on account of the departure of her new relation, a boy she seldom took any notice of, but to reconcile her to her fate; besides, it was necessary she should have a female companion, and there was not any maiden aunt in the family, or cousin of the same class.

CHAPTER VI

Mary was allowed to pay the rent which gave her so much uneasiness, and she exerted every nerve to prevail on her father effectually to succour the family; but the utmost she could obtain was a small sum very inadequate to the purpose, to enable the poor woman to carry into execution a little scheme of industry near the metropolis.

Her intention of leaving that part of the country, had much more weight with him, than Mary's arguments, drawn from motives of philanthropy and friendship; this was a language he did not understand, expressive of occult qualities he never thought of, as they could not be seen or felt.

After the departure of her mother, Ann still continued to languish, though she had a nurse who was entirely engrossed by the desire of amusing her. Had her health been re-established, the time would have passed in a tranquil, improving manner.

During the year of mourning they lived in retirement; music, drawing, and reading, filled up the time; and Mary's taste and judgment were both improved by contracting a habit of observation, and permitting the simple beauties of Nature to occupy her thoughts.

She had a wonderful quickness in discerning distinctions and combining ideas, that at the first glance did not appear to be similar. But these various pursuits did not banish all her cares, or carry off all her constitutional black bile.[11] Before she enjoyed Ann's society, she imagined it would have made her completely happy: she was disappointed, and yet knew not what to complain of.

As her friend could not accompany her in her walks, and wished to be alone, for a very obvious reason, she would return to her old haunts, retrace her anticipated pleasures – and wonder how they changed their colour in possession, and proved so futile.

She had not yet found the companion she looked for. Ann and she were not congenial minds, nor did she contribute to her comfort in the degree she expected. She shielded her from poverty; but this was only a negative blessing; when under the pressure it was very grievous, and still more so were the apprehensions; but when exempt from them, she was not contented.

Such is human nature, its laws were not to be inverted to gratify our heroine, and stop the progress of her understanding, happiness only flourished in paradise – we cannot taste and live.

Another year passed away with increasing apprehensions. Ann had a hectic[12] cough, and many unfavourable prognostics: Mary then forgot every thing but the fear of losing her, and even imagined that her recovery would have made her happy.

Her anxiety led her to study physic, and for some time she only read books of that cast; and this knowledge, literally speaking, ended in vanity and vexation of spirit,[13] as it enabled her to foresee what she could not prevent.

As her mind expanded, her marriage appeared a dreadful misfortune; she was sometimes reminded of the heavy yoke, and bitter was the recollection!

In one thing there seemed to be a sympathy between them, for she wrote formal answers to his as formal letters. An extreme dislike took root in her mind; the sound of his name made her turn sick; but she forgot all, listening to Ann's cough, and supporting her languid frame. She would then catch her to her bosom with convulsive eagerness, as if to save her from sinking into an opening grave.

CHAPTER VII

It was the will of Providence that Mary should experience almost every species of sorrow. Her father was thrown from his horse, when his blood was in a very inflammatory state, and as the bruises were very dangerous; his recovery was not expected by the physical tribe.

Terrified at seeing him so near death, and yet so ill prepared for it, his daughter sat by his bed, oppressed by the keenest anguish, which her piety increased.

Her grief had nothing selfish in it; he was not a friend or protector; but he was her father, an unhappy wretch, going into eternity, depraved and thoughtless. Could a life of sensuality be a preparation for a peaceful death? Thus meditating, she passed the still midnight hour by his bedside.

The nurse fell asleep, nor did a violent thunder storm interrupt her repose, though it made the night appear still more terrific to Mary. Her father's unequal breathing alarmed her, when she heard a long drawn breath, she feared it was his last, and watching for another, a dreadful peal of thunder struck her ears. Considering the separation of the soul and body, this night seemed sadly solemn, and the hours long.

Death is indeed a king of terrors when he attacks the vicious man! The compassionate heart finds not any comfort; but dreads an eternal separation. No transporting greetings are anticipated, when the survivors also shall have finished their course; but all is black! – the grave may truly be said to receive the departed – this is the sting of death!

Night after night Mary watched, and this excessive fatigue impaired her own health, but had a worse effect on Ann; though she constantly went to bed, she could not rest; a number of uneasy thoughts obtruded themselves; and apprehensions about Mary, whom she loved as well as her exhausted heart could love, harassed her mind. After a sleepless, feverish night she had a violent fit of coughing, and burst a blood-vessel. The physician, who was in the house, was sent for, and when he left the patient, Mary, with an authoritative voice, insisted on knowing his real opinion. Reluctantly he gave it, that her friend was in a critical state; and if she passed the approaching winter in England, he imagined she would die in the spring; a season fatal to consumptive disorders. The spring! – Her husband was then expected. – Gracious Heaven, could she bear all this.

In a few days her father breathed his last. The horrid sensations his death occasioned were too poignant to be durable: and Ann's danger, and her own situation, made Mary deliberate what mode of conduct she should pursue.

She feared this event might hasten the return of her husband, and prevent her putting into execution a plan she had determined on. It was to accompany Ann to a more salubrious climate.

CHAPTER VIII

I mentioned before, that Mary had never had any particular attachment, to give rise to the disgust that daily gained ground. Her friendship for Ann occupied her heart, and resembled a passion. She had had, indeed, several transient likings; but they did not amount to love. The society of men of genius delighted her, and improved her faculties. With beings of this class she did not often meet; it is a rare genus; her first favourites were men past the meridian of life, and of a philosophic turn.

Determined on going to the South of France, or Lisbon; she wrote to the man she had promised to obey. The physicians had said change of air was necessary for her as well as her friend. She mentioned this, and added, 'Her comfort, almost her existence, depended on the recovery of the invalid she wished to attend; and that should she neglect to follow the medical advice she had received, she should never forgive herself, or those who endeavoured to prevent her.' Full of her design, she wrote with more than usual freedom; and this letter was like most of her others, a transcript of her heart.

'This dear friend,' she exclaimed, 'I love for her agreeable qualities, and substantial virtues. Continual attention to her health, and the tender office of a nurse, have created an affection very like a maternal one – I am her only support, she leans on me – could I forsake the forsaken, and break the bruised reed[14] – No – I would die first! I must – I will go.'

She would have added, 'you would very much oblige me by consenting;' but her heart revolted – and irresolutely she wrote something about wishing him happy. – 'Do I not wish all the world well?' she cried, as she subscribed her name – It was blotted, the letter sealed in a hurry, and sent out of her sight; and she began to prepare for her journey.

By the return of the post she received an answer; it contained some common-place remarks on her romantic friendship, as he termed it; 'But as the physicians advised change of air, he had no objection.'

CHAPTER IX

There was nothing now to retard their journey; and Mary chose Lisbon rather than France, on account of its being further removed from the only person she wished not to see.

They set off accordingly for Falmouth, in their way to that city. The journey was of use to Ann, and Mary's spirits were raised by her recovered looks – She had been in despair – now she gave way to hope, and was intoxicated with it. On ship-board Ann always remained in the cabin; the sight of the water terrified her: on the contrary, Mary, after she was gone to bed, or when she fell asleep in the day, went on deck, conversed with the sailors, and surveyed the boundless expanse before her with delight. One instant she would regard the ocean, the next the beings who braved its fury. Their insensibility and want of fear, she could not name courage; their thoughtless mirth was quite of an animal kind, and their feelings as impetuous and uncertain as the element they plowed.

They had only been a week at sea when they hailed the rock of Lisbon, and the next morning anchored at the castle. After the customary visits, they were permitted to go on shore, about three miles from the city; and while one of the crew, who understood the language, went to procure them one of the ugly carriages peculiar to the country, they waited in the Irish convent, which is situated close to the Tagus.[15]

Some of the people offered to conduct them into the church, where there was a fine organ playing; Mary followed them, but Ann preferred staying with a nun she had entered into conversation with.

One of the nuns, who had a sweet voice, was singing; Mary was struck with awe; her heart joined in the devotion; and tears of gratitude and tenderness flowed from her eyes. My Father, I thank thee! burst from her – words were inadequate to express her feelings. Silently, she surveyed the lofty dome; heard unaccustomed sounds; and saw faces, strange ones, that she could not yet greet with fraternal love.

In an unknown land, she considered that the Being she adored inhabited eternity, was ever present in unnumbered worlds.[16] When she had not any one she loved near her, she was particularly sensible of the presence of her Almighty Friend.

The arrival of the carriage put a stop to her speculations; it was to conduct them to an hotel, fitted up for the reception of invalids. Unfortunately, before they could reach it there was a violent shower of rain; and as the wind was very high, it beat against the leather curtains, which they drew along the front of the vehicle, to shelter themselves from it; but it availed not, some of the rain forced its way, and Ann felt the effects of it, for she caught cold, spite of Mary's precautions.

As is the custom, the rest of the invalids, or lodgers, sent to enquire after their health; and as soon as Ann left her chamber, in which her complaints seldom confined her the whole day, they came in person to pay their compliments. Three fashionable females, and two gentlemen; the one a brother of the eldest of the young ladies, and the other an invalid, who came, like themselves, for the benefit of the air. They entered into conversation immediately.

People who meet in a strange country, and are all together in a house, soon get acquainted, without the formalities which attend visiting in separate houses, where they are surrounded by domestic friends. Ann was particularly delighted at meeting with agreeable society; a little hectic fever generally made her low-spirited in the morning, and lively in the evening, when she wished for company. Mary, who only thought of her, determined to cultivate their acquaintance, as she knew, that if her mind could be diverted, her body might gain strength.

They were all musical, and proposed having little concerts. One of the gentlemen played on the violin, and the other on the german-flute. The instruments were brought in, with all the eagerness that attends putting a new scheme in execution.

Mary had not said much, for she was diffident; she seldom joined in general conversations; though her quickness of penetration enabled her soon to enter into the characters of those she conversed with; and her sensibility made her desirous of pleasing every human creature. Besides, if her mind was not occupied by any particular sorrow, or study, she caught reflected pleasure, and was glad to see others happy, though their mirth did not interest her.

This day she was continually thinking of Ann's recovery, and encouraging the cheerful hopes, which though they dissipated the spirits that had been condensed by melancholy, yet made her wish to be silent. The music, more than the conversation, disturbed her reflections; but not at first. The gentleman who played on the german-flute, was a handsome, well-bred, sensible man; and his observations, if not original, were pertinent.

The other, who had not said much, began to touch the violin, and played a little Scotch ballad; he brought such a thrilling sound out of the instrument, that Mary started, and looking at him with more attention than she had done before, and saw, in a face rather ugly, strong lines of genius.[17] His manners were awkward, that kind of awkwardness which is often found in literary men: he seemed a thinker, and delivered his opinions in elegant expressions, and musical tones of voice.

When the concert was over, they all retired to their apartments. Mary always slept with Ann, as she was subject to terrifying dreams; and frequently in the night was obliged to be supported, to avoid suffocation. They chatted about their new acquaintance in their own apartment, and, with respect to the gentlemen, differed in opinion.

CHAPTER X

Every day almost they saw their new acquaintance; and civility produced intimacy. Mary sometimes left her friend with them; while she indulged herself in viewing new modes of life, and searching out the causes which produced them. She had a metaphysical turn, which inclined her to reflect on every object that passed by her; and her mind was not like a mirror, which receives every floating image, but does not retain them: she had not any prejudices, for every opinion was examined before it was adopted.

The Roman Catholic ceremonies attracted her attention, and gave rise to conversations when they all met; and one of the gentlemen continually introduced deistical notions, when he ridiculed the pageantry they all were surprised at observing. Mary thought of both the subjects, the Romish tenets, and the deistical doubts; and though not a sceptic, thought it right to examine the evidence on which her faith was built. She read Butler's Analogy,[18] and some other authors: and these researches made her a christian from conviction, and she learned charity, particularly with respect to sectaries; saw that apparently good and solid arguments might take their rise from different points of view; and she rejoiced to find that those she should not concur with had some reason on their side.

CHAPTER XI

When I mentioned the three ladies, I said they were fashionable women; and it was all the praise, as a faithful historian, I could bestow on them; the only thing in which they were consistent. I forgot to mention that they were all of one family, a mother, her daughter, and niece. The daughter was sent by her physician, to avoid a northerly winter; the mother, her niece, and nephew, accompanied her.

They were people of rank; but unfortunately, though of an ancient family, the title had descended to a very remote branch – a branch they took care to be intimate with; and servilely copied the Countess's airs. Their minds were shackled with a set of notions concerning propriety, the fitness of things for the world's eye, trammels which always hamper weak people. What will the world say? was the first thing that was thought of, when they intended doing any thing they had not done before. Or what would the Countess do on such an occasion? And when this question was answered, the right or wrong was discovered without the trouble of their having any idea of the matter in their own heads. This same Countess was a fine planet, and the satellites observed a most harmonic dance around her.

After this account it is scarcely necessary to add, that their minds had received very little cultivation. They were taught French, Italian, and Spanish; English was their vulgar tongue. And what did they learn? Hamlet will tell you – words – words.[19] But let me not forget that they squalled Italian songs in the true *gusta*. Without having any seeds sown in their understanding, or the affections of the heart set to work, they were brought out of their nursery, or the place they were secluded in, to prevent their faces being common; like blazing stars, to captivate Lords.

They were pretty, and hurrying from one party of pleasure to another, occasioned the disorder which required change of air. The mother, if we except her being near twenty years older, was just the same creature; and these additional years only served to make her more tenaciously adhere to her habits of folly, and decide with stupid gravity, some trivial points of ceremony, as a matter of the last importance; of which she was a competent judge, from having lived in the fashionable world so long: that world to which the ignorant look up as we do to the sun.

It appears to me that every creature has some notion – or rather relish, of the sublime. Riches, and the consequent state, are the sublime of weak minds: – These images fill, nay, are too big for their narrow souls.

One afternoon, which they had engaged to spend together, Ann was so ill, that Mary was obliged to send an apology for not attending the tea-table. The apology brought them on the carpet; and the mother, with a look of solemn importance, turned to the sick man, whose name was Henry, and said: 'Though people of the first fashion are frequently at places of this kind, intimate with they know not who; yet I do not choose that my daughter, whose family is so respectable, should be intimate with any one she would blush to know elsewhere. It is only on that account, for I never suffer her to be with any one but in my company,' added she, sitting more erect; and a smile of self-complacency dressed her countenance.

'I have enquired concerning these strangers, and find that the one who has the most dignity in her manners, is really a woman of fortune.' 'Lord, mamma, how ill she dresses:' mamma went on; 'She is a romantic creature, you must not copy her, miss; yet she is an heiress of the large fortune in ——shire, of which you may remember to have heard the Countess speak the night you had on the dancing-dress that was so much admired; but she is married.'

She then told them the whole story as she heard it from her maid, who picked it out of Mary's servant. 'She is a foolish creature, and this friend that she pays as much attention to as if she was a lady of quality, is a beggar.' 'Well, how strange!' cried the girls.

'She is, however, a charming creature,' said her nephew. Henry sighed, and strode across the room once or twice; then took up his violin, and played the air which first struck Mary; he had often heard her praise it.

The music was uncommonly melodious, 'And came stealing on the senses like the sweet south.'[20] The well-known sounds reached Mary as she sat by her friend – she listened without knowing that she did – and shed tears almost without being conscious of it. Ann soon fell asleep, as she had taken an opiate. Mary, then brooding over her fears, began to imagine she had deceived herself – Ann was still very ill; hope had beguiled many heavy hours; yet she was displeased with herself for admitting this welcome guest. – And she worked up her mind to such a degree of anxiety, that she determined, once more, to seek medical aid.

No sooner did she determine, than she ran down with a discomposed look, to enquire of the ladies who she should send for. When she entered the room she could not articulate her fears – it appeared like pronouncing Ann's sentence of death; her faultering tongue dropped some broken words, and she remained silent. The ladies wondered that a person of her sense should be so little mistress of herself; and began to administer some common-place comfort, as, that it was our duty to submit to the will of Heaven, and the like trite consolations, which Mary did not answer; but waving her hand, with an air of impatience, she exclaimed, 'I cannot live without her! – I have no other friend; if I lose her, what a desart will the world be to me.' 'No other friend,' re-echoed they, 'have you not a husband?'

Mary shrunk back, and was alternately pale and red. A delicate sense of propriety prevented her replying; and recalled her bewildered reason. – Assuming, in consequence of her recollection, a more composed manner, she made the intended enquiry, and left the room. Henry's eyes followed her while the females very freely animadverted on her strange behaviour.

CHAPTER XII

The physician was sent for; his prescription afforded Ann a little temporary relief; and they again joined the circle. Unfortunately, the weather happened to be constantly wet for more than a week, and confined them to the house. Ann then found the ladies not so agreeable; when they sat whole hours together, the thread-bare topics were exhausted; and, but for cards or music, the long evenings would have been yawned away in listless indolence.

The bad weather had had as ill an effect on Henry as on Ann. He was frequently very thoughtful, or rather melancholy; this melancholy would of itself have attracted Mary's notice, if she had not found his conversation so infinitely superior to the rest of the group. When she conversed with him, all the faculties of her soul unfolded themselves; genius animated her expressive countenance; and the most graceful, unaffected gestures gave energy to her discourse.

They frequently discussed very important subjects, while the rest were singing or playing cards, nor were they observed for doing so, as Henry, whom they all were pleased with, in the way of gallantry shewed them all more attention than her. Besides, as there was nothing alluring in her dress or manner, they never dreamt of her being preferred to them.

Henry was a man of learning; he had also studied mankind, and knew many of the intricacies of the human heart, from having felt the infirmities of his own. His taste was just, as it had a standard – Nature, which he observed with a critical eye. Mary could not help thinking that in his company her mind expanded, as he always went below the surface. She increased her stock of ideas, and her taste was improved.

He was also a pious man; his rational religious sentiments received warmth from his sensibility; and, except on very particular occasions, kept it in proper bounds; these sentiments had likewise formed his temper; he was gentle, and easily to be intreated. The ridiculous ceremonies they were every day witness to, led them into what are termed grave subjects, and made him explain his opinions, which, at other times, he was neither ashamed of, nor unnecessarily brought forward to notice.

CHAPTER XIII

When the weather began to clear up, Mary sometimes rode out alone, purposely to view the ruins that still remained of the earthquake:[21] or she would ride to the banks of the Tagus, to feast her eyes with the sight of that magnificent river. At other times she would visit the churches, as she was particularly fond of seeing historical paintings.

One of these visits gave rise to the subject, and the whole party descanted on it; but as the ladies could not handle it well, they soon adverted to portraits; and talked of the attitudes and characters in which they should wish to be drawn. Mary did not fix on one – when Henry, with more apparent warmth than usual, said, 'I would give the world for your picture, with the expression I have seen in your face, when you have been supporting your friend.'

This delicate compliment did not gratify her vanity, but it reached her heart. She then recollected that she had once sat for her picture – for whom was it designed? For a boy! Her cheeks flushed with indignation, so strongly did she feel an emotion of contempt at having been thrown away – given in with an estate.

As Mary again gave way to hope, her mind was more disengaged; and her thoughts were employed about the objects around her.

She visited several convents, and found that solitude only eradicates some passions, to give strength to others; the most baneful ones. She saw that religion does not consist in ceremonies; and that many prayers may fall from the lips without purifying the heart.

They who imagine they can be religious without governing their tempers, or exercising benevolence in its most extensive sense, must certainly allow, that their religious duties are only practised from selfish principles; how then can they be called good? The pattern of all goodness went about *doing* good. Wrapped up in themselves, the nuns only thought of inferior gratifications. And a number of intrigues were carried on to accelerate certain points on which their hearts were fixed:

Such as obtaining offices of trust or authority; or avoiding those that were servile or laborious. In short, when they could be neither wives nor mothers, they aimed at being superiors, and became the most selfish creatures in the world: the passions that were curbed gave strength to the appetites, or to those mean passions which only tend to provide for the gratification of them. Was this seclusion from the world? or did they conquer its vanities or avoid its vexations?

In these abodes the unhappy individual, who, in the first paroxysm of grief, flies to them for refuge, finds too late she took a wrong step. The same warmth which determined her will make her repent; and sorrow, the rust of the mind, will never have a chance of being rubbed off by sensible conversation, or new-born affections of the heart.

She will find that those affections that have once been called forth and strengthened by exercise, are only smothered, not killed, by disappointment; and that in one form or other discontent will corrode the heart, and produce those maladies of the imagination, for which there is no specific.

The community at large Mary disliked; but pitied many of them whose private distress she was informed of; and to pity and relieve were the same things with her.

The exercise of her various virtues gave vigor to her genius, and dignity to her mind; she was sometimes inconsiderate, and violent; but never mean or cunning.

CHAPTER XIV

The Portuguese are certainly the most uncivilized nation in Europe. Dr Johnson would have said, 'They have the least mind.'[22] And can such serve their Creator in spirit and in truth? No, the gross ritual of Romish ceremonies is all they can comprehend: they can do penance, but not conquer their revenge, or lust. Religion, or love, has never humanized their hearts; they want the vital part; the mere body worships. Taste is unknown; Gothic finery, and unnatural decorations, which they term ornaments, are conspicuous in their churches and dress. Reverence for mental excellence is only to be found in a polished nation.

Could the contemplation of such a people gratify Mary's heart? No: she turned disgusted from the prospects – turned to a man of refinement. Henry had been some time ill and low-spirited; Mary would have been attentive to any one in that situation; but to him she was particularly so; she thought herself bound in gratitude, on account of his constant endeavours to amuse Ann, and prevent her dwelling on the dreary prospect before her, which sometimes she could not help anticipating with a kind of quiet despair.

She found some excuse for going more frequently into the room they all met in; nay, she avowed her desire to amuse him: offered to read to him, and tried to draw him into amusing conversations; and when she was full of these little schemes, she looked at him with a degree of tenderness that she was not conscious of. This divided attention was of use to her, and prevented her continually thinking of Ann, whose fluctuating disorder often gave rise to false hopes.

A trifling thing occurred now which occasioned Mary some uneasiness. Her maid, a well-looking girl, had captivated the clerk of a neighbouring compting-house. As the match was an advantageous one, Mary could not raise any objection to it, though at this juncture it was very disagreeable to her to have a stranger about her person. However, the girl consented to delay the marriage, as she had some affection for her mistress; and, besides, looked forward to Ann's death as a time of harvest.

Henry's illness was not alarming, it was rather pleasing, as it gave Mary an excuse to herself for shewing him how much she was interested about him; and giving little artless proofs of affection, which the purity of her heart made her never wish to restrain.

The only visible return he made was not obvious to common observers. He would sometimes fix his eyes on her, and take them off with a sigh that was coughed away; or when he was leisurely walking into the room, and did not expect to see her, he would quicken his steps, and come up to her with eagerness to ask some trivial question. In the same style, he would try to detain her when he had nothing to say – or said nothing.

Ann did not take notice of either his or Mary's behaviour, nor did she suspect that he was a favourite, on any other account than his appearing neither well nor happy. She had often seen that when a person was unfortunate, Mary's pity might easily be mistaken for love, and, indeed, it was a temporary sensation of that kind. Such it was – why it was so, let others define, I cannot argue against instincts. As reason is cultivated in man, they are supposed to grow weaker, and this may have given rise to the assertion, 'That as judgment improves, genius evaporates.'[25]

CHAPTER XV

One morning they set out to visit the aqueduct; though the day was very fine when they left home, a very heavy shower fell before they reached it; they lengthened their ride, the clouds dispersed, and the sun came from behind them uncommonly bright.

Mary would fain have persuaded Ann not to have left the carriage; but she was in spirits, and obviated all her objections, and insisted on walking, tho' the ground was damp. But her strength was not equal to her spirits; she was soon obliged to return to the carriage so much fatigued, that she fainted, and remained insensible a long time.

Henry would have supported her; but Mary would not permit him; her recollection was instantaneous, and she feared sitting on the damp ground might do him a material injury; she was on that account positive, though the company did not guess the cause of her being so. As to herself, she did not fear bodily pain; and, when her mind was agitated, she could endure the greatest fatigue without appearing sensible of it.

When Ann recovered, they returned slowly home; she was carried to bed, and the next morning Mary thought she observed a visible change for the worse. The physician was sent for, who pronounced her to be in the most imminent danger.

All Mary's former fears now returned like a torrent, and carried every other care away; she even added to her present anguish by upbraiding herself for her late tranquillity – it haunted her in the form of a crime.

The disorder made the most rapid advances – there was no hope! – Bereft of it, Mary again was tranquil; but it was a very different kind of tranquillity.

She stood to brave the approaching storm, conscious she only could be overwhelmed by it.

She did not think of Henry, or if her thoughts glanced towards him, it was only to find fault with herself for suffering a thought to have strayed from Ann! – Ann! – this dear friend was soon torn from her – she died suddenly as Mary was assisting her to walk across the room. – The first string was fevered from her heart – and this 'slow, sudden-death'[24] disturbed her reasoning faculties; she seemed stunned by it; unable to reflect, or even to feel her misery.

The body was stolen out of the house the second night, and Mary refused to see her former companions.[25] She desired her maid to conclude her marriage, and request her intended husband to inform her when the first merchantman was to leave the port, as the packet had just sailed, and she determined not to stay in that hated place any longer than was absolutely necessary.

She then sent to request the ladies to visit her; she wished to avoid a parade of grief – her sorrows were her own, and appeared to her not to admit of increase or softening. She was right; the sight of them did not affect her, or turn the stream of her sullen sorrow; the black wave rolled along in the same course; it was equal to her when she cast her eyes; all was impenetrable gloom.

CHAPTER XVI

Soon after the ladies left her, she received a message from Henry, requesting, as she saw company, to be permitted to visit her: she consented, and he entered immediately, with an unassured pace. She ran eagerly up to him – saw the tear trembling in his eye, and his countenance softened by the tenderest compassion; the hand which pressed hers seemed that of a fellow-creature. She burst into tears; and, unable to restrain them, she hid her face with both her hands: these tears relieved her, (she had before had a difficulty in breathing,) and she sat down by him more composed than she had appeared since Ann's death; but her conversation was incoherent.

She called herself 'a poor disconsolate creature!' – 'Mine is a selfish grief,' she exclaimed – 'Yet, Heaven is my witness, I do not wish her back now she has reached those peaceful mansions, where the weary rest. Her pure spirit is happy; but what a wretch am I!'

Henry forgot his cautious reserve. 'Would you allow me to call you friend?' said he in a hesitating voice. 'I feel, dear girl, the tenderest interest in whatever concerns thee.' His eyes spoke the rest. They were both silent a few moments; then Henry resumed the conversation. 'I have also been acquainted with grief! I mourn the loss of a woman who was not worthy of my regard. Let me give thee some account of the man who now solicits thy friendship; and who, from motives of the purest benevolence, wishes to give comfort to thy wounded heart.

'I have myself,' said he, mournfully, 'shaken hands with happiness, and am dead to the world; I wait patiently for my dissolution; but, for thee, Mary, there may be many bright days in store.'

'Impossible,' replied she, in a peevish tone, as if he had insulted her by the supposition; her feelings were so much in unison with his, that she was in love with misery.

He smiled at her impatience, and went on. 'My father died before I knew him, and my mother was so attached to my eldest brother, that she took very little pains to fit me for the profession to which I was destined: and, may I tell thee, I left my family, and, in many different stations, rambled about the world; saw mankind in every rank of life; and, in order to be independent, exerted those talents Nature has given me: these exertions improved my understanding; and the miseries I was witness to, gave a keener edge to my sensibility. My constitution is naturally weak; and, perhaps, two or three lingering disorders in my youth, first gave me a habit of reflecting, and enabled me to obtain some dominion over my passions. At least,' added he, stifling a sigh, 'over the violent ones, though I fear, refinement and reflection only renders the tender ones more tyrannic.

'I have told you already I have been in love, and disappointed – the object is now no more; let her faults sleep with her! Yet this passion has pervaded my whole soul, and mixed itself with all my affections and pursuits. – I am not peacefully indifferent; yet it is only to my violin I tell the sorrows I now confide with thee. The object I loved forfeited my esteem; yet, true to the sentiment, my fancy has too frequently delighted to form a creature that I could love, that could convey to my soul sensations which the gross part of mankind have not any conception of.'

He stopped, as Mary seemed lost in thought; but as she was still in a listening attitude, continued his little narrative. 'I kept up an irregular correspondence with my mother; my brother's extravagance and ingratitude had almost broken her heart, and made her feel something like a pang of remorse, on account of her behaviour to me. I hastened to comfort her – and was a comfort to her.

'My declining health prevented my taking orders, as I had intended; but I with warmth entered into literary pursuits; perhaps my heart, not having an object, made me embrace the substitute with more eagerness. But, do not imagine I have always been a die-away swain. No: I have frequented the cheerful haunts of men, and wit! – enchanting wit! has made many moments fly free from care. I am too fond of the elegant arts; and woman – lovely woman! thou hast charmed me, though, perhaps, it would not be easy to find one to whom my reason would allow me to be constant.

'I have now only to tell you, that my mother insisted on my spending this winter in a warmer climate; and I fixed on Lisbon, as I had before visited the Continent.' He then looked Mary full in the face; and, with the most insinuating accents, asked 'if he might hope for her friendship? If she would rely on him as if he was her father; and that the tenderest father could not more anxiously interest himself in the fate of a darling child, than he did in her's.'

Such a crowd of thoughts all at once rushed into Mary's mind, that she in vain attempted to express the sentiments which were most predominant. Her heart longed to receive a new guest; there was a void in it: accustomed to have some one to love, she was alone, and comfortless, if not engrossed by a particular affection.

Henry saw her distress, and not to increase it, left the room. He had exerted himself to turn her thoughts into a new channel, and had succeeded; she thought of him till she began to chide herself for defrauding the dead, and, determining to grieve for Ann, she dwelt on Henry's misfortunes and ill health; and the interest he took in her fate was a balm to her sick mind. She did not reason on the subject; but she felt he was attached to her: lost in this delirium, she never asked herself what kind of an affection she had for him, or what it tended to; nor did she know that love and friendship are very distinct; she thought with rapture, that there was one person in the world who had an affection for her, and that person she admired – had a friendship for.

He had called her his dear girl; the words might have fallen from him by accident; but they did not fall to the ground. My child! His child, what an association of ideas! If I had had a father, such a father! – She could not dwell on the thoughts, the wishes which obtruded themselves. Her mind was unhinged, and passion unperceived filled her whole soul. Lost, in waking dreams, she considered and reconsidered Henry's account of himself; till she actually thought she would tell Ann – a bitter recollection then roused her out of her reverie; and aloud she begged forgiveness of her.

By these kind of conflicts the day was lengthened; and when she went to bed, the night passed away in feverish slumbers; though they did not refresh her, she was spared the labour of thinking, of restraining her imagination; it sported uncontrouled; but took its colour from her waking train of thoughts. One instant she was supporting her dying mother; then Ann was breathing her last, and Henry was comforting her.

The unwelcome light visited her languid eyes; yet, I must tell the truth, she thought she should see Henry, and this hope set her spirits in motion: but they were quickly depressed by her maid, who came to tell her that she had heard of a vessel on board of which she could be accommodated, and that there was to be another female passenger on board, a vulgar one; but perhaps she would be more useful on that account – Mary did not want a companion.

As she had given orders for her passage to be engaged in the first vessel that sailed, she could not now retract; and must prepare for the lonely voyage, as the Captain intended taking advantage of the first fair wind. She had too much strength of mind to waver in her determination; but to determine wrung her very heart, opened all her old wounds, and made them bleed afresh. What was she to do? where go? Could she set a seal to a hasty vow, and tell a deliberate lie; promise to love one man, when the image of another was ever present to her – her soul revolted. 'I might gain the applause of the world by such mock heroism; but should I not forfeit my own? forfeit thine, my father!'

There is a solemnity in the shortest ejaculation, which, for a while, stills the tumult of passion. Mary's mind had been thrown off its poise; her devotion had been, perhaps, more fervent for some time past; but less regular. She forgot that happiness was not to be found on earth, and built a terrestrial paradise liable to be destroyed by the first serious thought: when she reasoned she became inexpressibly sad, to render life bearable she gave way to fancy – this was madness.

In a few days she must again go to sea; the weather was very tempestuous –what of that, the tempest in her soul rendered every other trifling – it was not the contending elements, but *herself* she feared!

CHAPTER XVII

In order to gain strength to support the expected interview, she went out in a carriage. The day was fine; but all nature was to her a universal blank; she could neither enjoy it, nor weep that she could not. She passed by the ruins of an old monastery on a very high hill; she got out to walk amongst the ruins; the wind blew violently, she did not avoid its fury, on the contrary, wildly bid it blow on, and seemed glad to contend with it, or rather walk against it. Exhausted, she returned to the carriage, was soon at home, and in the old room.

Henry started at the sight of her altered appearance; the day before her complexion had been of the most pallid hue; but now her cheeks were flushed, and her eyes enlivened with a false vivacity, an unusual fire. He was not well, his illness was apparent in his countenance, and he owned he had not closed his eyes all night; this roused her dormant tenderness, she forgot they were so soon to part – engrossed by the present happiness of seeing, of hearing him.

Once or twice she essayed to tell him that she was, in a few days, to depart; but she could not; she was irresolute; it will do to-morrow; should the wind change they could not sail in such a hurry; thus she thought, and insensibly grew more calm. The Ladies prevailed on her to spend the evening with them; but she retired very early to rest, and sat on the side of her bed several hours, then threw herself on it, and waited for the dreaded to-morrow.

CHAPTER XVIII

The ladies heard that her servant was to be married that day, and that she was to sail in the vessel which was then clearing out at the Custom-house. Henry heard, but did not make any remarks; and Mary called up all her fortitude to support her, and enable her to hide from the females her internal struggles. She durst not encounter Henry's glances when she found he had been informed of her intention; and, trying to draw a veil over her wretched state of mind, she talked incessantly, she knew not what; flashes of wit burst from her, and when she began to laugh she could not stop herself.

Henry smiled at some of her sallies, and looked at her with such benignity and compassion, that he recalled her scattered thoughts; and, the ladies going to dress for dinner, they were left alone; and remained silent a few moments: after the noisy conversation it appeared solemn. Henry began. 'You are going Mary, and going by yourself; your mind is not in a state to be left to its own operations – yet I cannot dissuade you; if I attempted to do it, I should ill deserve the title I wish to merit. I only think of your happiness; could I obey the strongest impulse of my heart, I should accompany thee to England; but such a step might endanger your future peace.'

Mary, then, with all the frankness which marked her character, explained her situation to him, and mentioned her fatal tie with such disgust that he trembled for her. 'I cannot see him; he is not the man formed for me to love!' Her delicacy did not restrain her, for her dislike to her husband had taken root in her mind long before she knew Henry. Did she not fix on Lisbon rather than France on purpose to avoid him? and if Ann had been in tolerable health she would have flown with her to some remote corner to have escaped from him.

'I intend,' said Henry, 'to follow you in the next packet; where shall I hear of your health?' 'Oh! let me hear of thine,' replied Mary. 'I am well, very well; but thou art very ill – thy health is in the most precarious state.' She then mentioned her intention of going to Ann's relations. 'I am her representative, I have duties to fulfil for her: during my voyage I shall have time enough for reflection; though I think I have already determined.'

'Be not too hasty, my child,' interrupted Henry; 'far be it from me to persuade thee to do violence to thy feelings – but consider that all thy future life may probably take its colour from thy present mode of conduct. Our affections as well as our sentiments are fluctuating; you will not perhaps always either think or feel as you do at present: the object you now shun may appear in a different light.' He paused. 'In advising thee in this style, I have only thy good at heart, Mary.'

She only answered to expostulate. 'My affections are involuntary – yet they can only be fixed by reflection, and when they are they make quite a part of my soul, are interwoven in it, animate my actions, and form my taste: certain qualities are calculated to call forth my sympathies, and make me all I am capable of being. The governing affection gives its stamp to the rest – because I am capable of loving one, I have that kind of charity to all my fellow-creatures which is not easily provoked. Milton has asserted, That earthly love is the scale by which to heavenly we may ascend.'[26]

She went on with eagerness. 'My opinions on some subjects are not wavering; my pursuit through life has ever been the same: in solitude were my sentiments formed; they are indelible, and nothing can efface them but death – No, death itself cannot efface them, or my soul must be created afresh, and not improved. Yet a little while am I parted from my Ann – I could not exist without the hope of seeing her again – I could not bear to think that time could wear away an affection that was founded on what is not liable to perish; you might as well attempt to persuade me that my soul is matter, and that its feelings arose from certain modifications of it.'

'Dear enthusiastic creature,' whispered Henry, 'how you steal into my soul.' She still continued. 'The same turn of mind which leads me to adore the Author of all Perfection – which leads me to conclude that he only can fill my soul; forces me to admire the faint image – the shadows of his attributes here below; and my imagination gives still bolder strokes to them. I know I am in some degree under the influence of a delusion – but does not this strong delusion prove that I myself "am *of subtiler essence than the trodden clod*:"[27] these flights of the imagination point to futurity; I cannot banish them. Every cause in nature produces an effect; and am I an exception to the general rule? have I desires implanted in me only to make me miserable? will they never be gratified? shall I never be happy? My feelings do not accord with the notion of solitary happiness. In a state of bliss, it will be the society of beings we can love, without the alloy that earthly infirmities mix with our best affections, that will constitute great part of our happiness.

'With these notions can I conform to the maxims of worldly wisdom? can I listen to the cold dictates of worldly prudence, and bid my tumultuous passions cease to vex me, be still, find content in grovelling pursuits, and the admiration of the misjudging crowd, when it is only one I wish to please – one who could be all the world to me. Argue not with me, I am bound by human ties; but did my spirit ever promise to love, or could I consider when forced to bind myself – to take a vow, that at the awful day of judgment I must give an account of. My conscience does not smite me, and that Being who is greater than the internal monitor, may approve of what the world condemns; sensible that in Him I live, could I brave His presence, or hope in solitude to find peace, if I acted contrary to conviction, that the world might approve of my conduct – what could the world give to compensate for my own esteem? it is ever hostile and armed against the feeling heart!

'Riches and honours await me, and the cold moralist might desire me to sit down and enjoy them – I cannot conquer my feelings, and till I do, what are these baubles to me? you may tell me I follow a fleeting good, an *ignis fatuus*; but this chase, these struggles prepare me for eternity – when I no longer see through a glass darkly I shall not reason about, but *feel* in what happiness consists.'[28]

Henry had not attempted to interrupt her; he saw she was determined, and that these sentiments were not the effusion of the moment, but well digested ones, the result of strong affections, a high sense of honour, and respect for the source of all virtue and truth. He was startled, if not entirely convinced by her arguments; indeed her voice, her gestures were all persuasive.

Some one now entered the room; he looked an answer to her long harangue; it was fortunate for him, or he might have been led to say what in a cooler moment he had determined to conceal; but were words necessary to reveal it? He wished not to influence her conduct – vain precaution; she knew she was beloved; and could she forget that such a man loved her, or rest satisfied with any inferior gratification. When passion first enters the heart, it is only a return of affection that is sought after, and every other remembrance and wish is blotted out.

CHAPTER XIX

Two days passed away without any particular conversation; Henry, trying to be indifferent, or to appear so, was more assiduous than ever. The conflict was too violent for his present state of health; the spirit was willing, but the body suffered; he lost his appetite, and looked wretchedly; his spirits were calmly low – the world seemed to fade away – what was that world to him that Mary did not inhabit; she lived not for him.

He was mistaken; his affection was her only support; without this dear prop she had sunk into the grave of her lost – long-loved friend; – his attention snatched her from despair. Inscrutable are the ways of Heaven!

The third day Mary was desired to prepare herself; for if the wind continued in the same point, they should set sail the next evening. She tried to prepare her mind, and her efforts were not useless; she appeared less agitated than could have been expected, and talked of her voyage with composure. On great occasions she was generally calm and collected, her resolution would brace her unstrung nerves; but after the victory she had no triumph; she would sink into a state of moping melancholy, and feel ten-fold misery when the heroic enthusiasm was over.

The morning of the day fixed on for her departure she was alone with Henry only a few moments, and an awkward kind of formality made them slip away without their having said much to each other. Henry was afraid to discover his passion, or give any other name to his regard but friendship; yet his anxious solicitude for her welfare was ever breaking out – while she as artlessly expressed again and again, her fears with respect to his declining health.

'We shall soon meet,' said he, with a faint smile; Mary smiled too; she caught the sickly beam; it was still fainter by being reflected, and not knowing what she wished to do, started up and left the room. When she was alone she regretted she had left him so precipitately. 'The few precious moments I have thus thrown away may never return,' she thought – the reflection led to misery.

She waited for, nay, almost wished for the summons to depart. She could not avoid spending the intermediate time with the ladies and Henry; and the trivial conversations she was obliged to bear a part in harassed her more than can be well conceived.

The summons came, and the whole party attended her to the vessel. For a while the remembrance of Ann banished her regret at parting with Henry, though his pale figure pressed on her sight; it may seem a paradox, but he was more present to her when she sailed; her tears then were all his own.

'My poor Ann!' thought Mary, 'along this road we came, and near this spot you called me your guardian angel – and now I leave thee here! ah! no, I do not – thy spirit is not confined to its mouldering tenement! Tell me, thou soul of her I love, tell me, ah! whither art thou fled?' Ann occupied her until they reached the ship.

The anchor was weighed. Nothing can be more irksome than waiting to say farewel. As the day was serene, they accompanied her a little way, and then got into the boat; Henry was the last; he pressed her hand, it had not any life in it; she leaned over the side of the ship without looking at the boat, till it was so far distant, that she could not see the countenances of those that were in it: a mist spread itself over her sight – she longed to exchange one look – tried to recollect the last; – the universe contained no being but Henry! – The grief of parting with him had swept all others clean away. Her eyes followed the keel of the boat, and when she could no longer perceive its traces: she looked round on the wide waste of waters, thought of the precious moments which had been stolen from the waste of mur-dered time.

She then descended into the cabin, regardless of the surrounding beauties of nature, and throwing herself on her bed in the little hole which was called the state-room – she wished to forget her existence. On this bed she remained two days, listening to the dashing waves, unable to close her eyes. A small taper made the darkness visible;[29] and the third night, by its glimmering light, she wrote the following fragment.

'Poor solitary wretch that I am; here alone do I listen to the whistling winds and dashing waves; – on no human support can I rest – when not lost to hope I found pleasure in the society of those rough beings; but now they appear not like my fellow creatures; no social ties draw me to them. How long, how dreary has this day been; yet I scarcely wish it over – for what will to-morrow bring – to-morrow, and to-morrow[30] will only be marked with unvaried characters of wretchedness. Yet surely, I am not alone!'

Her moistened eyes were lifted up to heaven; a crowd of thoughts darted into her mind, and pressing her hand against her forehead, as if to bear the intellectual weight, she tried, but tried in vain, to arrange them. 'Father of Mercies, compose this troubled spirit: do I indeed wish it to be composed – to forget my Henry?' the *my*, the pen was directly drawn across in an agony.

CHAPTER XX

The mate of the ship, who heard her stir, came to offer her some refreshment; and she, who formerly received every offer of kindness or civility with pleasure, now shrunk away disgusted: peevishly she desired him not to disturb her; but the words were hardly articulated when her heart smote her, she called him back, and requested something to drink. After drinking it, fatigued by her mental exertions, she fell into a death-like slumber, which lasted some hours; but did not refresh her, on the contrary, she awoke languid and stupid.

The wind still continued contrary; a week, a dismal week, had she struggled with her sorrows; and the struggle brought on a flow fever, which sometimes gave her false spirits.

The winds then became very tempestuous, the Great Deep was troubled, and all the passengers appalled. Mary then left her bed, and went on deck, to survey the contending elements: the scene accorded with the present state of her soul; she thought in a few hours I may go home; the prisoner may be released. The vessel rose on a wave and descended into a yawning gulph – Not slower did her mounting soul return to earth, for – Ah! her treasure and her heart was there. The squalls rattled amongst the sails, which were quickly taken down; the wind would then die away, and the wild undirected waves rushed on every side with a tremendous roar. In a little vessel in the midst of such a storm she was not dismayed; she felt herself independent.

Just then one of the crew perceived a signal of distress; by the help of a glass he could plainly discover a small vessel dismasted, drifted about, for the rudder had been broken by the violence of the storm. Mary's thoughts were now all engrossed by the crew on the brink of destruction. They bore down to the wreck; they reached it, and hailed the trembling wretches: at the sound of the friendly greeting, loud cries of tumultuous joy were mixed with the roaring of the waves, and with ecstatic transport they leaped on the shattered deck, launched their boat in a moment, and committed themselves to the mercy of the sea. Stowed between two casks, and leaning on a sail, she watched the boat, and when a wave intercepted it from her view — she ceased to breathe, or rather held her breath until it rose again.

At last the boat arrived safe along-side the ship, and Mary caught the poor trembling wretches as they stumbled into it, and joined them in thanking that gracious Being, who though He had not thought fit to still the raging of the sea, had afforded them unexpected succour.

Amongst the wretched crew was one poor woman, who fainted when she was hauled on board: Mary undressed her, and when she had recovered, and soothed her, left her to enjoy the rest she required to recruit her strength, which fear had quite exhausted. She returned again to view the angry deep, and when she gazed on its perturbed state, she thought of the Being who rode on the wings of the wind, and stilled the noise of the sea; and the madness of the people — He only could speak peace to her troubled spirit! she grew more calm; the late transaction had gratified her benevolence, and stole her out of herself.

One of the sailors, happening to say to another, 'that he believed the world was going to be at an end;' this observation led her into a new train of thoughts: some of Handel's sublime compositions occurred to her, and she sung them to the grand accompaniment. The Lord God Omnipotent reigned, and would reign for ever, and ever![31] Why then did she fear the sorrows that were passing away, when she knew that He would bind up the broken-hearted, and receive those who came out of great tribulation. She retired to her cabin; and wrote in the little book that was now her only confident. It was after midnight.

'At this solemn hour, the great day of judgment fills my thoughts; the day of retribution, when the secrets of all hearts will be revealed; when all worldly distinctions will fade away, and be no more seen. I have not words to express the sublime images which the bare contemplation of this awful day raises in my mind. Then, indeed, the Lord Omnipotent will reign, and He will wipe the tearful eye, and support the trembling heart — yet a little while He hideth his face, and the dun shades of sorrow, and the thick clouds of folly separate us from our God; but when the glad dawn of an eternal day breaks, we shall know even as we are known.[32] Here we walk by faith, and not by sight; and we have this alternative, either to enjoy the pleasures of life, which are but for a season, or look forward to the prize of our high calling, and with fortitude, and that wisdom which is from above, endeavour to bear the warfare of life. We know that many run the race; but he that striveth obtaineth the crown of victory. Our race is an arduous one! How many are betrayed by traitors lodged in their own breasts, who wear the garb of Virtue, and are so near akin; we sigh to think they should ever lead into folly, and slide imperceptibly into vice. Surely any thing like happiness is madness! Shall probationers of an hour presume to pluck the fruit of immortality, before they have conquered death? it is guarded, when the great day, to which I allude, arrives, the way will again be opened. Ye dear delusions, gay deceits, farewell! and yet I cannot banish ye for ever; still does my panting soul push forward, and live in futurity, in the deep shades o'er which darkness hangs. – I try to pierce the gloom, and find a resting-place, where my thirst of knowledge will be gratified, and my ardent affections find an object to fix them. Every thing material must change; happiness and this fluctating principle is not compatible. Eternity, immateriality, and happiness, – what are ye? How shall I grasp the mighty and fleeting conceptions ye create?'

After writing, serenely she delivered her soul into the hands of the Father of Spirits; and slept in peace.

CHAPTER XXI

Mary rose early, refreshed by the reasonable rest, and went to visit the poor woman, whom she found quite recovered: and, on enquiry, heard that she had lately buried her husband, a common sailor; and that her only surviving child had been washed over-board the day before. Full of her own danger, she scarcely thought of her child till that was over; and then she gave way to boisterous[33] emotions.

Mary endeavoured to calm her at first, by sympathizing with her; and she tried to point out the only solid source of comfort; but in doing this she encountered many difficulties; she found her grossly ignorant, yet she did not despair: and as the poor creature could not receive comfort from the operations of her own mind, she laboured to beguile the hours which grief made heavy, by adapting her conversation to her capacity.

There are many minds that only receive impressions through the medium of the senses: to them did Mary address herself; she made her some presents, and promised to assist her when they should arrive in England. This employment roused her out of her late stupor, and again set the faculties of her soul in motion; made the understanding contend with the

imagination, and the heart throbbed not so irregularly during the conten-
tion. How short-lived was the calm! when the English coast was descried,
her sorrows returned with redoubled vigor. – She was to visit and comfort
the mother of her lost friend – And where then should she take up her
residence? These thoughts suspended the exertions of her understanding;
abstracted reflections gave way to alarming apprehensions; and tenderness
undermined fortitude.

CHAPTER XXII

In England then landed the forlorn wanderer. She looked round for some
few moments – her affections were not attracted to any particular part of
the Island. She knew none of the inhabitants of the vast city to which she
was going: the mass of buildings appeared to her a huge body without an
informing soul. As she passed through the streets in an hackney-coach,
disgust and horror alternately filled her mind. She met some women drunk;
and the manners of those who attacked the sailors, made her shrink into
herself and exclaim, are these my fellow creatures!

Detained by a number of carts near the water-side, for she came up the
river in the vessel, not having reason to hasten on shore, she saw vulgarity,
dirt, and vice – her soul sickened; this was the first time such complicated
misery obtruded itself on her sight. – Forgetting her own griefs, she gave the
world a much indebted tear;[*] mourned for a world in ruins. She then
perceived, that great part of her comfort must arise from viewing the
smiling face of nature, and be reflected from the view of innocent enjoyments; she was fond of seeing animals play, and could not bear to see her
own species sink below them.

In a little dwelling in one of the villages near London, lived the mother of
Ann; two of her children still remained with her; but they did not resemble
Ann. To her house Mary directed the coach, and told the unfortunate
mother of her loss. The poor woman, oppressed by it, and her many other
cares, after an inundation of tears, began to enumerate all her past misfortunes, and present cares. The heavy tale lasted until midnight, and the
impression it made on Mary's mind was so strong, that it banished sleep till
towards morning; when tired nature sought forgetfulness, and the soul
ceased to ruminate about many things.

She sent for the poor woman they took up at sea, provided her a lodging,
and relieved her present necessities. A few days were spent in a kind of
listless way; then the mother of Ann began to enquire when she thought of
returning home. She had hitherto treated her with the greatest respect, and

concealed her wonder at Mary's choosing a remote room in the house near the garden, and ordering some alterations to be made, as if she intended living in it.

Mary did not choose to explain herself; had Ann lived, it is probable she would never have loved Henry so fondly; but if she had, she could not have talked of her passion to any human creature. She deliberated, and at last informed the family, that she had a reason for not living with her husband, which must some time remain a secret – they stared – Not live with him! how will you live then? this was a question she could not answer; she had only about eighty pounds remaining, of the money she took with her to Lisbon; when it was exhausted where could she get more? I will work, she cried, do any thing rather than be a slave.

CHAPTER XXIII

Unhappy, she wandered about the village, and relieved the poor; it was the only employment that eased her aching heart; she became more intimate with misery – the misery that rises from poverty and the want of education. She was in the vicinity of a great city; the vicious poor in and about it must ever grieve a benevolent contemplative mind.

One evening a man who stood weeping in a little lane, near the house she resided in, caught her eye. She accosted him; in a confused manner, he informed her, that his wife was dying, and his children crying for the bread he could not earn. Mary desired to be conducted to his habitation; it was not very distant, and was the upper room in an old mansion-house, which had been once the abode of luxury. Some tattered shreds of rich hangings still remained, covered with cobwebs and filth; round the ceiling, through which the rain drop'd, was a beautiful cornice mouldering; and a spacious gallery was rendered dark by the broken windows being blocked up; through the apertures the wind forced its way in hollow sounds, and reverberated along the former scene of festivity.

It was crowded with inhabitants: some were scolding, others swearing, or singing indecent songs. What a sight for Mary! Her blood ran cold; yet she had sufficient resolution to mount to the top of the house. On the floor, in one corner of a very small room, lay an emaciated figure of a woman; a window over her head scarcely admitted any light, for the broken panes were stuffed with dirty rags. Near her were five children, all young, and covered with dirt; their sallow cheeks, and languid eyes, exhibited none of the charms of childhood. Some were fighting, and others crying for food; their yells were mixed with their mother's groans, and the wind which rushed through the passage. Mary was petrified; but soon assuming more courage, approached the bed, and, regardless of the surrounding nastiness, knelt down by the poor wretch, and breathed the most poisonous air; for the unfortunate creature was dying of a putrid fever, the consequence of dirt and want.

Their state did not require much explanation. Mary sent the husband for a poor neighbour, whom she hired to nurse the woman, and take care of the children; and then went herself to buy them some necessaries at a shop not far distant. Her knowledge of physic had enabled her to prescribe for the woman; and she left the house, with a mixture of horror and satisfaction.

She visited them every day, and procured them every comfort; contrary to her expectation, the woman began to recover; cleanliness and wholesome food had a wonderful effect; and Mary saw her rising as it were from the grave. Not aware of the danger she ran into, she did not think of it till she perceived she had caught the fever. It made such an alarming progress, that she was prevailed on to send for a physician; but the disorder was so violent, that for some days it baffled his skill; and Mary felt not her danger, as she was delirious. After the crisis, the symptoms were more favourable, and she slowly recovered, without regaining much strength or spirits; indeed they were intolerably low: she wanted a tender nurse.

For some time she had observed, that she was not treated with the same respect as formerly; her favors were forgotten when no more were expected. This ingratitude hurt her, as did a similar instance in the woman who came out of the ship. Mary had hitherto supported her; as her finances were growing low, she hinted to her, that she ought to try to earn her own subsistence: the woman in return loaded her with abuse.

Two months were elapsed; she had not seen, or heard from Henry. He was sick – nay, perhaps had forgotten her; all the world was dreary, and all the people ungrateful.

She sunk into apathy, and endeavouring to rouse herself out of it, she wrote in her book another fragment:

'Surely life is a dream, a frightful one! and after those rude, disjointed images are fled, will light ever break in? Shall I ever feel joy? Do all suffer like me; or am I framed so as to be particularly susceptible of misery? It is true, I have experienced the most rapturous emotions – short-lived delight! – ethereal beam, which only serves to shew my present misery – yet lie still, my throbbing heart, or burst; and my brain – why dost thou whirl about at such a terrifying rate? why do thoughts so rapidly rush into my mind, and yet when they disappear leave such deep traces? I could almost wish for the madman's happiness, and in a strong imagination lose a sense of woe.

'Oh! reason, thou boasted guide, why desert me, like the world, when I most need thy assistance! Canst thou not calm this internal tumult, and drive away the death-like sadness which presses so sorely on me, – a sadness surely very nearly allied to despair. I am now the prey of apathy – I could wish for the former storms! a ray of hope sometimes illumined my path; I had a pursuit; but now *it visits not my haunts forlorn*.[35] Too well have I loved my fellow creatures! I have been wounded by ingratitude; from every one it has something of the serpent's tooth.

'When overwhelmed by sorrow, I have met unkindness; I looked for some one to have pity on me; but found none! – The healing balm of sympathy is denied; I weep, a solitary wretch, and the hot tears scald my cheeks. I have not the medicine of life, the dear chimera I have so often chased, a friend. Shade of my loved Ann! dost thou ever visit thy poor Mary? Refined spirit, thou wouldst weep, could angels weep, to see her struggling with passions she cannot subdue; and feelings which corrode her small portion of comfort.'

She could not write any more; she wished herself far distant from all human society; a thick gloom spread itself over her mind: but did not make her forget the very beings she wished to fly from. She sent for the poor woman she found in the garret; gave her money to clothe herself and children, and buy some furniture for a little hut, in a large garden, the master of which agreed to employ her husband, who had been bred a gardener. Mary promised to visit the family, and see their new abode when she was able to go out.

CHAPTER XXIV

Mary still continued weak and low, though it was spring, and all nature began to look gay; with more than usual brightness the sun shone, and a little robin which she had cherished during the winter sung one of his best songs. The family were particularly civil this fine morning, and tried to prevail on her to walk out. Any thing like kindness melted her; she consented.

Softer emotions banished her melancholy, and she directed her steps to the habitation she had rendered comfortable.

Emerging out of a dreary chamber, all nature looked cheerful; when she had last walked out, snow covered the ground, and bleak winds pierced her through and through: now the hedges were green, the blossoms adorned the trees, and the birds sung. She reached the dwelling, without being much exhausted; and while she rested there, observed the children sporting on the grass, with improved complexions. The mother with tears thanked her deliverer, and pointed out her comforts. Mary's tears flowed not only from sympathy, but a complication of feelings and recollections; the affections which bound her to her fellow creatures began again to play, and reanimated nature. She observed the change in herself, tried to account for it, and wrote with her pencil a rhapsody on sensibility.

'Sensibility is the most exquisite feeling of which the human soul is susceptible: when it pervades us, we feel happy; and could it last unmixed, we might form some conjecture of the bliss of those paradisiacal days, when the obedient passions were under the dominion of reason, and the impulses of the heart did not need correction.

'It is this quickness, this delicacy of feeling, which enables us to relish the sublime touches of the poet, and the painter; it is this, which expands the soul, gives an enthusiastic greatness, mixed with tenderness, when we view the magnificent objects of nature; or hear of a good action. The same effect we experience in the spring, when we hail the returning sun, and the consequent renovation of nature; when the flowers unfold themselves, and exhale their sweets, and the voice of music is heard in the land. Softened by tenderness; the soul is disposed to be virtuous. Is any sensual gratification to be compared to that of feeling the eyes moistened after having comforted the unfortunate?

'Sensibility is indeed the foundation of all our happiness; but these raptures are unknown to the depraved sensualist, who is only moved by what strikes his gross senses; the delicate embellishments of nature escape his notice; as do the gentle and interesting affections. – But it is only to be felt; it escapes discussion.'

She then returned home, and partook of the family meal, which was rendered more cheerful by the presence of a man, past the meridian of life, of polished manners, and dazzling wit. He endeavoured to draw Mary out, and succeeded; she entered into conversation, and some of her artless flights of genius struck him with surprise; he found she had a capacious mind, and that her reason was as profound as her imagination was lively. She glanced from earth to heaven, and caught the light of truth. Her expressive countenance shewed what passed in her mind, and her tongue was ever the faithful interpreter of her heart; duplicity never threw a shade over her words or actions. Mary found him a man of learning; and the exercise of her understanding would frequently make her forget her griefs, when nothing else could, except benevolence.

This man had known the mistress of the house in her youth; good nature induced him to visit her; but when he saw Mary he had another inducement. Her appearance, and above all, her genius, and cultivation of mind, roused his curiosity; but her dignified manners had such an effect on him, he was obliged to suppress it. He knew men, as well as books; his conversation was entertaining and improving. In Mary's company he doubted whether heaven was peopled with spirits masculine; and almost forgot that he had called the sex 'the pretty play things that render life tolerable.'

He had been the slave of beauty, the captive of sense; love he ne'er had felt; the mind never rivetted the chain, nor had the purity of it made the body appear lovely in his eyes. He was humane, despised meanness; but was vain of his abilities, and by no means a useful member of society. He talked often of the beauty of virtue; but not having any solid foundation to build the practice on, he was only a shining, or rather a sparkling character: and though his fortune enabled him to hunt down pleasure, he was discontented.

Mary observed his character, and wrote down a train of reflections, which these observations led her to make; these reflections received a tinge from her mind; the present state of it, was that kind of painful quietness which arises from reason clouded by disgust; she had not yet learned to be resigned; vague hopes agitated her.

'There are some subjects that are so enveloped in clouds, as you dissipate one, another overspreads it. Of this kind are our reasonings concerning happiness, till we are obliged to cry out with the Apostle, *That it hath not entered into the heart of man to conceive in what it could consist*, or how satiety could be prevented.[36] Man seems formed for action, though the passions are seldom properly managed; they are either so languid as not to serve as a spur, or else so violent, as to overleap all bounds.

'Every individual has its own peculiar trials; and anguish, in one shape or other, visits every heart. Sensibility produces flights of virtue; and not curbed by reason, is on the brink of vice talking, and even thinking of virtue.

'Christianity can only afford just principles to govern the wayward feelings and impulses of the heart: every good disposition runs wild, if not transplanted into this soil; but how hard is it to keep the heart diligently, though convinced that the issues of life depend on it.

'It is very difficult to discipline the mind of a thinker, or reconcile him to the weakness, the inconsistency of his understanding; and a still more laborious task for him to conquer his passions, and learn to seek content, instead of happiness. Good dispositions, and virtuous propensities, without the light of the Gospel, produce eccentric characters: comet-like, they are always in extremes; while revelation resembles the laws of attraction, and produces uniformity; but too often is the attraction feeble; and the light so obscured by passion, as to force the bewildered soul to fly into void space, and wander in confusion.'

CHAPTER XXV

A few mornings after, as Mary was sitting ruminating, harassed by perplexing thoughts, and fears, a letter was delivered to her: the servant waited for an answer. Her heart palpitated; it was from Henry; she held it some time in her hand, then tore it open; it was not a long one; and only contained an account of a relapse, which prevented his sailing in the first packet, as he had intended. Some tender enquiries were added, concerning her health, and state of mind; but they were expressed in rather a formal style: it vexed her, and the more so, as it stopped the current of affection, which the account of his arrival and illness had made flow to her heart – it ceased to beat for a moment – she read the passage over again; but could not tell what she was hurt by – only that it did not answer the expectations of her affection. She wrote a laconic, incoherent note in return, allowing him to call on her the next day – he had requested permission at the conclusion of his letter.

Her mind was then painfully active; she could not read or walk; she tried to fly from herself, to forget the long hours that were yet to run before to-morrow could arrive: she knew not what time he would come; certainly in the morning, she concluded; the morning then was anxiously wished for; and every wish produced a sigh, that arose from expectation on the stretch, damped by fear and vain regret.

To beguile the tedious time, Henry's favorite tunes were sung; the books they read together turned over; and the short epistle read at least a hundred times. – Any one who had seen her, would have supposed that she was trying to decypher Chinese characters.

After a sleepless night, she hailed the tardy day, watched the rising sun, and then listened for every footstep, and started if she heard the street door opened. At last he came, and she who had been counting the hours, and doubting whether the earth moved, would gladly have escaped the approaching interview.

With an unequal, irresolute pace, she went to meet him; but when she beheld his emaciated countenance, all the tenderness, which the formality of his letter had damped, returned, and a mournful presentiment stilled the internal conflict. She caught his hand, and looking wistfully at him, exclaimed, 'Indeed, you are not well!'

'I am very far from well; but it matters not,' added he with a smile of resignation; 'my native air may work wonders, and besides, my mother is a tender nurse, and I shall sometimes see thee.'

Mary felt for the first time in her life, envy; she wished involuntarily, that all the comfort he received should be from her. She enquired about the symptoms of his disorder; and heard that he had been very ill; she hastily drove away the fears, that former dear bought experience suggested: and again and again did she repeat, that she was sure he would soon recover. She would then look in his face, to see if he assented, and ask more questions to the same purport. She tried to avoid speaking of herself, and Henry left her, with a promise of visiting her the next day.

Her mind was now engrossed by one fear – yet she would not allow herself to think that she feared an event she could not name. She still saw his pale face; the sound of his voice still vibrated on her ears; she tried to retain it; she listened, looked round, wept, and prayed.

Henry had enlightened the desolate scene: was this charm of life to fade away, and, like the baseless fabric of a vision,[37] leave not a wreck behind? These thoughts disturbed her reason, she shook her head, as if to drive them out of it; a weight, a heavy one, was on her heart; all was not well there.

Out of this reverie she was soon woke to keener anguish, by the arrival of a letter from her husband; it came to Lisbon after her departure: Henry had forwarded it to her, but did not choose to deliver it himself, for a very obvious reason; it might have produced a conversation he wished for some time to avoid; and his precaution took its rise almost equally from benevolence and love.

She could not muster up sufficient resolution to break the seal: her fears were not prophetic, for the contents gave her comfort. He informed her that he intended prolonging his tour, as he was now his own master, and wished to remain some time on the continent, and in particular to visit Italy without any restraint: but his reasons for it appeared childish; it was not to cultivate his taste, or tread on classic ground, where poets and philosophers caught their lore; but to join in the masquerades, and such burlesque amusements.

These instances of folly relieved Mary, in some degree reconciled her to herself, added fuel to the devouring flame – and silenced something like a pang, which reason and conscience made her feel, when she reflected, that it is the office of Religion to reconcile us to the seemingly hard dispensations of providence; and that no inclination, however strong, should oblige us to desert the post assigned us, or force us to forget that virtue should be an active principle; and that the most desirable station, is the one that exercises our faculties, refines our affections, and enables us to be useful.

One reflection continually wounded her repose; she feared not poverty; her wants were few; but in giving up a fortune, she gave up the power of comforting the miserable, and making the sad heart sing for joy.

Heaven had endowed her with uncommon humanity, to render her one of His benevolent agents, a messenger of peace; and should she attend to her own inclinations?

These suggestions, though they could not subdue a violent passion, increased her misery. One moment she was a heroine, half determined to bear whatever fate should inflict; the next, her mind would recoil – and tenderness possessed her whole soul. Some instances, of Henry's affection, his worth and genius, were remembered: and the earth was only a vale of tears, because he was not to sojourn with her.

CHAPTER XXVI

Henry came the next day, and once or twice in the course of the following week; but still Mary kept up some little formality, a certain consciousness restrained her; and Henry did not enter on the subject which he found she wished to avoid. In the course of conversation, however, she mentioned to him, that she earnestly desired to obtain a place in one of the public offices for Ann's brother, as the family were again in a declining way.

Henry attended, made a few enquiries, and dropped the subject; but the following week, she heard him enter with unusual haste; it was to inform her, that he had made interest with a person of some consequence, whom he had once obliged in a very disagreeable exigency, in a foreign country; and that he had procured a place for her friend, which would infallibly lead to something better, if he behaved with propriety. Mary could not speak to thank him; emotions of gratitude and love suffused her face; her blood eloquently spoke. She delighted to receive benefits through the medium of her fellow creatures; but to receive them from Henry was exquisite pleasure.

As the summer advanced, Henry grew worse; the closeness of the air, in the metropolis, affected his breath; and his mother insisted on his fixing on some place in the country, where she would accompany him. He could not think of going far off, but chose a little village on the banks of the Thames, near Mary's dwelling: he then introduced her to his mother.

They frequently went down the river in a boat; Henry would take his violin, and Mary would sometimes sing, or read, to them. She pleased his mother; she inchanted him. It was an advantage to Mary that friendship first possessed her heart; it opened it to all the softer sentiments of humanity: — and when this first affection was torn away, a similar one sprung up, with a still tenderer sentiment added to it.

The last evening they were on the water, the clouds grew suddenly black, and broke in violent showers, which interrupted the solemn stillness that had prevailed previous to it. The thunder roared; and the oars plying quickly, in order to reach the shore, occasioned a not unpleasing sound. Mary drew still nearer Henry; she wished to have sought with him a watry grave; to have escaped the horror of surviving him. — She spoke, but Henry saw the workings of her mind — he felt them; threw his arm round her waist — and they enjoyed the luxury of wretchedness. — As they touched the shore, Mary perceived that Henry was wet; with eager anxiety she cried, What shall I do! — this day will kill thee, and I shall not die with thee!

This accident put a stop to their pleasurable excursions; it had injured him, and brought on the spitting of blood he was subject to – perhaps it was not the cold that he caught, that occasioned it. In vain did Mary try to shut her eyes; her fate pursued her! Henry every day grew worse and worse.

CHAPTER XXVII

Oppressed by her foreboding fears, her sore mind was hurt by new instances of ingratitude: disgusted with the family, whose misfortunes had often disturbed her repose, and lost in anticipated sorrow, she rambled she knew not where; when turning down a shady walk, she discovered her feet had taken the path they delighted to tread. She saw Henry sitting in his garden alone; he quickly opened the garden-gate, and she sat down by him.

'I did not,' said he, 'expect to see thee this evening, my dearest Mary; but I was thinking of thee. Heaven has endowed thee with an uncommon portion of fortitude, to support one of the most affectionate hearts in the world. This is not a time for disguise; I know I am dear to thee – and my affection for thee is twisted with every fibre of my heart. – I loved thee ever since I have been acquainted with thine: thou art the being my fancy has delighted to form; but which I imagined existed only there! In a little while the shades of death will encompass me – ill-fated love perhaps added strength to my disease, and smoothed the rugged path. Try, my love, to fulfil thy destined course – try to add to thy other virtues patience. I could have wished, for thy sake, that we could have died together – or that I could live to shield thee from the assaults of an unfeeling world! Could I but offer thee an asylum in these arms – a faithful bosom, in which thou couldst repose all thy griefs' – He pressed her to it, and she returned the pressure – he felt her throbbing heart. A mournful silence ensued! when he resumed the conversation. 'I wished to prepare thee for the blow – too surely do I feel that it will not be long delayed! The passion I have nursed is so pure, that death cannot extinguish it – or tear away the impression thy virtues have made on my soul. I would fain comfort thee –'

'Talk not of comfort,' interrupted Mary, 'it will be in heaven with thee and Ann – while I shall remain on earth the veriest wretch!' – She grasped his hand.

'There we shall meet, my love, my Mary, in our Father's' – His voice faultered; he could not finish the sentence; he was almost suffocated – they both wept, their tears relieved them; they walked slowly to the garden-gate (Mary would not go into the house); they could not say farewel when they reached it – and Mary hurried down the lane, to spare Henry the pain of witnessing her emotions.

When she lost sight of the house she sat down on the ground, till it grew late, thinking of all that had passed. Full of these thoughts, she crept along, regardless of the descending rain; when lifting up her eyes to heaven, and then turning them wildly on the prospects around, without marking them; she only felt that the scene accorded with her present state of mind. It was the last glimmering of twilight, with a full moon, over which clouds continually flitted. Where am I wandering, God of Mercy! she thought; she alluded to the wanderings of her mind. In what a labyrinth am I lost! What miseries have I already encountered and what a number lie still before me.

Her thoughts flew rapidly to something. I could be happy listening to him, soothing his cares. – Would he not smile upon me – call me his own Mary? I am not his – said she with fierceness – I am a wretch! and she heaved a sigh that almost broke her heart, while the big tears rolled down her burning cheeks; but still her exercised mind, accustomed to think, began to observe its operation, though the barrier of reason was almost carried away, and all the faculties not restrained by her, were running into confusion. Wherefore am I made thus? Vain are my efforts – I cannot live without loving – and love leads to madness. – Yet I will not weep; and her eyes were now fixed by despair, dry and motionless; and then quickly whirled about with a look of distraction.

She looked for hope; but found none – all was troubled waters. – No where could she find rest. I have already paced to and fro in the earth; it is not my abiding place – may I not too go home! Ah! no. Is this complying with my Henry's request, could a spirit thus disengaged expect to associate with his? Tears of tenderness strayed down her relaxed countenance, and her softened heart heaved more regularly. She felt the rain, and turned to her solitary home.

Fatigued by the tumultuous emotions she had endured, when she entered the house she ran to her own room, sunk on the bed, and exhausted nature soon closed her eyes; but active fancy was still awake, and a thousand fearful dreams interrupted her slumbers.

Feverish and languid, she opened her eyes, and saw the unwelcome sun dart his rays through a window, the curtains of which she had forgotten to draw. The dew hung on the adjacent trees, and added to the lustre; the little robin began his song, and distant birds joined. She looked; her countenance was still vacant – her sensibility was absorbed by one object.

Did I ever admire the rising sun, she slightly thought, turning from the window, and shutting her eyes: she recalled to view the last night's scene. His faltering voice, lingering step, and the look of tender woe, were all graven on her heart; as were the words 'Could these arms shield thee from sorrow – afford thee an asylum from an unfeeling world.' The pressure to his bosom was not forgot. For a moment she was happy; but in a long-drawn sigh every delightful sensation evaporated. Soon – yes, very soon, will the grave again receive all I love! and the remnant of my days – she could not proceed – Were there then days to come after that?

CHAPTER XXVIII

Just as she was going to quit her room, to visit Henry, his mother called on her.

'My son is worse to-day,' said she. 'I come to request you to spend not only this day, but a week or two with me. – Why should I conceal any thing from you? Last night my child made his mother his confident, and, in the anguish of his heart, requested me to be thy friend – when I shall be childless. I will not attempt to describe what I felt when he talked thus to me. If I am to lose the support of my age, and be again a widow – may I call her 'Child whom my Henry wishes me to adopt?'

This new instance of Henry's disinterested affection, Mary felt most forcibly; and striving to restrain the complicated emotions, and sooth the wretched mother, she almost fainted: when the unhappy parent forced tears from her by saying, 'I deserve this blow; my partial fondness made me neglect him, when most he wanted a mother's care; this neglect, perhaps, first injured his constitution: righteous Heaven has made my crime its own punishment; and now I am indeed a mother, I shall lose my child – my only child!'

When they were a little more composed they hastened to the invalid; but during the short ride, the mother related several instances of Henry's goodness of heart. Mary's tears were not those of unmixed anguish; the display of his virtues gave her extreme delight – yet human nature prevailed; she trembled to think they would soon unfold themselves in a more genial clime.

CHAPTER XXIX

She found Henry very ill. The physician had some weeks before declared he never knew a person with a similar pulse recover. Henry was certain he could not live long; all the rest he could obtain, was procured by opiates. Mary now enjoyed the melancholy pleasure of nursing him, and softened by her tenderness the pains she could not remove. Every sigh did she stifle, every tear restrain, when he could see or hear them. She would boast of her resignation – yet catch eagerly at the least ray of hope. While he slept she would support his pillow, and rest her head where she could feel his breath. She loved him better than herself – she could not pray for his recovery; she could only say, The will of Heaven be done.

While she was in this state, she labored to acquire fortitude; but one tender look destroyed it all – she rather laboured, indeed, to make him believe she was resigned, than really to be so.

She wished to receive the sacrament with him, as a bond of union which was to extend beyond the grave. She did so, and received comfort from it; she rose above her misery.

His end was now approaching. Mary sat on the side of the bed. His eyes appeared fixed – no longer agitated by passion, he only felt that it was a fearful thing to die. The soul retired to the citadel; but it was not now solely filled by the image of her who in silent despair watched for his last breath. Collected, a frightful calmness stilled every turbulent emotion.

The mother's grief was more audible. Henry had for some time only attended to Mary – Mary pitied the parent, whose stings of conscience increased her sorrow; she whispered him, 'Thy mother weeps, disregarded by thee; oh! comfort her! – My mother, thy son blesses thee. –' The oppressed parent left the room. And Mary *waited* to see him die.

She pressed with trembling eagerness his parched lips – he opened his eyes again; the spreading film retired, and love relumed[38] them – he gave a look – it was never forgotten. My Mary, will you be comforted?

Yes, yes, she exclaimed in a firm voice; you go to be happy – I am not a complete wretch! The words almost choked her.

He was a long time silent; the opiate produced a kind of stupor. At last, in an agony, he cried, It is dark; I cannot see thee; raise me up. Where is Mary? did she not say she delighted to support me? let me die in her arms.

Her arms were opened to receive him; they trembled not. Again he was obliged to lie down, resting on her: as the agonies increased he leaned towards her: the soul seemed flying to her, as it escaped out of its prison. The breathing was interrupted; she heard distinctly the last sigh – and lifting up to Heaven her eyes, Father, receive his spirit, she calmly cried.

The attendants gathered round; she moved not, nor heard the clamor; the hand seemed yet to press hers; it still was warm. A ray of light from an opened window discovered the pale face.

She left the room, and retired to one very near it; and sitting down on the floor, fixed her eyes on the door of the apartment which contained the body. Every event of her life rushed across her mind with wonderful rapidity – yet all was still – fate had given the finishing stroke. She sat till midnight. – Then rose in a phrensy, went into the apartment, and desired those who watched the body to retire.

She knelt by the bed side; – an enthusiastic devotion overcame the dictates of despair. – She prayed most ardently to be supported, and dedicated herself to the service of that Being into whose hands, she had committed the spirit she almost adored – again – and again, – she prayed wildly – and fervently – but attempting to touch the lifeless hand – her head swum – she sunk –

CHAPTER XXX

Three months after, her only friend, the mother of her lost Henry began to be alarmed, at observing her altered appearance; and made her own health a pretext for travelling. These complaints roused Mary out of her torpid state; she imagined a new duty now forced her to exert herself – a duty love made sacred! –

They went to Bath, from that to Bristol; but the latter place they quickly left; the sight of the sick that resort there, they neither of them could bear. From Bristol they flew to Southampton. The road was pleasant – yet Mary shut her eyes; – or if they were open, green fields and commons, passed in quick succession, and left no more traces behind than if they had been waves of the sea.

Some time after they were settled at Southampton, they met the man who took so much notice of Mary, soon after her return to England. He renewed his acquaintance; he was really interested in her fate, as he had heard her uncommon story; besides, he knew her husband; knew him to be a good-natured, weak man. He saw him soon after his arrival in his native country, and prevented his hastening to enquire into the reasons of Mary's strange conduct. He desired him not to be too precipitate, if he ever wished to possess an invaluable treasure. He was guided by him, and allowed him to follow Mary to Southampton, and speak first to her friend.

This friend determined to trust to her native strength of mind, and informed her of the circumstance; but she overrated it: Mary was not able, for a few days after the intelligence, to fix on the mode of conduct she ought now to pursue. But at last she conquered her disgust, and wrote her *husband* an account of what had passed since she had dropped his correspondence.

He came in person to answer the letter. Mary fainted when he approached her unexpectedly. Her disgust returned with additional force, in spite of previous reasonings, whenever he appeared; yet she was prevailed on to promise to live with him, if he would permit her to pass one year, travelling from place to place; he was not to accompany her.

The time too quickly elapsed, and she gave him her hand – the struggle was almost more than she could endure. She tried to appear calm; time mellowed her grief, and mitigated her torments; but when her husband would take her hand, or mention any thing like love, she would instantly feel a sickness, a faintness at her heart, and wish, involuntarily, that the earth would open and swallow her.

CHAPTER XXXI

Mary visited the continent, and sought health in different climates; but her nerves were not to be restored to their former state. She then retired to her house in the country, established manufactories, threw the estate into small farms; and continually employed herself this way to dissipate care, and banish unavailing regret. She visited the sick, supported the old, and educated the young.

These occupations engrossed her mind; but there were hours when all her former woes would return and haunt her. – Whenever she did, or said, any thing she thought Henry would have approved of – she could not avoid thinking with anguish, of the rapture his approbation ever conveyed to her heart – a heart in which there was a void, that even benevolence and religion could not fill. The latter taught her to struggle for resignation; and the former rendered life supportable. Her delicate state of health did not promise long life. In moments of solitary sadness, a gleam of joy would dart across her mind – She thought she was hastening to that world *where there is neither marrying*, nor giving in marriage.[39]

Maria

PREFACE

The public are here presented with the last literary attempt of an author, whose fame has been uncommonly extensive, and whose talents have probably been most admired, by the persons by whom talents are estimated with the greatest accuracy and discrimination. There are few, to whom her writings could in any case have given pleasure, that would have wished that this fragment should have been suppressed, because it is a fragment. There is a sentiment, very dear to minds of taste and imagination, that finds a melancholy delight in contemplating these unfinished productions of genius, these sketches of what, if they had been filled up in a manner adequate to the writer's conception, would perhaps have given a new impulse to the manners of a world.

The purpose and structure of the following work, had long formed a favourite subject of meditation with its author, and she judged them capable of producing an important effect. The composition had been in progress for a period of twelve months. She was anxious to do justice to her conception, and recommenced and revised the manuscript several different times. So much of it as is here given to the public, she was far from considering as finished, and, in a letter to a friend directly written on this subject, she says, 'I am perfectly aware that some of the incidents ought to be transposed, and heightened by more harmonious shading; and I wished in some degree to avail myself of criticism, before I began to adjust my events into a story, the outline of which I had sketched in my mind.'* The only friends to whom the author communicated her manuscript, were Mr Dyson,[1] the translator of the Sorceror, and the present editor; and it was impossible for the most inexperienced author to display a stronger desire of profiting by the censures and sentiments that might be suggested.†

In revising these sheets for the press, it was necessary for the editor, in some places, to connect the more finished parts with the pages of an older copy, and a line or two in addition sometimes appeared requisite for that purpose. Wherever such a liberty has been taken, the additional phrases will be found inclosed in brackets; it being the editor's most earnest desire, to intrude nothing of himself into the work, but to give to the public the words, as well as ideas, of the real author.

What follows in the ensuing pages, is not a preface regularly drawn out

---

* A more copious extract of this letter is subjoined to the author's preface.
† The part communicated consisted of the first fourteen chapters.

by the author, but merely hints for a preface, which, though never filled up
in the manner the writer intended, appeared to be worth preserving.

W. GODWIN

The Wrongs of Woman, like the wrongs of the oppressed part of mankind, may be deemed necessary by their oppressors: but surely there are a few, who will dare to advance before the improvement of the age, and grant that my sketches are not the abortion of a distempered fancy, or the strong delineations of a wounded heart.

In writing this novel, I have rather endeavoured to pourtray passions than manners.

In many instances I could have made the incidents more dramatic, would I have sacrificed my main object, the desire of exhibiting the misery and oppression, peculiar to women, that arise out of the partial laws and customs of society.

In the invention of the story, this view restrained my fancy and the history ought rather to be considered, as of woman, than of an individual.

The sentiments I have embodied.

In many works of this species, the hero is allowed to be mortal, and to become wise and virtuous as well as happy, by a train of events and circumstances. The heroines, on the contrary, are to be born immaculate; and to act like goddesses of wisdom, just come forth highly finished Minervas from the head of Jove.[2]

[The following is an extract of a letter from the author to a friend, to whom she communicated her manuscript.]

For my part, I cannot suppose any situation more distressing, than for a woman of sensibility, with an improving mind, to be bound to such a man as I have described for life; obliged to renounce all the humanizing affections, and to avoid cultivating her taste, lest her perception of grace and refinement of sentiment, should sharpen to agony the pangs of disappointment. Love, in which the imagination mingles its bewitching colouring, must be fostered by delicacy. I should despise, or rather call her an ordinary woman, who could endure such a husband as I have sketched.

These appear to me (matrimonial despotism of heart and conduct) to be the peculiar Wrongs of Woman, because they degrade the mind. What are termed great misfortunes, may more forcibly impress the mind of common readers; they have more of what may justly be termed *stage-effect*; but it is the delineation of finer sensations, which, in my opinion, constitutes the merit of our best novels. This is what I have in view; and to show the wrongs of different classes of women, equally oppressive, though, from the difference of education, necessarily various.

MARIA[3]

CHAPTER I

Abodes of horror have frequently been described, and castles, filled with spectres and chimeras, conjured up by the magic spell of genius to harrow the soul, and absorb the wondering mind. But, formed of such stuff as dreams are made of,[4] what were they to the mansion of despair, in one corner of which Maria sat, endeavouring to recal her scattered thoughts!

Surprise, astonishment, that bordered on distraction, seemed to have suspended her faculties, till, waking by degrees to a keen sense of anguish, a whirlwind of rage and indignation roused her torpid pulse. One recollection with frightful velocity following another, threatened to fire her brain, and make her a fit companion for the terrific inhabitants, whose groans and shrieks were no unsubstantial sounds of whistling winds, or startled birds, modulated by a romantic fancy, which amuse while they affright; but such tones of misery as carry a dreadful certainty directly to the heart. What effect must they then have produced on one, true to the touch of sympathy, and tortured by maternal apprehension!

Her infant's image was continually floating on Maria's sight, and the first smile of intelligence remembered, as none but a mother, an unhappy mother, can conceive. She heard her half speaking half cooing, and felt the little twinkling fingers on her burning bosom – a bosom bursting with the nutriment for which this cherished child might now be pining in vain. From a stranger she could indeed receive the maternal aliment, Maria was grieved at the thought – but who would watch her with a mother's tenderness, a mother's self-denial?

The retreating shadows of former sorrows rushed back in a gloomy train, and seemed to be pictured on the walls of her prison, magnified by the state of mind in which they were viewed – Still she mourned for her child, lamented she was a daughter, and anticipated the aggravated ills of life that her sex rendered almost inevitable, even while dreading she was no more. To think that she was blotted out of existence was agony, when the imagination had been long employed to expand her faculties; yet to suppose her turned adrift on an unknown sea, was scarcely less afflicting.

After being two days the prey of impetuous, varying emotions, Maria began to reflect more calmly on her present situation, for she had actually been rendered incapable of sober reflection, by the discovery of the act of atrocity of which she was the victim. She could not have imagined, that, in all the fermentation of civilized depravity, a similar plot could have entered a human mind. She had been stunned by an unexpected blow; yet life, however joyless, was not to be indolently resigned, or misery endured without exertion, and proudly termed patience. She had hitherto meditated only to point the dart of anguish, and suppressed the heart heavings of indignant nature merely by the force of contempt. Now she endeavoured to brace her mind to fortitude, and to ask herself what was to be her employment in her dreary cell? Was it not to effect her escape, to fly to the succour of her child, and to baffle the selfish schemes of her tyrant – her husband?

These thoughts roused her sleeping spirit, and the self-possession returned, that seemed to have abandoned her in the infernal solitude into which she had been precipitated. The first emotions of overwhelming impatience began to subside, and resentment gave place to tenderness, and more tranquil meditation; though anger once more stopt the calm current of reflection, when she attempted to move her manacled arms. But this was an outrage that could only excite momentary feelings of scorn, which evaporated in a faint smile; for Maria was far from thinking a personal insult the most difficult to endure with magnanimous indifference.

She approached the small grated window of her chamber, and for a considerable time only regarded the blue expanse; though it commanded a view of a desolate garden, and of part of a huge pile of buildings, that, after having been suffered, for half a century, to fall to decay, had undergone some clumsy repairs, merely to render it habitable. The ivy had been torn off the turrets, and the stones not wanted to patch up the breaches of time, and exclude the warring elements, left in heaps in the disordered court. Maria contemplated this scene she knew not how long; or rather gazed on the walls, and pondered on her situation. To the master of this most horrid of prisons, she had, soon after her entrance, raved of injustice, in accents that would have justified his treatment, had not a malignant smile, when she appealed to his judgment, with a dreadful conviction stifled her remonstrating complaints. By force, or openly, what could be done? But surely some expedient might occur to an active mind, without any other employment, and possessed of sufficient resolution to put the risk of life into the balance with the chance of freedom.

A woman entered in the midst of these reflections, with a firm, deliberate step, strongly marked features, and large black eyes, which she fixed steadily on Maria's, as if she designed to intimidate her, saying at the same time – 'You had better sit down and eat your dinner, than look at the clouds.'

'I have no appetite,' replied Maria, who had previously determined to speak mildly; 'why then should I eat?'

'But, in spite of that, you must and shall eat something. I have had many ladies under my care, who have resolved to starve themselves; but, soon or late, they gave up their intent, as they recovered their senses.'

'Do you really think me mad?' asked Maria, meeting the searching glance of her eye.

'Not just now. But what does that prove? – only that you must be the more carefully watched, for appearing at times so reasonable. You have not touched a morsel since you entered the house.' – Maria sighed intelligibly. – 'Could any thing but madness produce such a disgust for food?'

'Yes, grief; you would not ask the question if you knew what it was.' The attendant shook her head; and a ghastly smile of desperate fortitude served as a forcible reply, and made Maria pause, before she added – 'Yet I will take some refreshment: I mean not to die. – No; I will preserve my senses; and convince even you, sooner than you are aware of, that my intellects have never been disturbed, though the exertion of them may have been suspended by some infernal drug.'

Doubt gathered still thicker on the brow of her guard, as she attempted to convict her of mistake.

'Have patience!' exclaimed Maria, with a solemnity that inspired awe. 'My God! how have I been schooled into the practice!' A suffocation of voice betrayed the agonizing emotions she was labouring to keep down; and conquering a qualm of disgust, she calmly endeavoured to eat enough to prove her docility, perpetually turning to the suspicious female, whose observation she courted, while she was making the bed and adjusting the room.

'Come to me often,' said Maria, with a tone of persuasion, in consequence of a vague plan that she had hastily adopted, when, after surveying this woman's form and features, she felt convinced that she had an understanding above the common standard; 'and believe me mad, till you are obliged to acknowledge the contrary.' The woman was no fool, that is, she was superior to her class; nor had misery quite petrified the life's-blood of humanity, to which reflections on our own misfortunes only give a more orderly course. The manner, rather than the expostulations, of Maria made a slight suspicion dart into her mind with corresponding sympathy, which various other avocations, and the habit of banishing compunction, prevented her, for the present, from examining more minutely.

But when she was told that no person, excepting the physician appointed by her family, was to be permitted to see the lady at the end of the gallery, she opened her keen eyes still wider, and uttered a – 'hem!' before she enquired – 'Why?' She was briefly told, in reply, that the malady was hereditary, and the fits not occurring but at very long and irregular intervals, she must be carefully watched; for the length of these lucid periods only rendered her more mischievous, when any vexation or caprice brought on the paroxysm of phrensy.

Had her master trusted her, it is probable that neither pity nor curiosity would have made her swerve from the straight line of her interest; for she had suffered too much in her intercourse with mankind, not to determine to look for support, rather to humouring their passions, than courting their approbation by the integrity of her conduct. A deadly blight had met her at the very threshold of existence; and the wretchedness of her mother seemed a heavy weight fastened on her innocent neck, to drag her down to perdition. She could not heroically determine to succour an unfortunate; but, offended at the bare supposition that she could be deceived with the same ease as a common servant, she no longer curbed her curiosity; and, though she never seriously fathomed her own intentions, she would sit, every moment she could steal from observation, listening to the tale, which Maria was eager to relate with all the persuasive eloquence of grief.

It is so cheering to see a human face, even if little of the divinity of virtue beam in it, that Maria anxiously expected the return of the attendant, as of a gleam of light to break the gloom of idleness. Indulged sorrow, she perceived, must blunt or sharpen the faculties to the two opposite extremes; producing stupidity, the moping melancholy of indolence; or the restless activity of a disturbed imagination. She sunk into one state, after being fatigued by the other: till the want of occupation became even more painful than the actual pressure or apprehension of sorrow; and the confinement that froze her into a nook of existence, with an unvaried prospect before her, the most insupportable of evils. The lamp of life seemed to be spending itself to chase the vapours of a dungeon which no art could dissipate. – And to what purpose did she rally all her energy? – Was not the world a vast prison, and women born slaves?

Though she failed immediately to rouse a lively sense of injustice in the mind of her guard, because it had been sophisticated into misanthropy, she touched her heart. Jemima (she had only a claim to a Christian name, which had not procured her any Christian privileges) could patiently hear of Maria's confinement on false pretences; she had felt the crushing hand of power, hardened by the exercise of injustice, and ceased to wonder at the perversions of the understanding, which systematize oppression; but, when told that her child, only four months old, had been torn from her, even while she was discharging the tenderest maternal office, the woman awoke in a bosom long estranged from feminine emotions, and Jemima determined to alleviate all in her power, without hazarding the loss of her place, the sufferings of a wretched mother, apparently injured, and certainly unhappy. A sense of right seems to result from the simplest act of reason, and to preside over the faculties of the mind, like the master-sense of feeling, to rectify the rest; but (for the comparison may be carried still farther) how often is the exquisite sensibility of both weakened or destroyed by the vulgar occupations, and ignoble pleasures of life?

The preserving her situation was, indeed, an important object to Jemima, who had been hunted from hole to hole, as if she had been a beast of prey, or infected with a moral plague. The wages she received, the greater part of which she hoarded, as her only chance for independence, were much more considerable than she could reckon on obtaining any where else, were it possible that she, an outcast from society, could be permitted to earn a subsistence in a reputable family. Hearing Maria perpetually complain of listlessness, and the not being able to beguile grief by resuming her customary pursuits, she was easily prevailed on, by compassion, and that involuntary respect for abilities, which those who possess them can never eradicate, to bring her some books and implements for writing. Maria's conversation had amused and interested her, and the natural consequence was a desire, scarcely observed by herself, of obtaining the esteem of a person she admired. The remembrance of better days was rendered more lively; and the sentiments then acquired appearing less romantic than they had for a long period, a spark of hope roused her mind to new activity.

How grateful was her attention to Maria! Oppressed by a dead weight of existence, or preyed on by the gnawing worm of discontent, with what eagerness did she endeavour to shorten the long days, which left no traces behind! She seemed to be sailing on the vast ocean of life, without seeing any land-mark to indicate the progress of time; to find employment was then to find variety, the animating principle of nature.

CHAPTER II

Earnestly as Maria endeavoured to soothe, by reading, the anguish of her wounded mind, her thoughts would often wander from the subject she was led to discuss, and tears of maternal tenderness obscured the reasoning page. She descanted on 'the ills which flesh is heir to,'[5] with bitterness, when the recollection of her babe was revived by a tale of fictitious woe, that bore any resemblance to her own; and her imagination was continually employed, to conjure up and embody the various phantoms of misery, which folly and vice had let loose on the world. The loss of her babe was the tender string; against other cruel remembrances she laboured to steel her bosom; and even a ray of hope, in the midst of her gloomy reveries, would sometimes gleam on the dark horizon of futurity, while persuading herself that she ought to cease to hope, since happiness was no where to be found. – But of her child, debilitated by the grief with which its mother had been assailed before it saw the light, she could not think without an impatient struggle.

'I, alone, by my active tenderness, could have saved,' she would exclaim, 'from an early blight, this sweet blossom; and, cherishing it, I should have something still to love.'

In proportion as other expectations were torn from her, this tender one had been fondly clung to, and knit into her heart.

The books she had obtained, were soon devoured, by one who had no other resource to escape from sorrow, and the feverish dreams of ideal wretchedness or felicity, which equally weaken the intoxicated sensibility. Writing was then the only alternative, and she wrote some rhapsodies descriptive of the state of her mind; but the events of her past life pressing on her, she resolved circumstantially to relate them, with the sentiments that experience, and more matured reason, would naturally suggest. They might perhaps instruct her daughter, and shield her from the misery, the tyranny, her mother knew not how to avoid.

This thought gave life to her diction, her soul flowed into it, and she soon found the task of recollecting almost obliterated impressions very interesting. She lived again in the revived emotions of youth, and forgot her present in the retrospect of sorrows that had assumed an unalterable character.

Though this employment lightened the weight of time, yet, never losing sight of her main object, Maria did not allow any opportunity to slip of winning on the affections of Jemima; for she discovered in her a strength of mind, that excited her esteem, clouded as it was by the misanthropy of despair.

An insulated being, from the misfortune of her birth, she despised and preyed on the society by which she had been oppressed, and loved not her fellow-creatures, because she had never been beloved. No mother had ever fondled her, no father or brother had protected her from outrage; and the man who had plunged her into infamy, and deserted her when she stood in greatest need of support, deigned not to smooth with kindness the road to ruin. Thus degraded, was she let loose on the world; and virtue, never nurtured by affection, assumed the stern aspect of selfish independence.

This general view of her life, Maria gathered from her exclamations and dry remarks. Jemima indeed displayed a strange mixture of interest and suspicion; for she would listen to her with earnestness, and then suddenly interrupt the conversation, as if afraid of resigning, by giving way to her sympathy, her dear-bought knowledge of the world.

Maria alluded to the possibility of an escape, and mentioned a compensation, or reward; but the style in which she was repulsed made her cautious, and determine not to renew the subject, till she knew more of the character she had to work on. Jemima's countenance, and dark hints, seemed to say, 'You are an extraordinary woman; but let me consider, this may only be one of your lucid intervals.' Nay, the very energy of Maria's character, made her suspect that the extraordinary animation she perceived might be the effect of madness. 'Should her husband then substantiate his charge, and get possession of her estate, from whence would come the promised annuity, or more desired protection? Besides, might not a woman, anxious to escape, conceal some of the circumstances which made against her? Was truth to be expected from one who had been entrapped, kidnapped, in the most fraudulent manner?'

In this train Jemima continued to argue, the moment after compassion and respect seemed to make her swerve; and she still resolved not to be wrought on to do more than soften the rigour of confinement, till she could advance on surer ground.

Maria was not permitted to walk in the garden; but sometimes, from her window, she turned her eyes from the gloomy walls, in which she pined life away, on the poor wretches who strayed along the walks, and contemplated the most terrific of ruins – that of a human soul. What is the view of the fallen column, the mouldering arch, of the most exquisite workmanship, when compared with this living memento of the fragility, the instability, of reason, and the wild luxuriancy of noxious passions? Enthusiasm turned adrift, like some rich stream overflowing its banks, rushes forward with destructive velocity, inspiring a sublime concentration of thought. Thus thought Maria – These are the ravages over which humanity must ever mournfully ponder, with a degree of anguish not excited by crumbling marble, or cankering brass, unfaithful to the trust of monumental fame. It is not over the decaying productions of the mind, embodied with the happiest art, we grieve most bitterly. The view of what has been done by man, produces a melancholy, yet aggrandizing, sense of what remains to be achieved by human intellect; but a mental convulsion, which, like the devastation of an earthquake, throws all the elements of thought and imagination into confusion, makes contemplation giddy, and we fearfully ask on what ground we ourselves stand.

Melancholy and imbecility marked the features of the wretches allowed to breathe at large; for the frantic, those who in a strong imagination had lost a sense of woe, were closely confined. The playful tricks and mis-chievous devices of their disturbed fancy, that suddenly broke out, could not be guarded against, when they were permitted to enjoy any portion of freedom; for, so active was their imagination, that every new object which accidentally struck their senses, awoke to phrenzy their restless passions; as Maria learned from the burden of their incessant ravings.

Sometimes, with a strict injunction of silence, Jemima would allow Maria, at the close of evening, to stray along the narrow avenues that separated the dungeon-like apartments, leaning on her arm. What a change of scene! Maria wished to pass the threshold of her prison, yet, when by chance she met the eye of rage glaring on her, yet unfaithful to its office, she shrunk back with more horror and affright, than if she had stumbled over a mangled corpse. Her busy fancy pictured the misery of a fond heart, watching over a friend thus estranged, absent, though present – over a poor wretch lost to reason and the social joys of existence; and losing all consciousness of misery in its excess. What a task, to watch the light of reason quivering in the eye, or with agonizing expectation to catch the beam of recollection; tantalized by hope, only to feel despair more keenly, at finding a much loved face or voice, suddenly remembered, or pathetically implored, only to be immediately forgotten, or viewed with indifference or abhorrence!

The heart-rending sigh of melancholy sunk into her soul; and when she retired to rest, the petrified figures she had encountered, the only human forms she was doomed to observe, haunting her dreams with tales of mysterious wrongs, made her wish to sleep to dream no more.

Day after day rolled away, and tedious as the present moment appeared, they passed in such an unvaried tenor, Maria was surprised to find that she had already been six weeks buried alive, and yet had such faint hopes of effecting her enlargement. She was, earnestly as she had sought for employment, now angry with herself for having been amused by writing her narrative; and grieved to think that she had for an instant thought of any thing, but contriving to escape.

Jemima had evidently pleasure in her society: still, though she often left her with a glow of kindness, she returned with the same chilling air; and, when her heart appeared for a moment to open, some suggestion of reason forcibly closed it, before she could give utterance to the confidence Maria's conversation inspired.

Discouraged by these changes, Maria relapsed into despondency, when she was cheered by the alacrity with which Jemima brought her a fresh parcel of books; assuring her, that she had taken some pains to obtain them from one of the keepers, who attended a gentleman confined in the opposite corner of the gallery.

Maria took up the books with emotion. 'They come,' said she, 'perhaps, from a wretch condemned, like me, to reason on the nature of madness, by having wrecked minds continually under his eye; and almost to wish himself – as I do – mad, to escape from the contemplation of it.' Her heart throbbed with sympathetic alarm; and she turned over the leaves with awe, as if they had become sacred from passing through the hands of an unfortunate being, oppressed by a similar fate.

Dryden's Fables, Milton's Paradise Lost,[6] with several modern productions, composed the collection. It was a mine of treasure. Some marginal notes, in Dryden's Fables, caught her attention: they were written with force and taste; and, in one of the modern pamphlets, there was a fragment left, containing various observations on the present state of society and government, with a comparative view of the politics of Europe and America. These remarks were written with a degree of generous warmth, when alluding to the enslaved state of the labouring majority, perfectly in unison with Maria's mode of thinking.

She read them over and over again; and fancy, treacherous fancy, began to sketch a character, congenial with her own, from these shadowy outlines. – 'Was he mad?' She re-perused the marginal notes, and they seemed the production of an animated, but not of a disturbed imagination. Confined to this speculation, every time she re-read them, some fresh refinement of sentiment, or acuteness of thought impressed her, which she was astonished at herself for not having before observed.

What a creative power has an affectionate heart! There are beings who cannot live without loving, as poets love; and who feel the electric spark of genius, wherever it awakens sentiment or grace. Maria had often thought, when disciplining her wayward heart, 'that to charm, was to be virtuous.' 'They who make me wish to appear the most amiable and good in their eyes, must possess in a degree,' she would exclaim, 'the graces and virtues they call into action.'

She took up a book on the powers of the human mind; but, her attention strayed from cold arguments on the nature of what she felt, while she was feeling, and she snapt the chain of the theory to read Dryden's Guiscard and Sigismunda.[7]

Maria, in the course of the ensuing day, returned some of the books; with the hope of getting others – and more marginal notes. Thus shut out from human intercourse, and compelled to view nothing but the prison of vexed spirits, to meet a wretch in the same situation, was more surely to find a friend, than to imagine a countryman one, in a strange land, where the human voice conveys no information to the eager ear.

'Did you ever see the unfortunate being to whom these books belong?' asked Maria, when Jemima brought her supper. 'Yes. He sometimes walks out, between five and six, before the family is stirring, in the morning, with two keepers; but even then his hands are confined.'

'What! is he so unruly?' enquired Maria, with an accent of disappointment.

'No, not that I perceive,' replied Jemima; 'but he has an untamed look, a vehemence of eye, that excites apprehension. Were his hands free, he looks as if he could soon manage both his guards: yet he appears tranquil.'

'If he be so strong, he must be young,' observed Maria.

'Three or four and thirty, I suppose; but there is no judging of a person in his situation.'

'Are you sure that he is mad?' interrupted Maria with eagerness. Jemima quitted the room, without replying.

'No, no, he certainly is not!' exclaimed Maria, answering herself; 'the man who could write those observations was not disordered in his intellects.'

She sat musing, gazing at the moon, and watching its motion as it seemed to glide under the clouds. Then, preparing for bed, she thought, 'Of what use could I be to him, or he to me, if it be true that he is unjustly confined? – Could he aid me to escape, who is himself more closely watched? – Still I should like to see him.' She went to bed, dreamed of her child, yet woke exactly at half after five o'clock, and starting up, only wrapped a gown around her, and ran to the window. The morning was chill, it was the latter end of September; yet she did not retire to warm herself and think in bed, till the sound of the servants, moving about the house, convinced her that the unknown would not walk in the garden that morning. She was ashamed at feeling disappointed; and began to reflect, as an excuse to herself, on the little objects which attract attention when there is nothing to divert the mind; and how difficult it was for women to avoid growing romantic, who have no active duties or pursuits.

At breakfast, Jemima enquired whether she understood French? for, unless she did, the stranger's stock of books was exhausted. Maria replied in the affirmative; but forbore to ask any more questions respecting the person to whom they belonged. And Jemima gave her a new subject for contemplation, by describing the person of a lovely maniac, just brought into an adjoining chamber. She was singing the pathetic ballad of old Robin Gray with the most heart-melting falls and pauses.[8] Jemima had half-opened the door, when she distinguished her voice, and Maria stood close to it, scarcely daring to respire, lest a modulation should escape her, so exquisitely sweet, so passionately wild. She began with sympathy to pourtray to herself another victim, when the lovely warbler flew, as it were, from the spray, and a torrent of unconnected exclamations and questions burst from her, interrupted by fits of laughter, so horrid, that Maria shut the door, and, turning her eyes up to heaven, exclaimed – 'Gracious God!'

Several minutes elapsed before Maria could enquire respecting the rumour of the house (for this poor wretch was obviously not confined without a cause); and then Jemima could only tell her, that it was said, 'she had been married, against her inclination, to a rich old man, extremely jealous (no wonder, for she was a charming creature); and that, in consequence of his treatment, or something which hung on her mind, she had, during her first lying-in, lost her senses.'

What a subject of meditation – even to the very confines of madness.

'Woman, fragile flower! why were you suffered to adorn a world exposed to the inroad of such stormy elements?' thought Maria, while the poor maniac's strain was still breathing on her ear, and sinking into her very soul.

Towards the evening, Jemima brought her Rousseau's *Heloïse*,[9] and she sat reading with eyes and heart, till the return of her guard to extinguish the light. One instance of her kindness was, the permitting Maria to have one, till her own hour of retiring to rest. She had read this work long since; but now it seemed to open a new world to her – the only one worth inhabiting. Sleep was not to be wooed; yet, far from being fatigued by the restless rotation of thought, she rose and opened her window, just as the thin watery clouds of twilight made the long silent shadows visible. The air swept across her face with a voluptuous freshness that thrilled to her heart, awakening indefinable emotions; and the sound of a waving branch, or the twittering of a startled bird, alone broke the stillness of reposing nature. Absorbed by the sublime sensibility which renders the consciousness of existence felicity, Maria was happy, till an autumnal scent, wafted by the breeze of morn from the fallen leaves of the adjacent wood, made her recollect that the season had changed since her confinement; yet life afforded no variety to solace an afflicted heart. She returned dispirited to her couch, and thought of her child till the broad glare of day again invited her to the window. She looked not for the unknown, still how great was her vexation at perceiving the back of a man, certainly he, with his two attendants, as he turned into a side-path which led to the house! A confused recollection of having seen somebody who resembled him, immediately occurred, to puzzle and torment her with endless conjectures. Five minutes sooner, and she should have seen his face, and been out of suspense – was ever any thing so unlucky! His steady, bold step, and the whole air of his person, bursting as it were from a cloud, pleased her, and gave an outline to the imagination to sketch the individual form she wished to recognize.

Feeling the disappointment more severely than she was willing to believe, she flew to Rousseau, as her only refuge from the idea of him, who might prove a friend, could she but find a way to interest him in her fate; still the personification of Saint Preux, or of an ideal lover far superior, was after this imperfect model, of which merely a glance had been caught, even to the minutiae of the coat and hat of the stranger. But if she lent St Preux, or the demi-god of her fancy, his form, she richly repaid him by the donation of all St Preux's sentiments and feelings, culled to gratify her own, to which he seemed to have an undoubted right, when she read on the margin of an impassioned letter, written in the well-known hand – 'Rousseau alone, the true Prometheus of sentiment,[10] possessed the fire of genius necessary to pourtray the passion, the truth of which goes so directly to the heart.'

Maria was again true to the hour, yet had finished Rousseau, and begun to transcribe some selected passages; unable to quit either the author or the window, before she had a glimpse of the countenance she daily longed to see; and, when seen, it conveyed no distinct idea to her mind where she had seen it before. He must have been a transient acquaintance; but to discover an acquaintance was fortunate, could she contrive to attract his attention, and excite his sympathy.

Every glance afforded colouring for the picture she was delineating on her heart; and once, when the window was half open, the sound of his voice reached her. Conviction flashed on her; she had certainly, in a moment of distress, heard the same accents. They were manly, and characteristic of a noble mind; nay, even sweet – or sweet they seemed to her attentive ear.

She started back, trembling, alarmed at the emotion a strange coincidence of circumstances inspired, and wondering why she thought so much of a stranger, obliged as she had been by his timely interference; [for she recollected, by degrees, all the circumstances of their former meeting.] She found however that she could think of nothing else; or, if she thought of her daughter, it was to wish that she had a father whom her mother could respect and love.

CHAPTER III

When perusing the first parcel of books, Maria had, with her pencil, written in one of them a few exclamations, expressive of compassion and sympathy, which she scarcely remembered, till turning over the leaves of one of the volumes, lately brought to her, a slip of paper dropped out, which Jemima hastily snatched up.

'Let me see it,' demanded Maria impatiently, 'You surely are not afraid of trusting me with the effusions of a madman?' 'I must consider,' replied Jemima; and withdrew, with the paper in her hand.

In a life of such seclusion, the passions gain undue force; Maria therefore felt a great degree of resentment and vexation, which she had not time to subdue, before Jemima, returning, delivered the paper.

'Whoever you are, who partake of my fate, accept my sincere commiseration – I would have said protection; but the privilege of man is denied me.

'My own situation forces a dreadful suspicion on my mind – I may not always languish in vain for freedom – say are you – I cannot ask the question; yet I will remember you when my remembrance can be of any use. I will enquire, *why* you are so mysteriously detained – and I *will* have an answer.

'HENRY DARNFORD.'

By the most pressing intreaties, Maria prevailed on Jemima to permit her to write a reply to this note. Another and another succeeded, in which explanations were not allowed relative to their present situation; but Maria, with sufficient explicitness, alluded to a former obligation; and they insensibly entered on an interchange of sentiments on the most important subjects. To write these letters was the business of the day, and to receive them the moment of sunshine. By some means, Darnford having discovered Maria's window, when she next appeared at it, he made her, behind his keepers, a profound bow of respect and recognition.

Two or three weeks glided away in this kind of intercourse, during which period Jemima, to whom Maria had given the necessary information respecting her family, had evidently gained some intelligence, which increased her desire of pleasing her charge, though she could not yet determine to liberate her. Maria took advantage of this favourable change, without too minutely enquiring into the cause; and such was her eagerness to hold human converse, and to see her former protector, still a stranger to her, that she incessantly requested her guard to gratify her more than curiosity.

Writing to Darnford, she was led from the sad objects before her, and frequently rendered insensible to the horrid noises around her, which previously had continually employed her feverish fancy. Thinking it selfish to dwell on her own sufferings, when in the midst of wretches, who had not only lost all that endears life, but their very selves, her imagination was occupied with melancholy earnestness to trace the mazes of misery, through which so many wretches must have passed to this gloomy receptacle of disjointed souls, to the grand source of human corruption. Often at midnight was she waked by the dismal shrieks of demoniac rage, or of excruciating despair, uttered in such wild tones of indescribable anguish as proved the total absence of reason, and roused phantoms of horror in her mind, far more terrific than all that dreaming superstition ever drew. Besides, there was frequently something so inconceivably picturesque in the varying gestures of unrestrained passion, so irresistibly comic in their sallies, or so heart-piercingly pathetic in the little airs they would sing, frequently bursting out after an awful silence, as to fascinate the attention, and amuse the fancy, while torturing the soul. It was the uproar of the passions which she was compelled to observe; and to mark the lucid beam of reason, like a light trembling in a socket, or like the flash which divides the threatening clouds of angry heaven only to display the horrors which darkness shrouded.

Jemima would labour to beguile the tedious evenings, by describing the persons and manners of the unfortunate beings, whose figures or voices awoke sympathetic sorrow in Maria's bosom; and the stories she told were the more interesting, for perpetually leaving room to conjecture something extraordinary. Still Maria, accustomed to generalize her observations, was led to conclude from all she heard, that it was a vulgar error to suppose that people of abilities were the most apt to lose the command of reason. On the contrary, from most of the instances she could investigate, she thought it resulted, that the passions only appeared strong and disproportioned, because the judgment was weak and unexercised; and that they gained strength by the decay of reason, as the shadows lengthen during the sun's decline.

Maria impatiently wished to see her fellow-sufferer; but Darnford was still more earnest to obtain an interview. Accustomed to submit to every åmpulse of passion, and never taught, like women, to restrain the most natural, and acquire, instead of the bewitching frankness of nature, a factitious propriety of behaviour, every desire became a torrent that bore down all opposition.

His travelling trunk, which contained the books lent to Maria, had been sent to him, and with a part of its contents he bribed his principal keeper; who, after receiving the most solemn promise that he would return to his apartment without attempting to explore any part of the house, conducted him, in the dusk of the evening, to Maria's room.

Jemima had apprized her charge of the visit, and she expected with trembling impatience, inspired by a vague hope that he might again prove her deliverer, to see a man who had before rescued her from oppression.[11] He entered with an animation of countenance, formed to captivate an enthusiast; and, hastily turned his eyes from her to the apartment, which he surveyed with apparent emotions of compassionate indignation. Sympathy illuminated his eye, and, taking her hand, he respectfully bowed on it, exclaiming – 'This is extraordinary! – again to meet you, and in such circumstances!' Still, impressive as was the coincidence of events which brought them once more together, their full hearts did not overflow. –*

[And though, after this first visit, they were permitted frequently to repeat their interviews, they were for some time employed in] a reserved conversation, to which all the world might have listened; excepting, when discussing some literary subject, flashes of sentiment, inforced by each relaxing feature, seemed to remind them that their minds were already acquainted.

[By degrees, Darnford entered into the particulars of his story.] In a few words, he informed her that he had been a thoughtless, extravagant young man; yet, as he described his faults, they appeared to be the generous luxuriancy of a noble mind. Nothing like meanness tarnished the lustre of his youth, nor had the worm of selfishness lurked in the unfolding bud, even while he had been the dupe of others. Yet he tardily acquired the experience necessary to guard him against future imposition.

'I shall weary you,' continued he, 'by my egotism; and did not powerful emotions draw me to you,' – his eyes glistened as he spoke, and a trembling seemed to run through his manly frame, – 'I would not waste these precious moments in talking of myself.

'My father and mother were people of fashion; married by their parents. He was fond of the turf, she of the card-table. I, and two or three other children since dead, were kept at home till we became intolerable. My father and mother had a visible dislike to each other, continually displayed; the servants were of the depraved kind usually found in the houses of people of fortune. My brothers and parents all dying, I was left to the care of guardians, and sent to Eton. I never knew the sweets of domestic affection, but I felt the want of indulgence and frivolous respect at school. I will not disgust you with a recital of the vices of my youth, which can scarcely be comprehended by female delicacy. I was taught to love by a creature I am ashamed to mention; and the other women with whom I afterwards became intimate, were of a class of which you can have no knowledge. I formed my acquaintance with them at the theatres; and, when vivacity danced in their eyes, I was not easily disgusted by the vulgarity which flowed from their

---

* The copy which had received the author's last corrections, breaks off in this place, and the pages which follow, to the end of Chap. IV, are printed from a copy in a less finished state.

lips. Having spent, a few years after I was of age, [the whole of] a considerable patrimony, excepting a few hundreds, I had no resource but to purchase a commission in a new-raised regiment, destined to subjugate America. The regret I felt to renounce a life of pleasure, was counterbalanced by the curiosity I had to see America, or rather to travel; [nor had any of those circumstances occurred to my youth, which might have been calculated] to bind my country to my heart. I shall not trouble you with the details of a military life. My blood was still kept in motion; till, towards the close of the contest, I was wounded and taken prisoner.

'Confined to my bed, or chair, by a lingering cure, my only refuge from the preying activity of my mind, was books, which I read with great avidity, profiting by the conversation of my host, a man of sound understanding. My political sentiments now underwent a total change; and, dazzled by the hospitality of the Americans, I determined to take up my abode with freedom. I, therefore, with my usual impetuosity, sold my commission, and travelled into the interior parts of the country, to lay out my money to advantage. Added to this, I did not much like the puritanical manners of the large towns. Inequality of condition was there most disgustingly galling. The only pleasure wealth afforded, was to make an ostentatious display of it; for the cultivation of the fine arts, or literature, had not introduced into the first circles that polish of manners which renders the rich so essentially superior to the poor in Europe. Added to this, an influx of vices had been let in by the Revolution, and the most rigid principles of religion shaken to the centre, before the understanding could be gradually emancipated from the prejudices which led their ancestors undauntedly to seek an inhospitable clime and unbroken soil. The resolution, that led them, in pursuit of independence, to embark on rivers like seas, to search for unknown shores, and to sleep under the hovering mists of endless forests, whose baleful damps agued their limbs was now turned into commercial speculations, till the national character exhibited a phenomenon in the history of the human mind – a head. enthusiastically enterprising, with cold selfishness of heart. And woman, lovely woman! – they charm every where – still there is a degree of prudery, and a want of taste and ease in the manners of the American women, that renders them, in spite of their roses and lilies, far inferior to our European charmers. In the country, they have often a bewitching simplicity of character; but, in the cities, they have all the airs and ignorance of the ladies who give the tone to the circles of the large trading towns in England. They are fond of their ornaments, merely because they are good, and not because they embellish their persons; and are more gratified to inspire the women with jealousy of these exterior advantages, than the men with love. All the frivolity which often (excuse me, Madam) renders the society of modest women so stupid in England, here seemed to throw still more leaden fetters on their charms. Not being an adept in gallantry, I found that I could only keep myself awake in their company by making downright love to them.

'But, not to intrude on your patience, I retired to the track of land which I had purchased in the country, and my time passed pleasantly enough while I cut down the trees, built my house, and planted my different crops. But winter and idleness came, and I longed for more elegant society, to hear what was passing in the world, and to do something better than vegetate with the animals that made a very considerable part of my household. Consequently, I determined to travel. Motion was a substitute for variety of objects; and, passing over immense tracks of country, I exhausted my exuberant spirits, without obtaining much experience. I every where saw industry the forerunner and not the consequence, of luxury; but this country, every thing being on an ample scale, did not afford those picturesque views, which a certain degree of cultivation is necessary gradually to produce. The eye wandered without an object to fix upon over immeasureable plains, and lakes that seemed replenished by the ocean, whilst eternal forests of small clustering trees, obstructed the circulation of air, and embarrassed the path, without gratifying the eye of taste. No cottage smiling in the waste, no travellers hailed us, to give life to silent nature; or, if perchance we saw the print of a footstep in our path, it was a dreadful warning to turn aside; and the head ached as if assailed by the scalping knife. The Indians who hovered on the skirts of the European settlements had only learned of their neighbours to plunder, and they stole their guns from them to do it with more safety.

'From the woods and back settlements, I returned to the towns, and learned to eat and drink most valiantly; but without entering into commerce (and I detested commerce) I found I could not live there; and, growing heartily weary of the land of liberty and vulgar aristocracy, seated on her bags of dollars, I resolved once more to visit Europe. I wrote to a distant relation in England, with whom I had been educated, mentioning the vessel in which I intended to sail. Arriving in London, my senses were intoxicated. I ran from street to street, from theatre to theatre, and the women of the town (again I must beg pardon for my habitual frankness) appeared to me like angels.

'A week was spent in this thoughtless manner, when, returning very late to the hotel in which I had lodged ever since my arrival, I was knocked down in a private street, and hurried, in a state of insensibility, into a coach, which brought me hither, and I only recovered my senses to be treated like one who had lost them. My keepers are deaf to my remonstrances and enquiries, yet assure me that my confinement shall not last long. Still I cannot guess, though I weary myself with conjectures, why I am confined, or in what part of England this house is situated. I imagine sometimes that I hear the sea roar, and wished myself again on the Atlantic, till I had a glimpse of you.'*

---

* The introduction of Darnford as the deliverer of Maria in a former instance, appears to have been an after-thought of the author. This has occasioned the omission of any allusion to that circumstance in the preceding narration.

A few moments were only allowed to Maria to comment on this narrative, when Darnford left her to her own thoughts, to the 'never ending, still beginning,' task of weighing his words, recollecting his tones of voice, and feeling them reverberate on her heart.

CHAPTER IV

Pity, and the forlorn seriousness of adversity, have both been considered as dispositions favourable to love, while satirical writers have attributed the propensity to the relaxing effect of idleness; what chance then had Maria of escaping, when pity, sorrow, and solitude all conspired to soften her mind, and nourish romantic wishes, and, from a natural progress, romantic expectations?

Maria was six-and-twenty. But, such was the native soundness of her constitution, that time had only given to her countenance the character of her mind. Revolving thought, and exercised affections had banished some of the playful graces of innocence, producing insensibly that irregularity of features which the struggles of the understanding to trace or govern the strong emotions of the heart, are wont to imprint on the yielding mass. Grief and care had mellowed, without obscuring, the bright tints of youth, and the thoughtfulness which resided on her brow did not take from the feminine softness of her features; nay, such was the sensibility which often mantled over it, that she frequently appeared, like a large proportion of her sex, only born to feel; and the activity of her well-proportioned, and even almost voluptuous figure, inspired the idea of strength of mind, rather than of body. There was a simplicity sometimes indeed in her manner, which bordered on infantine ingenuousness, that led people of common discernment to under-rate her talents, and smile at the flights of her imagination. But those who could not comprehend the delicacy of her sentiments, were attached by her unfailing sympathy, so that she was very generally beloved by characters of very different descriptions; still, she was too much under the influence of an ardent imagination to adhere to common rules.

There are mistakes of conduct which at five-and-twenty prove the strength of the mind, that, ten or fifteen years after, would demonstrate its weakness, its incapacity to acquire a sane judgment. The youths who are satisfied with the ordinary pleasures of life, and do not sigh after ideal phantoms of love and friendship, will never arrive at great maturity of understanding; but if these reveries are cherished, as is too frequently the case with women, when experience ought to have taught them in what human happiness consists, they become as useless as they are wretched.

Besides, their pains and pleasures are so dependent on outward circumstances, on the objects of their affections, that they seldom act from the impulse of a nerved mind, able to choose its own pursuit.

Having had to struggle incessantly with the vices of mankind, Maria's imagination found repose in pourtraying the possible virtues the world might contain. Pygmalion formed an ivory maid, and longed for an informing soul.[12] She, on the contrary, combined all the qualities of a hero's mind, and fate presented a statue in which she might enshrine them.

We mean not to trace the progress of this passion, or recount how often Darnford and Maria were obliged to part in the midst of an interesting conversation. Jemima ever watched on the tip-toe of fear, and frequently separated them on a false alarm, when they would have given worlds to remain a little longer together.

A magic lamp now seemed to be suspended in Maria's prison, and fairy landscapes flitted round the gloomy walls, late so blank. Rushing from the depth of despair, on the seraph wing of hope, she found herself happy. – She was beloved, and every emotion was rapturous.

To Darnford she had not shown a decided affection; the fear of outrunning his, a sure proof of love, made her often assume a coldness and indifference foreign from her character; and, even when giving way to the playful emotions of a heart just loosened from the frozen bond of grief, there was a delicacy in her manner of expressing her sensibility, which made him doubt whether it was the effect of love.

One evening, when Jemima left them, to listen to the sound of a distant footstep, which seemed cautiously to approach, he seized Maria's hand – it was not withdrawn. They conversed with earnestness of their situation; and, during the conversation, he once or twice gently drew her towards him. He felt the fragrance of her breath, and longed, yet feared, to touch the lips from which it issued; spirits of purity seemed to guard them, while all the enchanting graces of love sported on her cheeks, and languished in her eyes.

Jemima entering, he reflected on his diffidence with poignant regret, and, she once more taking alarm, he ventured, as Maria stood near his chair, to approach her lips with a declaration of love. She drew back with solemnity, he hung down his head abashed; but lifting his eyes timidly, they met her's; she had determined, during that instant, and suffered their rays to mingle. He took, with more ardour, reassured, a half-consenting, half-reluctant kiss, reluctant only from modesty; and there was a sacredness in her dignified manner of reclining her glowing face on his shoulder, that powerfully impressed him. Desire was lost in more ineffable emotions, and to protect her from insult and sorrow – to make her happy, seemed not only the first wish of his heart, but the most noble duty of his life. Such angelic confidence demanded the fidelity of honour; but could he, feeling her in every pulsation, could he ever change, could he be a villain? The emotion with which she, for a moment, allowed herself to be pressed to his bosom, the tear of rapturous sympathy, mingled with a soft melancholy sentiment of recollected disappointment, said – more of truth and faithfulness, than the tongue could have given utterance to in hours! They were silent – yet discoursed, how eloquently? till, after a moment's reflection, Maria drew her chair by the side of his, and, with a composed sweetness of voice, and supernatural benignity of countenance, said, 'I must open my whole heart to you; you must be told who I am, why I am here, and why, telling you I am a wife, I blush not to' – the blush spoke the rest.

Jemima was again at her elbow, and the restraint of her presence did not prevent an animated conversation, in which love, sly urchin, was ever at bo-peep.

So much of heaven did they enjoy, that paradise bloomed around them; or they, by a powerful spell, had been transported into Armida's garden.[13] Love, the grand enchanter, 'lapt them in Elysium,'[14] and every sense was harmonized to joy and social extacy. So animated, indeed, were their accents of tenderness, in discussing what, in other circumstances, would have been common-place subjects, that Jemima felt, with surprise, a tear of pleasure trickling down her rugged cheeks. She wiped it away, half ashamed; and when Maria kindly enquired the cause, with all the eager solicitude of a happy being wishing to impart to all nature its overflowing felicity. Jemima owned that it was the first tear that social enjoyment had ever drawn from her. She seemed indeed to breathe more freely; the cloud of suspicion cleared away from her brow; she felt herself, for once in her life, treated like a fellow-creature.

Imagination! who can paint thy power; or reflect the evanescent tints of hope fostered by thee? A despondent gloom had long obscured Maria's horizon – now the sun broke forth, the rainbow appeared, and every prospect was fair. Horror still reigned in the darkened cells, suspicion lurked in the passages, and whispered along the walls. The yells of men possessed, sometimes made them pause, and wonder that they felt so happy, in a tomb of living death. They even chid themselves for such apparent insensibility; still the world contained not three happier beings. And Jemima, after again patrolling the passage, was so softened by the air of confidence which breathed around her, that she voluntarily began an account of herself.

CHAPTER V

'My father,' said Jemima, 'seduced my mother, a pretty girl, with whom he lived fellow-servant; and she no sooner perceived the natural, the dreaded consequence, than the terrible conviction flashed on her – that she was ruined. Honesty, and a regard for her reputation, had been the only principles inculcated by her mother; and they had been so forcibly impressed, that she feared shame, more than the poverty to which it would lead. Her incessant importunities to prevail upon my father to screen her from reproach by marrying her, as he had promised in the fervour of seduction, estranged him from her so completely, that her very person became distasteful to him; and he began to hate, as well as despise me, before I was born.

'My mother, grieved to the soul by his neglect, and unkind treatment, actually resolved to famish herself; and injured her health by the attempt; though she had not sufficient resolution to adhere to her project, or renounce it entirely. Death came not at her call; yet sorrow, and the methods she adopted to conceal her condition, still doing the work of a house-maid, had such an effect on her constitution, that she died in the wretched garret, where her virtuous mistress had forced her to take refuge in the very pangs of labour, though my father, after a slight reproof, was allowed to remain in his place – allowed by the mother of six children, who, scarcely permitting a footstep to be heard, during her month's indulgence, felt no sympathy for the poor wretch, denied every comfort required by her situation.

'The day my mother died, the ninth after my birth, I was consigned to the care of the cheapest nurse my father could find; who suckled her own child at the same time, and lodged as many more as she could, in two cellar-like apartments.

'Poverty, and the habit of seeing children die off her hands, had so hardened her heart, that the office of a mother did not awaken the tenderness of a woman; nor were the feminine caresses which seem a part of the rearing of a child, ever bestowed on me. The chicken has a wing to shelter under; but I had no bosom to nestle in, no kindred warmth to foster me. Left in dirt, to cry with cold and hunger till I was weary, and sleep without ever being prepared by exercise, or lulled by kindness to rest; could I be expected to become any thing but a weak and rickety babe? Still, in spite of neglect, I continued to exist, to learn to curse existence, [her countenance grew ferocious as she spoke,] and the treatment that rendered me miserable, seemed to sharpen my wits. Confined then in a damp hovel, to rock the cradle of the succeeding tribe, I looked like a little old woman, or a hag shrivelling into nothing. The furrows of reflection and care contracted the youthful cheek, and gave a sort of supernatural wildness to the ever watchful eye. During this period, my father had married another fellow-servant, who loved him less, and knew better how to manage his passion, than my mother. She likewise proving with child, they agreed to keep a shop: my step-mother, if, being an illegitimate offspring, I may venture thus to characterize her, having obtained a sum of a rich relation, for that purpose.

'Soon after her lying-in, she prevailed on my father to take me home, to save the expence of maintaining me, and of hiring a girl to assist her in the care of the child. I was young, it was true, but appeared a knowing little thing, and might be made handy. Accordingly I was brought to her house; but not to a home – for a home I never knew. Of this child, a daughter, she was extravagantly fond; and it was a part of my employment, to assist to spoil her, by humouring all her whims, and bearing all her caprices. Feeling her own consequence, before she could speak, she had learned the art of tormenting me, and if I ever dared to resist, I received blows, laid on with no compunctious hand, or was sent to bed dinnerless, as well as supperless. I said that it was a part of my daily labour to attend this child, with the servility of a slave; still it was but a part. I was sent out in all seasons, and from place to place, to carry burdens far above my strength, without being allowed to draw near the fire, or ever being cheered by encouragement or kindness. No wonder then, treated like a creature of another species, that I began to envy, and at length to hate, the darling of the house. Yet, I perfectly remember, that it was the caresses, and kind expressions of my step-mother, which first excited my jealous discontent. Once, I cannot forget it, when she was calling in vain her wayward child to kiss her, I ran to her, saying, "I will kiss you, ma'am!" and how did my heart, which was in my mouth, sink, what was my debasement of soul, when pushed away with – "I do not want you, pert thing!" Another day, when a new gown had excited the highest good humour, and she uttered the appropriate *dear*, addressed unexpectedly to me, I thought I could never do enough to please her; I was all alacrity, and rose proportionably in my own estimation.

'As her daughter grew up, she was pampered with cakes and fruit, while I was, literally speaking, fed with the refuse of the table, with her leavings. A liquorish tooth[15] is, I believe, common to children, and I used to steal any thing sweet, that I could catch up with a chance of concealment. When detected, she was not content to chastize me herself at the moment, but, on my father's return in the evening (he was a shopman), the principal discourse was to recount my faults, and attribute them to the wicked disposition which I had brought into the world with me; inherited from my mother. He did not fail to leave the marks of his resentment on my body, and then solaced himself by playing with my sister. – I could have murdered her at those moments. To save myself from these unmerciful corrections, I resorted to falshood, and the untruths which I sturdily maintained, were brought in judgment against me, to support my tyrant's inhuman charge of my natural propensity to vice. Seeing me treated with contempt, and always being fed and dressed better, my sister conceived a contemptuous opinion of me, that proved an obstacle to all affection; and my father, hearing continually of my faults, began to consider me as a curse entailed on him for his sins: he was therefore easily prevailed on to bind me apprentice to one of my step-mother's friends, who kept a slop-shop[16] in Wapping. I was represented (as it was said) in my true colours; but she, "warranted," snapping her fingers, "that she should break my spirit or heart".

'My mother replied, with a whine, "that if any body could make me better, it was such a clever woman as herself; though, for her own part, she had tried in vain; but good-nature was her fault."

'I shudder with horror, when I recollect the treatment I had not to endure. Not only under the lash of my task-mistress, but the drudge of the maid, apprentices and children, I never had a taste of human kindness to soften the rigour of perpetual labour. I had been introduced as an object of abhorrence into the family; as a creature of whom my step-mother, though she had been kind enough to let me live in the house with her own child, could make nothing. I was described as a wretch, whose nose must be kept to the grinding stone – and it was held there with an iron grasp. It seemed indeed the privilege of their superior nature to kick me about, like the dog or cat. If I were attentive, I was called fawning, if refractory, an obstinate mule, and like a mule I received their censure on my loaded back. Often has my mistress, for some instance of forgetfulness, thrown me from one side of the kitchen to the other, knocked my head against the wall, spit in my face, with various refinements on barbarity that I forbear to enumerate, though they were all acted over again by the servant, with additional insults, to which the appellation of *bastard*, was commonly added, with taunts or sneers. But I will not attempt to give you an adequate idea of my situation, lest you, who probably have never been drenched with the dregs of human misery, should think I exaggerate.

'I stole now, from absolute necessity, – bread; yet whatever else was taken, which I had it not in my power to take, was ascribed to me. I was the filching cat, the ravenous dog, the dumb brute, who must bear all; for if I endeavoured to exculpate myself, I was silenced, without any enquiries being made, with "Hold your tongue, you never tell truth." Even the very air I breathed was tainted with scorn; for I was sent to the neighbouring shops with Glutton, Liar, or Thief, written on my forehead. This was, at first, the most bitter punishment; but sullen pride, or a kind of stupid desperation, made me, at length, almost regardless of the contempt, which had wrung from me so many solitary tears at the only moments when I was allowed to rest.

'Thus was I the mark of cruelty till my sixteenth year; and then I have only to point out a change of misery; for a period I never knew. Allow me first to make one observation. Now I look back, I cannot help attributing the greater part of my misery, to the misfortune of having been thrown into the world without the grand support of life – a mother's affection. I had no one to love me; or to make me respected, to enable me to acquire respect. I was an egg dropped on the sand; a pauper by nature, hunted from family to family, who belonged to nobody – and nobody cared for me. I was despised from my birth, and denied the chance of obtaining a footing for myself in society. Yes; I had not even the chance of being considered as a fellow-creature – yet all the people with whom I lived, brutalized as they were by the low cunning of trade, and the despicable shifts of poverty, were not without bowels,[17] though they never yearned for me. I was, in fact, born a slave, and chained by infamy to slavery during the whole of existence, without having any companions to alleviate it by sympathy, or teach me how to rise above it by their example. But, to resume the thread of my tale –

'At sixteen, I suddenly grew tall, and something like comeliness appeared on a Sunday, when I had time to wash my face, and put on clean clothes. My master had once or twice caught hold of me in the passage; but I instinctively avoided his disgusting caresses. One day however, when the family were at a methodist meeting, he contrived to be alone in the house with me, and by blows – yes; blows and menaces, compelled me to submit to his ferocious desire; and, to avoid my mistress's fury, I was obliged in future to comply, and skulk to my loft at his command, in spite of increasing loathing.

'The anguish which was now pent up in my bosom, seemed to open a new world to me: I began to extend my thoughts beyond myself, and grieve for human misery, till I discovered, with horror – ah! what horror! – that I was with child. I know not why I felt a mixed sensation of despair and tenderness, excepting that, ever called a bastard, a bastard appeared to me an object of the greatest compassion in creation.

'I communicated this dreadful circumstance to my master, who was almost equally alarmed at the intelligence; for he feared his wife, and public censure at the meeting. After some weeks of deliberation had elapsed, I in continual fear that my altered shape would be noticed, my master gave me a medicine in a phial, which he desired me to take, telling me, without any circumlocution, for what purpose it was designed. I burst into tears, I thought it was killing myself – yet was such a self worth preserving? He cursed me for a fool, and left me to my own reflections. I could not resolve to take this infernal potion; but I wrapped it up in an old gown, and hid it in a corner of my box.

'Nobody yet suspected me, because they had been accustomed to view me as a creature of another species. But the threatening storm at last broke over my devoted head – never shall I forget it! One Sunday evening when I was left, as usual, to take care of the house, my master came home intoxicated, and I became the prey of his brutal appetite. His extreme intoxication made him forget his customary caution, and my mistress entered and found us in a situation that could not have been more hateful to her than me. Her husband was "pot-valiant," he feared her not at the moment, nor had he then much reason, for she instantly turned the whole force of her anger another way. She tore off my cap, scratched, kicked and buffetted me, till she had exhausted her strength, declaring, as she rested her arm, "that I had wheedled her husband from her. – But, could any thing better be expected from a wretch, whom she had taken into her house out of pure charity?" What a torrent of abuse rushed out? till, almost breathless, she concluded with saying, "that I was born a strumpet; it ran in my blood, and nothing good could come to those who harboured me."

'My situation was, of course, discovered, and she declared that I should not stay another night under the same roof with an honest family. I was therefore pushed out of doors, and my trumpery thrown after me, when it had been contemptuously examined in the passage, lest I should have stolen any thing.

'Behold me then in the street, utterly destitute! Whither could I creep for shelter? To my father's roof I had no claim, when not pursued by shame – now I shrunk back as from death, from my mother's cruel reproaches, my father's execrations. I could not endure to hear him curse the day I was born, though life had been a curse to me. Of death I thought, but with a confused emotion of terror, as I stood leaning my head on a post, and starting at every footstep, lest it should be my mistress coming to tear my heart out. One of the boys of the shop passing by, heard my tale, and immediately repaired to his master, to give him a description of my situation; and he touched the right key – the scandal it would give rise to, if I were left to repeat my tale to every enquirer. This plea came home to his reason, who had been sobered by his wife's rage, the fury of which fell on him when I was out of her reach, and he sent the boy to me with half-a-guinea, desiring him to conduct me to a house, where beggars, and other wretches, the refuse of society, nightly lodged.

'This night was spent in a state of stupefaction, or desperation. I detested mankind, and abhorred myself.

'In the morning I ventured out, to throw myself in my master's way, at his usual hour of going abroad. I approached him, he "damned me for a b——, declared I had disturbed the peace of the family, and that he had sworn to his wife, never to take any more notice of me." He left me; but, instantly returning, he told me that he should speak to his friend, a parish-officer, to get a nurse for the brat I laid to him; and advised me, if I wished to keep out of the house of correction, not to make free with his name.

'I hurried back to my hole, and, rage giving place to despair, sought for the potion that was to procure abortion, and swallowed it, with a wish that it might destroy me, at the same time that it stopped the sensations of new-born life, which I felt with indescribable emotion. My head turned round, my heart grew sick, and in the horrors of approaching dissolution, mental anguish was swallowed up. The effect of the medicine was violent, and I was confined to my bed several days; but, youth and a strong constitution prevailing, I once more crawled out, to ask myself the cruel question, "Whither I should go?" I had but two shillings left in my pocket, the rest had been expended, by a poor woman who slept in the same room, to pay for my lodging, and purchase the necessaries of which she partook.

'With this wretch I went into the neighbouring streets to beg, and my disconsolate appearance drew a few pence from the idle, enabling me still to command a bed; till, recovering from my illness, and taught to put on my rags to the best advantage, I was accosted from different motives, and yielded to the desire of the brutes I met, with the same detestation that I had felt for my still more brutal master. I have since read in novels of the blandishments of seduction, but I had not even the pleasure of being enticed into vice.

'I shall not,' interrupted Jemima, 'lead your imagination into all the scenes of wretchedness and depravity, which I was condemned to view; or mark the different stages of my debasing misery. Fate dragged me through the very kennels of society; I was still a slave, a bastard, a common property. Become familiar with vice, for I wish to conceal nothing from you, I picked the pockets of the drunkards who abused me; and proved by my conduct, that I deserved the epithets, with which they loaded me at moments when distrust ought to cease.

'Detesting my nightly occupation, though valuing, if I may so use the word, my independence, which only consisted in choosing the street in which I should wander, or the roof, when I had money, in which I should hide my head, I was some time before I could prevail on myself to accept of a place in a house of ill fame, to which a girl, with whom I had accidentally conversed in the street, had recommended me. I had been hunted almost into a fever, by the watchmen of the quarter of the town I frequented; one, whom I had unwittingly offended, giving the word to the whole pack. You can scarcely conceive the tyranny exercised by these wretches: considering themselves as the instruments of the very laws they violate, the pretext which steels their conscience, hardens their heart. Not content with receiving from us, outlaws of society (let other women talk of favours) a brutal gratification gratuitously as a privilege of office, they extort a tithe of prostitution, and harrass with threats the poor creatures whose occupation affords not the means to silence the growl of avarice. To escape from this persecution, I once more entered into servitude.

'A life of comparative regularity restored my health; and – do not start – my manners were improved, in a situation where vice sought to render itself alluring, and taste was cultivated to fashion the person, if not to refine the mind. Besides, the common civility of speech, contrasted with the gross vulgarity to which I had been accustomed, was something like the polish of civilization. I was not shut out from all intercourse of humanity. Still I was galled by the yoke of service, and my mistress often flying into violent fits of passion, made me dread a sudden dismission, which I understood was always the case. I was therefore prevailed on, though I felt a horror of men, to accept the offer of a gentleman, rather in the decline of years, to keep his house, pleasantly situated in a little village near Hampstead.

'He was a man of great talents, and of brilliant wit; but, a worn-out votary of voluptuousness, his desires became fastidious in proportion as they grew weak, and the native tenderness of his heart was undermined by a vitiated imagination. A thoughtless career of libertinism and social enjoyment, had injured his health to such a degree, that, whatever pleasure his conversation afforded me (and my esteem was ensured by proofs of the generous humanity of his disposition), the being his mistress was purchasing it at a very dear rate. With such a keen perception of the delicacies of sentiment, with an imagination invigorated by the exercise of genius, how could he sink into the grossness of sensuality!

'But, to pass over a subject which I recollect with pain, I must remark to you, as an answer to your often-repeated question, "Why my sentiments and language were superior to my station?" that I now began to read, to beguile the tediousness of solitude, and to gratify an inquisitive, active mind. I had often, in my childhood, followed a ballad-singer, to hear the sequel of a dismal story, though sure of being severely punished for delaying to return with whatever I was sent to purchase. I could just spell and put a sentence together, and I listened to the various arguments, though often mingled with obscenity, which occurred at the table where I was allowed to preside: for a literary friend or two frequently came home with my master, to dine and pass the night. Having lost the privileged respect of my sex, my presence, instead of restraining, perhaps gave the reins to their tongues; still I had the advantage of hearing discussions, from which, in the common course of life, women are excluded.

'You may easily imagine, that it was only by degrees that I could comprehend some of the subjects they investigated, or acquire from their reasoning what might be termed a moral sense. But my fondness of reading increasing, and my master occasionally shutting himself up in this retreat, for weeks together, to write, I had many opportunities of improvement. At first, considering money (I was right!' exclaimed Jemima, altering her tone of voice) 'as the only means, after my loss of reputation, of obtaining respect, or even the toleration of humanity, I had not the least scruple to secrete a part of the sums intrusted to me, and to screen myself from detection by a system of falshood. But, acquiring new principles, I began to have the ambition of returning to the respectable part of society, and was weak enough to suppose it possible. The attention of my unassuming instructor, who, without being ignorant of his own powers, possessed great simplicity of manners, strengthened the illusion. Having sometimes caught up hints for thought, from my untutored remarks, he often led me to discuss the subjects he was treating, and would read to me his productions, previous to their publication, wishing to profit by the criticism of unsophisticated feeling. The aim of his writings was to touch the simple springs of the heart; for he despised the would-be oracles, the self-elected philosophers, who fright away fancy, while sifting each grain of thought to prove that slowness of comprehension is wisdom.

'I should have distinguished this as a moment of sunshine, a happy period in my life, had not the repugnance the disgusting libertinism of my protector inspired, daily become more painful. – And, indeed, I soon did recollect it as such with agony, when his sudden death (for he had recourse to the most exhilarating cordials to keep up the convivial tone of his spirits) again threw me into the desert of human society. Had he had any time for reflection, I am certain he would have left the little property in his power to me: but, attacked by the fatal apoplexy in town, his heir, a man of rigid morals, brought his wife with him to take possession of the house and effects, before I was even informed of his death, – "to prevent," as she took care indirectly to tell me, "such a creature as she supposed me to be, from purloining any of them, had I been apprized of the event in time."

'The grief I felt at the sudden shock the information gave me, which at first had nothing selfish in it, was treated with contempt, and I was ordered to pack up my clothes; and a few trinkets and books, given me by the generous deceased, were contested, while they piously hoped, with a reprobating shake of the head, "that God would have mercy on his sinful soul!" With some difficulty, I obtained my arrears of wages; but asking – such is the spirit-grinding consequence of poverty and infamy – for a character for honesty and economy, which God knows I merited, I was told by this – why must I call her woman? – "that it would go against her conscience to recommend a kept mistress." Tears started in my eyes, burning tears; for there are situations in which a wretch is humbled by the contempt they are conscious they do not deserve.

'I returned to the metropolis; but the solitude of a poor lodging was inconceivably dreary, after the society I had enjoyed. To be cut off from human converse, now I had been taught to relish it, was to wander a ghost among the living. Besides, I foresaw, to aggravate the severity of my fate, that my little pittance would soon melt away. I endeavoured to obtain needlework; but, not having been taught early, and my hands being rendered clumsy by hard work, I did not sufficiently excel to be employed by the ready-made linen shops, when so many women, better qualified, were suing for it. The want of a character prevented my getting a place; for, irksome as servitude would have been to me, I should have made another trial, had it been feasible. Not that I disliked employment, but the inequality of condition to which I must have submitted. I had acquired a taste for literature, during the five years I had lived with a literary man, occasionally conversing with men of the first abilities of the age; and now to descend to the lowest vulgarity, was a degree of wretchedness not to be imagined unfelt. I had not, it is true, tasted the charms of affection, but I had been familiar with the graces of humanity.

'One of the gentlemen, whom I had frequently dined in company with, while I was treated like a companion, met me in the street, and enquired after my health. I seized the occasion, and began to describe my situation; but he was in haste to join, at dinner, a select party of choice spirits; therefore, without waiting to hear me, he impatiently put a guinea in my hand, saying, "It was a pity such a sensible woman should be in distress – he wished me well from his soul."

'To another I wrote, stating my case, and requesting advice. He was an advocate for unequivocal sincerity; and had often, in my presence, descanted on the evils which arise in society from the despotim of rank and riches.

'In reply, I received a long essay on the energy of the human mind, with continual allusions to his own force of character. He added, "That the woman who could write such a letter as I had sent him, could never be in want of resources, were she to look into herself, and exert her powers; misery was the consequence of indolence, and, as to my being shut out from society, it was the lot of man to submit to certain privations."

'How often have I heard,' said Jemima, interrupting her narrative, 'in conversation, and read in books, that every person willing to work may find employment? It is the vague assertion, I believe, of insensible indolence, when it relates to men; but, with respect to women, I am sure of its fallacy, unless they will submit to the most menial bodily labour; and even to be employed at hard labour is out of the reach of many, whose reputation misfortune or folly has tainted.

'How writers, professing to be friends to freedom, and the improvement of morals, can assert that poverty is no evil, I cannot imagine.'

'No more can I,' interrupted Maria, 'yet they even expatiate on the peculiar happiness of indigence, though in what it can consist, excepting in brutal rest, when a man can barely earn a subsistence, I cannot imagine. The mind is necessarily imprisoned in its own little tenement; and, fully occupied by keeping it in repair, has not time to rove abroad for improvement. The book of knowledge is closely clasped, against those who must fulfil their daily task of severe manual labour or die; and curiosity, rarely excited by thought or information, seldom moves on the stagnate lake of ignorance.'

'As far as I have been able to observe,' replied Jemima, 'prejudices, caught up by chance, are obstinately maintained by the poor, to the exclusion of improvement; they have not time to reason or reflect to any extent, or minds sufficiently exercised to adopt the principles of action, which form perhaps the only basis of contentment in every station.'*

'And independence,' said Darnford, 'they are necessarily strangers to, even the independence of despising their persecutors. If the poor are happy, or can be happy, *things are very well as they are*. And I cannot conceive on what principle those writers contend for a change of system, who support this opinion. The authors on the other side of the question are much more consistent, who grant the fact; yet, insisting that it is the lot of the majority to be oppressed in this life, kindly turn them over to another, to rectify the false weights and measures of this, as the only way to justify the dispensations of Providence. I have not,' continued Darnford, 'an opinion more firmly fixed by observation in my mind, than that, though riches may fail to produce proportionate happiness, poverty most commonly excludes it, by shutting up all the avenues to improvement.'

'And as for the affections,' added Maria, with a sigh, 'how gross, and even tormenting do they become, unless regulated by an improving mind! The

---

* The copy which appears to have received the author's last corrections, ends at this place.

culture of the heart ever, I believe, keeps pace with that of the mind. But pray go on,' addressing Jemima, 'though your narrative gives rise to the most painful reflections on the present state of society.'

'Not to trouble you,' continued she, 'with a detailed description of all the painful feelings of unavailing exertion, I have only to tell you, that at last I got recommended to wash in a few families, who did me the favour to admit me into their houses, without the most strict enquiry, to wash from one in the morning till eight at night, for eighteen or twenty-pence a day. On the happiness to be enjoyed over a washing-tub I need not comment; yet you will allow me to observe, that this was a wretchedness of situation peculiar to my sex. A man with half my industry, and, I may say, abilities, could have procured a decent livelihood, and discharged some of the duties which knit mankind together; whilst I, who had acquired a taste for the rational, nay, in honest pride let me assert it, the virtuous enjoyments of life, was cast aside as the filth of society. Condemned to labour, like a machine, only to earn bread, and scarcely that, I became melancholy and desperate.

'I have now to mention a circumstance which fills me with remorse, and fear it will entirely deprive me of your esteem. A tradesman became attached to me, and visited me frequently, – and I at last obtained such a power over him, that he offered to take me home to his house. – Consider, dear madam, I was famishing: wonder not that I became a wolf! – The only reason for not taking me home immediately, was the having a girl in the house, with child by him – and this girl – I advised him – yes, I did! would I could forget it! – to turn out of doors: and one night he determined to follow my advice. Poor wretch! she fell upon her knees, reminded him that he had promised to marry her, that her parents were honest! – What did it avail? – She was turned out.

'She approached her father's door, in the skirts of London, – listened at the shutters, – but could not knock. A watchman had observed her go and return several times – Poor wretch! – [The remorse Jemima spoke of, seemed to be stinging her to the soul, as she proceeded.]

'She left it, and, approaching a tub where horses were watered, she sat down in it, and, with desperate resolution, remained in that attitude – till resolution was no longer necessary!

'I happened that morning to be going out to wash, anticipating the moment when I should escape from such hard labour. I passed by, just as some men, going to work, drew out the stiff, cold corpse – Let me not recal the horrid moment! – I recognized her pale visage; I listened to the tale told by the spectators, and my heart did not burst. I thought of my own state, and wondered how I could be such a monster! – I worked hard; and, returning home, I was attacked by a fever. I suffered both in body and mind. I determined not to live with the wretch. But he did not try me; he left the neighbourhood. I once more returned to the wash-tub.

'Still in this state, miserable as it was, admitted of aggravation. Lifting one day a heavy load, a tub fell against my shin, and gave me great pain. I did not pay much attention to the hurt, till it became a serious wound; being obliged to work as usual, or starve. But, finding myself at length unable to stand for any time, I thought of getting into an hospital. Hospitals, it should seem (for they are comfortless abodes for the sick) were expressly endowed for the reception of the friendless; yet I, who had on that plea a right to assistance, wanted the recommendation of the rich and respectable, and was several weeks languishing for admittance; fees were demanded on entering; and, what was still more unreasonable, security for burying me, that expence not coming into the letter of the charity. A guinea was the stipulated sum – I could as soon have raised a million; and I was afraid to apply to the parish for an order, lest they should have passed me, I knew not whither.[18] The poor woman at whose house I lodged, compassionating my state, got me into the hospital; and the family where I received the hurt, sent me five shillings, three and six-pence of which I gave at my admittance – I know not for what.

'My leg grew quickly better; but I was dismissed before my cure was completed, because I could not afford to have my linen washed to appear decently, as the virago of a nurse said, when the gentlemen (the surgeons) came. I cannot give you an adequate idea of the wretchedness of an hospital; every thing is left to the care of people intent on gain. The attendants seem to have lost all feeling of compassion in the bustling discharge of their offices; death is so familiar to them, that they are not anxious to ward it off. Every thing appeared to be conducted for the accommodation of the medical men and their pupils, who came to make experiments on the poor, for the benefit of the rich. One of the physicians, I must not forget to mention, gave me half-a-crown, and ordered me some wine, when I was at the lowest ebb. I thought of making my case known to the lady-like matron; but her forbidding countenance prevented me. She condescended to look on the patients, and make general enquiries, two or three times a week; but the nurses knew the hour when the visit of ceremony would commence, and every thing was as it should be.

'After my dismission, I was more at a loss than ever for a subsistence, and, not to weary you with a repetition of the same unavailing attempts, unable to stand at the washing-tub, I began to consider the rich and poor as natural enemies, and became a thief from principle. I could not now cease to reason, but I hated mankind. I despised myself, yet I justified my conduct. I was taken, tried, and condemned to six months' imprisonment in a house of correction. My soul recoils with horror from the remembrance of the insults I had to endure, till, branded with shame, I was turned loose in the street, pennyless. I wandered from street to street, till, exhausted by hunger and fatigue, I sunk down senseless at a door, where I had vainly demanded a morsel of bread. I was sent by the inhabitant to the work-house, to which he had surlily bid me go, saying, he "paid enough in conscience to the poor," when, with parched tongue, I implored his charity. If those well-meaning people who exclaim against beggars, were acquainted with the treatment the poor receive in many of these wretched asylums, they would not stifle so easily involuntary sympathy, by saying that they have all parishes to go to, or wonder that the poor dread to enter the gloomy walls. What are the common run of work-houses, but prisons, in which many respectable old people, worn out by immoderate labour, sink into the grave in sorrow, to which they are carried like dogs!'

Alarmed by some indistinct noise, Jemima rose hastily to listen, and Maria, turning to Darnford, said, 'I have indeed been shocked beyond expression when I have met a pauper's funeral. A coffin carried on the shoulders of three or four ill-looking wretches, whom the imagination might easily convert into a band of assassins, hastening to conceal the corpse, and quarrelling about the prey on their way. I know it is of little consequence how we are consigned to the earth; but I am led by this brutal insensibility, to what even the animal creation appears forcibly to feel, to advert to the wretched, deserted manner in which they died.'

'True,' rejoined Darnford, 'and, till the rich will give more than a part of their wealth, till they will give time and attention to the wants of the distressed, never let them boast of charity. Let them open their hearts, and not their purses, and employ their minds in the service, if they are really actuated by humanity; or charitable institutions will always be the prey of the lowest order of knaves.'[19]

Jemima returning, seemed in haste to finish her tale. 'The overseer farmed the poor of different parishes, and out of the bowels of poverty was wrung the money with which he purchased this dwelling, as a private receptacle for madness. He had been a keeper at a house of the same description, and conceived that he could make money much more readily in his old occupation. He is a shrewd – shall I say it? – villain. He observed something resolute in my manner, and offered to take me with him, and instruct me how to treat the disturbed minds he meant to intrust to my care. The offer of forty pounds a year, and to quit a workhouse, was not to be despised, though the condition of shutting my eyes and hardening my heart was annexed to it.

'I agreed to accompany him; and four years have I been attendant on many wretches, and' – she lowered her voice, – 'the witness of many enormities. In solitude my mind seemed to recover its force, and many of the sentiments which I imbibed in the only tolerable period of my life, returned with their full force. Still what should induce me to be the champion for suffering humanity? – Who ever risked any thing for me? – Who ever acknowledged me to be a fellow-creature?' –

Maria took her hand, and Jemima, more overcome by kindness than she had ever been by cruelty, hastened out of the room to conceal her emotions.

Darnford soon after heard his summons, and, taking leave of him, Maria promised to gratify his curiosity, with respect to herself, the first opportunity.

CHAPTER VI

Active as love was in the heart of Maria, the story she had just heard made her thoughts take a wider range. The opening buds of hope closed, as if they had put forth too early, and the happiest day of her life was overcast by the most melancholy reflections. Thinking of Jemima's peculiar fate and her own, she was led to consider the oppressed state of woman, and to lament that she had given birth to a daughter. Sleep fled from her eyelids, while she dwelt on the wretchedness of unprotected infancy, till sympathy with Jemima changed to agony, when it seemed probable that her own babe might even now be in the very state she so forcibly described.

Maria thought, and thought again. Jemima's humanity had rather been benumbed than killed, by the keen frost she had to brave at her entrance into life; an appeal then to her feelings, on this tender point, surely would not be fruitless; and Maria began to anticipate the delight it would afford her to gain intelligence of her child. This project was now the only subject of reflection; and she watched impatiently for the dawn of day, with that determinate purpose which generally insures success.

At the usual hour, Jemima brought her breakfast, and a tender note from Darnford. She ran her eye hastily over it, and her heart calmly hoarded up the rapture a fresh assurance of affection, such as she wished to inspire, gave her, without diverting her mind a moment from its design. While Jemima waited to take away the breakfast, Maria alluded to the reflections, that had haunted her during the night to the exclusion of sleep. She spoke with energy of Jemima's unmerited sufferings, and of the fate of a number of deserted females, placed within the sweep of a whirlwind, from which it was next to impossible to escape. Perceiving the effect her conversation produced on the countenance of her guard, she grasped the arm of Jemima with that irresistible warmth which defies repulse, exclaiming – 'With your heart, and such dreadful experience, can you lend your aid to deprive my babe of a mother's tenderness, a mother's care? In the name of God, assist me to snatch her from destruction! Let me but give her an education – let me but prepare her body and mind to encounter the ills which await her sex, and I will teach her to consider you as her second mother, and herself as the prop of your age. Yes, Jemima, look at me – observe me closely, and read my very soul; you merit a better fate;' she held out her hand with a firm gesture of assurance; 'and I will procure it for you, as a testimony of my esteem, as well as of my gratitude.'

Jemima had not power to resist this persuasive torrent; and, owning that the house in which she was confined, was situated on the banks of the Thames, only a few miles from London, and not on the sea-coast, as Darnford had supposed, she promised to invent some excuse for her absence, and go herself to trace the situation, and enquire concerning the health, of this abandoned daughter. Her manner implied an intention to do something more, but she seemed unwilling to impart her design; and Maria, glad to have obtained the main point, thought it best to leave her to the workings of her own mind; convinced that she had the power of interesting her still more in favour of herself and child, by a simple recital of facts.

In the evening, Jemima informed the impatient mother, that on the morrow she should hasten to town before the family hour of rising, and received all the information necessary, as a clue to her search. The 'Good night!' Maria uttered was peculiarly solemn and affectionate. Glad expectation sparkled in her eye; and, for the first time since her detention, she pronounced the name of her child with pleasureable fondness; and, with all the garrulity of a nurse, described her first smile when she recognized her mother. Recollecting herself, a still kinder 'Adieu!' with a 'God bless you!' – that seemed to include a maternal benediction, dismissed Jemima.

The dreary solitude of the ensuing day, lengthened by impatiently dwelling on the same idea, was intolerably wearisome. She listened for the sound of a particular clock, which some directions of the wind allowed her to hear distinctly. She marked the shadow gaining on the wall; and, twilight thickening into darkness, her breath seemed oppressed while she anxiously counted nine. – The last sound was a stroke of despair on her heart; for she expected every moment, without seeing Jemima, to have her light extinguished by the savage female who supplied her place. She was even obliged to prepare for bed, restless as she was, not to disoblige her new attendant. She had been cautioned not to speak too freely to her; but the caution was needless, her countenance would still more emphatically have made her shrink back. Such was the ferocity of manner, conspicuous in every word and gesture of this hag, that Maria was afraid to enquire, why Jemima, who had faithfully promised to see her before her door was shut for the night, came not? – and, when the key turned in the lock, to consign her to a night of suspence, she felt a degree of anguish which the circumstances scarcely justified.

Continually on the watch, the shutting of a door, or the sound of a footstep, made her start and tremble with apprehension, something like what she felt, when, at her entrance, dragged along the gallery, she began to doubt whether she were not surrounded by demons?

Fatigued by an endless rotation of thought and wild alarms, she looked like a spectre, when Jemima entered in the morning; especially as her eyes darted out of her head, to read in Jemima's countenance, almost as pallid, the intelligence she dared not trust her tongue to demand. Jemima put down the tea-things, and appeared very busy in arranging the table. Maria took up a cup with trembling hand, then forcibly recovering her fortitude, and restraining the convulsive movement which agitated the muscles of her mouth, she said, 'Spare yourself the pain of preparing me for your information, I adjure you! – My child is dead!' Jemima solemnly answered, 'Yes;' with a look expressive of compassion and angry emotions. 'Leave me,' added Maria, making a fresh effort to govern her feelings, and hiding her face in her handkerchief, to conceal her anguish – 'It is enough – I know that my babe is no more – I will hear the particulars when I am' – *calmer*, she could not utter; and Jemima, without importuning her by idle attempts to console her, left the room.

Plunged in the deepest melancholy, she would not admit Darnford's visits; and such is the force of early associations even on strong minds, that, for a while, she indulged the superstitious notion that she was justly punished by the death of her child, for having for an instant ceased to regret her loss. Two or three letters from Darnford, full of soothing, manly tenderness, only added poignancy to these accusing emotions; yet the passionate style in which he expressed, what he termed the first and fondest wish of his heart, 'that his affection might make her some amends for the cruelty and injustice she had endured,' inspired a sentiment of gratitude to heaven; and her eyes filled with delicious tears, when, at the conclusion of his letter, wishing to supply the place of her unworthy relations, whose want of principle he execrated, he assured her, calling her his dearest girl, 'that it should henceforth be the business of his life to make her happy.'

He begged, in a note sent the following morning, to be permitted to see her, when his presence would be no intrusion on her grief; and so earnestly intreated to be allowed, according to promise, to beguile the tedious moments of absence, by dwelling on the events of her past life, that she sent him the memoirs which had been written for her daughter, promising Jemima the perusal as soon as he returned them.

CHAPTER VII

'Addressing these memoirs to you, my child, uncertain whether I shall ever have an opportunity of instructing you, many observations will probably flow from my heart, which only a mother – a mother schooled in misery, could make.

'The tenderness of a father who knew the world, might be great; but could it equal that of a mother – of a mother, labouring under a portion of the misery, which the constitution of society seems to have entailed on all her kind? It is, my child, my dearest daughter, only such a mother, who will dare to break through all restraint to provide for your happiness – who will voluntarily brave censure herself, to ward off sorrow from your bosom. From my narrative, my dear girl, you may gather the instruction, the counsel, which is meant rather to exercise than influence your mind. – Death may snatch me from you, before you can weigh my advice, or enter into my reasoning: I would then, with fond anxiety, lead you very early in life to form your grand principle of action, to save you from the vain regret of having, through irresolution, let the spring-tide of existence pass away, unimproved, unenjoyed. – Gain experience – ah! gain it – while experience is worth having, and acquire sufficient fortitude to pursue your own happiness; it includes your utility, by a direct path. What is wisdom too often, but the owl of the goddess,[20] who sits moping in a desolated heart; around me she shrieks, but I would invite all the gay warblers of spring to nestle in your blooming bosom. – Had I not wasted years in deliberating, after I ceased to doubt, how I ought to have acted – I might now be useful and happy. – For my sake, warned by my example, always appear what you are, and you will not pass through existence without enjoying its genuine blessings, love and respect.

'Born in one of the most romantic parts of England; an enthusiastic fondness for the varying charms of nature is the first sentiment I recollect; or rather it was the first consciousness of pleasure that employed and formed my imagination.

'My father had been a captain of a man of war; but, disgusted with the service, on account of the preferment of men whose chief merit was their family connections or borough interest,[21] he retired into the country; and, not knowing what to do with himself – married. In his family, to regain his lost consequence, he determined to keep up the same passive obedience, as in the vessels in which he had commanded. His orders were not to be disputed; and the whole house was expected to fly, at the word of command, as if to man the shrouds, or mount aloft in an elemental strife, big with life or death. He was to be instantaneously obeyed, especially by my mother, whom he very benevolently married for love; but took care to remind her of the obligation, when she dared, in the slightest instance, to question his absolute authority. My eldest brother, it is true, as he grew up, was treated with more respect by my father; and became in due form the deputy-tyrant of the house. The representative of my father, a being privileged by nature – a boy, and the darling of my mother, he did not fail to act like an heir apparent. Such indeed was my mother's extravagant partiality, that, in comparison with her affection for him, she might be said not to love the rest of her children. Yet none of the children seemed to have so little affection for her. Extreme indulgence had rendered him so selfish, that he only thought of himself; and from tormenting insects and animals, he became the despot of his brothers, and still more of his sisters.

'It is perhaps difficult to give you an idea of the petty cares which obscured the morning of my life; continual restraint in the most trivial matters; unconditional submission to orders, which, as a mere child, I soon discovered to be unreasonable, because inconsistent and contradictory. Thus are we destined to experience a mixture of bitterness, with the recollection of our most innocent enjoyments.

'The circumstances which, during my childhood, occurred to fashion my mind, were various; yet, as it would probably afford me more pleasure to revive the fading remembrance of new-born delight, than you, my child, could feel in the perusal, I will not entice you to stray with me into the verdant meadow, to search for the flowers that youthful hopes scatter in every path; though, as I write, I almost scent the fresh green of spring – of that spring which never returns!

'I had two sisters, and one brother, younger than myself; my brother Robert was two years older, and might truly be termed the idol of his parents, and the torment of the rest of the family. Such indeed is the force of prejudice, that what was called spirit and wit in him, was cruelly repressed as forwardness in me.

'My mother had an indolence of character, which prevented her from paying much attention to our education. But the healthy breeze of a neighbouring heath, on which we bounded at pleasure, volatilized the humours that improper food might have generated. And to enjoy open air and freedom, was paradise, after the unnatural restraints of our fire-side, where we were often obliged to sit three or four hours together, without daring to utter a word, when my father was out of humour, from want of employment, or of a variety of boisterous amusement. I had however one advantage, an instructor, the brother of my father, who, intended for the church, had of course received a liberal education. But, becoming attached to a young lady of great beauty and large fortune, and acquiring in the world some opinions not consonant with the profession for which he was designed, he accepted, with the most sanguine expectations of success, the offer of a nobleman to accompany him to India, as his confidential secretary.

'A correspondence was regularly kept up with the object of his affection; and the intricacies of business, peculiarly wearisome to a man of a romantic turn of mind, contributed, with a forced absence, to increase his attachment. Every other passion was lost in this master-one, and only served to swell the torrent. Her relations, such were his waking dreams, who had despised him, would court in their turn his alliance, and all the blandishments of taste would grace the triumph of love. – While he basked in the warm sunshine of love, friendship also promised to shed its dewy freshness; for a friend, whom he loved next to his mistress, was the confident, who forwarded the letters from one to the other, to elude the observation of prying relations. A friend false in similar circumstances, is, my dearest girl, an old tale; yet, let not this example, or the frigid caution of cold-blooded moralists, make you endeavour to stifle hopes, which are the buds that naturally unfold themselves during the spring of life! Whilst your own heart is sincere, always expect to meet one glowing with the same sentiments; for to fly from pleasure, is not to avoid pain!

'My uncle realized, by good luck, rather than management, a handsome fortune; and returning on the wings of love, lost in the most enchanting reveries, to England, to share it with his mistress and his friend, he found them – united.

'There were some circumstances, not necessary for me to recite, which aggravated the guilt of the friend beyond measure, and the deception, that had been carried on to the last moment, was so base, it produced the most violent effect on my uncle's health and spirits. His native country, the world! lately a garden of blooming sweets, blasted by treachery, seemed changed into a parched desert, the abode of hissing serpents. Disappointment rankled in his heart; and, brooding over his wrongs, he was attacked by a raging fever, followed by a derangement of mind, which only gave place to habitual melancholy, as he recovered more strength of body.

'Declaring an intention never to marry, his relations were ever clustering about him, paying the grossest adulation to a man, who, disgusted with mankind, received them with scorn, or bitter sarcasms. Something in my countenance pleased him, when I began to prattle. Since his return, he appeared dead to affection; but I soon, by showing him innocent fondness, became a favourite; and endeavouring to enlarge and strengthen my mind, I grew dear to him in proportion as I imbibed his sentiments. He had a forcible manner of speaking, rendered more so by a certain impressive wildness of look and gesture, calculated to engage the attention of a young and ardent mind. It is not then surprising that I quickly adopted his opinions in preference, and reverenced him as one of a superior order of beings. He inculcated, with great warmth, self-respect, and a lofty consciousness of acting right, independent of the censure or applause of the world; nay, he almost taught me to brave, and even despise its censure, when convinced of the rectitude of my own intentions.

'Endeavouring to prove to me that nothing which deserved the name of love or friendship, existed in the world, he drew such animated pictures of his own feelings, rendered permanent by disappointment, as imprinted the sentiments strongly on my heart, and animated my imagination. These remarks are necessary to elucidate some peculiarities in my character, which by the world are indefinitely termed romantic.

'My uncle's increasing affection led him to visit me often. Still, unable to rest in any place, he did not remain long in the country to soften domestic tyranny; but he brought me books, for which I had a passion, and they conspired with his conversation, to make me form an ideal picture of life. I shall pass over the tyranny of my father, much as I suffered from it; but it is necessary to notice, that it undermined my mother's health; and that her temper, continually irritated by domestic bickering, became intolerably peevish.

'My eldest brother was articled to a neighbouring attorney, the shrewdest, and, I may add, the most unprincipled man in that part of the country. As my brother generally came home every Saturday, to astonish my mother by exhibiting his attainments, he gradually assumed a right of directing the whole family, not excepting my father. He seemed to take a peculiar pleasure in tormenting and humbling me; and if I ever ventured to complain of this treatment to either my father or mother, I was rudely rebuffed for presuming to judge of the conduct of my eldest brother.

'About this period a merchant's family came to settle in our neighbourhood. A mansion-house in the village, lately purchased, had been preparing the whole spring, and the sight of the costly furniture, sent from London, had excited my mother's envy, and roused my father's pride. My sensations were very different, and all of a pleasurable kind. I longed to see new characters, to break the tedious monotony of my life; and to find a friend, such as fancy had pourtrayed. I cannot then describe the emotion I felt, the Sunday they made their appearance at church. My eyes were rivetted on the pillar round which I expected first to catch a glimpse of them, and darted forth to meet a servant who hastily preceded a group of ladies, whose white robes and waving plumes, seemed to stream along the gloomy aisle, diffusing the light, by which I contemplated their figures.

'We visited them in form; and I quickly selected the eldest daughter for my friend. The second son, George, paid me particular attention, and finding his attainments and manners superior to those of the young men of the village, I began to imagine him superior to the rest of mankind. Had my home been more comfortable, or my previous acquaintance more numerous, I should not probably have been so eager to open my heart to new affections.

"Mr Venables, the merchant, had acquired a large fortune by unremitting attention to business; but his health declining rapidly, he was obliged to retire, before his son, George, had acquired sufficient experience, to enable him to conduct their affairs on the same prudential plan, his father had invariably pursued. Indeed, he had laboured to throw off his authority, having despised his narrow plans and cautious speculation. The eldest son could not be prevailed on to enter the firm; and, to oblige his wife, and have peace in the house, Mr Venables had purchased a commission for him in the guards.

'I am now alluding to circumstances which came to my knowledge long after; but it is necessary, my dearest child, that you should know the character of your father, to prevent your despising your mother; the only parent inclined to discharge a parent's duty. In London, George had acquired habits of libertinism, which he carefully concealed from his father and his commercial connections. The mask he wore, was so complete a covering of his real visage, that the praise his father lavished on his conduct, and, poor mistaken man! on his principles, contrasted with his brother's, rendered the notice he took of me peculiarly flattering. Without any fixed design, as I am now convinced, he continued to single me out at the dance, press my hand at parting, and utter expressions of unmeaning passion, to which I gave a meaning naturally suggested by the romantic turn of my thoughts. His stay in the country was short; his manners did not entirely please me; but, when he left us, the colouring of my picture became more vivid – Whither did not my imagination lead me? In short, I fancied myself in love – in love with the disinterestedness, fortitude, generosity, dignity, and humanity, with which I had invested the hero I dubbed. A circumstance which soon after occurred, rendered all these virtues palpable. [The incident is perhaps worth relating on other accounts, and therefore I shall describe it distinctly.]

'I had a great affection for my nurse, old Mary, for whom I used often to work, to spare her eyes. Mary had a younger sister, married to a sailor, while she was suckling me; for my mother only suckled my eldest brother, which might be the cause of her extraordinary partiality. Peggy, Mary's sister, lived with her, till her husband, becoming a mate in a West-India trader, got a little before-hand in the world. He wrote to his wife from the first port in the Channel, after his most successful voyage, to request her to come to London to meet him; he even wished her to determine on living there for the future, to save him the trouble of coming to her the moment he came on shore; and to turn a penny by keeping a green-stall. It was too much to set out on a journey the moment he had finished a voyage, and fifty miles by land, was worse than a thousand leagues by sea.

'She packed up her alls, and came to London – but did not meet honest Daniel. A common misfortune prevented her, and the poor are bound to suffer for the good of their country – he was pressed in the river – and never came on shore.[22]

'Peggy was miserable in London, not knowing, as she said, "the face of any living soul." Besides, her imagination had been employed, anticipating a month or six weeks' happiness with her husband. Daniel was to have gone with her to Sadler's Wells, and Westminster Abbey, and to many sights, which he knew she never heard of in the country. Peggy too was thrifty, and how could she manage to put his plan in execution alone? He had acquaintance; but she did not know the very name of their places of abode. His letters were made up of – How do you does, and God bless yous, – information was reserved for the hour of meeting.

'She too had her portion of information, near at heart. Molly and Jacky were grown such little darlings, she was almost angry that daddy did not see their tricks. She had not half the pleasure she should have had from their prattle, could she have recounted to him each night the pretty speeches of the day. Some stories, however, were stored up – and Jacky could say papa with such a sweet voice, it must delight his heart. Yet when she came, and found no Daniel to greet her, when Jacky called papa, she wept, bidding "God bless his innocent soul, that did not know what sorrow was." – But more sorrow was in store for Peggy, innocent as she was. – Daniel was killed in the first engagement, and then the *papa* was agony, sounding to the heart.

'She had lived sparingly on his wages, while there was any hope of his return; but, that gone, she returned with a breaking heart to the country, to a little market town, nearly three miles from our village. She did not like to go to service, to be snubbed about, after being her own mistress. To put her children out to nurse was impossible: how far would her wages go? and to send them to her husband's parish, a distant one, was to lose her husband twice over.

'I had heard all from Mary, and made my uncle furnish a little cottage for her, to enable her to sell – so sacred was poor Daniel's advice, now he was dead and gone – a little fruit, toys, and cakes. The minding of the shop did not require her whole time, nor even the keeping her children clean; so she took in washing, and altogether made a shift to earn bread for her children, still weeping for Daniel, when Jacky's arch looks made her think of his father. – It was pleasant to work for her children. – "Yes; from morning till night, could she have had a kiss from their father, God rest his soul! Yes; had it pleased Providence to have let him come back without a leg or an arm, it would have been the same thing to her – for she did not love him because he maintained them – no; she had hands of her own."

'The country people were honest, and Peggy left her linen out to dry very late. A recruiting party, as she supposed, passing through, made free with a large wash; for it was all swept away, including her own and her children's little stock.

'This was a dreadful blow; two dozen of shirts, stocks and handkerchiefs. She gave the money which she had laid by for half a year's rent, and promised to pay two shillings a week till all was cleared; so she did not lose her employment. This two shillings a week, and the buying a few necessaries for the children, drove her so hard, that she had not a penny to pay her rent with, when a twelvemonth's became due.

'She was now with Mary, and had just told her tale, which Mary instantly repeated – it was intended for my ear. Many houses in this town, producing a borough-interest,[23] were included in the estate purchased by Mr Venables, and the attorney with whom my brother lived, was appointed his agent, to collect and raise the rents.

'He demanded Peggy's, and, in spite of her intreaties, her poor goods had been seized and sold. So that she had not, and what was worse her children, "for she had known sorrow enough," a bed to lie on. She knew that I was good-natured – right charitable, yet not liking to ask for more than needs must, she scorned to petition while people could any how be made to wait. But now, should she be turned out of doors, she must expect nothing less than to lose all her customers, and then she must beg or starve – and what would become of her children? – "had Daniel not been pressed – but God knows best – all this could not have happened."

"I had two mattrasses on my bed; what did I want with two, when such a worthy creature must lie on the ground? My mother would be angry, but I could conceal it till my uncle came down; and then I would tell him all the whole truth, and if he absolved me, heaven would.

'I begged the house-maid to come up stairs with me (servants always feel for the distresses of poverty, and so would the rich if they knew what it was). She assisted me to tie up the mattrass; I discovering, at the same time, that one blanket would serve me till winter, could I persuade my sister who slept with me, to keep my secret. She entering in the midst of the package, I gave her some new feathers, to silence her. We got the mattrass down the back stairs, unperceived, and I helped to carry it, taking with me all the money I had, and what I could borrow from my sister.

'When I got to the cottage, Peggy declared that she would not take what I had brought secretly; but, when, with all the eager eloquence inspired by a decided purpose, I grasped her hand with weeping eyes, assuring her that my uncle would screen me from blame, when he was once more in the country, describing, at the same time, what she would suffer in parting with her children, after keeping them so long from being thrown on the parish, she reluctantly consented.

'My project of usefulness ended not here; I determined to speak to the attorney; he frequently paid me compliments. His character did not intimidate me; but, imagining that Peggy must be mistaken, and that no man could turn a deaf ear to such a tale of complicated distress, I determined to walk to the town with Mary the next morning, and request him to wait for the rent, and keep my secret, till my uncle's return.

'My repose was sweet; and, waking with the first dawn of day, I bounded to Mary's cottage. What charms do not a light heart spread over nature! Every bird that twittered in a bush, every flower that enlivened the hedge, seemed placed there to awaken me to rapture – yes; to rapture. The present moment was full fraught with happiness; and on futurity I bestowed not a thought, excepting to anticipate my success with the attorney.

'This man of the world, with rosy face and simpering features, received me politely, nay kindly; listened with complacency to my remonstrances, though he scarcely heeded Mary's tears. I did not then suspect, that my eloquence was in my complexion, the blush of seventeen, or that, in a world where humanity to women is the characteristic of advancing civilization, the beauty of a young girl was so much more interesting than the distress of an old one. Pressing my hand, he promised to let Peggy remain in the house as long as I wished. – I more than returned the pressure – I was so grateful and so happy. Emboldened by my innocent warmth, he then kissed me – and I did not draw back – I took it for a kiss of charity.

'Gay as a lark, I went to dine at Mr Venables'. I had previously obtained five shillings from my father, towards re-clothing the poor children of my care, and prevailed on my mother to take one of the girls into the house, whom I determined to teach to work and read.

'After dinner, when the younger part of the circle retired to the music-room, I recounted with energy my tale; that is, I mentioned Peggy's distress, without hinting at the steps I had taken to relieve her. Miss Venables gave me half-a-crown; the heir five shillings; but George sat unmoved. I was cruelly distressed by the disappointment – I scarcely could remain on my chair; and, could I have got out of the room unperceived, I should have flown home, as if to run away from myself. After several vain attempts to rise, I leaned my head against the marble chimney-piece, and gazing on the evergreens that filled the fire-place, moralized on the vanity of human expectations; regardless of the company. I was roused by a gentle tap on my shoulder from behind Charlotte's chair. I turned my head, and George slid a guinea into my hand, putting his finger to his mouth, to enjoin me silence.

'What a revolution took place, not only in my train of thoughts, but feelings! I trembled with emotion – now, indeed, I was in love. Such delicacy too, to enhance his benevolence! I felt in my pocket every five minutes, only to feel the guinea; and its magic touch invested my hero with more than mortal beauty. My fancy had found a basis to erect its model of perfection on; and quickly went to work, with all the happy credulity of youth, to consider that heart as devoted to virtue, which had only obeyed a virtuous impulse. The bitter experience was yet to come, that has taught me how very distinct are the principles of virtue, from the casual feelings from which they germinate.

CHAPTER VIII

'I have perhaps dwelt too long on a circumstance, which is only of importance as it marks the progress of a deception that has been so fatal to my peace; and introduces to your notice a poor girl, whom, intending to serve, I led to ruin. Still it is probable that I was not entirely the victim of mistake; and that your father, gradually fashioned by the world, did not quickly become what I hesitate to call him – out of respect to my daughter.

'But, to hasten to the more busy scenes of my life. Mr Venables and my mother died the same summer; and, wholly engrossed by my attention to her, I thought of little else. The neglect of her darling, my brother Robert, had a violent effect on her weakened mind; for, though boys may be reckoned the pillars of the house without doors, girls are often the only comfort within. They but too frequently waste their health and spirits attending a dying parent, who leaves them in comparative poverty. After closing, with filial piety, a father's eyes, they are chased from the paternal roof; to make room for the first-born, the son, who is to carry the empty family-name down to posterity; though, occupied with his own pleasures, he scarcely thought of discharging, in the decline of his parent's life, the debt contracted in his childhood. My mother's conduct led me to make these reflections. Great as was the fatigue I endured, and the affection my unceasing solicitude evinced, of which my mother seemed perfectly sensible, still, when my brother, whom I could hardly persuade to remain a quarter of an hour in her chamber, was with her alone, a short time before her death, she gave him a little hoard, which she had been some years accumulating.

'During my mother's illness, I was obliged to manage my father's temper, who, from the lingering nature of her malady, began to imagine that it was merely fancy. At this period, an artful kind of upper servant attracted my father's attention, and the neighbours made many remarks on the finery, not honestly got, exhibited at evening service. But I was too much occupied with my mother to observe any change in her dress or behaviour, or to listen to the whisper of scandal.

'I shall not dwell on the death-bed scene, lively as is the remembrance, or on the emotion produced by the last grasp of my mother's cold hand; when blessing me, she added, "A little patience, and all will be over!" Ah! my child, how often have those words rung mournfully in my ears – and I have exclaimed – "A little more patience, and I too shall be at rest!"

'My father was violently affected by her death, recollected instances of his unkindness, and wept like a child.

'My mother had solemnly recommended my sisters to my care, and bid me be a mother to them. They, indeed, became more dear to me as they became more forlorn; for, during my mother's illness, I discovered the ruined state of my father's circumstances, and that he had only been able to keep up appearances, by the sums which he borrowed of my uncle.

'My father's grief, and consequent tenderness to his children, quickly abated, the house grew still more gloomy or riotous; and my refuge from care was again at Mr Venables'; the young 'squire having taken his father's place, and allowing, for the present, his sister to preside at his table. George, though dissatisfied with his portion of the fortune, which had till lately been all in trade, visited the family as usual. He was now full of speculations in trade, and his brow became clouded by care. He seemed to relax in his attention to me, when the presence of my uncle gave a new turn to his behaviour. I was too unsuspecting, too disinterested, to trace these changes to their source.

'My home every day became more and more disagreeable to me; my liberty was unnecessarily abridged, and my books, on the pretext that they made me idle, taken from me. My father's mistress was with child, and he, doating on her, allowed or overlooked her vulgar manner of tyrannizing over us. I was indignant, especially when I saw her endeavouring to attract, shall I say seduce? my younger brother. By allowing women but one way of rising in the world, the fostering the libertinism of men, society makes monsters of them, and then their ignoble vices are brought forward as a proof of inferiority of intellect.

'The wearisomeness of my situation can scarcely be described. Though my life had not passed in the most even tenour with my mother, it was paradise to that I was destined to endure with my father's mistress, jealous of her illegitimate authority. My father's former occasional tenderness, in spite of his violence of temper, had been soothing to me; but now he only met me with reproofs or portentous frowns. The house-keeper, as she was now termed, was the vulgar despot of the family; and assuming the new character of a fine lady, she could never forgive the contempt which was sometimes visible in my countenance, when she uttered with pomposity her bad English, or affected to be well bred.

'To my uncle I ventured to open my heart; and he, with his wonted benevolence, began to consider in what manner he could extricate me out of my present irksome situation. In spite of his own disappointment, or, most probably, actuated by the feelings that had been petrified, not cooled, in all their sanguine fervour, like a boiling torrent of lava suddenly dashing into the sea, he thought a marriage of mutual inclination (would envious stars permit it) the only chance for happiness in this disastrous world. George Venables had the reputation of being attentive to business, and my father's example gave great weight to this circumstance; for habits of order in business would, he conceived, extend to the regulation of the affections in domestic life. George seldom spoke in my uncle's company, except to utter a short, judicious question, or to make a pertinent remark, with all due deference to his superior judgment; so that my uncle seldom left his company without observing, that the young man had more in him than people supposed.

'In this opinion he was not singular; yet, believe me, and I am not swayed by resentment, these speeches so justly poized, this silent deference, when the animal spirits of other young people were throwing off youthful ebullitions, were not the effect of thought or humility, but sheer barrenness of mind, and want of imagination. A colt of mettle will curvet and shew his paces. Yes; my dear girl, these prudent young men want all the fire necessary to ferment their faculties, and are characterized as wise, only because they are not foolish. It is true, that George was by no means so great a favourite of mine as during the first year of our acquaintance; still, as he often coincided in opinion with me, and echoed my sentiments; and having myself no other attachment, I heard with pleasure my uncle's proposal; but thought more of obtaining my freedom, than of my lover. But, when George, seemingly anxious for my happiness, pressed me to quit my present painful situation, my heart swelled with gratitude – I knew not that my uncle had promised him five thousand pounds.

'Had this truly generous man mentioned his intention to me, I should have insisted on a thousand pounds being settled on each of my sisters; George would have contested; I should have seen his selfish soul; and – gracious God! have been spared the misery of discovering, when too late, that I was united to a heartless, unprincipled wretch. All my schemes of usefulness would not then have been blasted. The tenderness of my heart would not have heated my imagination with visions of the ineffable delight of happy love; nor would the sweet duty of a mother have been so cruelly interrupted.

'But I must not suffer the fortitude I have so hardly acquired, to be under-mined by unavailing regret. Let me hasten forward to describe the turbid stream in which I had to wade – but let me exultingly declare that it is passed – my soul holds fellowship with him no more. He cut the Gordian knot, which my principles, mistaken ones, respected; he dissolved the tie, the fetters rather, that ate into my very vitals – and I should rejoice, conscious that my mind is freed, though confined in hell itself; the only place that even fancy can imagine more dreadful than my present abode.

'These varying emotions will not allow me to proceed. I heave sigh after sigh; yet my heart is still oppressed. For what am I reserved? Why was I not born a man, or why was I born at all?'

VOLUME 2

CHAPTER IX

'I resume my pen to fly from thought. I was married; and we hastened to London. I had purposed taking one of my sisters with me; for a strong motive for marrying, was the desire of having a home at which I could receive them, now their own grew so uncomfortable, as not to deserve the cheering appellation. An objection was made to her accompanying me, that appeared plausible; and I reluctantly acquiesced. I was however willingly allowed to take with me Molly, poor Peggy's daughter. London and preferment, are ideas commonly associated in the country; and, as blooming as May, she bade adieu to Peggy with weeping eyes. I did not even feel hurt at the refusal in relation to my sister, till hearing what my uncle had done for me, I had the simplicity to request, speaking with warmth of their situation, that he would give them a thousand pounds a-piece, which seemed to me but justice. He asked me, giving me a kiss, "If I had lost my senses?" I started back, as if I had found a wasp in a rose-bush. I expostulated. He sneered, and the demon of discord entered our paradise, to poison with his pestiferous breath every opening joy.

'I had sometimes observed defects in my husband's understanding; but, led astray by a prevailing opinion, that goodness of disposition is of the first importance in the relative situations of life, in proportion as I perceived the narrowness of his understanding, fancy enlarged the boundary of his heart. Fatal error! How quickly is the so much vaunted milkiness of nature turned into gall, by an intercourse with the world, if more generous juices do not sustain the vital source of virtue!

'One trait in my character was extreme credulity; but, when my eyes were once opened, I saw but too clearly all I had before overlooked. My husband was sunk in my esteem; still there are youthful emotions, which, for a while, fill up the chasm of love and friendship. Besides, it required some time to enable me to see his whole character in a just light, or rather to allow it to become fixed. While circumstances were ripening my faculties, and cultivating my taste, commerce and gross relaxations were shutting his against any possibility of improvement, till, by stifling every spark of virtue in himself, he began to imagine that it no where existed.

'Do not let me lead you astray, my child, I do not mean to assert, that any human being is entirely incapable of feeling the generous emotions, which are the foundation of every true principle of virtue; but they are frequently, I fear, so feeble, that, like the inflammable quality which more or less lurks in all bodies, they often lie for ever dormant; the circumstances never occurring, necessary to call them into action.

'I discovered however by chance, that, in consequence of some losses in trade, the natural effect of his gambling desire to start suddenly into riches, the five thousand pounds given me by my uncle, had been paid very opportunely. This discovery, strange as you may think the assertion, gave me pleasure; my husband's embarrassments endeared him to me. I was glad to find an excuse for his conduct to my sisters, and my mind became calmer.

'My uncle introduced me to some literary society; and the theatres were a never-failing source of amusement to me. My delighted eye followed Mrs Siddons,[24] when, with dignified delicacy, she played Calista;[25] and I involuntarily repeated after her, in the same tone, and with a long-drawn sigh,

"Hearts like our's were pair'd – – – not match'd." [26]

'These were, at first, spontaneous emotions, though, becoming acquainted with men of wit and polished manners, I could not sometimes help regretting my early marriage; and that, in my haste to escape from a temporary dependence, and expand my newly fledged wings, in an unknown sky, I had been caught in a trap, and caged for life. Still the novelty of London, and the attentive fondness of my husband, for he had some personal regard for me, made several months glide away. Yet, not forgetting the situation of my sisters, who were still very young, I prevailed on my uncle to settle a thousand pounds on each; and to place them in a school near town, where I could frequently visit, as well as have them at home with me.

'I now tried to improve my husband's taste, but we have few subjects in common; indeed he soon appeared to have little relish for my society, unless he was hinting to me the use he could make of my uncle's wealth. When we had company, I was disgusted by an ostentatious display of riches, and I have often quitted the room, to avoid listening to exaggerated tales of money obtained by lucky hits.

'With all my attention and affectionate interest, I perceived that I could not become the friend or confident of my husband. Every thing I learned relative to his affairs I gathered up by accident; and I vainly endeavoured to establish, at our fire-side, that social converse, which often renders people of different characters dear to each other. Returning from the theatre, or any amusing party, I frequently began to relate what I had seen and highly relished; but with sullen taciturnity he soon silenced me. I seemed therefore gradually to lose, in his society, the soul, the energies of which had just been in action. To such a degree, in fact, did his cold, reserved manner affect me, that, after spending some days with him alone, I have imagined myself the most stupid creature in the world, till the abilities of some casual visitor convinced me that I had some dormant animation, and sentiments above the dust in which I had been groveling. The very countenance of my husband changed; his complexion became sallow, and all the charms of youth were vanishing with its vivacity.

'I give you one view of the subject; but these experiments and alterations took up the space of five years; during which period, I had most reluctantly extorted several sums from my uncle, to save my husband, to use his own words, from destruction. At first it was to prevent bills being noted, to the injury of his credit; then to bail him; and afterwards to prevent an execution from entering the house. I began at last to conclude, that he would have made more exertions of his own to extricate himself, had he not relied on mine, cruel as was the task he imposed on me; and I firmly determined that I would make use of no more pretexts.

'From the moment I pronounced this determination, indifference on his part was changed into rudeness, or something worse.

'He now seldom dined at home, and continually returned at a late hour, drunk, to bed. I retired to another apartment; I was glad, I own, to escape from his; for personal intimacy without affection, seemed, to me the most degrading, as well as the most painful state in which a woman of any taste, not to speak of the peculiar delicacy of fostered sensibility, could be placed. But my husband's fondness for women was of the grossest kind, and imagination was so wholly out of the question, as to render his indulgences of this sort entirely promiscuous, and of the most brutal nature. My health suffered, before my heart was entirely estranged by the loathsome information; could I then have returned to his sullied arms, but as a victim to the prejudices of mankind, who have made women the property of their husbands? I discovered even, by his conversation, when intoxicated, that his favourites were wantons of the lowest class, who could by their vulgar, indecent mirth, which he called nature, rouse his sluggish spirits. Meretricious ornaments and manners were necessary to attract his attention. He seldom looked twice at a modest woman, and sat silent in their company; and the charms of youth and beauty had not the slightest effect on his senses, unless the possessors were initiated in vice. His intimacy with profligate women, and his habits of thinking, gave him a contempt for female endowments; and he would repeat, when wine had loosed his tongue, most of the common-place sarcasms levelled at them, by men who do not allow them to have minds, because mind would be an impediment to gross enjoyment. Men who are inferior to their fellow men, are always most anxious to establish their superiority over women. But where are these reflections leading me?

'Women who have lost their husband's affection, are justly reproved for neglecting their persons, and not taking the same pains to keep, as to gain a heart; but who thinks of giving the same advice to men, though women are continually stigmatized for being attached to fops; and from the nature of their education, are more susceptible of disgust? Yet why a woman should be expected to endure a sloven, with more patience than a man, and magnanimously to govern herself, I cannot conceive; unless it be supposed arrogant in her to look for respect as well as a maintenance. It is not easy to be pleased, because, after promising to love, in different circumstances, we are told that it is our duty. I cannot, I am sure (though, when attending the sick, I never felt disgust) forget my own sensations, when rising with health and spirit, and after scenting the sweet morning, I have met my husband at the breakfast table. The active attention I had been giving to domestic regulations, which were generally settled before he rose, or a walk, gave a glow to my countenance, that contrasted with his squallid appearance. The squeamishness of stomach alone, produced by the last night's intemperance, which he took no pains to conceal, destroyed my appetite. I think I now see him lolling in an arm-chair, in a dirty powdering gown,[27] soiled linen, ungartered stockings, and tangled hair, yawning and stretching himself. The newspaper was immediately called for, if not brought in on the tea-board, from which he would scarcely lift his eyes while I poured out the tea, excepting to ask for some brandy to put into it, or to declare that he could not eat. In answer to any question, in his best humour, it was a drawling, "What do you say, child?" But if I demanded money for the house expences, which I put off till the last moment, his customary reply, often prefaced with an oath, was, "Do you think me, madam, made of money?" – The butcher, the baker, must wait; and, what was worse, I was often obliged to witness his surly dismission of tradesmen, who were in want of their money, and whom I sometimes paid with the presents my uncle gave me for my own use.

At this juncture my father's mistress, by terrifying his conscience, prevailed on him to marry her; he was already become a methodist; and my brother, who now practised for himself, had discovered a flaw in the settlement made on my mother's children, which set it aside, and he allowed my father, whose distress made him submit to any thing, a tithe of his own, or rather our fortune.

My sisters had left school, but were unable to endure home, which my father's wife rendered as disagreeable as possible, to get rid of girls whom she regarded as spies on her conduct. They were accomplished, yet you can (may you never be reduced to the same destitute state!) scarcely conceive the trouble I had to place them in the situation of governesses, the only one in which even a well-educated woman, with more than ordinary talents, can struggle for a subsistence; and even this is a dependence next to menial. Is it then surprising, that so many forlorn women, with human passions and feelings, take refuge in infamy? Alone in large mansions, I say alone, because they had no companions with whom they could converse on equal terms, or from whom they could expect the endearments of affection, they grew melancholy, and the sound of joy made them sad; and the youngest, having a more delicate frame, fell into a decline. It was with great difficulty that I, who now almost supported the house by loans from my uncle, could prevail on the *master* of it, to allow her a room to die in. I watched her sick bed for some months, and then closed her eyes, gentle spirit! for ever. She was pretty, with very engaging manners; yet had never an opportunity to marry, excepting to a very old man. She had abilities sufficient to have shone in any profession, had there been any professions for women, though she shrunk at the name of milliner or mantua-maker as degrading to a gentlewoman. I would not term this feeling false pride to any one but you, my child, whom I fondly hope to see (yes; I will indulge the hope for a moment!) possessed of that energy of character which gives dignity to any station; and with that clear, firm spirit that will enable you to choose a situation for yourself, or submit to be classed in the lowest, if it be the only one in which you can be the mistress of your own actions.

'Soon after the death of my sister, an incident occurred, to prove to me that the heart of a libertine is dead to natural affection; and to convince me, that the being who has appeared all tenderness, to gratify a selfish passion, is as regardless of the innocent fruit of it, as of the object, which the fit is over. I had casually observed an old, mean-looking woman, who called on my husband every two or three months to receive some money. One day entering the passage of his little counting-house, as she was going out, I heard her say, "The child is very weak; she cannot live long, she will soon die out of your way, so you need not grudge her a little physic."

'"So much the better," he replied, "and pray mind your own business, good woman."

'I was struck by his unfeeling, inhuman tone of voice, and drew back, determined when the woman came again, to try to speak to her, not out of curiosity, I had heard enough, but with the hope of being useful to a poor, outcast girl.

'A month or two elapsed before I saw this woman again; and then she had a child in her hand that tottered along, scarcely able to sustain her own weight. They were going away, to return at the hour Mr Venables was expected; he was now from home. I desired the woman to walk into the parlour. She hesitated, yet obeyed. I assured her that I should not mention to my husband (the word seemed to weigh on my respiration), that I had seen her, or his child. The woman stared at me with astonishment; and I turned my eyes on the squalid object [that accompanied her.] She could hardly support herself, her complexion was sallow, and her eyes inflamed, with an indescribable look of cunning, mixed with the wrinkles produced by the peevishness of pain.

'"Poor child!" I exclaimed. "Ah! you may well say poor child," replied the woman. "I brought her here to see whether he would have the heart to look at her, and not get some advice. I do not know what they deserve who nursed her. Why, her legs bent under her like a bow when she came to me, and she has never been well since; but, if they were no better paid than I am, it is not to be wondered at, sure enough."

'On further enquiry I was informed, that this miserable spectacle was the daughter of a servant, a country girl, who caught Mr Venables' eye, and whom he seduced. On his marriage he sent her away, her situation being too visible. After her delivery, she was thrown on the town; and died in an hospital within the year. The babe was sent to a parish-nurse, and afterwards to this woman, who did not seem much better; but what was to be expected from such a close bargain? She was only paid three shillings a week for board and washing.

'The woman begged me to give her some old clothes for the child, assuring me, that she was almost afraid to ask master for money to buy even a pair of shoes.

'I grew sick at heart. And, fearing Mr Venables might enter, and oblige me to express my abhorrence, I hastily enquired where she lived, promised to pay her two shillings a week more, and to call on her in a day or two; putting a trifle into her hand as a proof of my good intention.

'If the state of this child affected me, what were my feelings at a discovery I made respecting Peggy ——?*

CHAPTER X

'My father's situation was now so distressing, that I prevailed on my uncle to accompany me to visit him; and to lend me his assistance, to prevent the whole property of the family from becoming the prey of my brother's rapacity; for, to extricate himself out of present difficulties, my father was totally regardless of futurity. I took down with me some presents for my step-mother; it did not require an effort for me to treat her with civility, or to forget the past.

'This was the first time I had visited my native village, since my marriage. But with what different emotions did I return from the busy world, with a heavy weight of experience benumbing my imagination, to scenes, that whispered recollections of joy and hope most eloquently to my heart! The first scent of the wild flowers from the heath, thrilled through my veins, awakening every sense to pleasure. The icy hand of despair seemed to be removed from my bosom; and – forgetting my husband – the nurtured visions of a romantic mind, bursting on me with all their original wildness and gay exuberance, were again hailed as sweet realities. I forgot, with equal facility, that I ever felt sorrow, or knew care in the country; while a

---

* The manuscript is imperfect here. An episode seems to have been intended, which was never committed to paper.

transient rainbow stole athwart the cloudy sky of despondency. The picturesque form of several favourite trees, and the porches of rude cottages, with
their smiling hedges, were recognized with the gladsome playfulness of
childish vivacity. I could have kissed the chickens that pecked on the
common; and longed to pat the cows, and frolic with the dogs that sported
on it. I gazed with delight on the windmill, and thought it lucky that it
should be in motion, at the moment I passed by; and entering the dear
green-lane, which led directly to the village, the sound of the well-known
rookery gave that sentimental tinge to the varying sensations of my active
soul, which only served to heighten the lustre of the luxuriant scenery. But,
spying, as I advanced, the spire, peeping over the withered tops of the aged
elms that composed the rookery, my thoughts flew immediately to the
church-yard, and tears of affection, such was the effect of my imagination,
bedewed my mother's grave! Sorrow gave place to devotional feelings. I
wandered through the church in fancy, as I used sometimes to do on a
Saturday evening. I recollected with what fervour I addressed the God of
my youth: and once more with rapturous love looked above my sorrows to
the Father of nature. I pause − feeling forcibly all the emotions I am
describing; and (reminded, as I register my sorrows, of the sublime calm I
have felt, when in some tremendous solitude, my soul rested on itself, and
seemed to fill the universe) I insensibly breathe soft, hushing every wayward
emotion, as if fearing to sully with a sigh, a contentment so extatic.

'Having settled my father's affairs, and, by my exertions in his favour,
made my brother my sworn foe, I returned to London. My husband's
conduct was now changed; I had during my absence, received several
affectionate, penitential letters from him; and he seemed on my arrival, to
wish by his behaviour to prove his sincerity. I could not then conceive why
he acted thus; and, when the suspicion darted into my head, that it might
arise from observing my increasing influence with my uncle, I almost
despised myself for imagining that such a degree of debasing selfishness
could exist.

'He became, unaccountable as was the change, tender and attentive; and,
attacking my weak side, made a confession of his follies, and lamented the
embarrassments in which I, who merited a far different fate, might be
involved. He besought me to aid him with my counsel, praised my understanding, and appealed to the tenderness of my heart.

'This conduct only inspired me with compassion. I wished to be his
friend; but love had spread his rosy pinions, and fled far, far away; and had
not (like some exquisite perfumes, the fine spirit of which is continually
mingling with the air) left a fragrance behind, to mark where he had shook
his wings. My husband's renewed caresses then became hateful to me; his
brutality was tolerable, compared to his distasteful fondness. Still, compassion, and the fear of insulting his supposed feelings, by a want of sympathy,
made me dissemble, and do violence to my delicacy. What a task!

'Those who support a system of what I term false refinement, and will not allow great part of love in the female, as well as male breast, to spring in some respects involuntarily, may not admit that charms are as necessary to feed the passion, as virtues to convert the mellowing spirit into friendship. To such observers I have nothing to say, any more than to the moralists, who insist that women ought to, and can love their husbands, because it is their duty. To you, my child, I may add, with a heart tremblingly alive to your future conduct, some observations, dictated by my present feelings, on calmly reviewing this period of my life. When novelists or moralists praise as a virtue, a woman's coldness of constitution, and want of passion; and make her yield to the ardour of her lover out of sheer compassion, or to promote a frigid plan of future comfort, I am disgusted. They may be good women, in the ordinary acceptation of the phrase, and do no harm; but they appear to me not to have those "finely fashioned nerves," which render the senses exquisite. They may possess tenderness; but they want that fire of the imagination, which produces *active* sensibility, and *positive* virtue. How does the woman deserve to be characterized, who marries one man, with a heart and imagination devoted to another? Is she not an object of pity or contempt, when thus sacrilegiously violating the purity of her own feelings? Nay, it is as indelicate, when she is indifferent, unless she be constitutionally insensible; then indeed it is a mere affair of barter; and I have nothing to do with the secrets of trade. Yes; eagerly as I wish you to possess true rectitude of mind, and purity of affection, I must insist that a heartless conduct is the contrary of virtuous. Truth is the only basis of virtue; and we cannot, without depraving our minds, endeavour to please a lover or husband, but in proportion as he pleases us. Men, more effectually to enslave us, may inculcate this partial morality, and lose sight of virtue in subdividing it into the duties of particular stations; but let us not blush for nature without a cause!

'After these remarks, I am ashamed to own, that I was pregnant. The greatest sacrifice of my principles in my whole life, was the allowing my husband again to be familiar with my person, though to this cruel act of self-denial, when I wished the earth to open and swallow me, you owe your birth; and I the unutterable pleasure of being a mother. There was something of delicacy in my husband's bridal attentions; but now his tainted breath, pimpled face, and blood-shot eyes, were not more repugnant to my senses, than his gross manners, and loveless familiarity to my taste.

'A man would only be expected to maintain; yes, barely grant a subsistence, to a woman rendered odious by habitual intoxication; but who would expect him, or think it possible to love her? And unless "youth, and genial years were flown," it would be thought equally unreasonable to insist, [under penalty of] forfeiting almost every thing reckoned valuable in life, that he should not love another: whilst woman, weak in reason, impotent in will, is required to moralize, sentimentalize herself to stone, and pine her life away, labouring to reform her embruted mate. He may even spend in dissipation, and intemperance, the very intemperance which renders him so hateful, her property, and by stinting her expences, not permit her to beguile in society, a wearisome, joyless life; for over their mutual fortune she has no power, it must all pass through his hand. And if she be a mother, and in the present state of women, it is a great misfortune to be prevented from discharging the duties, and cultivating the affections of one, what has she not to endure? – But I have suffered the tenderness of one to lead me into reflections that I did not think of making, to interrupt my narrative – yet the full heart will overflow.

'Mr Venables' embarrassments did not now endear him to me; still, anxious to befriend him, I endeavoured to prevail on him to retrench his expences; but he had always some plausible excuse to give, to justify his not following my advice. Humanity, compassion, and the interest produced by a habit of living together, made me try to relieve, and sympathize with him; but, when I recollected that I was bound to live with such a being for ever – my heart died within me; my desire of improvement became languid, and baleful, corroding melancholy took possession of my soul. Marriage had bastilled me for life. I discovered in myself a capacity for the enjoyment of the various pleasures existence affords; yet, fettered by the partial laws of society, this fair globe was to me an universal blank.[28]

'When I exhorted my husband to economy, I referred to himself. I was obliged to practise the most rigid, or contract debts, which I had too much reason to fear would never be paid. I despised this paltry privilege of a wife, which can only be of use to the vicious or inconsiderate, and determined not to increase the torrent that was bearing him down. I was then ignorant of the extent of his fraudulent speculations, whom I was bound to honour and obey.

'A woman neglected by her husband, or whose manners form a striking contrast with his, will always have men on the watch to soothe and flatter her. Besides, the forlorn state of a neglected woman, not destitute of personal charms, is particularly interesting, and rouses that species of pity, which is so near akin, it easily slides into love. A man of feeling thinks not of seducing, he is himself seduced by all the noblest emotions of his soul. He figures to himself all the sacrifices a woman of sensibility must make, and every situation in which his imagination places her, touches his heart, and fires his passions. Longing to take to his bosom the shorn lamb, and bid the drooping buds of hope revive, benevolence changes into passion: and should he then discover that he is beloved, honour binds him fast, though fore-seeing that he may afterwards be obliged to pay severe damages to the man, who never appeared to value his wife's society, till he found that there was a chance of his being indemnified for the loss of it.

'Such are the partial laws enacted by men; for, only to lay a stress on the dependent state of a woman in the grand question of the comforts arising from the possession of property, she is [even in this article] much more injured by the loss of the husband's affection, than he by that of his wife; yet where is she, condemned to the solitude of a deserted home, to look for a compensation from the woman, who seduces him from her? She cannot drive an unfaithful husband from his house, nor separate, or tear, his children from him, however culpable he may be; and he, still the master of his own fate, enjoys the smiles of a world, that would brand her with infamy, did she, seeking consolation, venture to retaliate.

'These remarks are not dictated by experience; but merely by the compassion I feel for many amiable women, the *out-laws* of the world. For myself, never encouraging any of the advances that were made to me, my lovers dropped off like the untimely shoots of spring. I did not even coquet with them; because I found, on examining myself, I could not coquet with a man without loving him a little; and I perceived that I should not be able to stop at the line of what are termed *innocent freedoms*, did I suffer any. My reserve was then the consequence of delicacy. Freedom of conduct has emancipated many women's minds; but my conduct has most rigidly been governed by my principles, till the improvement of my understanding has enabled me to discern the fallacy of prejudices at war with nature and reason.

'Shortly after the change I have mentioned in my husband's conduct, my uncle was compelled by his declining health, to seek the succour of a milder climate, and embark for Lisbon. He left his will in the hands of a friend, an eminent solicitor; he had previously questioned me relative to my situation and state of mind, and declared very freely, that he could place no reliance on the stability of my husband's professions. He had been deceived in the unfolding of his character; he now thought it fixed in a train of actions that would inevitably lead to ruin and disgrace.

'The evening before his departure, which we spent alone together, he folded me to his heart, uttering the endearing appellation of "child." – My more than father! why was I not permitted to perform the last duties of one, and smooth the pillow of death? He seemed by his manner to be convinced that he should never see me more; yet requested me, most earnestly, to come to him, should I be obliged to leave my husband. He had before expressed his sorrow at hearing of my pregnancy, having determined to prevail on me to accompany him, till I informed him of that circumstance. He expressed himself unfeignedly sorry that any new tie should bind me to a man whom he thought so incapable of estimating my value; such was the kind language of affection.

'I must repeat his own words; they made an indelible impression on my mind:

'"The marriage state is certainly that in which women, generally speaking, can be most useful; but I am far from thinking that a woman, once married, ought to consider the engagement as indissoluble (especially if there be no children to reward her for sacrificing her feelings) in case her husband merits neither her love, nor esteem. Esteem will often supply the place of love; and prevent a woman from being wretched, though it may not make her happy. The magnitude of a sacrifice ought always to bear some proportion to the utility in view; and for a woman to live with a man, for whom she can cherish neither affection nor esteem, or even be of any use to him, excepting in the light of a house-keeper, is an abjectness of condition, the enduring of which no concurrence of circumstances can ever make a duty in the sight of God or just men. If indeed she submits to it merely to be maintained in idleness, she has no right to complain bitterly of her fate; or to act, as a person of independent character might, as if she had a title to disregard general rules.

'"But the misfortune is, that many women only submit in appearance; and forfeit their own respect to secure their reputation in the world. The situation of a woman separated from her husband, is undoubtedly very different from that of a man who has left his wife. He, with lordly dignity, has shaken off[f] a clog; and the allowing her food and raiment, is thought sufficient to secure his reputation from taint. And, should she have been inconsiderate, he will be celebrated for his generosity and forbearance. Such is the respect paid to the master-key of property! A woman, on the contrary, resigning what is termed her natural protector (though he never was so, but in name) is despised and shunned, for asserting the independence of mind distinctive of a rational being, and spurning at slavery."

'During the remainder of the evening, my uncle's tenderness led him frequently to revert to the subject, and utter, with increasing warmth, sentiments to the same purport. At length it was necessary to say "Farewell!" – and we parted – gracious God! to meet no more.

CHAPTER XI

'A gentleman of large fortune and of polished manners, had lately visited very frequently at our house, and treated me, if possible, with more respect than Mr Venables paid him; my pregnancy was not yet visible. His society was a great relief to me, as I had for some time past, to avoid expence, confined myself very much at home. I ever disdained unnecessary, perhaps even prudent concealments; and my husband, with great ease, discovered the amount of my uncle's parting present. A copy of a writ was the stale pretext to extort it from me; and I had soon reason to believe that it was fabricated for the purpose. I acknowledge my folly in thus suffering myself to be continually imposed on. I had adhered to my resolution and not to apply to my uncle, on the part of my husband, any more; yet, when I had received a sum sufficient to supply my own wants, and to enable me to pursue a plan I had in view, to settle my younger brother in a respectable

employment, I allowed myself to be duped by Mr Venables' shallow
pretences, and hypocritical professions.

'Thus did he pillage me and my family, thus frustrate all my plans of
usefulness. Yet this was the man I was bound to respect and esteem: as if
respect and esteem depended on an arbitrary will of our own! But a wife
being as much a man's property as his horse, or his ass,[29] she has nothing
she can call her own. He may use any means to get at what the law
considers as his, the moment his wife is in possession of it, even to the
forcing of a lock, as Mr Venables did, to search for notes in my writing-desk
– and all this is done with a show of equity, because, forsooth, he is
responsible for her maintenance.

'The tender mother cannot *lawfully* snatch from the gripe of the gambling
spendthrift, or beastly drunkard, unmindful of his offspring, the fortune
which falls to her by chance; or (so flagrant is the injustice) what she earns
by her own exertions. No; he can rob her with impunity, even to waste
publicly on a courtezan; and the laws of her country – if women have a
country – afford her no protection or redress from the oppressor, unless she
have the plea of bodily fear; yet how many ways are there of goading the
soul almost to madness, equally unmanly, though not so mean?[30] When
such laws were framed, should not impartial lawgivers have first decreed, in
the style of a great assembly, who recognized the existence of an *être
suprême*,[31] to fix the national belief, that the husband should always be wiser
and more virtuous than his wife, in order to entitle him, with a show of
justice, to keep this idiot, or perpetual minor, for ever in bondage. But I
must have done – on this subject, my indignation continually runs away
with me.

'The company of the gentleman I have already mentioned, who had a
general acquaintance with literature and subjects of taste, was grateful to
me; my countenance brightened up as he approached, and I unaffectedly
expressed the pleasure I felt. The amusement his conversation afforded me,
made it easy to comply with my husband's request, to endeavour to render
our house agreeable to him.

'His attentions became more pointed; but, as I was not of the number of
women, whose virtue, as it is termed, immediately takes alarm, I
endeavoured, rather by raillery than serious expostulation, to give a different turn to his conversation. He assumed a new mode of attack, and I was,
for a while, the dupe of his pretended friendship.

'I had, merely in the style of *badinage*, boasted of my conquest, and
repeated his lover-like compliments to my husband. But he begged me, for
God's sake, not to affront his friend, or I should destroy all his projects, and
be his ruin. Had I had more affection for my husband, I should have
expressed my contempt of this time-serving politeness: now I imagined that
I only felt pity; yet it would have puzzled a casuist to point out in what the
exact difference consisted.

'This friend began now, in confidence, to discover to me the real state of

my husband's affairs. "Necessity," said Mr S——; why should I reveal his
name? for he affected to palliate the conduct he could not excuse, "had led
him to take such steps, by accommodation bills,³² buying goods on credit, to
sell them for ready money, and similar transactions, that his character in the
commercial world was gone. He was considered," he added, lowering his
voice, "on 'Change³³ as a swindler."

'I felt at that moment the first maternal pang. Aware of the evils my sex
have to struggle with, I still wished, for my own consolation, to be the
mother of a daughter; and I could not bear to think, that the *sins* of her
father's entailed disgrace, should be added to the ills to which woman is
heir.

'So completely was I deceived by these shows of friendship (nay, I
believe, according to his interpretation, Mr S—— really was my friend)
that I began to consult him respecting the best mode of retrieving my
husband's character: it is the good name of a woman only that sets to rise no
more. I knew not that he had been drawn into a whirlpool, out of which he
had not the energy to attempt to escape. He seemed indeed destitute of the
power of employing his faculties in any regular pursuit. His principles of
action were so loose, and his mind so uncultivated, that every thing like
order appeared to him in the shape of restraint; and, like men in the savage
state, he required the strong stimulus of hope or fear, produced by wild
speculations in which the interest of others went for nothing, to keep his
spirits awake. He one time professed patriotism, but he knew not what it
was to feel honest indignation; and pretended to be an advocate for liberty,
when, with as little affection for the human race as for individuals, he
thought of nothing but his own gratification. He was just such a citizen, as a
father. The sums he adroitly obtained by a violation of the laws of his
country, as well as those of humanity, he would allow a mistress to
squander; though she was with the same *sang froid*, consigned, as were his
children, to poverty, when another proved more attractive.

'On various pretences, his friend continued to visit me; and, observing
my want of money, he tried to induce me to accept of pecuniary aid; but
this offer I absolutely rejected, though it was made with such delicacy, I
could not be displeased.

'One day he came, as I thought accidentally, to dinner. My husband was
very much engaged in business, and quitted the room soon after the cloth
was removed. We conversed as usual, till confidential advice led again to
love. I was extremely mortified. I had a sincere regard for him, and hoped
that he had an equal friendship for me. I therefore began mildly to
expostulate with him. This gentleness he mistook for coy encouragement;
and he would not be diverted from the subject. Perceiving his mistake, I
seriously asked him how, using such language to me, he could profess to be
my husband's friend? A significant sneer excited my curiosity, and he,
supposing this to be my only scruple, took a letter deliberately out of his
pocket, saying, "Your husband's honour is not inflexible. How could you,

with your discernment, think it so? Why, he left the room this very day on purpose to give me an opportunity to explain myself; *he* thought me too timid – too tardy."

'I snatched the letter with indescribable emotion. The purport of it was to invite him to dinner, and to ridicule his chivalrous respect for me. He assured him, "that every woman had her price, and, with gross indecency, hinted, that he should be glad to have the duty of a husband taken off his hands. These he termed *liberal sentiments*. He advised him not to shock my romantic notions, but to attack my credulous generosity, and weak pity; and concluded with requesting him to lend him five hundred pounds for a month or six weeks." I read this letter twice over; and the firm purpose it inspired, calmed the rising tumult of my soul. I rose deliberately, requested Mr S——to wait a moment, and instantly going into the counting-house, desired Mr Venables to return with me to the dining-parlour.

'He laid down his pen, and entered with me, without observing any change in my countenance. I shut the door, and, giving him the letter, simply asked, "whether he wrote it, or was it a forgery?"

'Nothing could equal his confusion. His friend's eye met his, and he muttered something about a joke – But I interrupted him – "It is sufficient – We part for ever."

'I continued, with solemnity, "I have borne with your tyranny and infidelities. I disdain to utter what I have borne with. I thought you unprincipled, but not so decidedly vicious. I formed a tie, in the sight of heaven – I have held it sacred; even when men, more conformable to my taste, have made me feel – I despise all subterfuge! – that I was not dead to love. Neglected by you, I have resolutely stifled the enticing emotions, and respected the plighted faith you outraged. And you dare now to insult me, by selling me to prostitution! – Yes – equally lost to delicacy and principle – you dared sacrilegiously to barter the honour of the mother of your child."

'Then, turning to Mr S——, I added, "I call on you, Sir, to witness," and I lifted my hands and eyes to heaven, "that, as solemnly as I took his name, I now abjure it," I pulled off my ring, and put it on the table; "and that I mean immediately to quit his house, never to enter it more. I will provide for myself and child. I leave him as free as I am determined to be myself – he shall be answerable for no debts of mine."

'Astonishment closed their lips, till Mr Venables, gently pushing his friend, with a forced smile, out of the room, nature for a moment prevailed, and, appearing like himself, he turned round, burning with rage, to me: but there was no terror in the frown, excepting when contrasted with the malignant smile which preceded it. He bade me "leave the house at my peril; told me he despised my threats; I had no resource; I could not swear the peace against him! – I was not afraid of my life! – he had never struck me!"

'He threw the letter in the fire, which I had incautiously left in his hands; and, quitting the room, locked the door on me.

'When left alone, I was a moment or two before I could recollect myself. One scene had succeeded another with such rapidity, I almost doubted whether I was reflecting on a real event. "Was it possible? Was I, indeed, free?" – Yes; free I termed myself, when I decidedly perceived the conduct I ought to adopt. How had I panted for liberty – liberty, that I would have purchased at any price, but that of my own esteem! I rose, and shook myself; opened the window, and methought the air never smelled so sweet. The face of heaven grew fairer as I viewed it, and the clouds seemed to flit away obedient to my wishes, to give my soul room to expand. I was all soul, and (wild as it may appear) felt as if I could have dissolved in the soft balmy gale that kissed my cheek, or have glided below the horizon on the glowing, descending beams. A seraphic satisfaction animated, without agitating my spirits; and my imagination collected, in visions sublimely terrible, or soothingly beautiful, an immense variety of the endless images, which nature affords, and fancy combines, of the grand and fair. The lustre of these bright picturesque sketches faded with the setting sun; but I was still alive to the calm delight they had diffused through my heart.

'There may be advocates for matrimonial obedience, who, making a distinction between the duty of a wife and of a human being, may blame my conduct. – To them I write not – my feelings are not for them to analyze; and may you, my child, never be able to ascertain, by heart-rending experience, what your mother felt before the present emancipation of her mind!

'I began to write a letter to my father, after closing one to my uncle; not to ask advice, but to signify my determination; when I was interrupted by the entrance of Mr Venables. His manner was changed. His views on my uncle's fortune made him averse to my quitting his house, or he would, I am convinced, have been glad to have shaken off even the slight restraint my presence imposed on him; the restraint of showing me some respect. So far from having an affection for me, he really hated me, because he was convinced that I must despise him.

'He told me, that, "As I now had had time to cool and reflect, he did not doubt but that my prudence, and nice sense of propriety, would lead me to overlook what was passed."

'"Reflection," I replied, "had only confirmed my purpose, and no power on earth could divert me from it."

'Endeavouring to assume a soothing voice and look, when he would willingly have tortured me, to force me to feel his power, his countenance had an infernal expression, when he desired me, "Not to expose myself to the servants, by obliging him to confine me in my apartment; if then I would give my promise not to quit the house precipitately, I should be free – and – " I declared, interrupting him, "that I would promise nothing. I had no measures to keep with him – I was resolved, and would not condescend to subterfuge."

'He muttered, "that I should soon repent of these preposterous airs;"

and, ordering tea to be carried into my little study, which had a communication with my bed-chamber, he once more locked the door upon me, and left me to my own meditations. I had passively followed him up stairs, not wishing to fatigue myself with unavailing exertion.

'Nothing calms the mind like a fixed purpose. I felt as if I had heaved a thousand weight from my heart; the atmosphere seemed lightened; and, if I execrated the institutions of society, which thus enable men to tyrannize over women, it was almost a disinterested sentiment. I disregarded present inconveniences, when my mind had done struggling with itself, – when reason and inclination had shaken hands: and were at peace. I had no longer the cruel talk before me, in endless perspective, aye, during the tedious for ever of life, of labouring to overcome my repugnance – of labouring to extinguish the hopes, the may-bes of a lively imagination. Death I had hailed as my only chance for deliverance; but, while existence had still so many charms, and life promised happiness, I shrunk from the icy arms of an unknown tyrant, though far more inviting than those of the man, to whom I supposed myself bound without any other alternative; and was content to linger a little longer, waiting for I knew not what, rather than leave "the warm precincts of the cheerful day,"[34] and all the unenjoyed affection of my nature.

'My present situation gave a new turn to my reflection; and I wondered (now the film seemed to be withdrawn, that obscured the piercing sight of reason) how I could, previously to the deciding outrage, have considered myself as everlastingly united to vice and folly! "Had an evil genius cast a spell at my birth; or a demon stalked out of chaos, to perplex my understanding, and enchain my will, with delusive prejudices?"

'I pursued this train of thinking; it led me out of myself, to expatiate on the misery peculiar to my sex. "Are not," I thought, "the despots for ever stigmatized, who, in the wantonness of power, commanded even the most atrocious criminals to be chained to dead bodies? though surely those laws are much more inhuman, which forge adamantine fetters to bind minds together, that never can mingle in social communion! What indeed can equal the wretchedness of that state, in which there is no alternative, but to extinguish the affections, or encounter infamy?"

CHAPTER XII

'Towards midnight Mr Venables entered my chamber; and, with calm audacity preparing to go to bed, he bade me make haste, "for that was the best place for husbands and wives to end their differences." He had been drinking plentifully to aid his courage.

'I did not at first deign to reply. But perceiving that he affected to take my silence for consent, I told him that, "If he would not go to another bed, or allow me, I should sit up in my study all night." He attempted to pull me into the chamber, half joking. But I resisted; and, as he had determined not to give me any reason for saying that he used violence, after a few more efforts, he retired, cursing my obstinacy, to bed.

'I sat musing some time longer; then, throwing my cloak around me, prepared for sleep on a sopha. And, so fortunate seemed my deliverance, so sacred the pleasure of being thus wrapped up in myself, that I slept profoundly, and woke with a mind composed to encounter the struggles of the day. Mr Venables did not wake till some hours after; and then he came to me half-dressed, yawning and stretching, with haggard eyes, as if he scarcely recollected what had passed the preceding evening. He fixed his eyes on me for a moment, then, calling me a fool, asked "How long I intended to continue this pretty farce? For his part, he was devilish sick of it; but this was the plague of marrying women who pretended to know something."

'I made no other reply to this harangue, than to say, "That he ought to be glad to get rid of a woman so unfit to be his companion – and that any change in my conduct would be mean dissimulation; for maturer reflection only gave the sacred seal of reason to my first resolution."

'He looked as if he could have stamped with impatience, at being obliged to stifle his rage; but, conquering his anger (for weak people, whose passions seem the most ungovernable, restrain them with the greatest ease, when they have a sufficient motive), he exclaimed, "Very pretty, upon my soul! very pretty, theatrical flourishes! Pray, fair Roxana,[35] stoop from your altitudes, and remember that you are acting a part in real life."

'He uttered this speech with a self-satisfied air, and went down stairs to dress.

'In about an hour he came to me again; and in the same tone said, "That he came as my gentleman-usher to hand me down to breakfast."

' "Of the black rod?"[36] asked I.

'This question, and the tone in which I asked it, a little disconcerted him. To say the truth, I now felt no resentment; my firm resolution to free myself from my ignoble thraldom, had absorbed the various emotions which, during six years, had racked my soul. The duty pointed out by my principles seemed clear; and not one tender feeling intruded to make me swerve. The dislike which my husband had inspired was strong; but it only led me to wish to avoid, to wish to let him drop out of my memory; there was no misery, no torture that I would not deliberately have chosen, rather than renew my lease of servitude.

'During the breakfast, he attempted to reason with me on the folly of romantic sentiments; for this was the indiscriminate epithet he gave to every mode of conduct or thinking superior to his own. He asserted, "that all the world were governed by their own interest; those who pretended to be actuated by different motives, were only deeper knaves, or fools crazed by books, who took for gospel all the rodomantade[37] nonsense written by men who knew nothing of the world. For his part, he thanked God, he was no hypocrite; and, if he stretched a point sometimes, it was always with an intention of paying every man his own."

'He then artfully insinuated, "that he daily expected a vessel to arrive, a successful speculation, that would make him easy for the present, and that he had several other schemes actually depending, that could not fail. He had no doubt of becoming rich in a few years, though he had been thrown back by some unlucky adventures at the setting out."

'I mildly replied, "That I wished he might not involve himself still deeper."

'He had no notion that I was governed by a decision of judgment, not to be compared with a mere spurt of resentment. He knew not what it was to feel indignation against vice, and often boasted of his placable temper, and readiness to forgive injuries. True; for he only considered the being deceived, as an effort of skill he had not guarded against; and then, with a cant of candour, would observe, "that he did not know how he might himself have been tempted to act in the same circumstances." And, as his heart never opened to friendship, it never was wounded by disappointment. Every new acquaintance he protested, it is true, was "the cleverest fellow in the world;" and he really thought so; till the novelty of his conversation or manners ceased to have any effect on his sluggish spirits. His respect for rank or fortune was more permanent, though he chanced to have no design of availing himself of the influence of either to promote his own views.

'After a prefatory conversation, – my blood (I thought it had been cooler) flushed over my whole countenance as he spoke – he alluded to my situation. He desired me to reflect – "and act like a prudent woman, as the best proof of my superior understanding; for he must own I had sense, did I know how to use it. I was not," he laid a stress on his words, "without my passions; and a husband was a convenient cloke. – He was liberal in his way of thinking; and why might not we, like many other married people, who were above vulgar prejudices, tacitly consent to let each other follow their own inclination? – He meant nothing more, in the letter I made the ground of complaint; and the pleasure which I seemed to take in Mr S.'s company, led him to conclude, that he was not disagreeable to me."

'A clerk brought in the letters of the day, and I, as I often did, while he was discussing subjects of business, went to the *piano forte*, and began to play a favourite air to restore myself, as it were, to nature, and drive the sophisticated sentiments I had just been obliged to listen to, out of my soul.

'They had excited sensations similar to those I have felt, in viewing the squalid inhabitants of some of the lanes and back streets of the metropolis, mortified at being compelled to consider them as my fellow-creatures, as if an ape had claimed kindred with me. Or, as when surrounded by a mephitical[38] fog, I have wished to have a volley of cannon fired, to clear the incumbered atmosphere, and give me room to breathe and move.

'My spirits were all in arms, and I played a kind of extemporary prelude. The cadence was probably wild and impassioned, while, lost in thought, I made the sounds a kind of echo to my train of thinking.

'Pausing for a moment, I met Mr Venables' eyes. He was observing me with an air of conceited satisfaction, as much as to say – "My last insinuation has done the business – she begins to know her own interest." Then gathering up his letters, he said, "That he hoped he should hear no more romantic stuff, well enough in a miss just come from boarding school;" and went, as was his custom, to the counting-house. I still continued playing; and, turning to a sprightly lesson, I executed it with uncommon vivacity. I heard footsteps approach the door, and was soon convinced that Mr Venables was listening; the consciousness only gave more animation to my fingers. He went down into the kitchen, and the cook, probably by his desire, came to me, to know what I would please to order for dinner. Mr Venables came into the parlour again, with apparent carelessness. I perceived that the cunning man was over-reaching himself; and I gave my directions as usual, and left the room.

'While I was making some alteration in my dress, Mr Venables peeped in, and, begging my pardon for interrupting me, disappeared. I took up some work[39] (I could not read), and two or three messages were sent to me, probably for no other purpose, but to enable Mr Venables to ascertain what I was about.

'I listened whenever I heard the street-door open; at last I imagined I could distinguish Mr Venables' step, going out. I laid aside my work; my heart palpitated; still I was afraid hastily to enquire; and I waited a long half hour, before I ventured to ask the boy whether his master was in the counting-house?

'Being answered in the negative, I bade him call me a coach, and collecting a few necessaries hastily together, with a little parcel of letters and papers which I had collected the preceding evening, I hurried into it, desiring the coachman to drive to a distant part of the town.

'I almost feared that the coach would break down before I got out of the street; and, when I turned the corner, I seemed to breathe a freer air. I was ready to imagine that I was rising above the thick atmosphere of earth; or I felt, as wearied souls might be supposed to feel on entering another state of existence.

'I stopped at one or two stands of coaches to elude pursuit, and then drove round the skirts of the town to seek for an obscure lodging, where I wished to remain concealed, till I could avail myself of my uncle's protection. I had resolved to assume my own name immediately, and openly to avow my determination, without any formal vindication, the moment I had found a home, in which I could rest free from the daily alarm of expecting to see Mr Venables enter.

'I looked at several lodgings; but finding that I could not, without a reference to some acquaintance, who might inform my tyrant, get admittance into a decent apartment – men have not all this trouble – I thought of a woman whom I had assisted to furnish a little haberdasher's shop, and who I knew had a first floor to let.

'I went to her, and though I could not persuade her, that the quarrel between me and Mr Venables would never be made up, still she agreed to conceal me for the present; yet assuring me at the same time, shaking her head, that, when a woman was once married, she must bear every thing. Her pale face, on which appeared a thousand haggard lines and delving wrinkles, produced by what is emphatically termed fretting, inforced her remark; and I had afterwards an opportunity of observing the treatment she had to endure, which grizzled[40] her into patience. She toiled from morning till night; yet her husband would rob the till, and take away the money reserved for paying bills; and, returning home drunk, he would beat her if she chanced to offend him, though she had a child at the breast.

'These scenes awoke me at night; and, in the morning, I heard her, as usual, talk to her dear Johnny – he, forsooth, was her master; no slave in the West Indies had one more despotic; but fortunately she was of the true Russian breed of wives.[41]

'My mind, during the few past days, seemed, as it were, disengaged from my body; but, now the struggle was over, I felt very forcibly the effect which perturbation of spirits produces on a woman in my situation.

'The apprehension of a miscarriage, obliged me to confine myself to my apartment near a fortnight; but I wrote to my uncle's friend for money, promising "to call on him, and explain my situation, when I was well enough to go out; mean time I earnestly intreated him, not to mention my place of abode to any one, lest my husband – such the law considered him – should disturb the mind he could not conquer. I mentioned my intention of setting out for Lisbon, to claim my uncle's protection, the moment my health would permit."

'The tranquillity however, which I was recovering, was soon interrupted. My landlady came up to me one day, with eyes swollen with weeping, unable to utter what she was commanded to say. She declared, "That she was never so miserable in her life; that she must appear an ungrateful monster; and that she would readily go down on her knees to me, to intreat me to forgive her, as she had done to her husband to spare her the cruel task." Sobs prevented her from proceeding, or answering my impatient enquiries, to know what she meant.

'When she became a little more composed, she took a newspaper out of her pocket, declaring, "that her heart smote her, but what could she do? – she must obey her husband." I snatched the paper from her. An advertisement quickly met my eye, purporting, that "Maria Venables had, without any assignable cause, absconded from her husband; and any person harbouring her, was menaced with the utmost severity of the law."

'Perfectly acquainted with Mr Venables' meanness of soul, this step did not excite my surprise, and scarcely my contempt. Resentment in my breast, never survived love. I bade the poor woman, in a kind tone, wipe her eyes, and request her husband to come up, and speak to me himself.

'My manner awed him. He respected a lady, though not a woman; and began to mutter out an apology.

'"Mr Venables was a rich gentleman; he wished to oblige me, but he had suffered enough by the law already, to tremble at the thought; besides, for certain, we should come together again, and then even I should not thank him for being accessary to keeping us asunder. – A husband and wife were, God knows, just as one, – and all would come round at last." He uttered a drawling "Hem!" and then with an arch look, added – "Master might have had his little frolics – but – Lord bless your heart! – men would be men while the world stands."

'To argue with this privileged first-born of reason, I perceived, would be vain. I therefore only requested him to let me remain another day at his house, while I sought for a lodging; and not to inform Mr Venables that I had ever been sheltered there.

'He consented, because he had not the courage to refuse a person for whom he had an habitual respect; but I heard the pent-up choler burst forth in curses, when he met his wife, who was waiting impatiently at the foot of the stairs, to know what effect my expostulations would have on him.

'Without wasting any time in the fruitless indulgence of vexation, I once more set out in search of an abode in which I could hide myself for a few weeks.

'Agreeing to pay an exorbitant price, I hired an apartment, without any reference being required relative to my character: indeed, a glance at my shape seemed to say, that my motive for concealment was sufficiently obvious. Thus was I obliged to shroud my head in infamy.

'To avoid all danger of detection – I use the appropriate word, my child, for I was hunted out like a felon – I determined to take possession of my new lodgings that very evening.

'I did not inform my landlady where I was going. I knew that she had a sincere affection for me, and would willingly have run any risk to show her gratitude; yet I was fully convinced, that a few kind words from Johnny would have found the woman in her, and her dear benefactress, as she termed me in an agony of tears, would have been sacrificed, to recompense her tyrant for condescending to treat her like an equal. He could be kind-hearted, as she expressed it, when he pleased. And this thawed sternness, contrasted with his habitual brutality, was the more acceptable, and could not be purchased at too dear a rate.

'The sight of the advertisement made me desirous of taking refuge with my uncle, let what would be the consequence; and I repaired in a hackney coach (afraid of meeting some person who might chance to know me, had I walked) to the chambers of my uncle's friend.

'He received me with great politeness (my uncle had already prepossessed him in my favour), and listened, with interest, to my explanation of the motives which had induced me to fly from home, and skulk in obscurity, with all the timidity of fear that ought only to be the companion of guilt. He lamented, with rather more gallantry than, in my situation, I thought delicate, that such a woman should be thrown away on a man insensible to the charms of beauty or grace. He seemed at a loss what to advise me to do, to evade my husband's search, without hastening to my uncle, whom, he hesitating said, I might not find alive. He uttered this intelligence with visible regret; requested me, at least, to wait for the next packet;[42] offered me what money I wanted, and promised to visit me.

'He kept his word; still no letter arrived to put an end to my painful state of suspense. I procured some books and music, to beguile the tedious solitary days.

'"Come, ever smiling Liberty,
"And with thee bring thy jocund train:"[43]

I sung – and sung till, saddened by the strain of joy, I bitterly lamented the fate that deprived me of all social pleasure. Comparative liberty indeed I had possessed myself of; but the jocund train lagged far behind!

CHAPTER XIII

'By watching my only visitor, my uncle's friend, or by some other means, Mr Venables discovered my residence, and came to enquire for me. The maid-servant assured him there was no such person in the house. A bustle ensued – I caught the alarm – listened – distinguished his voice, and immediately locked the door. They suddenly grew still; and I waited near a quarter of an hour, before I heard him open the parlour door, and mount the stairs with the mistress of the house, who obsequiously declared that she knew nothing of me.

'Finding my door locked, she requested me to "open it, and prepare to go home with my husband, poor gentleman! to whom I had already occasioned sufficient vexation." I made no reply. Mr Venables then, in an assumed tone of softness, intreated me, "to consider what he suffered, and my own reputation, and get the better of childish resentment." He ran on in the same strain, pretending to address me, but evidently adapting his discourse to the capacity of the landlady; who, at every pause, uttered an exclamation of pity; or "Yes, to be sure – Very true, sir."

'Sick of the farce, and perceiving that I could not avoid the hated interview, I opened the door, and he entered. Advancing with easy assurance to take my hand, I shrunk from his touch, with an involuntary start, as I should have done from a noisome reptile, with more disgust than terror. His conductress was retiring, to give us, as she said, an opportunity to accommodate matters. But I bade her come in, or I would go out; and curiosity impelled her to obey me.

'Mr Venables began to expostulate; and this woman, proud of his confidence, to second him. But I calmly silenced her, in the midst of a vulgar harangue, and turning to him, asked, "Why he vainly tormented me? declaring that no power on earth should force me back to his house."

'After a long altercation, the particulars of which, it would be to no purpose to repeat, he left the room. Some time was spent in loud conversation in the parlour below, and I discovered that he had brought his friend, an attorney, with him.[44]

['J]The tumult on the landing place, brought out a gentleman, who had recently taken apartments in the house; he enquired why I was thus assailed?* The voluble attorney instantly repeated the trite tale. The stranger turned to me, observing, with the most soothing politeness and manly interest, that "my countenance told a very different story." He added, "that I should not be insulted, or forced out of the house, by any body."

'"Not by her husband?" asked the attorney.

'"No, sir, not by her husband." Mr Venables advanced towards him – But there was a decision in his attitude, that so well seconded that of his voice,[45]

They left the house: at the same time protesting, that any one that should dare to protect me, should be prosecuted with the utmost rigour.

'They were scarcely out of the house, when my landlady came up to me again, and begged my pardon, in a very different tone. For, though Mr Venables had bid her, at her peril, harbour me, he had not attended, I found, to her broad hints, to discharge the lodging. I instantly promised to pay her, and make her a present to compensate for my abrupt departure, if she would procure me another lodging, at a sufficient distance; and she, in return, repeating Mr Venables' plausible tale, I raised her indignation, and excited her sympathy, by telling her briefly the truth.

'She expressed her commiseration with such honest warmth, that I felt soothed; for I have none of that fastidious sensitiveness, which a vulgar accent or gesture can alarm to the disregard of real kindness. I was ever glad to perceive in others the humane feelings I delighted to exercise; and the recollection of some ridiculous characteristic circumstances, which have occurred in a moment of emotion, has convulsed me with laughter, though

---

* The introduction of Darnford as the deliverer of Maria, in an early stage of the history, is already stated (Chap. III.) to have been an afterthought of the author. This has probably caused the imperfectness of the manuscript in the above passage; though, at the same time, it must be acknowledged to be somewhat uncertain, whether Darnford is the stranger intended in this place. It appears from Chap. XVII, that an interference of a more decisive nature was designed to be attributed to him.

at the instant I should have thought it sacrilegious to have smiled. Your improvement, my dearest girl, being ever present to me while I write, I note these feelings, because women, more accustomed to observe manners than actions, are too much alive to ridicule. So much so, that their boasted sensibility is often stifled by false delicacy. True sensibility, the sensibility which is the auxiliary of virtue, and the soul of genius, is in society so occupied with the feelings of others, as scarcely to regard its own sensations. With what reverence have I looked up at my uncle, the dear parent of my mind! when I have seen the sense of his own sufferings, of mind and body, absorbed in a desire to comfort those, whose misfortunes were comparatively trivial. He would have been ashamed of being as indulgent to himself, as he was to others. "Genuine fortitude," he would assert, "consisted in governing our own emotions, and making allowance for the weaknesses in our friends, that we would not tolerate in ourselves." But where is my fond regret leading me!

'"Women must be submissive," said my landlady. "Indeed what could most women do? Who had they to maintain them, but their husbands? Every woman, and especially a lady, could not go through rough and smooth, as she had done, to earn a little bread."

'She was in a talking mood, and proceeded to inform me how she had been used in the world. "She knew what it was to have a bad husband, or she did not know who should." I perceived that she would be very much mortified, were I not to attend to her tale, and I did not attempt to interrupt her, though I wished her, as soon as possible, to go out in search of a new abode for me, where I could once more hide my head.

'She began by telling me, "That she had saved a little money in service; and was over-persuaded (we must all be in love once in our lives) to marry a likely man, a footman in the family, not worth a groat. My plan," she continued, "was to take a house, and let out lodgings; and all went on well, till my husband got acquainted with an impudent slut, who chose to live on other people's means – and then all went to rack and ruin. He ran in debt to buy her fine clothes, such clothes as I never thought of wearing myself, and – would you believe it? – he signed an execution on my very goods, bought with the money I worked so hard to get; and they came and took my bed from under me, before I heard a word of the matter. Aye, madam, these are misfortunes that you gentlefolks know nothing of; – but sorrow is sorrow, let it come which way it will.

'"I sought for a service again – very hard, after having a house of my own! – but he used to follow me, and kick up such a riot when he was drunk, that I could not keep a place; nay, he even stole my clothes, and pawned them; and when I went to the pawnbroker's, and offered to take my oath that they were not bought with a farthing of his money, they said, "It was all as one, my husband had a right to whatever I had."

'"At last he listed for a soldier, and I took a house, making an agreement to pay for the furniture by degrees; and I almost starved myself, till I once more got before-hand in the world.

'"After an absence of six years (God forgive me! I thought he was dead) my husband returned; found me out, and came with such a penitent face, I forgave him, and clothed him from head to foot. But he had not been a week in the house, before some of his creditors arrested him; and, he selling my goods, I found myself once more reduced to beggary; for I was not as well able to work, go to bed late, and rise early, as when I quitted service; and then I thought it hard enough. He was soon tired of me, when there was nothing more to be had, and left me again.

'"I will not tell you how I was buffeted about, till, hearing for certain that he had died in an hospital abroad, I once more returned to my old occupation; but have not yet been able to get my head above water: so, madam, you must not be angry if I am afraid to run any risk, when I know so well, that women have always the worst of it, when law is to decide."

'After uttering a few more complaints, I prevailed on my landlady to go out in quest of a lodging; and, to be more secure, I condescended to the mean shift of changing my name.

'But why should I dwell on similar incidents! − I was hunted, like an infected beast, from three different apartments, and should not have been allowed to rest in any, had not Mr Venables, informed of my uncle's dangerous state of health, been inspired with the fear of hurrying me out of the world as I advanced in my pregnancy, by thus tormenting and obliging me to take sudden journeys to avoid him; and then his speculations on my uncle's fortune must prove abortive.

'One day, when he had pursued me to an inn, I fainted, hurrying from him; and, falling down, the sight of my blood alarmed him, and obtained a respite for me. It is strange that he should have retained any hope, after observing my unwavering determination; but, from the mildness of my behaviour, when I found all my endeavours to change his disposition unavailing, he formed an erroneous opinion of my character, imagining that, were we once more together, I should part with the money he could not legally force from me, with the same facility as formerly. My forbearance and occasional sympathy he had mistaken for weakness of character; and, because he perceived that I disliked resistance, he thought my indulgence and compassion mere selfishness, and never discovered that the fear of being unjust, or of unnecessarily wounding the feelings of another, was much more painful to me, than any thing I could have to endure myself. Perhaps it was pride which made me imagine, that I could bear what I dreaded to inflict; and that it was often easier to suffer, than to see the sufferings of others.

'I forgot to mention that, during this persecution, I received a letter from my uncle, informing me, "that he only found relief from continual change of air; and that he intended to return when the spring was a little more advanced (it was now the middle of February), and then we would plan a journey to Italy, leaving the fogs and cares of England far behind." He approved of my conduct, promised to adopt my child, and seemed to have no doubt of obliging Mr Venables to hear reason. He wrote to his friend, by the same post, desiring him to call on Mr Venables in his name; and, in consequence of the remonstrances he dictated, I was permitted to lie-in tranquilly.

'The two or three weeks previous, I had been allowed to rest in peace; but, so accustomed was I to pursuit and alarm, that I seldom closed my eyes without being haunted by Mr Venables' image, who seemed to assume terrific or hateful forms to torment me, wherever I turned. – Sometimes a wild cat, a roaring bull, or hideous assassin, whom I vainly attempted to fly; at others he was a demon, hurrying me to the brink of a precipice, plunging me into dark waves, or horrid gulfs; and I woke, in violent fits of trembling anxiety, to assure myself that it was all a dream, and to endeavour to lure my waking thoughts to wander to the delightful Italian vales, I hoped soon to visit; or to picture some august ruins, where I reclined in fancy on a mouldering column, and escaped, in the contemplation of the heart-enlarging virtues of antiquity, from the turmoil of cares that had depressed all the daring purposes of my soul. But I was not long allowed to calm my mind by the exercise of my imagination; for the third day after your birth, my child, I was surprised by a visit from my elder brother; who came in the most abrupt manner, to inform me of the death of my uncle. He had left the greater part of his fortune to my child, appointing me its guardian; in short, every step was taken to enable me to be mistress of his fortune, without putting any part of it in Mr Venables' power. My brother came to vent his rage on me, for having, as he expressed himself, "deprived him, my uncle's eldest nephew, of his inheritance;" though my uncle's property, the fruit of his own exertion, being all in the funds, or on landed securities, there was not a shadow of justice in the charge.

'As I sincerely loved my uncle, this intelligence brought on a fever, which I struggled to conquer with all the energy of my mind; for, in my desolate state, I had it very much at heart to suckle you, my poor babe. You seemed my only tie to life, a cherub to whom I wished to be a father, as well as a mother; and the double duty appeared to me to produce a proportionate increase of affection. But the pleasure I felt, while sustaining you, snatched from the wreck of hope, was cruelly damped by melancholy reflections on my widowed state – widowed by the death of my uncle. Of Mr Venables I thought not, even when I thought of the felicity of loving your father, and how a mother's pleasure might be exalted, and her care softened by a husband's tenderness. – "Ought to be!" I exclaimed; and I endeavoured to drive away the tenderness that suffocated me; but my spirits were weak, and the unbidden tears would flow. "Why was I," I would ask thee, but thou didst not heed me, – "cut off from the participation of the sweetest pleasure of life?" I imagined with what extacy, after the pains of child-bed, I should have presented my little stranger, whom I had so long wished to view, to a respectable father, and with what maternal fondness I should have pressed them both to my heart! – Now I kissed her with less delight, though with the most endearing compassion, poor helpless one! when I perceived a slight resemblance of him, to whom she owed her existence; or, if any gesture reminded me of him, even in his best days, my heart heaved, and I pressed the innocent to my bosom, as if to purify it – yes, I blushed to think that its purity had been sullied, by allowing such a man to be its father.

'After my recovery, I began to think of taking a house in the country, or of making an excursion on the continent, to avoid Mr Venables; and to open my heart to new pleasures and affection. The spring was melting into summer, and you, my little companion, began to smile – that smile made hope bud out afresh, assuring me the world was not a desert. Your gestures were ever present to my fancy; and I dwelt on the joy I should feel when you would begin to walk and lisp. Watching your wakening mind, and shielding from every rude blast my tender blossom, I recovered my spirits – I dreamed not of the frost – "the killing frost",[46] to which you were destined to be exposed. – But I lose all patience – and execrate the injustice of the world – folly! ignorance! – I should rather call it; but, shut up from a free circulation of thought, and always pondering on the same griefs, I writhe under the torturing apprehensions, which ought to excite only honest indignation, or active compassion; and would, could I view them as the natural consequence of things. But, born a woman – and born to suffer, in endeavouring to repress my own emotions, I feel more acutely the various ills my sex are fated to bear – I feel that the evils they are subject to endure, degrade them so far below their oppressors, as almost to justify their tyranny; leading at the same time superficial reasoners to term that weakness the cause, which is only the consequence of short-sighted despotism.

CHAPTER XIV

'As my mind grew calmer, the visions of Italy again returned with their former glow of colouring; and I resolved on quitting the kingdom for a time, in search of the cheerfulness, that naturally results from a change of scene, unless we carry the barbed arrow with us, and only see what we feel.

'During the period necessary to prepare for a long absence, I sent a supply to pay my father's debts, and settled my brothers in eligible situations; but my attention was not wholly engrossed by my family, though I do not think it necessary to enumerate the common exertions of humanity. The manner in which my uncle's property was settled, prevented me from making the addition to the fortune of my surviving sister, that I could have wished; but I had prevailed on him to bequeath her two thousand pounds, and she determined to marry a lover, to whom she had been some time attached. Had it not been for this engagement, I should have invited her to accompany me in my tour; and I might have escaped the pit, so artfully dug in my path, when I was the least aware of danger.

'I had thought of remaining in England, till I weaned my child; but this state of freedom was too peaceful to last, and I had soon reason to wish to hasten my departure. A friend of Mr Venables, the same attorney who had accompanied him in several excursions to hunt me from my hiding places, waited on me to propose a reconciliation. On my refusal, he indirectly advised me to make over to my husband – for husband he would term him – the greater part of the property I had at command, menacing me with continual persecution unless I complied; and that, as a last resort, he would claim the child. I did not, though intimidated by the last insinuation, scruple to declare, that I would not allow him to squander the money left to me for far different purposes, but offered him five hundred pounds, if he would sign a bond not to torment me any more. My maternal anxiety made me thus appear to waver from my first determination, and probably suggested to him, or his diabolical agent, the infernal plot, which has succeeded but too well.

'The bond was executed; still I was impatient to leave England. Mischief hung in the air when we breathed the same; I wanted seas to divide us, and waters to roll between, till he had forgotten that I had the means of helping him through a new scheme. Disturbed by the late occurrences, I instantly prepared for my departure. My only delay was waiting for a maid-servant, who spoke French fluently, and had been warmly recommended to me. A valet I was advised to hire, when I fixed on my place of residence for any time.

'My God, with what a light heart did I set out for Dover! – It was not my country, but my cares, that I was leaving behind. My heart seemed to bound with the wheels, or rather appeared the centre on which they twirled. I clasped you to my bosom, exclaiming "And you will be safe – quite safe – when – we are once on board the packet. – Would we were there!" I smiled at my idle fears, as the natural effect of continual alarm; and I scarcely owned to myself that I dreaded Mr Venables's cunning, or was conscious of the horrid delight he would feel, at forming stratagem after stratagem to circumvent me. I was already in the snare – I never reached the packet – I never saw thee more. – I grow breathless. I have scarcely patience to write down the details. The maid – the plausible woman I had hired – put, doubtless, some stupifying potion in what I ate or drank, the morning I left town. All I know is, that she must have quitted the chaise, shameless wretch! and taken (from my breast) my babe with her. How could a creature in a female form see me caress thee, and steal thee from my arms! I must stop, stop to repress a mother's anguish; lest, in bitterness of soul, I imprecate the wrath of heaven on this tiger, who tore my only comfort from me.

'How long I slept I know not; certainly many hours, for I woke at the close of day, in a strange confusion of thought. I was probably roused to recollection by some one thundering at a huge, unwieldy gate. Attempting to ask where I was, my voice died away, and I tried to raise it in vain, as I have done in a dream. I looked for my babe with affright; feared that it had fallen out of my lap, while I had so strangely forgotten her; and, such was the vague intoxication, I can give it no other name, in which I was plunged, I could not recollect when or where I last saw you; but I sighed, as if my heart wanted room to clear my head.

'The gates opened heavily, and the sullen sound of many locks and bolts drawn back, grated on my very soul, before I was appalled by the creeking of the dismal hinges, as they closed after me. The gloomy pile was before me, half in ruins; some of the aged trees of the avenue were cut down, and left to rot where they fell; and as we approached some mouldering steps, a monstrous dog darted forwards to the length of his chain, and barked and growled infernally.

'The door was opened slowly, and a murderous visage peeped out, with a lantern. "Hush!" he uttered, in a threatening tone, and the affrighted animal stole back to his kennel. The door of the chaise flew back, the stranger put down the lantern, and clasped his dreadful arms around me. It was certainly the effect of the soporific draught, for, instead of exerting my strength, I sunk without motion, though not without sense, on his shoulder, my limbs refusing to obey my will. I was carried up the steps into a close-shut hall. A candle flaring in the socket, scarcely dispersed the darkness, though it displayed to me the ferocious countenance of the wretch who held me.

'He mounted a wide staircase. Large figures painted on the walls seemed to start on me, and glaring eyes to meet me at every turn. Entering a long gallery, a dismal shriek made me spring out of my conductor's arms, with I know not what mysterious emotion of terror; but I fell on the floor, unable to sustain myself.

'A strange-looking female started out of one of the recesses, and observed me with more curiosity than interest; till, sternly bid retire, she flitted back like a shadow. Other faces, strongly marked, or distorted, peeped through the half-opened doors, and I heard some incoherent sounds. I had no distinct idea where I could be – I looked on all sides, and almost doubted whether I was alive or dead.

'Thrown on a bed, I immediately sunk into insensibility again; and next day, gradually recovering the use of reason, I began, starting affrighted from the conviction, to discover where I was confined – I insisted on seeing the master of the mansion – I saw him – and perceived that I was buried alive. –

'Such, my child, are the events of thy mother's life to this dreadful moment – Should she ever escape from the fangs of her enemies, she will add the secrets of her prison-house – and –'

Some lines were here crossed out, and the memoirs broke off abruptly with the names of Jemima and Darnford.

APPENDIX

[ADVERTISEMENT

The performance, with a fragment of which the reader has now been presented, was designed to consist of three parts. The preceding sheets were considered as constituting one of those parts. Those persons who in the perusal of the chapters, already written and in some degree finished by the author, have felt their hearts awakened, and their curiosity excited as to the sequel of the story, will, of course, gladly accept even of the broken paragraphs and half-finished sentences, which have been found committed to paper, as materials for the remainder. The fastidious and cold-hearted critic may perhaps feel himself repelled by the incoherent form in which they are presented. But an inquisitive temper willingly accepts the most imperfect and mutilated information, where better is not to be had: and readers, who in any degree resemble the author in her quick apprehension of sentiment, and of the pleasures and pains of imagination, will, I believe, find gratification, in contemplating sketches, which were designed in a short time to have received the finishing touches of her genius; but which must now for ever remain a mark to record the triumphs of mortality, over schemes of usefulness, and projects of public interest.]

CHAPTER XV

Darnford returned the memoirs to Maria, with a most affectionate letter, in which he reasoned on 'the absurdity of the laws respecting matrimony, which, till divorces could be more easily obtained, was,' he declared, 'the most insufferable bondage. Ties of this nature could not bind minds governed by superior principles; and such beings were privileged to act above the dictates of laws they had no voice in framing, if they had sufficient strength of mind to endure the natural consequence. In her case, to talk of duty, was a farce, excepting what was due to herself. Delicacy, as well as reason, forbade her ever to think of returning to her husband: was she then to restrain her charming sensibility through mere prejudice? These arguments were not absolutely impartial, for he disdained to conceal, that, when he appealed to her reason, he felt that he had some interest in her heart. – The conviction was not more transporting, than sacred – a thousand times a day, he asked himself how he had merited such happiness? – and as often he determined to purify the heart she deigned to inhabit – He intreated to be again admitted to her presence.'

He was; and the tear which glistened in his eye, when he respectfully pressed her to his bosom, rendered him peculiarly dear to the unfortunate mother. Grief had stilled the transports of love, only to render their mutual tenderness more touching. In former interviews, Darnford had contrived, by a hundred little pretexts, to sit near her, to take her hand, or to meet her eyes – now it was all soothing affection, and esteem seemed to have rivalled love. He adverted to her narrative, and spoke with warmth of the oppression she had endured. – His eyes, glowing with a lambent flame, told her how much he wished to restore her to liberty and love; but he kissed her hand, as if it had been that of a saint; and spoke of the loss of her child, as if it had been his own. – What could have been more flattering to Maria? – Every instance of self-denial was registered in her heart, and she loved him, for loving her too well to give way to the transports of passion.

They met again and again; and Darnford declared, while passion suffused his cheeks, that he never before knew what it was to love. –

One morning Jemima informed Maria, that her master intended to wait on her, and speak to her without witnesses. He came, and brought a letter with him, pretending that he was ignorant of its contents, though he insisted on having it returned to him. It was from the attorney already mentioned, who informed her of the death of her child, and hinted, 'that she could not now have a legitimate heir, and that, would she make over the half of her fortune during life, she should be conveyed to Dover, and permitted to pursue her plan of travelling.'

Maria answered with warmth, 'That she had no terms to make with the murderer of her babe, nor would she purchase liberty at the price of her own respect.'

She began to expostulate with her jailor; but he sternly bade her 'Be silent – he had not gone so far, not to go further.'

Darnford came in the evening. Jemima was obliged to be absent, and she, as usual, locked the door on them, to prevent interruption or discovery. – The lovers were, at first, embarrassed; but fell insensibly into confidential discourse. Darnford represented, 'that they might soon be parted', and wished her 'to put it out of the power of fate to separate them'.

As her husband she now received him, and he solemnly pledged himself as her protector – and eternal friend. –

There was one peculiarity in Maria's mind: she was more anxious not to deceive, than to guard against deception; and had rather trust without sufficient reason, than be for ever the prey of doubt. Besides, what are we, when the mind has, from reflection, a certain kind of elevation, which exalts the contemplation above the little concerns of prudence! We see what we wish, and make a world of our own – and, though reality may sometimes open a door to misery, yet the moments of happiness procured by the imagination, may, without a paradox, be reckoned among the solid comforts of life. Maria now, imagining that she had found a being of celestial mould – was happy, – nor was she deceived. – He was then plastic in her impassioned hand – and reflected all the sentiments which animated and warmed her.[47]

CHAPTER XVI

One morning confusion seemed to reign in the house, and Jemima came in terror, to inform Maria, 'that her master had left it, with a determination, she was assured (and too many circumstances corroborated the opinion, to leave a doubt of its truth) of never returning. I am prepared then,' said Jemima, 'to accompany you in your flight.'

Maria started up, her eyes darting towards the door, as if afraid that some one should fasten it on her for ever.

Jemima continued, 'I have perhaps no right now to expect the performance of your promise; but on you it depends to reconcile me with the human race.'

'But Darnford!' – exclaimed Maria, mournfully – sitting down again, and crossing her arms – 'I have no child to go to, and liberty has lost its sweets.'

'I am much mistaken, if Darnford is not the cause of my master's flight – his keepers assure me, that they have promised to confine him two days longer, and then he will be free – you cannot see him; but they will give a letter to him the moment he is free. – In that inform him where he may find you in London; fix on some hotel. Give me your clothes; I will send them out of the house with mine, and we will slip out at the garden-gate. Write your letter while I make these arrangements, but lose no time!'

In an agitation of spirit, not to be calmed, Maria began to write to Darnford. She called him by the sacred name of 'husband', and bade him 'hasten to her, to share her fortune, or she would return to him'. – An hotel in the Adelphi[48] was the place of rendezvous.

The letter was sealed and given in charge; and with light footsteps, yet terrified at the sound of them, she descended, scarcely breathing, and with an indistinct fear that she should never get out at the garden gate. Jemima went first.

A being, with a visage that would have suited one possessed by a devil, crossed the path, and seized Maria by the arm. Maria had no fear but of being detained – 'Who are you? what are you?' for the form was scarcely human. 'If you are made of flesh and blood,' his ghastly eyes glared on her, 'do not stop me!'

'Woman,' interrupted a sepulchral voice, 'what have I to do with thee?' – Still he grasped her hand, muttering a curse.

'No, no; you have nothing to do with me,' she exclaimed, 'this is a moment of life and death!' –

With supernatural force she broke from him, and, throwing her arms round Jemima, cried, 'Save me!' The being, from whose grasp she had loosed herself, took up a stone as they opened the door, and with a kind of hellish sport threw it after them. They were out of his reach.

When Maria arrived in town, she drove to the hotel already fixed on. But she could not sit still – her child was ever before her; and all that had passed during her confinement, appeared to be a dream. She went to the house in the suburbs, where, as she now discovered, her babe had been sent: The moment she entered, her heart grew sick; but she wondered not that it had proved its grave. She made the necessary enquiries, and the church-yard was pointed out, in which it rested under a turf. A little frock which the nurse's child wore (Maria had made it herself) caught her eye. The nurse was glad to sell it for half-a-guinea, and Maria hastened away with the relic, and, re-entering the hackney-coach which waited for her, gazed on it, till she reached her hotel.

She then waited on the attorney who had made her uncle's will, and explained to him her situation. He readily advanced her some of the money which still remained in his hands, and promised to take the whole of the case into consideration. Maria only wished to be permitted to remain in quiet – She found that several bills, apparently with her signature, had been presented to her agent, nor was she for a moment at a loss to guess by whom they had been forged; yet, equally averse to threaten or intreat, she requested her friend [the solicitor] to call on Mr Venables. He was not to be found at home; but at length his agent, the attorney, offered a conditional promise to Maria, to leave her in peace, as long as she behaved with propriety, if she would give up the notes. Maria inconsiderately consented – Darnford was arrived, and she wished to be only alive to love; she wished to forget the anguish she felt whenever she thought of her child.

They took a ready-furnished lodging together, for she was above disguise; Jemima insisting on being considered as her house-keeper, and to receive the customary stipend. On no other terms would she remain with her friend.

Darnford was indefatigable in tracing the mysterious circumstances of his confinement. The cause was simply, that a relation, a very distant one, to whom he was heir, had died, intestate, leaving a considerable fortune. On the news of Darnford's arrival [in England, a person, intrusted with the management of the property, and who had the writings in his possession, determining, by one bold stroke, to strip Darnford of the succession,] had planned his confinement; and [as soon as he had taken the measures he judged most conducive to his object, this ruffian, together with his instrument,] the keeper of the private mad-house, left the kingdom. Darnford, who still pursued his enquiries, at last discovered that they had fixed their place of refuge at Paris.

Maria and he determined therefore, with the faithful Jemima, to visit that metropolis, and accordingly were preparing for the journey, when they were informed that Mr Venables had commenced an action against Darnford for seduction and adultery. The indignation Maria felt cannot be explained; she repented of the forbearance she had exercised in giving up the notes. Darnford could not put off his journey, without risking the loss of his property: Maria therefore furnished him with money for his expedition; and determined to remain in London till the termination of this affair.

She visited some ladies with whom she had formerly been intimate, but was refused admittance; and at the opera, or Ranelagh,[49] they could not recollect her. Among these ladies there were some, not her most intimate acquaintance, who were generally supposed to avail themselves of the cloke of marriage, to conceal a mode of conduct, that would for ever have damned their fame, had they been innocent, seduced girls. These particularly stood aloof. – Had she remained with her husband, practising insincerity, and neglecting her child to manage an intrigue, she would still have been visited and respected. If, instead of openly living with her lover, she could have condescended to call into play a thousand arts, which, degrading her own mind, might have allowed the people who were not deceived, to pretend to be so, she would have been caressed and treated like an honourable woman.

'And Brutus* is an honourable man!' said Mark-Antony with equal sincerity.[50]

With Darnford she did not taste uninterrupted felicity; there was a volatility in his manner which often distressed her; but love gladdened the scene; besides, he was the most tender, sympathizing creature in the world. A fondness for the sex often gives an appearance of humanity to the behaviour of men, who have small pretensions to the reality; and they seem to love others, when they are only pursuing their own gratification. Darnford appeared ever willing to avail himself of her taste and acquirements, while she endeavoured to profit by his decision of character, and to eradicate some of the romantic notions, which had taken root in her mind, while in adversity she had brooded over visions of unattainable bliss.

The real affections of life, when they are allowed to burst forth, are buds pregnant with joy and all the sweet emotions of the soul; yet they branch out with wild ease, unlike the artificial forms of felicity, sketched by an imagination painful alive. The substantial happiness, which enlarges and civilizes the mind, may be compared to the pleasure experienced in roving through nature at large, inhaling the sweet gale natural to the clime; while the reveries of a feverish imagination continually sport themselves in gardens full of aromatic shrubs, which cloy while they delight, and weaken the sense of pleasure they gratify. The heaven of fancy, below or beyond the stars, in this life, or in those ever-smiling regions surrounded by the unmarked ocean of futurity, have an insipid uniformity which palls. Poets have imagined scenes of bliss; but, fencing out sorrow, all the extatic emotions of the soul, and even its grandeur, seem to be equally excluded. We dose over the unruffled lake, and long to scale the rocks which fence the happy valley of contentment, though serpents hiss in the pathless desert, and danger lurks in the unexplored wiles.[51] Maria found herself more indulgent as she was happier, and discovered virtues, in characters, she had before disregarded, while chasing the phantoms of elegance and excellence, which sported in the meteors that exhale in the marshes of misfortune. The heart is often shut by romance against social pleasure; and, fostering a sickly sensibility, grows callous to the soft touches of humanity.

To part with Darnford was indeed cruel. — It was to feel most painfully alone; but she rejoiced to think, that she should spare him the care and perplexity of the suit, and meet him again, all his own. Marriage, as at present constituted, she considered as leading to immorality — yet, as the odium of society impedes usefulness, she wished to avow her affection to Darnford, by becoming his wife, according to established rules; not to be confounded with women who act from very different motives, though her conduct would be just the same without the ceremony as with it, and her expectations from him not less firm. The being summoned to defend herself from a charge which she was determined to plead guilty to, was still galling, as it roused bitter reflections on the situation of women in society.

* The name in the manuscript is by mistake written Caesar.

CHAPTER XVII

Such was her state of mind when the dogs of law were let loose on her. Maria took the task of conducting Darnford's defence upon herself. She instructed his counsel to plead guilty to the charge of adultery; but to deny that of seduction.

The counsel for the plaintiff opened the cause, by observing, 'that his client had ever been an indulgent husband, and had borne with several defects of temper, while he had nothing criminal to lay to the charge of his wife. But that she left his house without assigning any cause. He could not assert that she was then acquainted with the defendant; yet, when he was once endeavouring to bring her back to her home, this man put the peace-officers to flight, and took her he knew not whither. After the birth of her child, her conduct was so strange, and a melancholy malady having afflicted one of the family, which delicacy forbade the dwelling on, it was necessary to confine her. By some means the defendant enabled her to make her escape, and they had lived together, in despite of all sense of order and decorum. The adultery was allowed, it was not necessary to bring any witnesses to prove it; but the seduction, though highly probable from the circumstances which he had the honour to state, could not be so clearly proved. – It was of the most atrocious kind, as decency was set at defiance, and respect for reputation, which shows internal compunction, utterly disregarded.'

A strong sense of injustice had silenced every emotion, which a mixture of true and false delicacy might otherwise have excited in Maria's bosom. She only felt in earnest to insist on the privilege of her nature. The sarcasms of society, and the condemnation of a mistaken world, were nothing to her, compared with acting contrary to those feelings which were the foundation of her principles. [She therefore eagerly put herself forward, instead of desiring to be absent, on this memorable occasion.]

Convinced that the subterfuges of the law were disgraceful, she wrote a paper, which she expressly desired might be read in court:

'Married when scarcely able to distinguish the nature of the engagement, I yet submitted to the rigid laws which enslave women, and obeyed the man whom I could no longer love. Whether the duties of the state are reciprocal, I mean not to discuss; but I can prove repeated infidelities which I overlooked or pardoned.[52] Witnesses are not wanting to establish these facts. I at present maintain the child of a maid-servant, sworn to him, and born after our marriage. I am ready to allow, that education and circumstances lead men to think and act with less delicacy, than the preservation of order in society demands from women; but surely I may without assumption declare, that, though I could excuse the birth, I could not the desertion of this unfortunate babe: – and, while I despised the man, it was not easy to venerate the husband. With proper restrictions however, I revere the institution which fraternizes the world. I exclaim against the laws which throw the whole weight of the yoke on the weaker shoulders, and force women, when they claim protectorship as mothers, to sign a contract, which renders them dependent on the caprice of the tyrant, whom choice or necessity has appointed to reign over them. Various are the cases, in which a woman ought to separate herself from her husband; and mine, I may be allowed emphatically to insist, comes under the description of the most aggravated.

'I will not enlarge on those provocations which only the individual can estimate; but will bring forward such charges only, the truth of which is an insult upon humanity. In order to promote destructive speculations, Mr Venables prevailed on me to borrow certain sums of a wealthy relation; and, when I refused further compliance, he thought of bartering my person; and not only allowed opportunities to, but urged, a friend from whom he borrowed money, to seduce me. On the discovery of this act of atrocity, I determined to leave him, and in the most decided manner, for ever. I consider all obligation as made void by his conduct; and hold, that schisms which proceed from want of principles, can never be healed.

'He received a fortune with me to the amount of five thousand pounds. On the death of my uncle, convinced that I could provide for my child, I destroyed the settlement of that fortune. I required none of my property to be returned to me, nor shall enumerate the sums extorted from me during six years that we lived together.

'After leaving, what the law considers as my home, I was hunted like a criminal from place to place, though I contracted no debts, and demanded no maintenance – yet, as the laws sanction such proceeding, and make women the property of their husbands, I forbear to animadvert. After the birth of my daughter, and the death of my uncle, who left a very considerable fortune to myself and child, I was exposed to new persecution; and, because I had, before arriving at what is termed years of discretion, pledged my faith, I was treated by the world, as bound for ever to a man whose vices were notorious. Yet what are the vices generally known, to the various miseries that a woman may be subject to, which, though deeply felt, eating into the soul, elude description, and may be glossed over! A false morality is even established, which makes all the virtue of woman consist in chastity, submission, and the forgiveness of injuries.

'I pardon my oppressor – bitterly as I lament the loss of my child, torn from me in the most violent manner. But nature revolts, and my soul sickens at the bare supposition, that it could ever be a duty to pretend affection, when a separation is necessary to prevent my feeling hourly aversion.

'To force me to give my fortune, I was imprisoned – yes; in a private mad-house. – There, in the heart of misery, I met the man charged with seducing me. We became attached – I deemed, and ever shall deem, myself free. The death of my babe dissolved the only tie which subsisted between me and my, what is termed, lawful husband.

'To this person, thus encountered, I voluntarily gave myself, never considering myself as any more bound to transgress the laws of moral purity, because the will of my husband might be pleaded in my excuse, than to transgress those laws to which [the policy of artificial society has] annexed [positive] punishments. – While no command of a husband can prevent a woman from suffering for certain crimes, she must be allowed to consult her conscience, and regulate her conduct, in some degree, by her own sense of right. The respect I owe to myself, demanded my strict adherence to my determination of never viewing Mr Venables in the light of a husband, nor could it forbid me from encouraging another. If I am unfortunately united to an unprincipled man, am I for ever to be shut out from fulfilling the duties of a wife and mother?[53] – I wish my country to approve of my conduct; but, if laws exist, made by the strong to oppress the weak, I appeal to my own sense of justice, and declare that I will not live with the individual, who has violated every moral obligation which binds man to man.

'I protest equally against any charge being brought to criminate the man, whom I consider as my husband. I was six-and-twenty when I left Mr Venables' roof; if ever I am to be supposed to arrive at an age to direct my own actions, I must by that time have arrived at it. – I acted with deliberation. – Mr Darnford found me a forlorn and oppressed woman, and promised the protection women in the present state of society want. – But the man who now claims me – was he deprived of my society by this conduct? The question is an insult to common sense, considering where Mr Darnford met me. – Mr Venables' door was indeed open to me – nay, threats and intreaties were used to induce me to return; but why? Was affection or honour the motive? – I cannot, it is true, dive into the recesses of the human heart – yet I presume to assert, [borne out as I am by a variety of circumstances,] that he was merely influenced by the most rapacious avarice.

'I claim then a divorce, and the liberty of enjoying, free from molestation, the fortune left to me by a relation, who was well aware of the character of the man with whom I had to contend. – I appeal to the justice and humanity of the jury – a body of men, whose private judgment must be allowed to modify laws, that must be unjust, because definite rules can never apply to indefinite circumstances – and I deprecate punishment [upon the man of my choice, freeing him, as I solemnly do, from the charge of seduction.]

'I did not put myself into a situation to justify a charge of adultery, till I had, from conviction, shaken off the fetters which bound me to Mr Venables. – While I lived with him, I defy the voice of calumny to sully what is termed the fair fame of woman. – Neglected by my husband, I never encouraged a lover; and preserved with scrupulous care, what is termed my honour, at the expence of my peace, till he, who should have been its guardian, laid traps to ensnare me. From that moment I believed myself, in the sight of heaven, free – and no power on earth shall force me to renounce my resolution.'

The judge, in summing up the evidence, alluded to 'the fallacy of letting women plead their feelings, as an excuse for the violation of the marriage-vow. For his part, he had always determined to oppose all innovation, and the new-fangled notions which incroached on the good old rules of conduct. We did not want French principles in public or private life – and, if women were allowed to plead their feelings, as an excuse or palliation of infidelity, it was opening a flood-gate for immorality. What virtuous woman thought of her feelings? – It was her duty to love and obey the man chosen by her parents and relations, who were qualified by their experience to judge better for her, than she could for herself. As to the charges brought against the husband, they were vague, supported by no witnesses, excepting that of imprisonment in a private mad-house. The proofs of an insanity in the family, might render that however a prudent measure; and indeed the conduct of the lady did not appear that of a person of sane mind. Still such a mode of proceeding could not be justified, and might perhaps entitle the lady [in another court] to a sentence of separation from bed and board, during the joint lives of the parties;[54] but he hoped that no Englishman would legalize adultery, by enabling the adulteress to enrich her seducer. Too many restrictions could not be thrown in the way of divorces, if we wished to maintain the sanctity of marriage; and, though they might bear a little hard on a few, very few individuals, it was evidently for the good of the whole.'

CONCLUSION

BY THE EDITOR

Very few hints exist respecting the plan of the remainder of the work. I find only two detached sentences, and some scattered heads for the continuation of the story. I transcribe the whole.

I

'Darnford's letters were affectionate; but circumstances occasioned delays, and the miscarriage of some letters rendered the reception of wished-for answers doubtful: his return was necessary to calm Maria's mind.'

II

'As Darnford had informed her that his business was settled, his delaying to return seemed extraordinary; but love to excess, excludes fear or suspicion.'

The scattered heads for the continuation of the story, are as follow.*

I

'Trial for adultery – Maria defends herself – A separation from bed and board is the consequence – Her fortune is thrown into chancery – Darnford obtains a part of his property – Maria goes into the country.'

II

'A prosecution for adultery commenced – Trial – Darnford sets out for France – Letters – Once more pregnant – He returns – Mysterious behaviour – Visit – Expectation – Discovery – Interview – Consequence.'

III

'Sued by her husband – Damages awarded to him – Separation from bed and

* To understand these minutes, it is necessary the reader should consider each of them as setting out from the same point in the story, *viz.* the point to which it is brought down in the preceding chapter.

board – Darnford goes abroad – Maria into the country – Provides for her
father – Is shunned – Returns to London – Expects to see her lover – The
rack of expectation – Finds herself again with child – Delighted – A
discovery – A visit – A miscarriage – Conclusion.'

IV

'Divorced by her husband – Her lover unfaithful – Pregnancy – Miscarriage
– Suicide.'

[The following passage appears in some respects to deviate from the
preceding hints. It is superscribed.]

'THE END.

'She swallowed the laudanum; her soul was calm – the tempest had subsided
– and nothing remained but an eager longing to forget herself – to fly from
the anguish she endured to escape from thought – from this hell of
disappointment.

'Still her eyes closed not – one remembrance with frightful velocity
followed another – All the incidents of her life were in arms, embodied to
assail her, and prevent her sinking into the sleep of death. – Her murdered
child again appeared to her, mourning for the babe of which she was the
tomb. – "And could it have a nobler? – Surely it is better to die with me,
than to enter on life without a mother's care! I cannot live! – but could I
have deserted my child the moment it was born? – thrown it on the
troubled wave of life, without a hand to support it?" – She looked up:
"What have I not suffered! – may I find a father where I am going!" – Her
head turned; a stupor ensued; a faintness – "Have a little patience," said
Maria, holding her swimming head (she thought of her mother), "this
cannot last long; and what is a little bodily pain to the pangs I have
endured?"

'A new vision swam before her. Jemima seemed to enter – leading a little
creature, that, with tottering footsteps, approached the bed. The voice of
Jemima sounding as at a distance, called her – she tried to listen, to speak, to
look!

'"Behold your child!" exclaimed Jemima. Maria started off the bed, and
fainted. – Violent vomiting followed.

When she was restored to life, Jemima addressed her with great solemnity: "——— led me to suspect, that your husband and brother had deceived
you, and secreted the child. I would not torment you with doubtful hopes,
and I left you (at a fatal moment) to search for the child! – I snatched her
from misery – and (now she is alive again) would you leave her alone in the
world, to endure what I have endured?"

ized wildly at her, her whole frame was convulsed with emotion;
child, whom Jemima had been tutoring all the journey, uttered
'Mamma!" She caught her to her bosom, and burst into a passion
then, resting the child gently on the bed, as if afraid of killing it, –
she put her hand to her eyes, to conceal as it were the agonizing struggle of
her soul. She remained silent for five minutes, crossing her arms over her
bosom, and reclining her head, – then exclaimed: "The conflict is over! I will
live for my child!" '

A few readers perhaps, in looking over these hints, will wonder how it could
have been practicable, without tediousness, or remitting in any degree the
interest of the story, to have filled, from these slight sketches, a number of
pages, more considerable than those which have been already presented.
But, in reality, these hints, simple as they are, are pregnant with passion and
distress. It is the refuge of barren authors, only, to crowd their fictions with
so great a number of events, as to suffer no one of them to sink into the
reader's mind. It is the province of true genius to develop events, to
discover their capabilities, to ascertain the different passions and sentiments
with which they are fraught, and to diversify them with incidents, that give
reality to the picture, and take a hold upon the mind of a reader of taste,
from which they can never be loosened. It was particularly the design of the
author, in the present instance, to make her story subordinate to a great
moral purpose, that 'of exhibiting the misery and oppression, peculiar to
women, that arise out of the partial laws and customs of society. – This view
restrained her fancy.'* It was necessary for her, to place in a striking point
of view, evils that are too frequently overlooked, and to drag into light those
details of oppression, of which the grosser and more insensible part of
mankind make little account.

* See author's preface.

Matilda

MATILDA

CHAPTER I

It is only four o'clock; but it is winter and the sun has already set: there are
no clouds in the clear, frosty sky to reflect its slant beams, but the air itself is
tinged with a slight roseate colour which is again reflected on the snow that
covers the ground. I live in a lone cottage on a solitary, wide heath: no voice
of life reaches me. I see the desolate plain covered with white, save a few
black patches that the noonday sun has made at the top of those sharp
pointed hillocks from which the snow, sliding as it fell, lay thinner than on
the plain ground: a few birds are pecking at the hard ice that covers the
pools – for the frost has been of long continuance.

I am in a strange state of mind. I am alone – quite alone – in the world –
the blight of misfortune has passed over me and withered me; I know that I
am about to die and I feel happy – joyous. – I feel my pulse; it beats fast: I
place my thin hand on my cheek; it burns: there is a slight, quick spirit
within me which is now emitting its last sparks. I shall never see the snows
of another winter – I do believe that I shall never again feel the vivifying
warmth of another summer sun; and it is in this persuasion that I begin to
write my tragic history. Perhaps a history such as mine had better die with
me, but a feeling that I cannot define leads me on and I am too weak both in
body and mind to resist the slightest impulse. While life was strong within
me I thought indeed that there was a sacred horror in my tale that rendered
it unfit for utterance, and now about to die I pollute its mystic terrors. It is
as the wood of the Eumenides none but the dying may enter; and Oedipus is
about to die.[1]

What am I writing? – I must collect my thoughts. I do not know that
any will peruse these pages except you, my friend, who will receive them
at my death. I do not address them to you alone because it will give me
pleasure to dwell upon our friendship in a way that would be needless if
you alone read what I shall write. I shall relate my tale therefore as if I
wrote for strangers. You have often asked me the cause of my solitary life;
my tears; and above all of my impenetrable and unkind silence. In life I
dared not; in death I unveil the mystery. Others will toss these pages
lightly over: to you, Woodville, kind, affectionate friend, they will be dear
– the precious memorials of a heart-broken girl who, dying, is still
warmed by gratitude towards you: your tears will fall on the words that

record my misfortunes; I know they will – and while I have life I thank you for your sympathy.

But enough of this. I will begin my tale: it is my last task, and I hope I have strength sufficient to fulfil it. I record no crimes; my faults may easily be pardoned; for they proceeded not from evil motive but from want of judgement; and I believe few would say that they could, by a different conduct and superior wisdom, have avoided the misfortunes to which I am the victim. My fate has been governed by necessity, a hideous necessity. It required hands stronger than mine; stronger I do believe than any human force to break the thick, adamantine chain that has bound me, once breathing nothing but joy, ever possessed by a warm love and delight in goodness, – to misery only to be ended, and now about to be ended, in death. But I forget myself, my tale is yet untold. I will pause a few moments, wipe my dim eyes, and endeavour to lose the present obscure but heavy feeling of unhappiness in the more acute emotions of the past.

I was born in England. My father was a man of rank: he had lost his father early, and was educated by a weak mother with all the indulgence she thought due to a nobleman of wealth. He was sent to Eton and afterwards to college; and allowed from childhood the free use of large sums of money; thus enjoying from his earliest youth the independance which a boy with these advantages, always acquires at a public school.

Under the influence of these circumstances his passions found a deep soil wherein they might strike their roots and flourish either as flowers or weeds as was their nature. By being always allowed to act for himself his character became strongly and early marked and exhibited a various surface on which a quick sighted observer might see the seeds of virtues and of misfortunes. His careless extravagance, which made him squander immense sums of money to satisfy passing whims, which from their apparent energy he dignified with the name of passions, often displayed itself in unbounded generosity. Yet while he earnestly occupied himself about the wants of others his own desires were gratified to their fullest extent. He gave his money, but none of his own wishes were sacrifised to his gifts; he gave his time, which he did not value, and his affections which he was happy in any manner to have called into action.

I do not say that if his own desires had been put in competition with those of others that he would have displayed undue selfishness, but this trial was never made. He was nurtured in prosperity and attended by all its advantages; every one loved him and wished to gratify him. He was ever employed in promoting the pleasures of his companions – but their pleasures were his; and if he bestowed more attention upon the feelings of others than is usual with schoolboys it was because his social temper could never enjoy itself if every brow was not as free from care as his own.

While at school, emulation and his own natural abilities made him hold a conspicuous rank in the forms among his equals; at college he discarded books; he believed that he had other lessons to learn than those which they could teach him. He was now to enter into life and he was still young enough to consider study as a school-boy shackle, employed merely to keep the unruly out of mischief but as having no real connexion with life – whose wisdom of riding – gaming etc. he considered with far deeper interest – So he quickly entered into all college follies although his heart was too well moulded to be contaminated by them – it might be light but it was never cold. He was a sincere and sympathizing friend – but he had met with none who superior or equal to himself could aid him in unfolding his mind, or make him seek for fresh stores of thought by exhausting the old ones. He felt himself superior in quickness of judgement to those around him: his talents, his rank and wealth made him the chief of his party, and in that station he rested not only contented but glorying, conceiving it to be the only ambition worthy for him to aim at in the world.

By a strange narrowness of ideas he viewed all the world in connexion only as it was or was not related to his little society. He considered queer and out of fashion all opinions that were exploded by his circle of intimates, and he became at the same time dogmatic and yet fearful of not coinciding with the only sentiments he could consider orthodox. To the generality of spectators he appeared careless of censure, and with high disdain to throw aside all dependance on public prejudices; but at the same time that he strode with a triumphant stride over the rest of the world, he cowered, with self disguised lowliness, to his own party, and although its chief never dared express an opinion or a feeling until he was assured that it would meet with the approbation of his companions.

Yet he had one secret hidden from these dear friends; a secret he had nurtured from his earliest years, and although he loved his fellow collegiates he would not trust it to the delicacy or sympathy of any one among them. He loved. He feared that the intensity of his passion might become the subject of their ridicule; and he could not bear that they should blaspheme it by considering that trivial and transitory which he felt was the life of his life.

There was a gentleman of small fortune who lived near his family mansion who had three lovely daughters. The eldest was far the most beautiful, but her beauty was only an addition to her other qualities – her understanding was clear and strong and her disposition angelically gentle. She and my father had been playmates from infancy: Diana, even in her childhood had been a favourite with his mother; this partiality encreased with the years of this beautiful and lively girl and thus during his school and college vacations they were perpetually together. Novels and all the various methods by which youth in civilized life are led to a knowledge of the existence of passions before they really feel them, had produced a strong effect on him who was so peculiarly susceptible of every impression. At eleven years of age Diana was his favourite playmate but he already talked the language of love. Although she was elder than he by nearly two years the nature of her education made her more childish at least in the knowledge and expression of feeling; she received his warm protestations with innocence, and returned them unknowing of what they meant. She had read no novels and associated only with her younger sisters, what could she know of the difference between love and friendship? And when the development of her understanding disclosed the true nature of this intercourse to her, her affections were already engaged to her friend, and all she feared was lest other attractions and fickleness might make him break his infant vows.

But they became every day more ardent and tender. It was a passion that had grown with his growth; it had become entwined with every faculty and every sentiment and only to be lost with life. None knew of their love except their own two hearts; yet although in all things else, and even in this he dreaded the censure of his companions, for thus truly loving one inferior to him in fortune, nothing was ever able for a moment to shake his purpose of uniting himself to her as soon as he could muster courage sufficient to meet those difficulties he was determined to surmount.

Diana was fully worthy of his deepest affection. There were few who could boast of so pure a heart, and so much real humbleness of soul joined to a firm reliance on her own integrity and a belief in that of others. She had from her birth lived a retired life. She had lost her mother when very young, but her father had devoted himself to the care of her education – He had many peculiar ideas which influenced the system he had adopted with regard to her – She was well acquainted with the heroes of Greece and Rome or with those of England who had lived some hundred years ago, while she was nearly ignorant of the passing events of the day: she had read few authors who had written during at least the last fifty years but her reading with this exception was very extensive. Thus although she appeared to be less initiated in the mysteries of life and society than he her knowledge was of a deeper kind and laid on firmer foundations; and if even her beauty and sweetness had not fascinated him her understanding would ever have held his in thrall. He looked up to her as his guide, and such was his adoration that he delighted to augment to his own mind the sense of inferiority with which she sometimes impressed him.

When he was nineteen his mother died. He left college on this event and shaking off for a while his old friends he retired to the neighbourhood of his Diana and received all his consolation from her sweet voice and dearer caresses. This short separation from his companions gave him courage to assert his independance. He had a feeling that however they might express ridicule of his intended marriage they would not dare display it when it had taken place; therefore seeking the consent of his guardian which with some difficulty he obtained, and of the father of his mistress which was more easily given, without acquainting any one else of his intention, by the time he had attained his twentieth birthday he had become the husband of Diana.

He loved her with passion and her tenderness had a charm for him that would not permit him to think of aught but her. He invited some of his college friends to see him but their frivolity disgusted him. Diana had torn the veil which had before kept him in his boyhood: he was become a man and he was surprised how he could ever have joined in the cant words and ideas of his fellow collegiates or how for a moment he had feared the censure of such as these. He discarded his old friendships not from fickleness but because they were indeed unworthy of him. Diana filled up all his heart: he felt as if by his union with her he had received a new and better soul. She was his monitress as he learned what were the true ends of life. It was through her beloved lessons that he cast off his old pursuits and gradually formed himself to become one among his fellow men; a distinguished member of society, a Patriot; and an enlightened lover of truth and virtue. – He loved her for her beauty and for her amiable disposition but he seemed to love her more for what he considered her superior wisdom. They studied, they rode together; they were never separate and seldom admitted a third to their society.

Thus my father, born in affluence, and always prosperous, clombe without the difficulty and various disappointments that all human beings seem destined to encounter, to the very topmost pinacle of happiness: Around him was sunshine, and clouds whose shapes of beauty made the prospect divine concealed from him the barren reality which lay hidden below them. From this dizzy point he was dashed at once as he unawares congratulated himself on his felicity. Fifteen months after their marriage I was born, and my mother died a few days after my birth.

A sister of my father was with him at this period. She was nearly fifteen years older than he, and was the offspring of a former marriage of his father. When the latter died this sister was taken by her maternal relations: they had seldom seen one another, and were quite unlike in disposition. This aunt, to whose care I was afterwards consigned, has often related to me the effect that this catastrophe had on my father's strong and susceptible character. From the moment of my mother's death untill his departure she never heard him utter a single word: buried in the deepest melancholy he took no notice of any one; often for hours his eyes streamed tears or a more fearful gloom overpowered him. All outward things seemed to have lost their existence relatively to him and only one circumstance could in any degree recall him from his motionless and mute despair: he would never see me. He seemed insensible to the presence of any one else, but if, as a trial to awaken his sensibility, my aunt brought me into the room he would instantly rush out with every symptom of fury and distraction. At the end of a month he suddenly quitted his house and, unattended by any servant, departed from that part of the country without by word or writing informing any one of his intentions. My aunt was only relieved of her anxiety concerning his fate by a letter from him dated Hamburgh.

How often have I wept over that letter which until I was sixteen was the only relic I had to remind me of my parents. 'Pardon me,' it said, 'for the uneasiness I have unavoidably given you: but while in that unhappy island, where every thing breathes *her* spirit whom I have lost for ever, a spell held me. It is broken: I have quitted England for many years, perhaps for ever.

But to convince you that selfish feeling does not entirely engross me I shall remain in this town until you have made by letter every arrangement that you judge necessary. When I leave this place do not expect to hear from me: I must break all ties that at present exist. I shall become a wanderer, a miserable outcast – alone! alone!' – In another part of the letter he mentioned me – 'As for that unhappy little being whom I could not see, and hardly dare mention, I leave her under your protection. Take care of her and cherish her: one day I may claim her at your hands; but futurity is dark, make the present happy to her.'

My father remained three months at Hamburg; when he quitted it he changed his name, my aunt could never discover that which he adopted and only by faint hints, could conjecture that he had taken the road of Germany and Hungary to Turkey.

Thus this towering spirit who had excited interest and high expectation in all who knew and could value him became at once, as it were, extinct. He existed from this moment for himself only. His friends remembered him as a brilliant vision which would never again return to them. The memory of what he had been faded away as years passed; and he who before had been as a part of themselves and of their hopes was now no longer counted among the living.

CHAPTER II

I now come to my own story. During the early part of my life there is little to relate, and I will be brief; but I must be allowed to dwell a little on the years of my childhood that it may be apparent how when one hope failed all life was to be a blank; and how when the only affection I was permitted to cherish was blasted my existence was extinguished with it.

I have said that my aunt was very unlike my father. I believe that without the slightest tinge of a bad heart she had the coldest that ever filled a human breast: it was totally incapable of any affection. She took me under her protection because she considered it her duty; but she had too long lived alone and undisturbed by the noise and prattle of children to allow that I should disturb her quiet. She had never been married; and for the last five years had lived perfectly alone on an estate, that had descended to her through her mother, on the shores of Loch Lomond in Scotland. My father had expressed a wish in his letters that she should reside with me at his family mansion which was situated in a beautiful country near Richmond in Yorkshire. She would not consent to this proposition, but as soon as she had arranged the affairs which her brother's departure had caused to fall to her care, she quitted England and took me with her to her scotch estate.

The care of me while a baby, and afterwards until I had reached my eighth year devolved on a servant of my mother's, who had accompanied us in our retirement for that purpose. I was placed in a remote part of the house, and only saw my aunt at stated hours. These occurred twice a day; once about noon she came to my nursery, and once after her dinner I was taken to her. She never caressed me, and seemed all the time I stayed in the room to fear that I should annoy her by some childish freak. My good nurse always schooled me with the greatest care before she ventured into the parlour – and the awe my aunt's cold looks and few constrained words inspired was so great that I seldom disgraced her lessons or was betrayed from the exemplary stillness which I was taught to observe during these short visits.

Under my good nurse's care I ran wild about our park and the neighbouring fields. The offspring of the deepest love I displayed from my earliest years the greatest sensibility of disposition. I cannot say with what passion I loved every thing even the inanimate objects that surrounded me. I believe that I bore an individual attachment to every tree in our park; every animal that inhabited it knew me and I loved them. Their occasional deaths filled my infant heart with anguish. I cannot number the birds that I have saved during the long and severe winters of that climate; or the hares and rabbits that I have defended from the attacks of our dogs, or have nursed when accidentally wounded.

When I was seven years of age my nurse left me. I now forget the cause of her departure if indeed I ever knew it. She returned to England, and the bitter tears she shed at parting were the last I saw flow for love of me for many years. My grief was terrible: I had no friend but her in the whole world. By degrees I became reconciled to solitude but no one supplied her place in my affections. I lived in a desolate country where

> ———— there were none to praise
> And very few to love.*

It is true that I now saw a little more of my aunt, but she was in every way an unsocial being; and to a timid child she was as a plant beneath a thick covering of ice; I should cut my hands in endeavouring to get at it. So I was entirely thrown upon my own resources. The neighbouring minister was engaged to give me lessons in reading, writing and french, but he was without family and his manners even to me were always perfectly characteristic of the profession in the exercise of whose functions he chiefly shone, that of a schoolmaster. I sometimes strove to form friendships with the most attractive of the girls who inhabited the neighbouring village; but I believe I

* Wordsworth.[2]

should never have succeeded even had not my aunt interposed her authority to prevent all intercourse between me and the peasantry; for she was fearful lest I should acquire the scotch accent and dialect; a little of it I had, although great pains was taken that my tongue should not disgrace my English origin.

As I grew older my liberty increased with my desires, and my wanderings extended from our park to the neighbouring country. Our house was situated on the shores of the lake and the lawn came down to the water's edge. I rambled amidst the wild scenery of this lovely country and became a complete mountaineer: I passed hours on the steep brow of a mountain that overhung a waterfall or rowed myself in a little skiff to some one of the islands. I wandered for ever about these lovely solitudes, gathering flower after flower

> Ond' era pinta tutta la mia via*

singing as I might the wild melodies of the country, or occupied by pleasant day dreams. My greatest pleasure was the enjoyment of a serene sky amidst these verdant woods: yet I loved all the changes of Nature; and rain, and storm, and the beautiful clouds of heaven brought their delights with them. When rocked by the waves of the lake my spirits rose in triumph as a horseman feels with pride the motions of his high fed steed.

But my pleasures arose from the contemplation of nature alone, I had no companion: my warm affections finding no return from any other human heart were forced to run waste on inanimate objects. Sometimes indeed I wept when my aunt received my caresses with repulsive coldness, and when I looked round and found none to love; but I quickly dried my tears. As I grew older books in some degree supplied the place of human intercourse: the library of my aunt was very small; Shakespeare, Milton, Pope and Cowper were the strangely assorted poets of her collection; and among the prose authors a translation of Livy and Rollin's[4] ancient history were my chief favourites although as I emerged from childhood I found others highly interesting which I had before neglected as dull.

When I was twelve years old it occurred to my aunt that I ought to learn music; she herself played upon the harp. It was with great hesitation that she persuaded herself to undertake my instruction; yet believing this accomplishment a necessary part of my education, and balancing the evils of this measure or of having some one in the house to instruct me she submitted to the inconvenience. A harp was sent for that my playing might not interfere with hers, and I began: she found me a docile and when I had conquered the first rudiments a very apt scholar. I had acquired in my harp a companion in rainy days; a sweet soother of my feelings when any untoward accident ruffled them: I often addressed it as my only friend; I could pour forth to it

* Dante.[5]

my hopes and loves, and I fancied that its sweet accents answered me. I have now mentioned all my studies.

I was a solitary being, and from my infant years, ever since my dear nurse left me, I had been a dreamer. I brought Rosalind and Miranda and the lady of Comus to life to be my companions, or on my isle acted over their parts imagining myself to be in their situations.[5] Then I wandered from the fancies of others and formed affections and intimacies with the aerial creations of my own brain – but still clinging to reality I gave a name to these conceptions and nursed them in the hope of realization. I clung to the memory of my parents; my mother I should never see, she was dead: but the idea of my unhappy, wandering father was the idol of my imagination. I bestowed on him all my affections; there was a miniature of him that I gazed on continually; I copied his last letter and read it again and again. Sometimes it made me weep; and at other times I repeated with transport those words, – 'One day I may claim her at your hands.' I was to be his consoler, his companion in after years. My favourite vision was that when I grew up I would leave my aunt, whose coldness lulled my conscience, and disguised like a boy I would seek my father through the world. My imagination hung upon the scene of recognition; his miniature, which I should continually wear exposed on my breast, would be the means and I imaged the moment to my mind a thousand and a thousand times, perpetually varying the circumstances. Sometimes it would be in a desert; in a populous city; at a ball; we should perhaps meet in a vessel; and his first words constantly were, 'My daughter, I love thee'! What ecstatic moments have I passed in these dreams! How many tears I have shed; how often have I laughed aloud.

This was my life for sixteen years. At fourteen and fifteen I often thought that the time was come when I should commence my pilgrimage, which I had cheated my own mind into believing was my imperious duty: but a reluctance to quit my Aunt; a remorse for the grief which, I could not conceal from myself, I should occasion her for ever withheld me. Sometimes when I had planned the next morning for my escape a word of more than usual affection from her lips made me postpone my resolution. I reproached myself bitterly for what I called a culpable weakness; but this weakness returned upon me whenever the critical moment approached, and I never found courage to depart.

CHAPTER III

It was on my sixteenth birthday that my aunt received a letter from my father. I cannot describe the tumult of emotions that arose within me as I read it. It was dated from London; he had returned! I could only relieve my transports by tears, tears of unmingled joy. He had returned, and he wrote to know whether my aunt would come to London or whether he should visit her in Scotland. How delicious to me were the words of his letter that concerned me: 'I cannot tell you,' it said, 'how ardently I desire to see my Matilda. I look on her as the creature who will form the happiness of my future life: she is all that exists on earth that interests me. I can hardly prevent myself from hastening immediately to you but I am necessarily detained a week and I write because if you come here I may see you somewhat sooner.' I read these words with devouring eyes; I kissed them, wept over them and exclaimed, 'He will love me!' –

My aunt would not undertake so long a journey, and in a fortnight we had another letter from my father, it was dated Edinburgh: he wrote that he should be with us in three days. 'As he approached his desire of seeing me,' he said, 'became more and more ardent, and he felt that the moment when he should first clasp me in his arms would be the happiest of his life.'

How irksome were these three days to me! All sleep and appetite fled from me; I could only read and re-read his letter, and in the solitude of the woods imagine the moment of our meeting. On the eve of the third day I retired early to my room; I could not sleep but paced all night about my chamber and, as you may in Scotland at midsummer, watched the crimson track of the sun as it almost skirted the northern horizon. At day break I hastened to the woods; the hours past on while I indulged in wild dreams that gave wings to the slothful steps of time, and beguiled my eager impatience. My father was expected at noon but when I wished to return to meet him I found that I had lost my way: it seemed that in every attempt to find it I only became more involved in the intracacies of the woods, and the trees hid all trace by which I might be guided. I grew impatient, I wept; and wrung my hands but still I could not discover my path.

It was past two o'clock when by a sudden turn I found myself close to the lake near a cove where a little skiff was moored – It was not far from our house and I saw my father and aunt walking on the lawn. I jumped into the boat, and well accustomed to such feats, I pushed it from the shore, and exerted all my strength to row swiftly across. As I came, dressed in white, covered only by my tartan *rachan*,[6] my hair streaming on my shoulders, and shooting across with greater speed than it could be supposed I could give to my boat, my father has often told me that I looked more like a spirit than a human maid. I approached the shore, my father held the boat, I leapt lightly out, and in a moment was in his arms.

And now I began to live. All around me was changed from a dull uniformity to the brightest scene of joy and delight. The happiness I enjoyed in the company of my father far exceeded my sanguine expectations. We were for ever together; and the subjects of our conversations were inexhaustible. He had passed the sixteen years of absence among nations nearly unknown to Europe; he had wandered through Persia, Arabia and the north of India and had penetrated among the habitations of the natives with a freedom permitted to few Europeans. His relations of their manners, his anecdotes and descriptions of scenery whiled away delicious hours, when we were tired of talking of our own plans of future life.

The voice of affection was so new to me that I hung with delight upon words when he told me what he had felt concerning me during these long years of apparent forgetfulness. 'At first' – said he, 'I could not bear to think of my poor little girl; but afterwards as grief wore off and hope again revisited me I could only turn to her, and amidst cities and desarts her little fairy form, such as I imagined it, for ever flitted before me. The northern breeze as it refreshed me was sweeter and more balmy for it seemed to carry some of your spirit along with it. I often thought that I would instantly return and take you along with me to some fertile island where we should live at peace for ever. As I returned my fervent hopes were dashed by so many fears; my impatience became in the highest degree painful. I dared not think that the sun should shine and the moon rise not on your living form but on your grave. But, no, it is not so; I have my Matilda, my consolation, and my hope.' –

My father was very little changed from what he described himself to be before his misfortunes. It is intercourse with civilized society; it is the disappointment of cherished hopes, the falsehood of friends, or the perpetual clash of mean passions that changes the heart and damps the ardour of youthful feelings; lonely wanderings in a wild country among people of simple or savage manners may inure the body but will not tame the soul, or extinguish the ardour and freshness of feeling incident to youth. The burning sun of India, and the freedom from all restraint had rather encreased the energy of his character: before he bowed under, now he was impatient of any censure except that of his own mind. He had seen so many customs and witnessed so great a variety of moral creeds that he had been obliged to form an independant one for himself which had no relation to the peculiar notions of any one country: his early prejudices of course influenced his judgement in the formation of his principles, and some raw college ideas were strangely mingled with the deepest deductions of his penetrating mind.

The vacuity his heart endured of any deep interest in life during his long absence from his native country had had a singular effect upon his ideas. There was a curious feeling of unreality attached by him to his foreign life in comparison with the years of his youth. All the time he passed out of England was as a dream, and all the interest of his soul, all his affections belonged to events which had happened and persons who had existed sixteen years before. It was strange when you heard him talk to see how he passed over this lapse of time as a night of visions; while the remembrances of his youth standing separate as they did from his after life had lost none of their vigour. He talked of my Mother as if she had lived but a few weeks before; not that he expressed poignant grief, but his discription of her person, and his relation of all anecdotes connected with her was thus fervent and vivid.

In all this there was a strangeness that attracted and enchanted me. He was, as it were, now awakened from his long, visionary sleep, and he felt some what like one of the seven sleepers, or like Nourjahad,[7] in that sweet imitation of an eastern tale: Diana was gone; his friends were changed or dead, and now on his awakening I was all that he had to love on earth.

How dear to me were the waters, and mountains, and woods of Loch Lomond now that I had so beloved a companion for my rambles. I visited with my father every delightful spot, either on the islands, or by the side of the tree-sheltered waterfalls; every shady path, or dingle entangled with underwood and fern. My ideas were enlarged by his conversation. I felt as if I were recreated and had about me all the freshness and life of a new being: I was, as it were, transported since his arrival from a narrow spot of earth into a universe boundless to the imagination and the understanding. My life had been before as a pleasing country rill, never destined to leave its native fields, but when its task was fulfilled quietly to be absorbed, and leave no trace. Now it seemed to me to be as a various river flowing through a fertile and lovely lanscape, ever changing and ever beautiful. Alas! I knew not the desart it was about to reach; the rocks that would tear its waters, and the hideous scene that would be reflected in a more distorted manner in its waves. Life was then brilliant; I began to learn to hope and what brings a more bitter despair to the heart than hope destroyed?

Is it not strange that grief should quickly follow so divine a happiness? I drank of an enchanted cup but gall was at the bottom of its long drawn sweetness. My heart was full of deep affection, but it was calm from its very depth and fulness. I had no idea that misery could arise from love, and this lesson that all at last must learn was taught me in a manner few are obliged to receive it. I lament now, I must ever lament, those few short months of Paradisaical bliss; I disobeyed no command, I ate no apple, and yet I was ruthlessly driven from it. Alas! my companion did, and I was precipitated in his fall. But I wander from my relation – let woe come at its appointed time; I may at this stage of my story still talk of happiness.

Three months passed away in this delightful intercourse, when my aunt fell ill. I passed a whole month in her chamber nursing her, but her disease was mortal and she died, leaving me for some time inconsolable, Death is so dreadful to the living; the chains of habit are so strong even when affection does not link them that the heart must be agonized when they break. But my father was beside me to console me and to drive away bitter memories by bright hopes: methought that it was sweet to grieve that he might dry my tears.

Then again he distracted my thoughts from my sorrow by comparing it with his despair when he lost my mother. Even at that time I shuddered at the picture he drew of his passions: he had the imagination of a poet, and when he described the whirlwind that then tore his feelings he gave his words the impress of life so vividly that I believed while I trembled. I wondered how he could ever again have entered into the offices of life after his wild thoughts seemed to have given him affinity with the unearthly; while he spoke so tremendous were the ideas which he conveyed that it appeared as if the human heart were far too bounded for their conception. His feelings seemed better fitted for a spirit whose habitation is the earthquake and the volcano than for one confined to a mortal body and human lineaments. But these were merely memories; he was changed since then. He was now all love, all softness: and when I raised my eyes in wonder at him as he spoke the smile on his lips told me that his heart was possessed by the gentlest passions.

Two months after my aunt's death we removed to London where I was led by my father to attend to deeper studies than had before occupied me. My improvement was his delight; he was with me during all my studies and assisted or joined with me in every lesson. We saw a great deal of society, and no day passed that my father did not endeavour to embellish by some new enjoyment. The tender attachment that he bore me, and the love and veneration with which I returned it cast a charm over every moment. The hours were slow for each minute was employed; we lived more in one week than many do in the course of several months and the variety and novelty of our pleasures gave zest to each.

We perpetually made excursions together. And whether it were to visit beautiful scenery, or to see fine pictures, or sometimes for no object but to seek amusement as it might chance to arise, I was always happy when near my father. It was a subject of regret to me whenever we were joined by a third person, yet if I turned with a disturbed look towards my father, his eyes fixed on me and beaming with tenderness instantly restored joy to my heart. O, hours of intense delight! Short as ye were ye are made as long to me as a whole life when looked back upon through the mist of grief that rose immediately after as if to shut ye from my view. Alas! ye were the last of happiness that I ever enjoyed; a few, a very few weeks and all was destroyed. Like Psyche[8] I lived for awhile in an enchanted palace, amidst odours, and music, and every luxurious delight; when suddenly I was left on a barren rock; a wide ocean of despair rolled around me: above all was black, and my eyes closed while I still inhabited a universal death. Still I would not hurry on; I would pause for ever on the recollections of these happy weeks; I would repeat every word, and how many do I remember, record every enchantment of the faery habitation. But, no, my tale must not pause; it must be as rapid as was my fate, – I can only describe in short although strong expressions my precipitate and irremediable change from happiness to despair.

CHAPTER IV

Among our most assiduous visitors was a young man of rank, well informed, and agreeable in his person. After we had spent a few weeks in London his attentions towards me became marked and his visits more frequent. I was too much taken up by my own occupations and feelings to attend much to this, and then indeed I hardly noticed more than the bare surface of events as they passed around me; but I now remember that my father was restless and uneasy whenever this person visited us, and when we talked together watched us with the greatest apparent anxiety although he himself maintained a profound silence. At length these obnoxious visits suddenly ceased altogether, but from that moment I must date the change of my father: a change that to remember makes me shudder and then filled me with the deepest grief. There were no degrees which could break my fall from happiness to misery; it was as the stroke of lightning – sudden and entire. Alas! I now met frowns where before I had been welcomed only with smiles: he, my beloved father, shunned me, and either treated me with harshness or a more heart-breaking coldness. We took no more sweet counsel together; and when I tried to win him again to me, his anger, and the terrible emotions that he exhibited drove me to silence and tears.

And this was sudden. The day before we had passed alone together in the country; I remember we had talked of future travels that we should undertake together –. There was an eager delight in our tones and gestures that could only spring from deep and mutual love joined to the most unrestrained confidence; and now the next day, the next hour, I saw his brows contracted, his eyes fixed in sullen fierceness on the ground, and his voice so gentle and so dear made me shiver when he addressed me. Often, when my wandering fancy brought by its various images now consolation and now aggravation of grief to my heart, I have compared myself to Proserpine⁹ who was gaily and heedlessly gathering flowers on the sweet plain of Enna, when the King of Hell snatched her away to the abodes of death and misery. Alas! I who so lately knew of nought but the joy of life; who had slept only to dream sweet dreams and awoke to incomparable happiness, I now passed my days and nights in tears. I who sought and had found joy in the love-breathing countenance of my father now when I dared fix on him a supplicating look it was ever answered by an angry frown. I dared not speak to him; and when sometimes I had worked up courage to meet him and to ask an explanation one glance at his face where a chaos of mighty passion seemed for ever struggling made me tremble and shrink to silence. I was dashed down from heaven to earth as a silly sparrow when pounced on by a hawk; my eyes swam and my head was bewildered by the sudden apparition of grief. Day after day passed marked only by my complaints and my tears; often I lifted my soul in vain prayer for a softer descent from joy to woe, or if that were denied me that I might be allowed to die, and fade for ever under the cruel blast that swept over me,

> ———for what should I do here,
> Like a decaying flower, still withering
> Under his bitter words, whose kindly heat
> Should give my poor heart life?*

Sometimes I said to myself, this is an enchantment, and I must strive against it. My father is blinded by some malignant vision which I must remove. And then, like David, I would try music to win the evil spirit from him; and once while singing I lifted my eyes towards him and saw his fixed on me and filled with tears; all his muscles seemed relaxed to softness.[11] I sprung towards him with a cry of joy and would have thrown myself into his arms, but he pushed me roughly from him and left me. And even from this slight incident he contracted fresh gloom and an additional severity of manner.

There are many incidents that I might relate which shewed the diseased yet incomprehensible state of his mind; but I will mention one that occurred while we were in company with several other persons. On this occasion I chanced to say that I thought Myrrha the best of Alfieri's tragedies;[12] as I said this I chanced to cast my eyes on my father and met his: for the first time the expression of those beloved eyes displeased me, and I saw with affright that his whole frame shook with some concealed emotion that in spite of his efforts half conquered him: as this tempest faded from his soul he became melancholy and silent. Every day some new scene occured and displayed in him a mind working as it were with an unknown horror that now he could master but which at times threatened to overturn his reason, and to throw the bright seat of his intelligence into a perpetual chaos.

I will not dwell longer than I need on these disastrous circumstances. I might waste days in describing how anxiously I watched every change of fleeting circumstance that promised better days, and with what despair I found that each effort of mine aggravated his seeming madness. To tell all

* Fletcher's comedy of the Captain.[10]

my grief I might as well attempt to count the tears that have fallen from these eyes, or every sign that has torn my heart. I will be brief for there is in all this a horror that will not bear many words, and I sink almost a second time to death while I recall these sad scenes to my memory. Oh, my beloved father! Indeed you made me miserable beyond all words, but how truly did I even then forgive you, and how entirely did you possess my whole heart while I endeavoured, as a rainbow gleams upon a cataract,* to soften thy tremendous sorrows.[13]

Thus did this change come about. I seem perhaps to have dashed too suddenly into the description, but thus suddenly did it happen. In one sentence I have passed from the idea of unspeakable happiness to that of unspeakable grief but they were thus closely linked together. We had remained five months in London three of joy and two of sorrow. My father and I were now seldom alone or if we were he generally kept silence with his eyes fixed on the ground – the dark full orbs in which before I delighted to read all sweet and gentle feeling shadowed from my sight by their lids and the long lashes that fringed them. When we were in company he affected gaiety but I wept to hear his hollow laugh – begun by an empty smile and often ending in a bitter sneer such as never before this fatal period had wrinkled his lips. When others were there he often spoke to me and his eyes perpetually followed my slightest motion. His accents whenever he addressed me were cold and constrained although his voice would tremble when he perceived that my full heart choked the answer to words proffered with a mien yet new to me.

But days of peaceful melancholy were of rare occurence: they were often broken in upon by gusts of passion that drove me as a weak boat on a stormy sea to seek a cove for shelter; but the winds blew from my native harbour and I was cast far, far out until shattered I perished when the tempest had passed and the sea was apparently calm. I do not know that I can describe his emotions: sometimes he only betrayed them by a word or gesture, and then retired to his chamber and I crept as near it as I dared and listened with fear to every sound, yet still more dreading a sudden silence – dreading I knew not what, but ever full of fear.

It was after one tremendous day when his eyes had glared on me like lightning – and his voice sharp and broken seemed unable to express the extent of his emotion that in the evening when I was alone he joined me with a calm countenance, and not noticing my tears which I quickly dried when he approached, told me that in three days[14] he intended to remove with me to his estate in Yorkshire, and bidding me prepare left me hastily as if afraid of being questioned.

This determination on his part indeed surprised me. This estate was that which he had inhabited in childhood and near which my mother resided while a girl; this was the scene of their youthful loves and where they had

* Lord Byron.

lived after their marriage; in happier days my father had often told me that however he might appear weaned from his widow sorrow, and free from bitter recollections elsewhere, yet he would never dare visit the spot where he had enjoyed her society or trust himself to see the rooms that so many years ago they had inhabited together; her favourite walks and the gardens the flowers of which she had delighted to cultivate. And now while he suffered intense misery he determined to plunge into still more intense, and strove for greater emotion than that which already tore him. I was perplexed, and most anxious to know what this portended; ah, what could it portend but ruin!

I saw little of my father during this interval, but he appeared calmer although not less unhappy than before. On the morning of the third day he informed me that he had determined to go to Yorkshire first alone, and that I should follow him in a fortnight unless I heard any thing from him in the mean time that should contradict this command. He departed the same day, and four days afterwards I received a letter from his steward telling me in his name to join him with as little delay as possible. After travelling day and night I arrived with an anxious, yet a hoping heart, for why should he send for me if it were only to avoid me and to treat me with the apparent aversion that he had in London. I met him at the distance of thirty miles from our mansion. His demeanour was sad; for a moment he appeared glad to see me and then he checked himself as if unwilling to betray his feelings. He was silent during our ride, yet his manner was kinder than before and I thought I beheld a softness in his eyes that gave me hope.

When we arrived, after a little rest, he led me over the house and pointed out to me the rooms which my mother had inhabited. Although more than sixteen years had passed since her death nothing had been changed; her work box, her writing desk were still there and in her room a book lay open on the table as she had left it. My father pointed out these circumstances with a serious and unaltered mien, only now and then fixing his deep and liquid eyes upon me; there was something strange and awful in his look that overcame me, and in spite of myself I wept, nor did he attempt to console me, but I saw his lips quiver and the muscles of his countenance seemed convulsed.

We walked together in the gardens and in the evening when I would have retired he asked me to stay and read to him; and first said, 'When I was last here your mother read Dante to me; you shall go on where she left off.' And then in a moment he said, 'No, that must not be; you must not read Dante. Do you choose a book.' I took up Spencer and read the descent of Sir Guyon to the halls of Avarice;[15] while he listened his eyes fixed on me in sad profound silence.

I heard the next morning from the steward that upon his arrival he had been in a most terrible state of mind: he had passed the first night in the garden lying on the damp grass; he did not sleep but groaned perpetually. 'Alas!' said the old man, who gave me this account with tears in his eyes, 'it wrings my heart to see my lord in this state: when I heard that he was coming down here with you, my young lady, I thought we should have the happy days over again that we enjoyed during the short life of my lady your mother – But that would be too much happiness for us poor creatures born to tears – and that was why she was taken from us so soon; she was too beautiful and good for us. It was a happy day as we all thought it when my lord married her: I knew her when she was a child and many a good turn has she done for me in my old lady's time – You are like her although there is more of my lord in you – But has he been thus ever since his return? All my joy turned to sorrow when I first beheld him with that melancholy countenance enter these doors as it were the day after my lady's funeral – He seemed to recover himself a little after he had bidden me write to you – but still it is a woeful thing to see him so unhappy.' These were the feelings of an old, faithful servant: what must be those of an affectionate daughter. Alas! Even then my heart was almost broken.

We spent two months together in this house. My father spent the greater part of his time with me; he accompanied me in my walks, listened to my music, and leant over me as I read or painted. When he conversed with me his manner was cold and constrained; his eyes only seemed to speak, and as he turned their black, full lustre towards me they expressed a living sadness. There was something in those dark deep orbs so liquid, and intense that even in happiness I could never meet their full gaze that mine did not overflow. Yet it was with sweet tears; now there was a depth of affliction in their gentle appeal that rent my heart with sympathy; they seemed to desire peace for me; for himself a heart patient to suffer; a craving for sympathy, yet a perpetual self denial. It was only when he was absent from me that his passion subdued him, – that he clinched his hands – knit his brows – and with haggard looks called for death to his despair, raving wildly, until exhausted he sank down nor was revived until I joined him.

While we were in London there was a harshness and sullenness in his sorrow which had now entirely disappeared. There I shrunk and fled from him, now I only wished to be with him that I might soothe him to peace. When he was silent I tried to divert him, and when sometimes I stole to him during the energy of his passion I wept but did not desire to leave him. Yet he suffered fearful agony; during the day he was more calm, but at night when I could not be with him he seemed to give the reins to his grief: he often passed his nights either on the floor in my mother's room, or in the garden; and when in the morning he saw me view with poignant grief his exhausted frame, and his person languid almost to death with watching he wept; but during all this time he spoke no word by which I might guess the cause of his unhappiness. If I ventured to enquire he would either leave me or press his finger on his lips, and with a deprecating look that I could not resist, turn away. If I wept he would gaze on me in silence but he was no longer harsh and although he repulsed every caress yet it was with gentleness.

He seemed to cherish a mild grief and softer emotions although sad as a relief from despair – He contrived in many ways to nurse his melancholy as an antidote to wilder passion. He perpetually frequented the walks that had been favourites with him when he and my mother wandered together talking of love and happiness; he collected every relick that remained of her and always sat opposite her picture which hung in the room fixing on it a look of sad despair – and all this was done in a mystic and awful silence. If his passion subdued him he locked himself in his room; and at night when he wandered restlessly about the house, it was when every other creature slept.

It may easily be imagined that I wearied myself with conjecture to guess the cause of his sorrow. The solution that seemed to me the most probable was that during his residence in London he had fallen in love with some unworthy person, and that his passion mastered him although he would not gratify it: he loved me too well to sacrifice me to this inclination, and that he had now visited his house that by reviving the memory of my mother whom he so passionately adored he might weaken the present impression. This was possible; but it was a mere conjecture unfounded on any fact. Could there be guilt in it? He was too upright and noble to *do* aught that his conscience would not approve; I did not yet know of the crime there may be in involuntary feeling and therefore ascribed his tumultuous starts and gloomy looks wholly to the struggles of his mind and not any as they were partly due to the worst fiend of all – Remorse.

But still do I flatter myself that this would have passed away. His paroxisms of passions were terrific but his soul bore him through them triumphant, though almost destroyed by victory; but the day would finally have been won had not I, foolish and presumtuous wretch! hurried him on until there was no recall, no hope. My rashness gave the victory in this dreadful fight to the enemy who triumphed over him as he lay fallen and vanquished. I! I alone was the cause of his defeat and justly did I pay the fearful penalty. I said to myself, let him receive sympathy and these struggles will cease. Let him confide his misery to another heart and half the weight of it will be lightened. I will win him to me; he shall not deny his grief to me and when I know his secret then will I pour a balm into his soul and again I shall enjoy the ravishing delight of beholding his smile, and of again seeing his eyes beam if not with pleasure at least with gentle love and thankfulness. This will I do, I said. Half I accomplished; I gained his secret and we were both lost for ever.

CHAPTER V

Nearly a year had passed since my father's return, and the seasons had almost finished their round – It was now the end of May; the woods were clothed in their freshest verdure, and the sweet smell of the new mown grass was in the fields. I thought that the balmy air and the lovely face of Nature might aid me in inspiring him with mild sensations, and give him gentle feelings of peace and love preparatory to the confidence I determined to win from him.

I chose therefore the evening of one of these days for my attempt. I invited him to walk with me, and led him to a neighbouring wood of beech trees whose light shade shielded us from the slant and dazzling beams of the descending sun– After walking for some time in silence I seated my self with him on a mossy hillock – It is strange but even now I seem to see the spot – the slim and smooth trunks were many of them wound round by ivy whose shining leaves of the darkest green contrasted with the white bark and the light leaves of the young sprouts of beech that grew from their parent trunks – the short grass was mingled with moss and was partly covered by the dead leaves of the last autumn that driven by the winds had here and there collected in little hillocks – there were a few moss grown stumps about – The leaves were gently moved by the breeze and through their green canopy you could see the bright blue sky – As evening came on the distant trunks were reddened by the sun and the wind died entirely away while a few birds flew past us to their evening rest.

Well it was here we sat together, and when you hear all that past – all that of terrible tore our souls even in this placid spot, which but for strange passions might have been a paradise to us, you will not wonder that I remember it as I looked on it that its calm might give me calm, and inspire me not only with courage but with persuasive words. I saw all these things and in a vacant manner noted them in my mind while I endeavoured to arrange my thoughts in fitting order for my attempt. My heart beat fast as I worked myself up to speak to him, for I was determined not to be repulsed but I trembled to imagine what effect my words might have on him; at length, with much hesitation I began:

'Your kindness to me, my dearest father, and the affection – the excessive affection – that you had for me when you first returned will I hope excuse me in your eyes that I dare speak to you, although with the tender affection of a daughter, yet also with the freedom of a friend and equal. But pardon me, I entreat you and listen to me: do not turn away from me; do not be impatient; you may easily intimidate me into silence, but my heart is bursting, nor can I willingly consent to endure for one moment longer the agony of uncertitude which for the last four months has been my portion.

'Listen to me, dearest friend, and permit me to gain your confidence. Are the happy days of mutual love which have passed to be to me as a dream never to return? Alas! You have a secret grief that destroys us both: but you must permit me to win this secret from you. Tell me, can I do nothing? You well know that on the whole earth there is no sacrifice that I would not make, no labour that I would not undergo with the mere hope that I might bring you ease. But if no endeavour on my part can contribute to your happiness, let me at least know your sorrow, and surely my earnest love and deep sympathy must soothe your despair.

'I fear that I speak in a constrained manner: my heart is overflowing with the ardent desire I have of bringing calm once more to your thoughts and looks; but I fear to aggravate your grief, or to raise that in you which is death to me, anger and distaste. Do not then continue to fix your eyes on the earth; raise them on me for I can read your soul in them: speak to me,[16] and pardon my presumption. Alas! I am a most unhappy creature!'

I was breathless with emotion, and I paused fixing my earnest eyes on my father, after I had dashed away the intrusive tears that dimmed them. He did not raise his, but after a short silence he replied to me in a low voice: 'You are indeed presumptuous, Matilda, presumptuous and very rash. In the heart of one like me there are secret thoughts working, and secret tortures which you ought not to seek to discover. I cannot tell you how it adds to my grief to know that I am the cause of uneasiness to you; but this will pass away, and I hope that soon we shall be as we were a few months ago. Restrain your impatience or you may mar what you attempt to alleviate. Do not again speak to me in this strain; but wait in submissive patience the event of what is passing around you.'

'Oh, yes!' I passionately replied, 'I will be very patient; I will not be rash or presumptuous: I will see the agonies, and tears, and despair of my father, my only friend, my hope, my shelter, I will see it all with folded arms and downcast eyes. You do not treat me with candour; it is not true what you say; this will not soon pass away, it will last forever if you deign not to speak to me; to admit my consolations.

'Dearest, dearest father, pity me and pardon me: I entreat you do not drive me to despair; indeed I must not be repulsed; there is one thing that[17] although it may torture me to know, yet that you must tell me. I demand, and most solemnly I demand if in any way I am the cause of your unhappiness. Do you not see my tears which I in vain strive against – You hear unmoved my voice broken by sobs – Feel how my hand trembles: my whole heart is in the words I speak and you must not endeavour to silence me by mere words barren of meaning: the agony of my doubt hurries me on, and you must reply. I beseech you; by your former love for me now lost, I adjure you to answer that one question. Am I the cause of your grief?'

He raised his eyes from the ground, but still turning them away from me, said: 'Besought by that plea I will answer your rash question. Yes, you are the sole, the agonizing cause of all I suffer, of all I must suffer until I die. Now, beware! Be silent! Do not urge me to your destruction. I am struck by the storm, rooted up, laid waste: but you can stand against it; you are young and your passions are at peace. One word I might speak and then you would be implicated in my destruction; yet that word is hovering on my lips. Oh! There is a fearful chasm; but I adjure you to beware!'

'Ah, dearest friend!' I cried, 'do not fear! Speak that word; it will bring peace, not death. If there is a chasm our mutual love will give us wings to pass it, and we shall find flowers, and verdure, and delight on the other side,' I threw myself at his feet, and took his hand, 'Yes, speak, and we shall be happy; there will no longer be doubt, no dreadful uncertainty; trust me, my affection will soothe your sorrow; speak that word and all danger will be past, and we shall love each other as before, and for ever.'

He snatched his hand from me, and rose in violent disorder: 'What do you mean? You know not what you mean. Why do you bring me out, and torture me, and tempt me, and kill me – Much happier would it be for you and for me if in your frantic curiosity you tore my heart from my breast and tried to read its secrets in it as its life's blood was dropping from it. Thus you may console me by reducing me to nothing – but your words I cannot bear; soon they will make me mad, quite mad, and then I shall utter strange words, and you will believe them, and we shall be both lost for ever. I tell you I am on the verge of insanity; why, cruel girl, do you drive me on: you will repent and I shall die.'

When I repeat his words I wonder at my pertinacious folly; I hardly know what feelings resistlessly impelled me. I believe it was that coming out with a determination not to be repulsed I went right forward to my object without well weighing his replies: I was led by passion and drew him with frantic heedlessness into the abyss that he so fearfully avoided – I replied to his terrific words: 'You fill me with affright it is true, dearest father, but you only confirm my resolution to put an end to this state of doubt. I will not be put off thus: do you think that I can live thus fearfully from day to day – the sword in my bosom yet kept from its mortal wound by a hair – a word! – I demand that dreadful word; though it be as a flash of lightning to destroy me, speak it.

'Alas! Alas! What am I become? But a few months have elapsed since I believed that I was all the world to you; and that there was no happiness or grief for you on earth unshared by your Matilda – your child: that happy time is no longer, and what I most dreaded in this world is come upon me. In despair of my heart I see what you cannot conceal: you no longer love me. I adjure you, my father, has not an unnatural passion seized upon your heart? Am I not the most miserable worm that crawls? Do I not embrace your knees, and you most cruelly repulse me? I know it – I see it – you hate me!'

I was transported by violent emotion, and rising from his feet, at which I had thrown myself, I leant against a tree, wildly raising my eyes to heaven. He began to answer with violence: 'Yes, yes, I hate you! You are my bane, my poison, my disgust! Oh! No!' And then his manner changed, and fixing his eyes on me with an expression that convulsed every nerve and member of my frame – 'you are none of all these; you are my light, my only one, my life. – My daughter, I love you!' The last words died away in a hoarse whisper, but I heard them and sunk on the ground, covering my face and almost dead with excess of sickness and fear: a cold perspiration covered my forehead and I shivered in every limb – But he continued, clasping his hands with a frantic gesture:

'Now I have dashed from the top of the rock to the bottom! Now I have precipitated myself down the fearful chasm! The danger is over; she is alive! Oh, Matilda, lift up those dear eyes in the light of which I live. Let me hear the sweet tones of your beloved voice in peace and calm. Monster as I am, you are still, as you ever were, lovely, beautiful beyond expression. What I have become since this last moment I know not; perhaps I am changed in mien as the fallen archangel. I do believe I am for I have surely a new soul within me, and my blood riots through my veins: I am burnt up with fever. But these are precious moments; devil as I am become, yet that is my Matilda before me whom I love as one was never before loved: and she knows it now; she listens to these words which I thought, fool as I was, would blast her to death. Come, come, the worst is past: no more grief, tears or despair; were not those the words you uttered? – We have leapt the chasm I told you of, and now, mark me, Matilda, we are to find flowers, and verdure and delight, or is it hell, and fire, and tortures? Oh! Beloved One, I am borne away; I can no longer sustain myself; surely this is death that is coming. Let me lay my head near your heart; let me die in your arms!' – He sunk to the earth fainting, while I, nearly as lifeless, gazed on him in despair.

Yes it was despair I felt; for the first time that phantom seized me; the first and only time for it has never since left me – After the first moments of speechless agony I felt her fangs on my heart: I tore my hair; I raved aloud; at one moment in pity for his sufferings I would have clasped my father in my arms; and then starting back with horror I spurned him with my foot; I felt as if stung by a serpent, as if scourged by a whip of scorpions which drove me – Ah! Whither – Whither?

Well, this could not last. One idea rushed on my mind; never, never may I speak to him again. As this terrible conviction came upon me[18] it melted my soul to tenderness and love – I gazed on him as to take my last farewell – he lay insensible – his eyes closed and[19] his cheeks deathly pale – Above, the leaves of the beech wood cast a flickering shadow on his face, and waved in mournful melody over him – I saw all these things and said, 'Aye, this is his grave!' And then I wept aloud, and raised my eyes to heaven to entreat for a respite to my despair and an alleviation for his unnatural suffering – the tears that gushed in a warm and healing stream from my eyes relieved the burthen that oppressed my heart almost to madness. I wept for a long time until I saw him about to revive, when horror and misery again recurred, and the tide of my sensations rolled back to their former channel: with a terror I could not restrain – I sprung up and fled, with winged speed, along the paths of the wood and across the fields until nearly dead I reached our house and just ordering the servants to seek my father at the spot I indicated, I shut myself up in my own room.

CHAPTER VI

My chamber was in a retired part of the house, and looked upon the garden so that no sound of the other inhabitants could reach it; and here in perfect solitude I wept for several hours. When a servant came to ask me if I would take food I learnt from him that my father had returned, and was apparently well and this relieved me from a load of anxiety, yet I did not cease to weep bitterly. At[20] first, as the memory of former happiness contrasted to my present despair came across me, I gave relief to the oppression of heart that I felt by words, and groans, and heart rending sighs: but nature became wearied, and this more violent grief gave place to a passionate but mute flood of tears: my whole soul seemed to dissolve in them. I did not wring my hands, or tear my hair, or utter wild exclamations, but as Boccaccio describes the intense and quiet grief of Sigismunda over the heart of Guiscardo,[21] I sat with my hands folded, silently letting fall a perpetual stream from my eyes. Such was the depth of my emotion that I had no feeling of what caused my distress, my thoughts even wandered to many different objects; but still neither moving limb or feature my tears fell until, as if the fountains were exhausted, they gradually subsided, and I awoke to life as from a dream.

When I had ceased to weep reason and memory returned upon me, and I began to reflect with greater calmness on what had happened, and how it became me to act – A few hours only had passed but a mighty revolution had taken place with regard to me – the natural work of years had been transacted since the morning: my father was as dead to me, and I felt for a moment as if he with white hairs were laid in his coffin and I – youth vanished in approaching age, were weeping at his timely dissolution. But it was not so, I was yet young, Oh! far too young, nor was he dead to others; but I, most miserable, must never see or speak to him again. I must fly from him with more earnestness than from my greatest enemy: in solitude or in cities I must never more behold him. That consideration made me breathless with anguish, and impressing itself on my imagination I was unable for a

time to follow up any train of ideas. Ever after this, I thought, I would live in
the most dreary seclusion. I would retire to the Continent and become a
nun; not for religion's sake, for I was not a Catholic, but that I might for
ever be shut out from the world. I should there find solitude where I might
weep, and the voices of life might never reach me.

But my father; my beloved and most wretched father? Would he die?
Would he never overcome the fierce passion that now held pitiless dominion over him? Might he not many, many years hence, when age had
quenched the burning sensations that he now experienced, might he not
then be again a father to me? This reflection unwrinkled my brow, and I
could feel (and I wept to feel it) a half melancholy smile draw from my lips
their expression of suffering: I dared indulge better hopes for my future life;
years must pass but they would speed lightly away winged by hope, or if
they passed heavily, still they would pass and I had not lost my father for
ever. Let him spend another sixteen years of desolate wandering: let him
once more utter his wild complaints to the vast woods and the tremendous
cataracts of another clime: let him again undergo fearful danger and soul-
quelling hardships: let the hot sun of the south again burn his passion worn
cheeks and the cold night rains fall on him and chill his blood.

To this life, miserable father, I devote thee! – Go! – Be thy days passed
with savages, and thy nights under the cope of heaven! Be thy limbs worn
and thy heart chilled, and all youth be dead within thee! Let thy hairs be as
snow; thy walk trembling and thy voice have lost its mellow tones! Let the
liquid lustre of thine eyes be quenched; and then return to me, return to thy
Matilda, thy child, who may then be clasped in thy loved arms, while thy
heart beats with sinless emotion. Go, Devoted One, and return thus! – This
is my curse, a daughter's curse: go, and return pure to thy child, who will
never love aught but thee.

These were my thoughts; and with trembling hands I prepared to begin a
letter to my unhappy parent. I had now spent many hours in tears and
mournful meditation; it was past twelve o'clock; all was at peace in the
house, and the gentle air that stole in at my window did not rustle the leaves
of the twining plants that shadowed it. I felt the entire tranquillity of the
hour when my own breath and involuntary sobs were all the sounds that
struck upon the air. On a sudden I heard a gentle step ascending the stairs; I
paused breathless, and as it approached glided into an obscure corner of the
room; the steps paused at my door, but after a few moments they again
receded, descended the stairs and I heard no more.

This slight incident gave rise in me to the most painful reflections; nor do
I now dare express the emotions I felt. That he should be restless I
understood; that he should wander as an unlaid ghost and find no quiet
from the burning hell that consumed his heart. But why approach my
chamber? Was not that sacred? I felt almost ready to faint while he had
stood there, but I had not betrayed my wakefulness by the slightest motion,
although I had heard my own heart beat with violent fear. He had

withdrawn. Oh, never, never, may I see him again! Tomorrow night the same roof may not cover us; he or I must depart. The mutual link of our destinies is broken; we must be divided by seas – by land. The stars and the sun must not rise at the same period to us: he must not say, looking at the setting crescent of the moon, 'Matilda now watches its fall.' – No, all must be changed. Be it light with him when it is darkness with me! Let him feel the sun of summer while I am chilled by the snows of winter! Let there be the distance of the antipodes between us!

At length the east began to brighten, and the comfortable light of morning streamed into my room. I was weary with watching and for some time I had combated with the heavy sleep that weighed down my eyelids: but now, no longer fearful, I threw myself on my bed. I sought for repose although I did not hope for forgetfulness; I knew I should be pursued by dreams, but did not dread the frightful one that I really had. I thought that I had risen and went to seek my father to inform him of my determination to separate myself from him. I sought him in the house, in the park, and then in the fields and the woods, but I could not find him. At length I saw him at some distance, seated under a tree, and when he perceived me he waved his hand several times, beckoning me to approach; there was something unearthly in his mien that awed and chilled me, but I drew near. When at a short distance from him I saw that he was deadly pale, and clothed in flowing garments of white. Suddenly he started up and fled from me; I pursued him: we sped over the fields, and by the skirts of woods, and on the banks of the rivers; he flew fast and I followed. We came at last, methought, to the brow of a huge cliff that over hung the sea which, troubled by the winds, dashed against its base, at a distance. I heard the roar of the waters: he held his course right on towards the brink and I became breathless with fear lest he should plunge down the dreadful precipice; I tried to augment my speed, but my knees failed beneath me, yet I had just reached him; just caught a part of his flowing robe, when he leapt down and I awoke with a violent scream. I was trembling and my pillow was wet with tears; for a few moments my heart beat hard, but the bright beams of the sun and the chirping of the birds quickly restored me to myself, and I rose with a languid spirit, yet wondering what events the day would bring forth. Some time passed before I summoned courage to ring the bell for my servant, and when she came I still dared not utter my father's name. I ordered her to bring my breakfast to my room, and was again left alone – yet still I could make no resolve, but only thought that I might write a note to my father to beg his permission to pay a visit to a relation who lived about thirty miles off, and who had before invited me to her house, but I had refused for then I could not quit my suffering father. When the servant came back she gave me a letter.

'From whom is this letter?' I asked trembling.

'Your father left it, madam, with his servant, to be given to you when you should rise.'

'My father left it! Where is he? Is he not here?'

'No; he quitted the house before four this morning.'

'Good God! He is gone! But tell how this was; speak quick!'

Her relation was short. He had gone in the carriage to the nearest town where he took a post chaise and horses with orders for the London road. He dismissed his servants there, only telling them that he had a sudden call of business and that they were to obey me as their mistress until his return.

CHAPTER VII

With a beating heart and fearful, I knew not why, I dismissed the servant and locking my door, sat down to read my father's letter. These are the words that it contained.

'My dear Child

'I have betrayed your confidence; I have endeavoured to pollute your mind, and have made your innocent heart acquainted with the looks and language of unlawful and monstrous passion. I must expiate these crimes, and must endeavour in some degree to proportionate my punishment to my guilt. You are I doubt not prepared for what I am about to announce; we must separate and be divided for ever.

'I deprive you of your parent and only friend. You are cast out shelterless on the world: your hopes are blasted; the peace and security of your pure mind destroyed; memory will bring to you frightful images of guilt, and the anguish of innocent love betrayed. Yet I who draw down all this misery upon you; I who cast you forth and remorselessly have set the seal of distrust and agony on the heart and brow of my own child, who with devilish levity have endeavoured to steal away her loveliness to place in its stead the foul deformity of sin; I, in the overflowing anguish of my heart, supplicate you to forgive me.

'I do not ask your pity; you must and do abhor me: but pardon me, Matilda, and let not your thoughts follow me in my banishment with unrelenting anger. I must never more behold you; never more hear your voice; but the soft whisperings of your forgiveness will reach me and cool the burning of my disordered brain and heart; I am sure I feel it even in my grave. And I dare enforce this request by relating how miserably I was betrayed into this net of fiery anguish and all my struggles to release myself: indeed if your soul were less pure and bright I would not attempt to exculpate myself to you; I should fear that if I led you to regard me with less abhorrence you might hate vice less: but in addressing you I feel as if I appealed to an angelic judge. I cannot depart without your forgiveness and I must endeavour to gain it, or I must despair. I conjure you therefore to listen to my words, and if with the good guilt may be in any degree extenuated by sharp agony, and remorse that rends the brain as madness perhaps you may think, though I dare not, that I have some claim to your compassion.

'I entreat you to call to your remembrance our first happy life on the shores of Loch Lomond. I had arrived from a weary wandering of sixteen years, during which, although I had gone through many dangers and misfortunes, my affections had been an entire blank. If I grieved it was for your mother, if I loved it was your image; these sole emotions filled my heart in quietness. The human creatures around me excited in me no sympathy and I thought that the mighty change that the death of your mother had wrought within me had rendered me callous to any future impression. I saw the lovely and I did not love, I imagined therefore that all warmth was extinguished in my heart except that which led me ever to dwell on your then infantine image.

'It is a strange link in my fate that without having seen you I should passionately love you. During my wanderings I never slept without first calling down gentle dreams on your head. If I saw a lovely woman, I thought, does my Matilda resemble her? All delightful things, sublime scenery, soft breezes, exquisite music seemed to me associated with you and only through you to be pleasant to me. At length I saw you. You appeared as the deity of a lovely region, the ministering Angel of a Paradise to which of all human kind you admitted only me. I dared hardly consider you as my daughter; your beauty, artlessness and untaught wisdom seemed to belong to a higher order of beings; your voice breathed forth only words of love: if there was aught of earthly in you it was only what you derived from the beauty of the world; you seemed to have gained a grace from the mountain breezes – the waterfalls and the lake; and this was all of earthly except your affections that you had; there was no dross, no bad feeling in the composition. You yet even have not seen enough of the world to know the stupendous difference that exists between the women we meet in daily life and a nymph of the woods such as you were, in whose eyes alone mankind may study for centuries and grow wiser and purer. Those divine lights which shone on me as did those of Beatrice upon Dante, and well might I say with him yet with what different feelings

E quasi mi perdei gli occhi chini.*

Can you wonder, Matilda, that I dwelt on your looks, your words, your motions, and drank in unmixed delight?

'But I am afraid that I wander from my purpose. I must be more brief for

* Canto IV Vers Ult.[22]

night draws on apace and all my hours in this house are counted. Well, we removed to London, and still I felt only the peace of sinless passion. You were ever with me, and I desired no more than to gaze on your countenance, and to know that I was all the world to you; I was lapped in a fool's paradise of enjoyment and security. Was my love blamable? If it was I was ignorant of it; I desired only that which I possessed, and if I enjoyed from your looks, and words, and most innocent caresses a rapture usually excluded from the feelings of a parent towards his child, yet no uneasiness, no wish, no casual idea awoke me to a sense of guilt. I loved you as a human father might be supposed to love a daughter borne to him by a heavenly mother; as Anchises might have regarded the child of Venus if the sex had been changed;[23] love mingled with respect and adoration. Perhaps also my passion was lulled to content by the deep and exclusive affection you felt for me.

'But when I saw you become the object of another's love; when I imagined that you might be loved otherwise than as a sacred type and image of loveliness and excellence; or that you might love another with a more ardent affection than that which you bore to me, then the fiend awoke within me; I dismissed your lover; and from that moment I have known no peace. I have sought in vain for sleep and rest; my lids refused to close, and my blood was for ever in a tumult. I awoke to a new life as one who dies in hope might wake in Hell. I will not sully your imagination by recounting my combats, my self-anger and my despair. Let a veil be drawn over the unimaginable sensations of a guilty father; the secrets of so agonized a heart may not be made vulgar. All was uproar, crime, remorse and hate, yet still the tenderest love; and what first awoke me to the firm resolve of conquering my passion and of restoring her father to my child was the sight of your bitter and sympathizing sorrows. It was this that led me here: I thought that if I could again awaken in my heart the grief I had felt at the loss of your mother, and the many associations with her memory which had been laid to sleep for seventeen years, that all love for her child would become extinct. In a fit of heroism I determined to go alone; to quit you, the life of my life, and not to see you again until I might guiltlessly. But it would not do: I rated my fortitude too high, or my love too low. I should certainly have died if you had not hastened to me. Would that I had been indeed extinguished!

'And now, Matilda I must make you my last confession. I have been miserably mistaken in imagining that I could conquer my love for you; I never can. The sight of this house, these fields and woods which my first love inhabited seems to have encreased it: in my madness I dared say to myself – Diana died to give her birth; her mother's spirit was transferred into her frame, and she ought to be as Diana to me. With every effort to cast it off, this love clings closer, this guilty love more unnatural than hate, that withers your hopes and destroys me for ever.

Better have loved despair, & safer kissed her.

No time or space can tear from my soul that which makes a part of it. Since my arrival here I have not for a moment ceased to feel the hell of passion which has been implanted in me to burn until all be cold, and stiff, and dead. Yet I will not die; alas! how dare I go where I may meet Diana, when I have disobeyed her last request; her last words said in a faint voice when all feeling but love, which survives all things else was already dead, she then bade me make her child happy: that thought alone gives a double sting to death. I will wander away from you, away from all life – in the solitude I shall seek I alone shall breathe of human kind. I must endure life; and as it is my duty so I shall until the grave dreaded yet desired, receive me free from pain: for while I feel it will be pain that must make up the whole sum of my sensations. Is not this a fearful curse that I labour under? Do I not look forward to a miserable future? My child, if after this life I am permitted to see you again, if pain can purify the heart, mine will be pure: if remorse may expiate guilt, I shall be guiltless.

———————————

'I have been at the door of your chamber: every thing is silent. You sleep. Do you indeed sleep, Matilda? Spirits of Good, behold the tears of my earnest prayer! Bless my child! Protect her from the selfish among her fellow creatures: protect her from the agonies of passion, and the despair of disappointment! Peace, Hope and Love be thy guardians, oh, thou soul of my soul: thou in whom I breathe!

———————————

'I dare not read my letter over for I have no time to write another, and yet I fear that some expressions in it might displease me. Since I last saw you I have been constantly employed in writing letters, and have several more to write; for I do not intend that any one shall hear of me after I depart. I need not conjure you to look upon me as one of whom all links that once existed between us are broken. Your own delicacy will not allow you, I am convinced, to attempt to trace me. It is far better for your peace that you should be ignorant of my destination. You will not follow me, for when I banish myself would you nourish guilt by obtruding yourself upon me? You will not do this, I know you will not. You must forget me and all the evil that I have taught you. Cast off the only gift that I have bestowed upon you, your grief, and rise from under my blighting influence as no flower so sweet ever did rise from beneath so much evil.

'You will never hear from me again: receive these then as the last words of mine that will ever reach you; and although I have forfeited your filial love, yet regard them I conjure you as a father's command. Resolutely shake off the wretchedness that this first misfortune in early life must occasion you. Bear boldly up against the storm: continue wise and mild, but believe it, and indeed it is, your duty to be happy. You are very young; let not this check for more than a moment retard your glorious course; hold on, beloved one. The sun of youth is not set for you; it will restore vigour and life to you; do not resist with obstinate grief its beneficent influence, oh, my child! bless me with the hope that I have not utterly destroyed you.

'Farewell, Matilda. I go with the belief that I have your pardon. Your gentle nature would not permit you to hate your greatest enemy and though I be he, although I have rent happiness from your grasp; though I have passed over your young love and hopes as the angel of destruction, finding beauty and joy, and leaving blight and despair, yet you will forgive me, and with eyes overflowing with tears I thank you; my beloved one, I accept your pardon with a gratitude that will never die, and that will, indeed it will, outlive guilt and remorse.

'Farewell for ever!'

The moment I finished this letter I ordered the carriage and prepared to follow my father. The words of his letter by which he had dissuaded me from this step were those that determined me. Why did he write them? He must know that if I believed that his intention was merely to absent himself from me that instead of opposing him it would be that which I should myself require – or if he thought that any lurking feeling, yet he could not think that, should lead me to him would he endeavour to overthrow the only hope he could have of ever seeing me again; a lover, there was madness in the thought, yet he was my lover, would not act thus. No, he had determined to die, and he wished to spare me the misery of knowing it. The few ineffectual words he had said concerning his duty were to me a further proof – and the more I studied the letter the more did I perceive a thousand slight expressions that could only indicate a knowledge that life was now over for him. He was about to die! My blood froze at the thought: a sickening feeling of horror came over me that allowed not of tears. As I waited for the carriage I walked up and down with a quick pace; then kneeling and passionately clasping my hands I tried to pray but my voice was choked by convulsive sobs – Oh the sun shone, the air was balmy – he must yet live for if he were dead all would surely be black as night to me!

The motion of the carriage knowing that it carried me towards him and that I might perhaps find him alive somewhat revived my courage: yet I had a dreadful ride. Hope only supported me, the hope that I should not be too late. I did not weep, but I wiped the perspiration from my brow, and tried to still my brain and heart beating almost to madness. Oh! I must not be mad when I see him; or perhaps it were as well that I should be, my distraction might calm his, and recall him to the endurance of life. Yet until I find him I must force reason to keep her seat, and I pressed my forehead hard with my hands – Oh do not leave me; or I shall forget what I am about – instead of driving on as we ought with the speed of lightning they will attend to me, and we shall be too late. Oh! God help me! Let him be alive! It is all dark; in my abject misery I demand no more: no hope, no good: only passion, and guilt, and horror; but alive! My sensations choked me – No tears fell yet I sobbed, and breathed short and hard; one only thought possessed me, and I could only utter one word, that half screaming was perpetually on my lips; Alive! Alive! –

I had taken the steward with me for he, much better than I, could make the requisite enquiries – the poor old man could not restrain his tears as he saw my deep distress and knew the cause – he sometimes uttered a few broken words of consolation: in moments like these the mistress and servant become in a manner equals and when I saw his old dim eyes wet with sympathizing tears; his gray hair thinly scattered on an age-wrinkled brow I thought oh if my father were as he is – decrepid and hoary – then I should be spared this pain –

When I had arrived at the nearest town I took post horses and followed the road my father had taken. At every inn where we changed horses we heard of him, and I was possessed by alternate hope and fear. A length I found that he had altered his route; at first he had followed the London road; but now he changed it, and upon enquiry I found that the one which he now pursued led *towards the sea*. My dream recurred to my thoughts; I was not usually superstitious but in wretchedness every one is so. The sea was fifty miles off, yet it was towards it that he fled. The idea was terrible to my half crazed imagination, and almost overturned the little self possession that still remained to me. I journied all day; every moment my misery increased and the fever of my blood became intolerable. The summer sun shone in an unclouded sky; the air was close but all was cool to me except my own scorching skin. Towards evening dark thunder clouds arose above the horizon and I heard its distant roll – after sunset they darkened the whole sky and it began to rain, the lightning lighted up the whole country and the thunder drowned the noise of our carriage. At the next inn my father had not taken horses; he had left a box there saying he would return, and had walked over the fields to the town of —— a seacoast town eight miles off.

For a moment I was almost paralized by fear; but my energy returned and I demanded a guide to accompany me in following his steps. The night was tempestuous but my bribe was high and I easily procured a countryman. We passed through many lanes and over fields and wild downs; the rain poured down in torrents, and the loud thunder broke in terrible crashes over our heads. Oh! What a night it was! And I passed on with quick steps among the high, dank grass amid the rain and tempest. My dream was for ever in my thoughts, and with a kind of half insanity that often possesses the mind in despair, I said aloud; 'Courage! We are not near the sea; we are yet several miles from the ocean' – Yet it was towards the sea that our direction lay and that heightened the confusion of my ideas. Once, overcome by fatigue, I sunk on the wet earth; about two hundred yards distant, alone in a large meadow stood a magnificent oak; the lightnings shewed its myriad boughs torn by the storm. A strange idea seized me; a person must have felt all the agonies of doubt concerning the life and death of one who is the whole world to them before they can enter into my feelings – for in that state, the mind working unrestrained by the will makes strange and fanciful combinations with outward circumstances and weaves the chances and changes of nature into an immediate connexion with the event they dread. It was with this feeling that I turned to the old Steward who stood pale and trembling beside me; 'Mark, Gaspar, if the next flash of lightning rend not that oak my father will be alive.'

I had scarcely uttered these words than a flash instantly followed by a tremendous peal of thunder descended on it; and when my eyes recovered their sight after the dazzling light, the oak no longer stood in the meadow. – The old man uttered a wild exclamation of horror when he saw so sudden an interpretation given to my prophesy. I started up, my strength returned[24] with my terror; I cried, 'Oh, God! Is this thy decree? Yet perhaps I shall not be too late.'

Although still several miles distant we continued to approach the sea. We came at last to the road that led to the town of —— and at an inn there we heard that my father had passed by somewhat before sunset; he had observed the approaching storm and had hired a horse for the next town which was situated a mile from the sea that he might arrive there before it should commence: this town was five miles off. We hired a chaise here, and with four horses drove with speed through the storm. My garments were wet and clung around me, and my hair hung in straight locks on my neck when not blown aside by the wind. I shivered, yet my pulse was high with fever. Great God! What agony I endured. I shed no tears but my eyes wild and inflamed were starting from my head; I could hardly support the weight that pressed upon my brain. We arrived at the town of —— in a little more than half an hour. When my father had arrived the storm had already begun, but he had refused to stop and leaving his horse there he walked on – *towards the sea.* Alas! it was double cruelty in him to have chosen the sea for his fatal resolve; it was adding madness to my despair.

The poor old servant who was with me endeavoured to persuade me to remain here and to let him go alone – I shook my head silently and sadly; sick almost to death I leant upon his arm, and as there was no road for a chaise dragged my weary steps across the desolate downs to meet my fate, now too certain for the agony of doubt. Almost fainting I slowly approached the fatal waters; when we had quitted the town we heard their roaring. I whispered to myself in a muttering voice – 'The sound is the same as that which I heard in my dream. It is the knell of my father which I hear.'

The rain had ceased; there was no more thunder and lightning; the wind had paused. My heart no longer beat wildly; I did not feel any fever: but I was chilled; my knees sunk under me – I almost slept as I walked with excess of weariness; every limb trembled. I was silent: all was silent except the roaring of the sea which became louder and more dreadful. Yet we advanced slowly: sometimes I thought that we should never arrive; that the sound of waves would still allure us, and that we should walk on for ever and ever: field succeeding field, never would our weary journey cease, nor night nor day; but still we should hear the dashing of the sea, and to all this there would be no end. Wild beyond the imagination of the happy are the thoughts bred by misery and despair.

At length we reached the overhanging beach; a cottage stood beside the path; we knocked at the door and it was opened: the bed within instantly caught my eye; something stiff and straight lay on it, covered by a sheet; the cottagers looked aghast. The first words that they uttered confirmed what I before knew. I did not feel shocked or overcome: I believe that I asked one or two questions and listened to the answers. I hardly know, but in a few moments I sank lifeless to the ground; and so would that then all had been at an end!

CHAPTER VIII

I was carried to the next town: fever succeeded to convulsions and faintings, and for some weeks my unhappy spirit hovered on the very verge of death. But life was yet strong within me; I recovered: nor did it a little aid my returning health that my recollections were at first vague, and that I was too weak to feel any violent emotion. I often said to myself, my father is dead. he loved me with a guilty passion, and stung by remorse and despair he killed himself. Why is it that I feel no horror? Are these circumstances not dreadful? Is it not enough that I shall never more meet the eyes of my beloved father; never more hear his voice; no caress, no look? All cold, and stiff, and dead! Alas! I am quite callous: the night I was out in was fearful and the cold rain that fell about my heart has acted like the waters of the cavern of Antiparos[25] and has changed it to stone. I do not weep or sigh; but I must reason with myself, and force myself to feel sorrow and despair. This is not resignation that I feel, for I am dead to all regret.

I communed in this manner with myself, but I was silent to all around me. I hardly replied to the slightest question, and was uneasy when I saw a human creature near me. I was surrounded by my female relations, but they were all of them nearly strangers to me: I did not listen to their consolations, and so little did they work their designed effect that they seemed to me to be spoken in an unknown tongue. I found if sorrow was dead within me, so was love and desire of sympathy. Yet sorrow only slept to revive more fierce, but love never woke again – its ghost, ever hovering over my father's grave, alone survived – since his death all the world was to me a blank except where woe had stamped its burning words telling me to smile no more – the living were not fit companions for me, and I was ever meditating by what means I might shake them all off, and never be heard of again.

My convalescence rapidly advanced, yet this was the thought that haunted me, and I was for ever forming plans how I might hereafter contrive to escape the tortures that were prepared for me when I should mix in society, and to find that solitude which alone could suit one whom an untold grief separated from her fellow creatures. Who can be more solitary even in a crowd than one whose history and the never ending feelings and remembrances arising from it is known to no living soul. There was too deep a horror in my tale for confidence; I was on earth the sole depository of my own secret. I might tell it to the winds and to the desert heaths but I must never among my fellow creatures, either by word or look give allowance to the smallest conjecture of the dread reality: I must shrink before the eye of man lest he should read my father's guilt in my glazed eyes: I must be silent lest my faltering voice should betray unimagined horrors. Over the deep grave of my secret I must heap an impenetrable heap of false smiles and words: cunning frauds, treacherous laughter and a mixture of all light deceits would form a mist to blind others and be as the poisonous simoon to me.[26] I, the offspring of love, the child of the woods, the nursling of Nature's bright self was to submit to this? I dared not.

How must I escape? I was rich and young, and had a guardian appointed for me; and all about me would act as if I were one of their great society, while I must keep the secret that I really was cut off from them for ever. If I fled I should be pursued; in life there was no escape for me: why then I must die. I shuddered; I dared not die even though the cold grave held all I loved; although I might say with Job

> Where is now my hope? For my hope who shall see it?
> They shall go down together to the bars of the pit, when our rest together is in the dust –[27]

Yes my hope was corruption and dust and all to which death brings us. – Or after life – No, no, I will not persuade myself to die, I may not, dare not. And then I wept; yes, warm tears once more struggled into my eyes soothing yet bitter; and after I had wept much and called with unavailing anguish, with outstretched arms, for my cruel father; after my weak frame was exhausted by all variety of plaint I sank once more into reverie, and once more reflected on how I might find that which I most desired; dear to me if aught were dear, a death-like solitude.

I dared not die, but I might feign death, and thus escape from my comforters: they will believe me united to my father, and so indeed I shall be. For alone, when no voice can disturb my dream, and no cold eye meet mine to check its fire, then I may commune with his spirit; on a lone heath, at noon or at midnight, still I should be near him. His last injunction to me was that I should be happy; perhaps he did not mean the shadowy happiness that I promised myself, yet it was that alone which I could taste. He did not conceive that ever again I could make one of the smiling hunters that go coursing after bubbles that break to nothing when caught, and then after a new one with brighter colours; my hope also had proved a bubble, but it had been so lovely, so adorned that I saw none that could attract me after it; besides I was wearied with the pursuit, nearly dead with weariness.

I would feign to die; my contented heirs would seize upon my wealth, and I should purchase freedom. But then my plan must be laid with art; I would not be left destitute, I must secure some money. Alas! to what loathsome shifts must I be driven? Yet a whole life of falsehood was otherwise my portion: and when remorse at being the contriver of any cheat made me shrink from my design I was irresistibly led back and confirmed in it by the visit of some aunt or cousin, who would tell me that death was the end of all men. And then say that my father had surely lost his wits ever since my mother's death; that he was mad and that I was fortunate, for in one of his fits he might have killed me instead of destroying his own crazed being. And all this, to be sure, was delicately put; not in broad words for my feelings might be hurt but

> Whispered so and so
> In dark hint soft and low*

with downcast eyes, and sympathizing smiles or whimpers; and I listened with quiet countenance while every nerve trembled; I that dared not utter aye or no to all this blasphemy. Oh, this was a delicious life quite void of guile! I with my dove's look and fox's heart: for indeed I felt only the degradation of falsehood, and not any sacred sentiment of conscious innocence that might redeem it. I who had before clothed myself in the bright garb of sincerity must now borrow one of divers colours: it might sit awkwardly at first, but use would enable me to place it in elegant folds, to lie with grace. Aye, I might die my soul with falsehood until I had quite hid its native colour. Oh, beloved father! Accept the pure heart of your unhappy daughter; permit me to join you unspotted as I was or you will not recognize my altered semblance. As grief might change Constance[29] so would deceit change me until in heaven you would say, 'This is not my child' – My father, to be happy both now and when again we meet I must fly from all this life which is mockery to one like me. In solitude only shall I be myself; in solitude I shall be thine.

Alas! I even now look back with disgust at my artifices and contrivances by which, after many painful struggles, I effected my retreat. I might enter into a long detail of the means I used, first to secure myself a slight maintenance for the remainder of my life, and afterwards to ensure the conviction of my death: I might, but I will not. I even now blush at the falsehoods I uttered; my heart sickens: I will leave this complication of what I hope I may in a manner call innocent deceit to be imagined by the reader.

---

* Coleridge's Fire, Famine and Slaughter.[28]

The remembrance haunts me like a crime – I know that if I were to endeavour to relate it my tale would at length remain unfinished. I was led to London, and had to endure for some weeks cold looks, cold words and colder consolations: but I escaped; they tried to bind me with fetters that they thought silken, yet which weighed on me like iron, although I broke them more easily than a girth formed of a single straw and fled to freedom.

The few weeks that I spent in London were the most miserable of my life: a great city is a frightful habitation to one sorrowing. The sunset and the gentle moon, the blessed motion of the leaves and the murmuring of waters are all sweet physicians to a distempered mind. The soul is expanded and drinks in quiet, a lulling medicine – to me it was as the sight of the lovely water snakes to the bewitched mariner – in loving and blessing Nature I unawares, called down a blessing on my own soul.[30] But in a city all is closed shut like a prison, a wiry prison from which you can peep at the sky only. I can not describe to you what was[31] the frantic nature of my sensations while I resided there; I was often on the verge of madness. Nay, when I look back on many of my wild thoughts, thoughts with which actions sometimes endeavoured to keep pace; when I tossed my hands high calling down the cope 'of heaven to fall on me and bury me; when I tore my hair and throwing it to the winds cried, 'Ye are free, go seek my father!' And then, like the unfortunate Constance, catching at them again and tying them up, that nought might find him if I might not. How, on my knees I have fancied myself close to my father's grave and struck the ground in anger that it should cover him from me. Oft when I have listened with gasping attention for the sound of the ocean mingled with my father's groans; and then wept until my strength was gone and I was calm and faint, when I have recollected all this I have asked myself if this were not madness. While in London these and many other dreadful thoughts too harrowing for words were my portion: I lost all this suffering when I was free; when I saw the wild heath around me, and the evening star in the west, then I could weep, gently weep, and be at peace.

Do not mistake me; I never was really mad. I was always conscious of my state when my wild thoughts seemed to drive me to insanity, and never betrayed them to aught but silence and solitude. The people around me saw nothing of all this. They only saw a poor girl broken in spirit, who spoke in a low and gentle voice, and from underneath whose downcast lids tears would sometimes steal which she strove to hide. One who loved to be alone, and shrunk from observation; who never smiled; oh, no! I never smiled – and that was all.

Well, I escaped. I left my guardian's house and I was never heard of again; it was believed from the letters that I left and other circumstances that I planned that I had destroyed myself. I was sought after therefore with less care than would otherwise have been the case; and soon all trace and memory of me was lost. I left London in a small vessel bound for a port in the north of England. And now having succeeded in my attempt, and being quite alone peace returned to me. The sea was calm and the vessel moved gently onwards, I sat upon deck under the open canopy of heaven and methought I was an altered creature. Not the wild, raving and most miserable Matilda but a youthful Hermitess dedicated to seclusion and whose bosom she must strive to keep free from all tumult and unholy despair – The fanciful nunlike dress that I had adopted; the knowledge that my very existence was a secret known only to myself; the solitude to which I was for ever hereafter destined nursed gentle thoughts in my wounded heart. The breeze that played in my hair revived me, and I watched with quiet eyes the sunbeams that glittered on the waves, and the birds that coursed each other over the waters just brushing them with their plumes. I slept too undisturbed by dreams; and awoke refreshed to again enjoy my tranquil freedom.

In four days we arrived at the harbour to which we were bound. I would not remain on the sea coast, but proceeded immediately inland. I had already planned the situation where I would live. It should be a solitary house on a wide plain near no other habitation: where I could behold the whole horizon, and wander far without molestation from the sight of my fellow creatures. I was not misanthropic, but I felt that the gentle current of my feelings depended upon my being alone. I fixed myself on a wide solitude. On a dreary heath bestrewn with stones, among which short grass grew; and here and there a few rushes beside a little pool. Not far from my cottage was a small cluster of pines the only trees to be seen for many miles: I had a path cut through the furze from my door to this little wood, from whose topmost branches the birds saluted the rising sun and awoke me to my daily meditation. My view was bounded only by the horizon except on one side where a distant wood made a black spot on the heath, that every where else stretched out its faint hues as far as the eye could reach, wide and very desolate. Here I could mark the net work of the clouds as they wove themselves into thick masses: I could watch the slow rise of the heavy thunder clouds and could see the rack as it was driven across the heavens, or under the pine trees I could enjoy the stillness of the azure sky.

My life was very peaceful. I had one female servant who spent the greater part of the day at a village two miles off. My amusements were simple and very innocent; I fed the birds who built on the pines or among the ivy that covered the wall of my little garden, and they soon knew me: the bolder ones pecked the crumbs from my hands and perched on my fingers to sing their thankfulness. When I had lived here some time other animals visited me and a fox came every day for a portion of food appropriated for him and would suffer me to pat his head. I had besides many books and a harp with which when despairing I could soothe my spirits, and raise myself to sympathy and love.

Love! What had I to love? Oh many things: there was the moonshine, and the bright stars; the breezes and the refreshing rains; there was the whole earth and the sky that covers it: all lovely forms that visited my imagination, all memories of heroism and virtue. Yet this was very unlike my early life although as then I was confined to Nature and books. Then I bounded across the fields; my spirit often seemed to ride upon the winds, and to mingle in joyful sympathy with the ambient air. Then if I wandered slowly I cheered myself with a sweet song or sweeter day dreams. I felt a holy rapture spring from all I saw. I drank in joy with life; my steps were light; my eyes, clear from the love that animated them, sought the heavens, and with my long hair loosened to the winds I gave my body and my mind to sympathy and delight. But now my walk was slow – My eyes were seldom raised and often filled with tears; no song; no smiles; no careless motion that might bespeak a mind intent on what surrounded it – I was gathered up into myself – a selfish solitary creature ever pondering on my regrets and faded hopes.

Mine was an idle, useless life; it was so; but say not to the lily laid prostrate by the storm arise, and bloom as before. My heart was bleeding from its death's wound; I could live no otherwise – Often amid apparent calm I was visited by despair and melancholy; gloom that nought could dissipate or overcome; a hatred of life; a carelessness of beauty; all these would by fits hold me nearly annihilated by their powers. Never for one moment when most placid did I cease to pray for death. I could be found in no state of mind which I would not willingly have exchanged for nothingness. And morning and evening my tearful eyes raised to heaven, my hands clasped tight in the energy of prayer, I have repeated with the poet –

> Before I see another day
> Oh, let this body die away![32]

Let me not be reproached then with inutility; I believed that by suicide I should violate a divine law of nature, and I thought that I sufficiently fulfilled my part in submitting to the hard task of enduring the crawling hours and minutes[33] – in bearing the load of time that weighed miserably upon me and that in abstaining from what I in my calm moments considered a crime, I deserved the reward of virtue. There were periods, dreadful ones, during which I despaired – and doubted the existence of all duty and the reality of crime – but I shudder, and turn from the remembrance.

CHAPTER IX

Thus I passed two years. Day after day so many hundreds wore on; they brought no outward changes with them, but some few slowly operated on my mind as I glided on towards death. I began to study more; to sympathize more in the thoughts of others as expressed in books; to read history, and to lose my individuality among the crowd that had existed before me. Thus perhaps as the sensation of immediate suffering wore off, I became more human. Solitude also lost to me some of its charms: I began again to wish for sympathy; not that I was ever tempted to seek the crowd, but I wished for one friend to love me. You will say perhaps that I gradually became fitted to return to society. I do not think so. For the sympathy that I desired must be so pure, so divested of influence from outward circumstances that in the world I could not fail of being balked by the gross materials that perpetually mingle even with its best feelings. Believe me, I was then less fitted for any communion with my fellow creatures than before. When I left them they had tormented me but it was in the same way as pain and sickness may torment; something extraneous to the mind that galled it, and that I wished to cast aside. But now I should have desired sympathy; I should wish to knit my soul to some one of theirs, and should have prepared for myself plentiful draughts of disappointment and suffering; for I was tender as the sensitive plant, all nerve. I did not desire sympathy and aid in ambition or wisdom, but sweet and mutual affection; smiles to cheer me and gentle words of comfort. I wished for one heart in which I could pour unrestrained my plaints, and by the heavenly nature of the soil blessed fruit might spring from such bad seed. Yet how could I find this? The love that is the soul of friendship is a soft spirit seldom found except when two amiable creatures are knit from early youth, or when bound by mutual suffering and pursuits; it comes to some of the elect unsought and unaware; it descends as gentle dew on chosen spots which however barren they were before become under its benign influence fertile in all sweet plants; but when desired it flies; it scoffs at the prayers of its votaries; it will bestow, but not be sought.

I knew all this and did not go to seek sympathy; but there on my solitary heath, under my lowly roof where all around was desert, it came to me as a sun beam in winter to adorn while it helps to dissolve the drifted snow. – Alas the sun shone on blighted fruit; I did not revive under its radiance for I was too utterly undone to feel its kindly power. My father had been and his memory was the life of my life. I might feel gratitude to another but I never more could love or hope as I had done; it was all suffering; even my pleasures were endured, not enjoyed. I was as a solitary spot among mountains shut in on all sides by steep black precipices; where no ray of heat could penetrate; and from which there was no outlet to sunnier fields. And thus it was that although the spirit of friendship soothed me for a while it could not restore me. It came as some gentle visitation; it went and I hardly felt the loss. The spirit of existence was dead within me; be not surprised therefore that when it came I welcomed not more gladly, or when it departed I lamented not more bitterly the best gift of heaven – a friend.

The name of my friend was Woodville. I will briefly relate his history that you may judge how cold my heart must have been not to be warmed by his eloquent words and tender sympathy; and how he also being most unhappy we were well fitted to be a mutual consolation to each other, if I had not been hardened to stone by the Medusa head of Misery. The misfortunes of Woodville were not of the hearts core like mine; his was a natural grief, not to destroy but to purify the heart and from which he might, when its shadow had passed from over him, shine forth brighter and happier than before.

Woodville was the son of a poor clergyman and had received a classical education. He was one of those very few whom fortune favours from their birth; on whom she bestows all gifts of intellect and person with a profusion that knew no bounds, and whom under her peculiar protection, no imperfection however slight, or disappointment however transitory has leave to touch. She seemed to have formed his mind of that excellence which no dross can tarnish, and his understanding was such that no error could pervert. His genius was transcendant, and when it rose as a bright star in the east all eyes were turned towards it in admiration. He was a Poet. That name has so often been degraded that it will not convey the idea of all that he was. He was like a poet of old whom the muses had crowned in his cradle, and on whose lips bees had fed. As he walked among other men he seemed encompassed with a heavenly halo that divided him from and lifted him above them. It was his surpassing beauty, the dazzling fire of his eyes, and his words whose rich accents wrapped the listener in mute and ecstatic wonder, that made him transcend all others so that before him they appeared only formed to minister to his superior excellence.

He was glorious from his youth. Every one loved him; no shadow of envy or hate cast even from the meanest mind ever fell upon him, He was, as one the peculiar delight of the Gods, railed and fenced in by his own divinity, so that nought but love and admiration could approach him. His heart was simple like a child, unstained by arrogance or vanity. He mingled in society unknowing of his superiority over his companions, not because he undervalued himself but because he did not perceive the inferiority of others. He seemed incapable of conceiving of the full extent of the power that selfishness and vice possesses in the world: when I knew him, although he had suffered disappointment in his dearest hopes, he had not experienced any that arose from the meanness and self love of men: his station was too high to allow of his suffering through their hardheartedness; and too low for him to have experienced ingratitude and encroaching selfishness: it is one of the blessings of a moderate fortune, that by preventing the possessor from confering pecuniary favours it prevents him also from diving into the arcana of human weakness or malice – To bestow on your fellow men is a Godlike attribute – So indeed it is and as such not one fit for mortality; – the giver like Adam and Prometheus, must pay the penalty of rising above his nature by being the martyr to his own excellence. Woodville was free from all these evils; and if slight examples did come across him he did not notice them but passed on in his course as an angel with winged feet might glide along the earth unimpeded by all those little obstacles over which we of earthly origin stumble. He was a believer in the divinity of genius and always opposed a stern disbelief to the objections of those petty cavillers and minor critics who wish to reduce all men to their own miserable level – 'I will make a scientific simile' he would say, 'in the manner, if you will, of Dr Darwin[34] – I consider the alleged errors of a man of genius as the aberrations of the fixed stars. It is our distance from them and our imperfect means of communication that makes them appear to move; in truth they always remain stationary, a glorious centre, giving us a fine lesson of modesty if we would thus receive it.' ––

I have said that he was a poet: when he was three and twenty years of age he first published a poem, and it was hailed by the whole nation with enthusiasm and delight. His good star perpetually shone upon him; a reputation had never before been made so rapidly: it was universal. The multitude extolled the same poems that formed the wonder of the sage in his closet: there was not one dissentient voice.[35]

It was at this time, in the height of his glory, that he became acquainted with Elinor. She was a young heiress of exquisite beauty who lived under the care of her guardian: from the moment they were seen together they appeared formed for each other. Elinor had not the genius of Woodville but she was generous and noble, and exalted by her youth and the love that she every where excited above the knowledge of aught but virtue and excellence. She was lovely; her manners were frank and simple; her deep blue eyes swam in a lustre which could only be given by sensibility joined to wisdom.

They were formed for one another and they soon loved. Woodville for the first time felt the delight of love: and Elinor was enraptured in possessing the heart of one so beautiful and glorious among his fellow men. Could any thing but unmixed joy flow from such a union?

Woodville was a Poet – he was sought for by every society and all eyes were turned on him alone when he appeared; but he was the son of a poor clergyman and Elinor was a rich heiress. Her guardian was not displeased with their mutual affection: the merit of Woodville was too eminent to admit of cavil on account of his inferior wealth; but the dying will of her father did not allow her to marry before she was of age and her fortune depended upon her obeying this injunction. She had just entered her twentieth year, and she and her lover were obliged to submit to this delay. But they were ever together and their happiness seemed that of Paradise: they studied together: formed plans of future occupations, and drinking in love and joy from each other's eyes and words they hardly repined at the delay to their entire union. Woodville for ever rose in glory; and Elinor become more lovely and wise under the lessons of her accomplished lover.

In two months Elinor would be twenty one: every thing was prepared for their union. How shall I relate the catastrophe to so much joy; but the earth would not be the earth it is covered with blight and sorrow if one such pair as these angelic creatures had been suffered to exist for one another: search through the world and you will not find the perfect happiness which their marriage would have caused them to enjoy; there must have been a revolution in the order of things as established among us miserable earth-dwellers to have admitted of such consummate joy. The chain of necessity ever bringing misery must have been broken and the malignant fate that presides over it would not permit this breach of her eternal laws. But why should I repine at this? Misery was my element, and nothing but what was miserable could approach me; if Woodville had been happy I should never have known him. And can I who for many years was fed by tears, and nourished under the dew of grief, can I pause to relate a tale of woe and death?

Woodville was obliged to make a journey into the country and was detained from day to day in irksome absence from his lovely bride. He received a letter from her to say that she was slightly ill, but telling him to hasten to her, that from his eyes she would receive health and that his company would be her surest medicine. He was detained three days longer and then he hastened to her. His heart, he knew not why prognosticated misfortune; he had not heard from her again; he feared she might be worse and this fear made him impatient and restless for the moment of beholding her once more stand before him arrayed in health and beauty; for a sinister voice seemed always to whisper to him, 'You will never more behold her as she was.'

When he arrived at her habitation all was silent in it: he made his way through several rooms; in one he saw a servant weeping bitterly: he was faint with fear and could hardly ask, 'Is she dead?' and just listened to the dreadful answer, 'Not yet.' These astounding words came on him as of less fearful import than those which he had expected; and to learn that she was still in being, and that he might still hope was an alleviation to him. He remembered the words of her letter and he indulged the wild idea that his kisses breathing warm love and life would infuse new spirit into her, and that with him near her she could not die; that his presence was the talisman of her life.

He hastened to her sick room; she lay, her cheeks burning with fever, yet her eyes were closed and she was seemingly senseless. He wrapped her in his arms; he imprinted breathless kisses on her burning lips; he called to her in a voice of subdued anguish by the tenderest names; 'Return Elinor; I am with you; your life, your love. Return; dearest one, you promised me this boon, that I should bring you health. Let your sweet spirit revive; you cannot die near me: What is death? To see you no more? To part with what is a part of myself; without whom I have no memory and no futurity? Elinor die! This is frenzy and the most miserable despair: you cannot die while I am near.'

And again he kissed her eyes and lips, and hung over her inanimate form in agony, gazing on her countenance still lovely although changed, watching every slight convulsion, and varying colour which denoted life still lingering although about to depart. Once for a moment she revived and recognized his voice; a smile, a last lovely smile, played upon her lips. He watched beside her for twelve hours and then she died.

CHAPTER X

It was six months after this miserable conclusion to his long nursed hopes that I first saw him. He had retired to a part of the country where he was not known that he might peacefully indulge his grief. All the world, by the death of his beloved Elinor, was changed to him, and he could no longer remain in any spot where he had seen her or where her image mingled with the most rapturous hopes had brightened all around with a light of joy which would now be transformed to a darkness blacker than midnight since she, the sun of his life, was set for ever.

He lived for some time never looking on the light of heaven but shrouding his eyes in a perpetual darkness far from all that could remind him of what he had been; but as time softened his grief like a true child of Nature he sought in the enjoyment of her beauties for a consolation in his unhappiness. He came to a part of the country where he was entirely unknown and where in the deepest solitude he could converse only with his own heart. He found a relief to his impatient grief in the breezes of heaven and in the sound of waters and woods. He became fond of riding; this exercise distracted his mind and elevated his spirits; on a swift horse he could for a moment gain respite from the image that else for ever followed him; Elinor on her death bed, her sweet features changed, and the soft spirit that animated her gradually waning into extinction. For many months Woodville had in vain endeavoured to cast off this terrible remembrance; it still hung on him until memory was too great a burthen for his loaded soul, but when on horseback the spell that seemingly held him to this idea was snapped; then if he thought of his lost bride he pictured her radiant in beauty; he could hear her voice, and fancy her 'a sylvan Huntress by his side,' while his eyes brightened as he thought he gazed on her cherished form. I had several times seen him ride across the heath and felt angry that my solitude should be disturbed. It was so long since I had spoken to any but peasants that I felt a disagreeable sensation at being gazed on by one of superior rank. I feared also that it might be some one who had seen me before: I might be recognized, my impostures discovered and I dragged back to a life of worse torture than that I had before endured. These were dreadful fears and they even haunted my dreams.

I was one day seated on the verge of the clump of pines when Woodville rode past. As soon as I perceived him I suddenly rose to escape from his observation by entering among the trees. My rising startled his horse; he reared and plunged and the Rider was at length thrown. The horse then galloped swiftly across the heath and the stranger remained on the ground stunned by his fall. He was not materially hurt, a little fresh water soon recovered him. I was struck by his exceeding beauty, and as he spoke to thank me the sweet but melancholy cadence of his voice brought tears into my eyes.

A short conversation passed between us, but the next day he again stopped at my cottage and by degrees an intimacy grew between us. It was strange to him to see a female in extreme youth, I was not yet twenty, evidently belonging to the first classes of society and possessing every accomplishment an excellent education could bestow, living alone on a desolate heath[36] – One on whose forehead the impress of grief was strongly marked, and whose words and motions betrayed that her thoughts did not follow them but were intent on far other ideas; bitter and overwhelming miseries. I was dressed also in a whimsical nunlike habit which denoted that I did not retire to solitude from necessity, but that I might indulge in a luxury of grief, and fanciful seclusion.

He soon took great interest in me, and sometimes forgot his own grief to sit beside me and endeavour to cheer me. He could not fail to interest even one who had shut herself from the whole world, whose hope was death, and who lived only with the departed. His personal beauty; his conversation which glowed with imagination and sensibility; the poetry that seemed to hang upon his lips and to make the very air mute to listen to him were charms that no one could resist. He was younger, less worn, more passionless than my father and in no degree reminded me of him; he suffered under immediate grief yet its gentle influence instead of calling feelings otherwise dormant into action, seemed only to veil that which otherwise would have been too dazzling for me. When we were together I spoke little yet my selfish mind was sometimes borne away by the rapid course of his ideas; I would lift my eyes with momentary brilliancy until memories that never died and seldom slept would recur, and a tear would dim them.

Woodville for ever tried to lead me to the contemplation of what is beautiful and happy in the world.[37] His own mind was constitutionally bent to a firmer[38] belief in good than in evil and this feeling which must ever exhilarate the hopeless ever shone forth in his words. He would talk of the wonderful powers of man, of their present state and of their hopes: of what they had been and what they were, and when reason could no longer guide him, his imagination as if inspired shed light on the obscurity that veils the past and the future. He loved to dwell on what might have been the state of the earth before man lived on it, and how he first arose and gradually became the strange, complicated, but as he said, the glorious creature he now is. Covering the earth with their creations and forming by the power of their minds another world more lovely than the visible frame of things, even all the world that we find in their writings. A beautiful creation, he would say, which may claim this superiority to its model, that good and evil is more easily separated: the good rewarded in the way they themselves desire; the evil punished as in all things evil ought to be punished, not by pain which is revolting to all philanthropy to consider but by quiet obscurity, which simply deprives them of their harmful qualities; why kill the serpent when you have extracted his fangs?

The poetry of his language and ideas which my words ill convey held me enchained to his discourses. It was a melancholy pleasure to me to listen to his inspired words; to catch for a moment the light of his eyes; to feel a transient sympathy and then to awaken from the delusion, again to know that all this was nothing, – a dream – a shadow for which[39] there was no reality for me; my father had for ever deserted me, leaving me only memories which set an eternal barrier between me and my fellow creatures. I was indeed fellow to none. He – Woodville, mourned the loss of his bride: others wept the various forms of misery as they visited them: but infamy and guilt was mingled with my portion; unlawful and detestable passion had poured its poison into my ears and changed all my blood, so that it was no longer the kindly stream that supports life but a cold fountain of bitterness corrupted in its very source. It must be the excess of madness that could make me imagine that I could ever be aught but one alone; struck off from humanity; bearing no affinity to man or woman; a wretch on whom Nature had set her ban.

Sometimes Woodville talked to me of himself. He related his history brief in happiness and woe and dwelt with passion on his and Elinor's mutual love. 'She was,' he said, 'the brightest vision that ever came upon the earth: there was something in her frank countenance, in her voice, and in every motion of her graceful form that overpowered me, as if it were a celestial creature that deigned to mingle with me in intercourse more sweet than man had ever before enjoyed. Sorrow fled before her; and her smile seemed to possess an influence like light to irradiate all mental darkness. It was not like a human loveliness that these gentle smiles went and came; but as a sunbeam on a lake, now light and now obscure, flitting before as you strove to catch them, and fold them for ever to your heart. I saw this smile fade for ever. Alas! I could never have believed that it was indeed Elinor that died if once when I spoke she had not lifted her almost benighted eyes, and for one moment like nought beside on earth, more lovely than a sunbeam, slighter, quicker than the waving plumage of a bird, dazzling as lightning and like it giving day to night, yet mild and faint, that smile came; it went, and then there was an end of all joy to me.'

Thus his own sorrows, or the shapes copied from nature that dwelt in his mind with beauty greater than their own, occupied our talk while I railed in my own griefs with cautious secresy. If for a moment he shewed curiosity, my eyes fell, my voice died away and my evident suffering made him quickly endeavour to banish the ideas he had awakened; yet he for ever mingled consolation in his talk, and tried to soften my despair by demonstrations of deep sympathy and compassion. 'We are both unhappy –' he would say to me; 'I have told you my melancholy tale and we have wept together the loss of that lovely spirit that has so cruelly deserted me; but you hide your griefs: I do not ask you to disclose them, but tell me if I may not console you. It seems to me a wild adventure to find in this desert one like you quite solitary: you are young and lovely; your manners are refined and attractive; yet there is in your settled melancholy, and something, I know not what, in your expressive eyes that seems to separate you from your kind: you shudder; pardon me, I entreat you but I cannot help expressing this once at least the lively interest I feel in your destiny.

'You never smile: your voice is low, and you utter your words as if you were afraid of the slight sound they would produce: the expression of awful and intense sorrow never for a moment fades from your countenance. I have lost for ever the loveliest companion that any man could ever have possessed, one who rather appears to have been a superior spirit who by some strange accident wandered among us earthly creatures, than as belonging to our kind. Yet I smile, and sometimes I speak almost forgetful of the change I have endured. But your sad mien never alters; your pulses beat and you breathe, yet you seem already to belong to another world; and sometimes, pray pardon my wild thoughts, when you touch my hand I am surprised to find your hand warm when all the fire seems extinct within you.

'When I look upon you, the tears you shed, the soft deprecating look with which you withstand enquiry; the deep sympathy your voice expresses when I speak of my lesser sorrows add to my interest for you. You stand here shelterless. You have cast yourself from among us and you wither on this wild plain forlorn and helpless: some dreadful calamity must have befallen you. Do not turn from me; I do not ask you to reveal it: I only entreat you to listen to me and to become familiar with the voice of consolation and kindness. If pity, and admiration, and gentle affection can wean you from despair let me attempt the task. I cannot see your look of deep grief without endeavouring to restore you to happier feelings. Unbend your brow; relax the stern melancholy of your regard; permit a friend, a sincere, affectionate friend, I will be one, to convey some relief, some momentary pause to your sufferings.

'Do not think that I would intrude upon your confidence: I only ask your patience. Do not for ever look sorrow and never speak it; utter one word of bitter complaint and I will reprove it with gentle exhortation and pour on you the balm of compassion. You must not shut me from all communion with you: do not tell me why you grieve but only say the words, 'I am unhappy,' and you will feel relieved as if for some time excluded from all intercourse by some magic spell you should suddenly enter again the pale of human sympathy. I entreat you to believe in my most sincere professions and to treat me as an old and tried friend: promise me never to forget me, never causelessly to banish me; but try to love me as one who would devote all his energies to make you happy. Give me the name of friend; I will fulfill

its duties; and if for a moment complaint and sorrow would shape themselves into words let me be near to speak peace to your vexed soul.'

I repeat his persuasions in faint terms and cannot give you at the same
time the tone and gesture that animated them. Like a refreshing shower on
an arid soil they revived me, and although I still kept their cause secret he
led me to pour forth my bitter complaints and to clothe my woe in words of
gall and fire. With all the energy of desperate grief I told him how I had
fallen at once from bliss to misery; how that for me there was no joy, no
hope; that death however bitter would be the welcome seal to all my pangs;
death the skeleton was to be beautiful as love. I know not why but I found it
sweet to utter these words to human ears; and though I derided all
consolation yet I was pleased to see it offered me with gentleness and
kindness. I listened quietly, and when he paused would again pour out my
misery in expressions that shewed how far too deep my wounds were for
any cure.

But now also I began to reap the fruits of my perfect solitude. I had
become unfit for any intercourse, even with Woodville the most gentle and
sympathizing creature that existed. I had become captious and unreasonable: my temper was utterly spoilt. I called him my friend but I viewed all he
did with jealous eyes. If he did not visit me at the appointed hour I was
angry, very angry, and told him that if indeed he did feel interest in me it
was cold, and could not be fitted for me, a poor worn creature, whose deep
unhappiness demanded much more than his worldly heart could give. When
for a moment I imagined that his manner was cold I would fretfully say to
him – 'I was at peace before you came; why have you disturbed me? You
have given me new wants and now your trifle with me as if my heart were as
whole as yours, as if I were not in truth a shorn lamb thrust out on the bleak
hill side, tortured by every blast. I wished for no friend, no sympathy. I
avoided you, you know I did, but you forced yourself upon me and gave me
those wants which you see with triumph give you power over me. Oh the
brave power of the bitter north wind which freezes the tears it has caused to
shed! But I will not bear this; go: the sun will rise and set as before you
came, and I shall sit among the pines or wander on the heath weeping and
complaining without wishing for you to listen. You are cruel, very cruel, to
treat me who bleed at every pore in this rough manner.'

And then, when in answer to my peevish words, I saw his countenance
bent with living pity on me, when I saw him

> Gli occhi drizzo ver me con quel sembiante
> Che madre fa sopra figlioul deliro   Paradiso. C 1.[40]

I wept and said, 'Oh, pardon me! You are good and kind but I am not fit for
life. Why am I obliged to live? To drag hour after hour, to see the trees wave
their branches restlessly, to feel the air, and to suffer in all I feel keenest
agony. My frame is strong, but my soul sinks beneath this endurance of

living anguish. Death is the goal that I would attain, but, alas! I do not even see the end of the course. Do you, my compassionate friend, tell me how to die peacefully and innocently and I will bless you: all that I, poor wretch, can desire is a painless death.'

But Woodville's words had magic in them, when beginning with the sweetest pity, he would raise me by degrees out of myself and my sorrows until I wondered at my own selfishness: but he left me and despair returned; the work of consolation was ever to begin anew. I often desired his entire absence; for I found that I was grown out of the ways of life and that by long seclusion, although I could support my accustomed grief, and drink the bitter daily draught with some degree of patience, yet I had become unfit for the slightest novelty of feeling. Expectation, and hopes, and affection were all too much for me. I knew this, but at other times I was unreasonable and laid the blame upon him, who was most blameless, and peevishly thought that if his gentle soul were more gentle, if his intense sympathy were more intense, he could drive the fiend from my soul and make me more human. I am, I thought, a tragedy; a character that he comes to see act: now and then he gives me my cue that I may make a speech more to his purpose: perhaps he is already planning a poem in which I am to figure. I am a farce and play to him, but to me this is all dreary reality: he takes all the profit and I bear all the burthen.

CHAPTER XI

It is a strange circumstance but it often occurs that blessings by their use turn to curses; and that I who in solitude had desired sympathy as the only relief I could enjoy should now find it an additional torture to me. During my father's life time I had always been of an affectionate and forbearing disposition, but since those days of joy alas! I was much changed. I had become arrogant, peevish, and above all suspicious. Although the real interest of my narration is now ended and I ought quickly to wind up its melancholy catastrophe, yet I will relate one instance of my sad suspicion and despair and how Woodville with the goodness and almost the power of an angel, softened my rugged feelings and led me back to gentleness.

He had promised to spend some hours with me one afternoon but a violent and continual rain prevented him. I was alone the whole evening. I had passed two whole years alone unrepining, but now I was miserable. He could not really care for me, I thought, for if he did the storm would rather have made him come even if I had not expected him, than, as it did, prevent a promised visit. He would well know that this drear sky and gloomy rain would load my spirit almost to madness: if the weather had been fine I should not have regretted his absence as heavily as I necessarily must shut up in this miserable cottage with no companions but my own wretched thoughts. If he were truly my friend he would have calculated all this; and let me now calculate this boasted friendship, and discover its real worth. He got over his grief for Elinor, and the country became dull to him, so he was glad to find even me for amusement; and when he does not know what else to do he passes his lazy hours here, and calls this friendship – It is true that his presence is a consolation to me, and that his words are sweet, and, when he will he can pour forth thoughts that win me from despair. His words are sweet, – and so, truly, is the honey of the bee, but the bee has a sting, and unkindness is a worse smart that that received from an insect's venom. I will put him to the proof. He says all hope is dead to him, and I know that it is dead to me, so we are both equally fitted for death. Let me try if he will die with me; and as I fear to die alone, if he will accompany to cheer me, and thus he can shew himself my friend in the only manner my misery will permit.

It was madness I believe, but I so worked myself up to this idea that I could think of nothing else. If he dies with me it is well, and there will be an end of two miserable beings; and if he will not, then will I scoff at his friendship and drink the poison before him to shame his cowardice. I planned the whole scene with an earnest heart and frantically set my soul on this project. I procured Laudanum and placing it in two glasses on the table, filled my room with flowers and decorated the last scene of my tragedy with the nicest care. As the hour for his coming approached my heart softened and I wept; not that I gave up my plan, but even when resolved the mind must undergo several revolutions of feeling before it can drink its death.

Now all was ready and Woodville came. I received him at the door of my cottage and leading him solemnly into the room, I said: 'My friend, I wish to die. I am quite weary of enduring the misery which hourly I do endure, and I will throw it off. What slave will not, if he may, escape from his chains? Look, I weep: for more than two years I have never enjoyed one moment free from anguish. I have often desired to die; but I am a very coward. It is hard for one so young who was once so happy as I was[41] voluntarily to divest themselves of all sensation and to go alone to the dreary grave; I dare not. I must die, yet my fear chills me; I pause and shudder and then for months I endure my excess of wretchedness. But now the time is come when I may quit life, I have a friend who will not refuse to accompany me in this dark journey; such is my request: earnestly do I entreat and implore you to die with me. Then we shall find Elinor and what I have lost. Look, I am prepared; there is the death draught, let us drink it together and willingly and joyfully quit this hated round of daily life.

'You turn from me; yet before you deny me reflect, Woodville, how sweet it were to cast off the load of tears and misery under which we now labour: and surely we shall find light after we have passed the dark valley.

That drink will plunge us in a sweet slumber, and when we awaken what joy will be ours to find all our sorrows and fears past. *A little patience, and all will be over*; aye, a very little patience; for, look, there is the key of our prison; we hold it in our own hands, and are we more debased than slaves to cast it away and give ourselves up to voluntary bondage? Even now if we had courage we might be free. Behold, my cheek is flushed with pleasure at the imagination of death; all that we love are dead. Come, give me your hand, one look of joyous sympathy and we will go together and seek them; a lulling journey; where our arrival will bring bliss and our waking be that of angels. Do you delay? Are you a coward, Woodville? Oh fie! Cast off this blank look of human melancholy. Oh! that I had words to express the luxury of death that I might win you. I tell you we are no longer miserable mortals; we are about to become Gods; spirits free and happy as gods. What fool on a bleak shore, seeing a flowery isle on the other side with his lost love beckoning to him from it would pause because the wave is dark and turbid?

> 'What if some little payne the passage have
> That makes frayle flesh to fear the bitter wave?
> Is not short payne well borne that brings long ease,
> And lays the soul to sleep in quiet grave?*

'Do you mark my words; I have learned the language of despair: I have it all by heart; for I am Despair; and a strange being am I, joyous, triumphant Despair. But those words are false, for the wave may be dark but it is not bitter. We lie down, and close our eyes with a gentle good night, and when we wake, we are free. Come then, no more delay, thou tardy one! Behold the pleasant potion! Look, I am a spirit of good; and not a human maid that invites thee, and with winning accents, (oh, that they would win thee!) says, Come and drink.'

As I spoke I fixed my eyes upon his countenance, and his exquisite beauty, the heavenly compassion that beamed from his eyes, his gentle yet earnest look of deprecation and wonder even before he spoke wrought a change in my high strained feelings taking from me all the sternness of despair and filling me only with the softest grief. I saw his eyes humid also as he took both my hands in his; and sitting down near me, he said:

'This is a sad deed to which you would lead me, dearest friend, and your woe must indeed be deep that could fill you with these unhappy thoughts. You long for death and yet you fear it and wish me to be your companion. But I have less courage than you and even thus accompanied I dare not die. Listen to me, and then reflect if you ought to win me to your project, even if with the overbearing eloquence of despair you could make black death so inviting that the fair heaven should appear darkness. Listen I entreat you to

---

* Spencer's Faery Queen Book 1 – Canto 9.[42]

the words of one who has himself nurtured desperate thoughts, and longed with impatient desire for death, but who has at length trampled the phantom under foot, and crushed his sting. Come, as you have played Despair with me I will play the part of Una with you and bring you hurtless from his dark cavern. Listen to me, and let yourself be softened by words in which no selfish passion lingers.

'We know not what all this wide world means; its strange mixture of good and evil. But we have been placed here and bid live and hope. I know not what we are to hope; but there is some good beyond us that we must seek; and that is our earthly task. If misfortune come against us we must fight with her; we must cast her aside, and still go on to find out that which it is our nature to desire. Whether this prospect of future good be the preparation for another existence I know not; or whether that it is merely that we, as workmen in God's vineyard, must lend a hand to smooth the way for our posterity. If it indeed be that; if the efforts of the virtuous now, are to make the future inhabitants of this fair world more happy; if the labours of those who cast aside selfishness, and try to know the truth of things, are to free the men of ages, now far distant but which will one day come, from the burthen under which those who now live groan, and like you weep bitterly; if they free them but one of what are now the necessary evils of life, truly I will not fail but will with my whole soul aid the work. From my youth I have said, I will be virtuous; I will dedicate my life for the good of others; I will do my best to extirpate evil and if the spirit who protects ill should so influence circumstances that I should suffer through my endeavour, yet while there is hope and hope there ever must be, of success, cheerfully do I gird myself to my task.

'I have powers; my countrymen think well of them. Do you think I sow my seed in the barren air, and have no end in what I do? Believe me, I will never desert life until this last hope is torn from my bosom, that in some way my labours may form a link in the chain of gold with which we ought all to strive to drag Happiness from where she sits enthroned above the clouds, now far beyond our reach, to inhabit the earth with us. Let us suppose that Socrates, or Shakespeare, or Rousseau had been seized with despair and died in youth when they were as young as I am; do you think that we and all the world should not have lost incalculable improvement in our good feelings and our happiness thro' their destruction. I am not like one of these; they influenced millions but if I can influence but a hundred, but ten, but one solitary individual, so as in any way to lead him from ill to good, that will be a joy to repay me for all my sufferings, though they were a million times multiplied; and that hope will support me to bear them.

'And those who do not work for posterity; or working, as may be my case, will not be known by it; yet they, believe me, have also their duties. You grieve because you are unhappy; it is happiness you seek but you despair of obtaining it. But if you can bestow happiness on another; if you can give one other person only one hour of joy ought you not live to do it?

And every one has it in their power to do that. The inhabitants of this world suffer so much pain. In crowded cities, among cultivated plains, or on the desert mountains, pain is thickly sown, and if we can tear up but one of these noxious weeds, or more, if in its stead we can sow one seed of corn, or plant one fair flower, let that be motive sufficient against suicide. Let us not desert our task while there is the slightest hope that we may in a future day do this.

'Indeed I dare not die. I have a mother whose support and hope I am. I have a friend who loves me as his life, and in whose breast I should infix a mortal sting if I ungratefully left him. So I will not die. Nor shall you, my friend; cheer up; cease to weep, I entreat you. Are you not young, and fair, and good? Why should you despair? Or if you must for yourself, why for others? If you can never be happy, can you never bestow happiness? Oh! believe me, if you beheld on lips pale with grief one smile of joy and gratitude, and knew that you were parent of that smile, and that without you it had never been, you would feel so pure and warm a happiness that you would wish to live for ever again and again to enjoy the same pleasure.

'Come, I see that you have already cast aside the sad thoughts you before frantically indulged. Look in that mirror; when I came your brow was contracted, your eyes deep sunk in your head, your lips quivering; your hands trembled violently when I took them; but now all is tranquil and soft. You are grieved and there is grief in the expression of your countenance but it is gentle and sweet. You allow me to throw away this cursed drink; you smile; oh, Congratulate me, hope is triumphant, and I have done some good.'

These words are shadowy as I repeat them but they were indeed words of fire and produced a warm hope in me (I, miserable wretch, to hope!) that tingled like pleasure in my veins. He did not leave me for many hours; not until he had improved the spark that he had kindled, and with an angelic hand fostered the return of somthing that seemed like joy. He left me but I still was calm, and after I had saluted the starry sky and dewy earth with eyes of love and a contented good night, I slept sweetly, visited by dreams, the first of pleasure I had had for many long months.

But this was only a momentary relief and my old habits of feeling returned; for I was doomed while in life to grieve, and to the natural sorrow of my father's death and its most terrific cause, imagination added a tenfold weight of woe. I believed myself to be polluted by the unnatual love I had inspired, and that I was a creature cursed and set apart by nature. I thought that like another Cain, I had a mark set on my forehead to show mankind that there was a barrier between me and them.[43] Woodville had told me that there was in my countenance an expression as if I belonged to another world; so he had seen that sign: and there it lay a gloomy mark to tell the world that there was that within my soul that no silence could render sufficiently obscure. Why when fate drove me to become this outcast from human feeling; this monster with whom none might mingle in converse and love; why had she not from that fatal and most accursed moment, shrouded me in thick mists and placed real darkness between me and my fellows so that I might never more be seen? and as I passed, like a murky cloud loaded with blight, they might only perceive me by the cold chill I should cast upon them; telling them, how truly, that something unholy was near? Then I should have lived upon this dreary heath unvisited, and blasting none by my unhallowed gaze. Alas! I verily believe that if the near prospect of death did not dull and soften my bitter feelings, if for a few months longer I had continued to live as I then lived, strong in body, but my soul corrupted to its core by a deadly cancer, if day after day I had dwelt on these dreadful sentiments I should have become mad, and should have fancied myself a living pestilence: so horrible to my own solitary thoughts did this form, this voice, and all this wretched self appear; for had it not been the source of guilt that wants a name?

This was superstition. I did not feel thus frantically when first I knew that the holy name of father was become a curse to me: but my lonely life inspired me with wild thoughts; and then when I saw Woodville and day after day he tried to win my confidence and I never dared give words to my dark tale, I was impressed more strongly with the withering fear that I was in truth a marked creature, a pariah, only fit for death.

CHAPTER XII

As I was perpetually haunted by these ideas, you may imagine that the influence of Woodville's words was very temporary; and that although I did not again accuse him of unkindness, yet I soon became as unhappy as before. Soon after this incident we parted. He heard that his mother was ill, and he hastened to her. He came to take leave of me, and we walked together on the heath for the last time. He promised that he would come and see me again; and bade me take cheer, and to encourage what happy thoughts I could, until time and fortitude should overcome my misery, and I could again mingle in society.

'Above all other admonition on my part,' he said, 'cherish and follow this one: do not despair. That is the most dangerous gulph on which you perpetually totter; but you must reassure your steps, and take hope to guide you. Hope, and your wounds will be already half healed: but if you obstinately despair, there never more will be comfort for you. Believe me, my dearest friend, that there is a joy that the sun and earth and all its beauties can bestow that you will one day feel. The refreshing bliss of Love will again visit your heart, and undo the spell that binds you to woe, until you wonder how your eyes could be closed in the long night that burthens you. I dare not hope that I have inspired you with sufficient interest that the thought of me, and the affection that I shall ever bear you, will soften your melancholy and decrease the bitterness of your tears. But if my friendship can make you look on life with less disgust, beware how you injure it with suspicion. Love is a delicate sprite and easily hurt by rough jealousy. Guard, I entreat you, a firm persuasion of my sincerity in the inmost recesses of your heart out of the reach of the casual winds that may disturb its surface. Your temper is made unequal by suffering, and the tenor of your mind is, I fear, sometimes shaken by unworthy causes; but let your confidence in my sympathy and love be deeper far, and incapable of being reached by these agitations that come and go, and if they touch not your affections leave you uninjured.'

These were some of Woodville's last lessons. I wept as I listened to him; and after we had taken an affectionate farewell, I followed him far with my eyes until they saw the last of my earthly comforter. I had insisted on accompanying him across the heath towards the town where he dwelt: the sun was yet high when he left me, and I turned my steps towards my cottage. It was at the latter end of the month of September when the nights have become chill. But the weather was serene, and as I walked on I fell into no unpleasing reveries. I thought of Woodville with gratitude and kindness and did not, I know not why, regret his departure with any bitterness. It seemed that after one great shock all other change was trivial to me; and I walked on wondering when the time would come when we should all four, my dearest father restored to me, meet in some sweet Paradise. I pictured to myself a lovely river such as that on whose banks Dante describes Matilda gathering flowers, which ever flows

> —— bruna, bruna,
> Sotto l'ombra perpetua, che mai
> Raggiar non lascia sole ivi, nè Luna.[44]

And then I repeated to myself all that lovely passage that relates the entrance of Dante into the terrestrial Paradise; and thought it would be sweet when I wandered on those lovely banks to see the car of light descend with my long lost parent to be restored to me. As I waited there in expectation of that moment, I thought how, of the lovely flowers that grew there, I would wind myself a chaplet and crown myself for joy: I would sing *sul margine d'un rio*,[45] my father's favourite song, and that my voice gliding through the windless air would announce to him in whatever bower he sat expecting the moment of our union, that his daughter was come. Then the mark of misery would have faded from my brow, and I should raise my eyes fearlessly to meet his, which ever beamed with the soft lustre of innocent love. When I reflected on the magic look of those deep eyes I wept, but gently, lest my sobs should disturb the fairy scene.

I was so entirely wrapped in this reverie that I wandered on, taking no heed of my steps until I actually stooped down to gather a flower for my wreath on that bleak plain where no flower grew, when I awoke from my day dream and found myself I knew not where.

The sun had set and the roseate hue which the clouds had caught from him in his descent had nearly died away. A wind swept across the plain, I looked around me and saw no object that told me where I was; I had lost myself, and in vain attempted to find my path. I wandered on, and the coming darkness made every trace indistinct by which I might be guided. At length all was veiled in the deep obscurity of blackest night; I became weary and knowing that my servant was to sleep that night at the neighbouring village, so that my absence would alarm no one; and that I was safe in this wild spot from every intruder, I resolved to spend the night where I was. Indeed I was too weary to walk further: the air was chill but I was careless of bodily inconvenience, and I thought that I was well inured to the weather during my two years of solitude, when no change of seasons prevented my perpetual wanderings.

I lay upon the grass surrounded by a darkness which not the slightest beam of light penetrated – There was no sound for the deep night had laid to sleep the insects, the only creatures that lived on the lone spot where no tree or shrub could afford shelter to aught else – There was a wondrous silence in the air that calmed my senses yet which enlivened my soul, my mind hurried from image to image and seemed to grasp an eternity. All in my heart was shadowy yet calm, until my ideas became confused and at length died away in sleep.

When I awoke it rained:[46] I was already quite wet, and my limbs were stiff and my head giddy with the chill of night. It was a drizzling, penetrating shower; as my dank hair clung to my neck and partly covered my face, I had hardly strength to part with my fingers, the long strait locks that fell before my eyes. The darkness was much dissipated and in the east where the clouds were least dense the moon was visible behind the thin grey cloud –

> The moon is behind, and at the full
> And yet she looks both small and dull.[47]

Its presence gave me a hope that by its means I might find my home. But I was languid and many hours passed before I could reach the cottage, dragging as I did my slow steps, and often resting on the wet earth unable to proceed.

I particularly mark this night, for it was that which has hurried on the last scene of my tragedy, which else might have dwindled on through long years of listless sorrow. I was very ill when I arrived and quite incapable of taking off my wet clothes that clung about me. In the morning, on her return, my servant found me almost lifeless, while possessed by a high fever I was lying on the floor of my room.

I was very ill for a long time, and when I recovered from the immediate danger of fever, every symptom of a rapid consumption declared itself. I was for some time ignorant of this and thought that my excessive weakness was the consequence of the fever. But my strength became less and less; as winter came on I had a cough; and my sunken cheek, before pale, burned with a hectic fever. One by one these symptoms struck me; and I became convinced that the moment I had so much desired was about to arrive and that I was dying. I was sitting by my fire, the physician who had attended me ever since my fever had just left me, and I looked over his prescription in which digitalis[48] was the prominent medicine. 'Yes,' I said, 'I see how this is, and it is strange that I should have deceived myself so long; I am about to die an innocent death, and it will be sweeter even than that which the opium promised.'

I rose and walked slowly to the window; the wide heath was covered by snow which sparkled under the beams of the sun that shone brightly thro' the pure, frosty air: a few birds were pecking some crumbs under my window. I smiled with quiet joy; and in my thoughts, which through long habit would for ever connect themselves into one train, as if I shaped them into words, I thus addressed the scene before me:

'I salute thee, beautiful Sun, and thou, white Earth, fair and cold! Perhaps I shall never see thee again covered with green, and the sweet flowers of the coming spring will blossom on my grave. I am about to leave thee; soon this living spirit which is ever busy among strange shapes and ideas, which belong not to thee, soon it will have flown to other regions and this emaciated body will rest insensate on thy bosom

'Rolled round in earth's diurnal course
With rocks, and stones, and trees.[49]

'For it will be the same with thee, who art called our Universal Mother,' when I am gone. I have loved thee; and in my days both of happiness and sorrow I have peopled your solitudes with wild fancies of my own creation. The woods, the lakes, and mountains which I have loved, have for me a thousand associations; and thou, oh, Sun! hast smiled upon, and borne your part in many imaginations that sprung to life in my soul alone, and which will die with me. Your solitudes, sweet land, your trees and waters will still exist, moved by your winds, or still beneath the eye of noon, though what I have felt about ye, and all my dreams which have often strangely deformed thee, will die with me. You will exist to reflect other images in other minds, and ever will remain the same, although your reflected semblance vary in a thousand ways, changeable as the hearts of those who view thee. One of these fragile mirrors, that ever doted on thine image, is about to be broken, crumbled to dust. But everteeming Nature will create another and another, and thou wilt loose nought by my destruction.

'Thou wilt ever be the same. Receive then the grateful farewell of a fleeting shadow who is about to disappear, who joyfully leaves thee, yet with a last look of affectionate thankfulness. Farewell! Sky, and fields and woods; the lovely flowers that grow on thee; thy mountains and thy rivers; to the balmy air and the strong wind of the north, to all, a last farewell. I shall shed no more tears for my task is almost fulfilled, and I am about to be rewarded for long and most burthensome suffering. Bless thy child even[50] in death, as I bless thee; and let me sleep at peace in my quiet grave.'

I feel death to be near at hand and I am calm. I no longer despair, but look on all around me with placid affection. I find it sweet to watch the progressive decay of my strength, and to repeat to myself, another day and yet another, but again I shall not see the red leaves of autumn; before that time I shall be with my father. I am glad Woodville is not with me for perhaps he would grieve, and I desire to see smiles alone during the last scene of my life; when I last wrote to him of my ill health but not of its mortal tendency, lest he should conceive it to be his duty to come to me for I fear lest the tears of friendship should destroy the blessed calm of my mind. I take pleasure in arranging all the little details which will occur when I shall no longer be. In truth I am in love with death; no maiden ever took more pleasure in the contemplation of her bridal attire than I in fancying my limbs already enwrapped in their shroud: is it not my marriage dress? Alone it will unite me to my father when in an eternal mental union we shall never part.

I will not dwell on the last changes that I feel in the final decay of nature. It is rapid but without pain: I feel a strange pleasure in it. For long years these are the first days of peace that have visited me. I no longer exhaust my miserable heart by bitter tears and frantic complaints; I no longer[51] reproach the sun, the earth, the air, for pain and wretchedness. I wait in quiet expectation for the closing hours of a life which has been to me most sweet and bitter. I do not die not having enjoyed life; for sixteen years I was happy: during the first months of my father's return I had enjoyed ages of pleasure: now indeed I am grown old in grief; my steps are feeble like those of age; I have become peevish and unfit for life; so having passed little more than twenty years upon the earth I am more fit for my narrow grave than many are when they reach the natural term of their lives.

Again and again I have passed over in my remembrance the different scenes of my short life: if the world is a stage and I merely an actor on it my part has been strange, and, alas! tragical. Almost from infancy I was deprived of all the testimonies of affection which children generally receive; I was thrown entirely upon my own resources, and I enjoyed what I may almost call unnatural pleasures, for they were dreams and not realities. The earth was to me a magic lantern and I a gazer, and a listener but no actor; but then came the transporting and soul-reviving era of my existence: my father returned and I could pour my warm affections on a human heart; there was a new sun and a new earth created to me; the waters of existence sparkled: joy! joy! but, alas! what grief! My bliss was more rapid than the progress of a sunbeam on a mountain, which discloses its glades and woods, and then leaves it dark and blank; to my happiness followed madness and agony, closed by despair.

This was the drama of my life which I have now depicted upon paper. During three months I have been employed in this task. The memory of sorrow has brought tears; the memory of happiness a warm glow the lively shadow of that joy. Now my tears are dried; the glow has faded from my cheeks, and with a few words of farewell to you, Woodville, I close my work: the last that I shall perform.

Farewell, my only living friend; you are the sole tie that binds me to existence, and now I break it. It gives me no pain to leave you; nor can our separation give you much. You never regarded me as one of this world, but rather as a being, who for some penance was sent from the Kingdom of Shadows; and she passed a few days weeping on the earth and longing to return to her native soil. You will weep but they will be tears of gentleness. I would, if I thought that it would lessen your regret, tell you to smile and congratulate me on my departure from the misery you beheld me endure. I would say; Woodville, rejoice with your friend, I triumph now and am most happy. But I check these expressions; these may not be the consolations of the living; they weep for their own misery, and not for that of the being they have lost. No; shed a few natural tears due to my memory: and if you ever visit my grave, pluck from thence a flower, and lay it to your heart; for your heart is the only tomb in which my memory will be interred.

My death is rapidly approaching and you are not near to watch the flitting and vanishing of my spirit. Do not regret this; for death is a too terrible[52] object for the living. It is one of those adversities which hurt instead of purifying the heart; for it is so intense a misery that it hardens and dulls the feelings. Dreadful as the time was when I pursued my father towards the ocean, and found there only his lifeless corpse; yet for my own sake I should prefer that to the watching one by one his senses fade; his pulse weaken – and sleeplessly as it were devour his life in gazing. To see life in his limbs and to know that soon life would no longer be there; to see the warm breath issue from his lips and to know they would soon be chill – I will not continue to trace this frightful picture; you suffered this torture once; I never did. And the remembrance fills your heart sometimes with bitter despair when otherwise your feelings would have melted into soft sorrow.

So day by day I become weaker, and life flickers in my wasting form, as a lamp about to lose its vivifying oil. I now behold the glad sun of May. It was May, four years ago, that I first saw my beloved father; it was in May, three years ago that my folly destroyed the only being I was doomed to love. May is returned, and I die. Three days ago, the anniversary of our meeting; and, alas! of our eternal separation, after a day of killing emotion, I caused myself to be led once more to behold the face of nature. I caused myself to be carried to some meadows some miles distant from my cottage; the grass was being mowed, and there was the scent of hay in the fields; all the earth looked fresh and its inhabitants happy. Evening approached and I beheld the sun set. Three years ago and on that day and hour it shone through the branches and leaves of the beech wood and its beams flickered upon the countenance of him whom I then beheld for the last time. I now saw that divine orb, gilding all the clouds with unwonted splendour, sink behind the horizon; it disappeared from a world where he whom I would seek exists not; it approached a world where he exists not. Why do I weep so bitterly? Why does my heart heave with vain endeavour to cast aside the bitter anguish that covers it 'as the waters cover the sea'.[53] I go from this world where he is no longer and soon I shall meet him in another.

Farewell, Woodville, the turf will soon be green on my grave; and the violets will bloom on it. *There* is my hope and my expectation; yours are in this world; may they be fulfilled.

NOTES

[1] The idealized heroines of Samuel Richardson, *Clarissa* (1747–8), *Sir Charles Grandison* (1753–4) and of Rousseau, *Emile, ou de l'Education* (1762) respectively.

[2] *Paradise Lost*, III, 448–97, describes 'a Limbo large and broad, since call'd / The Paradise of Fools,' where wander 'all things vain, and all who in vain things / Built their fond hopes of glory or lasting fame, / Or happiness in this or th'other life'.

[3] Wollstonecraft's first novel appeared in a single edition in her lifetime; according to Godwin, *Memoirs of the Author of A Vindication of the Rights of Woman* (1789), ch. 4, she wrote it during the summer of 1787 whilst on holiday in Bristol with her employers, the Kingsboroughs. In a letter to the Rev. Henry Dyson Gabell, on 13 September 1787, Wollstonecraft called it 'a tale, to illustrate an opinion of mine, that a genius will educate itself. I have drawn from Nature.'

[4] A book of prayers for preparation for Holy Communion.

[5] Mrs H. Cartwright, *The Platonic Marriage* (1787); *The History of Eliza Warwick* (1777).

[6] Milton, 'L'Allegro', l. 34.

[7] James Thomson, *The Seasons* (1730); Edward Young, *The Complaint, or Night Thoughts on Life, Death and Immortality* (1742–5); Milton, *Paradise Lost* (1667).

[8] I Corinthians 13:12: 'For now we see through a glass, darkly.'

[9] Luke 2:14: 'Glory to God in the highest and on earth peace, good will toward men.'

[10] The court of the lord Chancellor of England was the chief equity court until 1873.

[11] According to the physiological theory of the humours, black bile caused melancholy.

[12] Samuel Johnson, *A Dictionary of the English Language* (1755): 'Habitual, constitutional.'

[13] cf. Ecclesiastes 1:4.

[14] Isaiah 42:3: 'A bruised reed shall he not break.'

[15] Lisbon was built around the Tagus estuary.

[16] Young, *The Complaint*, IV, 710. The idea of a plurality of worlds was made current by Fontanelle in *Entretiens sur la pluralité des mondes*, translated in 1688 by Aphra Behn.

[17] A reference to the theory of physiognomy, described by J. C. Lavater in his *Phyiognomical Fragments* (1775–80) which Wollstonecraft had begun to translate and which she used again in 'The Cave of Fancy' (1787).

[18] Joseph Butler, *Analogy of Religion, Natural and Revealed, to the Constitution and Course of Nature* (1736).

[19] *Hamlet*, II. ii. 192.

[20] *Twelfth Night*, I. i. 5–7: 'O, it came o'er my ear, like the sweet south / That breathes upon a bank of violets, / Stealing, and giving odour.'

[21] The Lisbon earthquake of November 1755 devastated the city.

[22] cf. James Boswell, *The Journal of a Tour to the Hebrides, with Samuel Johnson, LL.D.* (1785), 15 August, pp. 26–7: '*Robertson* said, one man had more judgement, another more imagination. – *Johnson*. No, Sir; it is only one man has more mind than another.'

[23] cf. Wollstonecraft, 'Hints. (Chiefly designed to have been incorporated in the second part of the Rights of Woman)' *The Works of Mary Wollstonecraft* V. 269, 'Genius decays as judgement increases'.

[24] Young, *The Complaint*, I, 388.

[25] cf. Godwin, *Memoirs*: 'The obsequies of Fanny, which it was necessary to perform by stealth and in darkness . . .' because of her Protestantism.

[26] *Paradise Lost*, VIII, 589–92.

[27] Young, *The Complaint*, I, 100.

[28] I Corinthians 13:12.

[29] *Paradise Lost*, I, 63.

[30] *Macbeth*, V. v. 19.

[31] Handel, *The Messiah*, words by Charles Jennens (1742), pt. II, Hallellujah chorus: 'Hallellujah, *for the Lord Omnipotent reigneth*, Hallellujah. *The Kingdom of this World, is become the Kingdom of our Lord and of Our Christ, and he shall Reign for ever and ever.*'

[32] I Corinthians 13:12.

[33] Johnson, *Dictionary*: 'furious.'

[34] Young, *The Complaint*, I, 304, 'Take then, O World! thy much-indebted tear.'

[35] cf. Charlotte Smith, *Elegaic Sonnets and Other Essays* (1784), 'To Hope', ll. 1–2: 'Oh, Hope! thou soother sweet of human woe! / How shall I lure thee to my haunts forlorn?'

[36] I Corinthians 2:9: 'But as it is written, Eye hath not seen, nor ear heard, neither have entered into the heart of man, the things which God hath prepared for them that love him.'

[37] *The Tempest*, IV. i. 151, 155.

[38] i.e. relit.

[39] Matthew 22:30: 'For in the resurrection they neither marry, nor are given in marriage, but are as the angels of God in heaven.' Also Mark 12:25; Luke 20:35.

NOTES TO MARIA

[1] George Dyson (d. 1822), London radical, painter and translator, to whom the letter in the author's preface was written. He was the translator of Veit Weber, *The Sorcerer*, (1795).

[2] The Roman deities Minerva and Jove were identified with the Greek Athene and Zeus respectively; according to Greek mythology, when Metis (wisdom), the first wife of Zeus, became pregnant, the chief god swallowed her and their unborn child,

having been warned that their offspring would be mightier than he. From his skull emerged Athene, goddess of wisdom and war, armed and fully grown.

[3] This novel first appeared in *Posthumous Works of the Author of A Vindication of the Rights of Woman* (1798), vols I and II, arranged and edited by William Godwin. In *Memoirs of the Author of A Vindication of the Rights of Woman* (1798), ch. 9, Godwin says that Wollstonecraft began it over a year before her death. Square brackets in the text indicate Godwin's own interpolations (see Godwin's preface).

[4] cf. *The Tempest*, IV i 156–7: 'We are such stuff / As dreams are made on.'

[5] *Hamlet*, III. i. 62–3: 'The heart-ache, and the thousand natural shocks / That flesh is heir to.'

[6] John Dryden, *Fables Ancient and Modern* (1700), Milton, *Paradise Lost* (1667).

[7] Dryden, *Fables*, p. 123, taken from Boccaccio's *Decameron* 4th day, 1st story.

[8] Lady Anne Lindsay, 'Auld Robin Gray', *Ancient and Modern Scottish Songs*, ed. David Herd (1776), II; after Jenny's beloved Jamie has gone to sea, her impoverished parents persuade her to marry the wealthy 'auld Robin Gray'; Jamie returns too late and takes his final farewell.

[9] Jean-Jacques Rousseau, *Lettres de deux Amants (. . .): Julie, ou la Nouvelle Héloïse* (1761); Julie and her tutor Saint-Preux fall in love, but their different social standing makes marriage impossible. When Julie marries Wolmar, the man of her father's choice, she devotes herself to her family, but both she and her husband retain a close friendship with Saint-Preux for whom she acknowledges her lasting love on her deathbed.

[10] In Greek mythology Prometheus created human beings from clay, provided them with fire and taught them arts.

[11] See Godwin's note, p. 76.

[12] In Greek mythology Pygmalion, a sculptor, created a statue of such beauty that he fell in love with it. At first the cold ivory could not respond to his kisses, but Aphrodite took pity on him, inspired the statue with life, and his love was returned.

[13] Torquato Tasso, *Gerusalemme Liberata* (1581), IV, V; Armida, a magician, lures a group of Christian knights into her gardens where they are overwhelmed with indolence.

[14] Milton, *Comus* (1637), l.256: 'And lap it in Elysium'.

[15] A sweet tooth.

[16] A shop selling cheap ready-made clothes.

[17] Johnson, *Dictionary*: 'Tenderness, compassion'.

[18] Poor relief was administered only in the parish where the people had last been legally settled and they would be sent there when they applied elsewhere for this relief.

[19] Overseers of the poor hired out the labour of inmates of the workhouse and kept part of the money received.

[20] In Greek mythology the owl was a symbol of Athene, goddess of wisdom.

[21] Offices, like dwellings, were commonly bartered in the electioneering bribery of the eighteenth century.

[22] The impressment of able-bodied but unwilling men into the navy continued in

Britain until the end of the Napoleonic wars in 1815; the recruits were taken from the poor, who were least able to resist.

[23] Ownership of property allowing a person to vote for borough offices and for the M.P.

[24] Sarah Siddons (*née* Kemble) (1755–1830).

[25] The heroine of Nicholas Rowe, *The Fair Penitent* (1703); Mrs Siddons played this role many times.

[26] Rowe, *The Fair Penitent*, II i 99–100: 'Such hearts as ours were never paired above; / Ill suited to each other; joined not matched'.

[27] Garment worn over the ordinary clothes to protect them while the hair was being powdered.

[28] cf. *Paradise Lost*, III, 48: '. . . for the Book of knowledge fair, / Presented with a universal blank / Of Natures works to me expung'd and ras'd'.

[29] cf. Exodus, 20:17: 'Thou shalt not covet thy neighbour's house, thou shalt not covet thy neighbour's wife, nor his manservant, nor his maidservant, nor his ox, nor his ass, nor anything that is thy neighbour's.'

[30] See William Blackstone, *Commentaries on the Laws of England* (1765–9), I. 15. iii. pp. 430, 432–3; II. 29. vi. p. 433.

[31] On 7 May, 1794, Robespierre persuaded the National Convention to decree that the French people acknowledged the existence of a Supreme Being and the immortality of the soul.

[32] Bill for raising money on credit.

[33] i.e. exchange.

[34] Thomas Gray, *An Elegy wrote in a Country Churchyard* (1751), l. 87.

[35] The murderess in Nathaniel Lee, *The Rival Queens, or the Death of Alexander the Great* (1677).

[36] An officer of the House of Lords, whose tasks include bringing defendants to trial.

[37] Extravagant boastfulness; after Rodomonte, the blustering warrior in the poems of Ariosto.

[38] Mephitis, a pestilential vapour coming from the earth.

[39] i.e. needlework.

[40] Fretted.

[41] Russian wives were notorious for their submission to brutal beatings by their husbands.

[42] i.e., packet boat, mail boat.

[43] Handel, *Judas Maccabaeus*, words by Thomas Morel (1746), part I.

[44] In *Posthumous Works* 3 lines of asterisks open the following paragraph.

[45] In *Posthumous Works* 2 lines of asterisks follow.

[46] *Henry VIII* III. ii. 355: 'The third day comes a frost, a killing frost'.

[47] In *Posthumous Works* 2 lines of dashes conclude the chapter.

[48] An Adams brothers development between the Strand and the Thames built 1768–72.

[49] Public riverside gardens in Chelsea.

[50] *Julius Caesar*, III ii 82.

[51] cf. the 'happy valley' of the discontented Rasselas in Johnson, *The Prince of Abyssinia. A Tale* (1759).

[52] This is legally irrelevant; though a husband could be granted a divorce on the grounds of his wife's adultery, a wife could only divorce on the grounds of incest, bigamy, impotence, or physically dangerous cruelty.

[53] Guardianship of children could only be removed from the father in very exceptional circumstances.

[54] Ecclesiastical courts could grant divorce from bed and board, a legal separation which provided the wife with alimony, but prohibited remarriage.

NOTES TO MATILDA

[1] In Sophocles's *Oedipus at Colonus*, the three Furies or Eumenides inhabit a grove which the remorseful and blinded Oedipus must enter.

[2] Wordsworth, 'She Dwelt Among the Untrodden Ways', *Lyrical Ballads* (1800).

[3] Dante, *Purgatorio*, canto 28, line 42. Entering the garden of Eden, Dante paused at a stream and looked over at a lady (Matelda) who was singing and picking flowers 'with which her whole path was painted'. The original quotation has 'sua via'.

[4] Livy (d. AD 17), author of a history of the Roman Empire; Charles Rollin, author of *The Ancient History of the Egyptians, Carthaginians, Assyrians* (1730–38).

[5] Characters from Shakespeare's *As You Like It* and *The Tempest*, and from Milton's *Comus*.

[6] According to the *Scottish National Dictionary* (Edinburgh, 1968) 'rachan' is a Scots word for a plaid or wrap, traditionally worn by shepherds.

[7] The Seven Sleepers of Ephesus, early Christians who slept in a cave for several centuries, initially to avoid the persecutions of Decius. *Illusion; or the Trances of Nourjahad*, play by Samuel James Arnold, briefly attributed to Byron and performed in London in November 1813. It was based on Frances Sheridan's novella, *The History of Nourjahad* (1767) in which Nourjahad is tricked into believing he periodically sleeps through many decades.

[8] In Apuleius, the nymph Psyche lived in an enchanted palace but left it for various uncomfortable places in search of Cupid or through the will of Venus. She later tried to commit suicide by throwing herself into a river.

[9] Proserpine, daughter of Ceres, lived in the plains of Enna in Sicily from which she was abducted by Pluto to become queen of the underworld.

[10] Act I, scene 3, lines 237–40 of *The Captain*, a comedy by Beaumont and Fletcher. Later in the play Lelia tries to seduce her father, whom she does not recognize after a long absence but, when she learns his identity, she still desires him.

[11] I *Samuel* 23: 'And it came to pass, when the evil spirit from God was upon Saul, that David took an harp, and played with his hand: so Saul was refreshed, and was well, and the evil spirit departed from him.'

[12] A reference to Vittorio Alfieri, *Myrrha*, *Tragedies*, trans. Charles Lloyd (1815).

[13] According to Nitchie, Mary Shelley wrote 'Lord B's Ch^de Harold' in the margin

of 'The Fields of Fancy' after this phrase. The reference is to 'Child Harold', IV, 71–2 where Byron compares an iris by the cataract to 'Hope upon a death-bed' and 'Love watching Madness with unalterable mien'.

[14] Nitchie text reads 'days that he intended'.

[15] Spencer, *Faerie Queene*, Book II, vii, where Mammon leads Sir Guyon down to his house adjoining the gate of Hell to urge him to accept riches.

[16] Nitchie text reads 'to me to me, and . . .'

[17] Nitchie text reads 'one thing that which although . . .'

[18] Nitchie text reads 'upon *him* it . . .'

[19] Nitchie text reads 'closed as his . . .'

[20] Nitchie text reads 'At [As] first . . .'

[21] A reference to Boccaccio's *Decameron* 4th day, 1st story, in which Ghismonda sheds tears over the golden goblet containing the heart of Guiscardo. Mary Shelley had been reading the *Decameron* earlier in the year. She changes 'Ghismonda' to 'Sigismunda', the name in Dryden's *Fables*, a work to which Wollstonecraft refers in *Maria*.

[22] Dante, *Paradiso*, 'E quasi mi perdei con gli occhi chini': Beatrice looked at him with eyes so full of divine love that he turned away 'and almost lost myself, with downcast eyes'.

[23] The beautiful Anchises was loved by Venus who bore him a son Aeneas, founder of Rome. In the 6th book of the *Aeneid* Anchises is in the Elysian fields with his son.

[24] Nitchie text reads 'returned; with my terror . . .'

[25] Aegean island, one of the Cyclades, famous for its grotto full of stalactites and stalagmites.

[26] Hot, dry, sandy wind of African and Asian deserts.

[27] Job 17: 15–16.

[28] Coleridge, 'Fire, Famine and Slaughter', lines 17–18, Famine says 'Whisper it, sister! so & so! In a dark hint, soft & slow.'

[29] Constance, Prince Arthur's mother in Shakespeare's *King John*, spends most of the play grieving.

[30] A possible reference to Coleridge's 'The Rime of the Ancient Mariner', Part IV, ll. 284–5, where the Mariner, watching the water snakes, felt 'a spring of love' and 'blessed them unawares', so releasing the burden of the albatross from his neck.

[31] Nitchie text reads 'what were the . . .'

[32] Wordsworth's 'The Complaint of a Forsaken Indian Woman' in *Lyrical Ballads* (1798).

[33] cf. *Prometheus Unbound* I, 48 'the wingless, crawling hours'.

[34] Erasmus Darwin (1731–1802), physician, botanist and poet, was famous for his long scientific poem, *The Botanic Garden*, much ridiculed for the incongruity of its language and subject matter.

[35] The description is closer to the effect of Byron's poetry than to that of Shelley which was not popular in his lifetime.

[36] Nitchie text reads 'desolate health —'

[37] cf. Shelley in *Queen Mab*, *Prometheus Unbound* and Julian's speeches in *Julian and Maddalo*.

[38] Nitchie text reads 'former'.

[39] Nitchie text reads 'for that'.

[40] Dante, *Paradiso*, 1, 101–2: 'she turned her eyes towards me with the expression of a mother who looks at her delirious child'.

[41] Nitchie text reads 'I was; voluntarily . . .'

[42] Spencer, *Faerie Queene*, 1, 40. Despair is tempting Redcrosse to kill himself but Una snatches the knife from him and urges him not to 'let vaine words bewitch thy manly hart'.

[43] Nitchie text reads 'me and they'.

[44] Dante, *Purgatorio*, 28, 31–3: a description of the flowing water across which Dante sees Matelda picking flowers: 'dark, dark beneath the perpetual shade, which never lets sun or moon shine there'.

[45] Nitchie identifies this song as an anonymous one published in about 1800.

[46] Possibly a reference to Coleridge's 'Ancient Mariner' Part V where the rain follows a spiritual change.

[47] From Coleridge's 'Christabel' Part I, where the moon is prelude to the enchantment of Christabel.

[48] Drug made from foxglove leaves used to stimulate a failing heart.

[49] Wordsworth's 'A Slumber Did My Spirit Seal' from *Lyrical Ballads*, in which the poet experiences a death or inanimation.

[50] Nitchie text reads 'child even even in . . .'

[51] Nitchie text reads 'longer the . . .'

[52] Nitchie text reads 'terrible an object . . .'

[53] Isaiah 11:7.

CHRONOLOGY

1759 *27 April*: Mary Wollstonecraft (MW) born in London to John Edward Wollstonecraft and Elizabeth Dickson. She is the second of six children.

1768 Family moves to farm in Beverley in Yorkshire.

1770 William Wordsworth born.

1772 Samuel Taylor Coleridge born.

1775 Family moves to Hoxton near London and MW meets Frances (Fanny) Blood, who becomes her closest friend.

1776 Family moves to Laugharne, a small town in Wales by the sea.

1777 Family returns to London and MW resumes friendship with Fanny Blood.

1779 MW moves to Bath to take up a position as companion to rich widow, Mrs Dawson.

1782 MW returns to London to nurse dying mother. Eliza, MW's sister, marries Meredith Bishop. MW moves in with Fanny Blood.

1783 After birth of daughter, Eliza leaves her husband (with MW's help).

1784 MW, Fanny and Eliza open school in Islington. MW's other sister, Everina, joins them. MW meets Dr Richard Price and other liberal Dissenters.

1785 MW goes to Portugal to nurse Fanny, who dies in childbirth. On return to London, MW closes school, which was losing students.

1786 MW meets liberal publisher and bookseller Joseph Johnson. MW writes first work, *Thoughts on the Education of Daughters*. She moves to Ireland to work as governess to daughters of Viscount and Viscountess Kingsborough.

1787 MW writes first novel, *Mary, A Fiction*. She leaves Kingsboroughs and sets up as writer and editorial assistant to Joseph Johnson.

1788 Lord Byron born. George III becomes insane but recovers by the following March.

1789 *July*: Fall of Bastille.

Johnson publishes MW's *The Female Reader*.

1790 MW writes *A Vindication of the Rights of Men* in response to Edmund Burke's *Reflections on the Revolution in France*.

1791 MW becomes infatuated with the artist Henry Fuseli. She begins work on *A Vindication of the Rights of Woman*.

1792 *A Vindication of the Rights of Woman* published. Percy Bysshe Shelley born. MW goes to France.

1793 MW meets Gilbert Imlay, an American speculator and trader. MW moves to the nearby village of Neuilly for safety during the Terror. After war breaks out between Britain and France, MW, although unmarried, is registered as Imlay's wife at the American Embassy to gain protection as American citizen. William Godwin's *Enquiry Concerning Political Justice* published in London. Imlay travels to Le Havre on business.

1794 MW joins Imlay in Le Havre.

14 May: gives birth to daughter, Fanny.

Godwin's *Things as They Are, or, The Adventures of Caleb Williams* published in London. Imlay returns to Paris and MW and Fanny follow. Imlay leaves for London. MW's *An Historical and Moral View of the Origin and Progress of the French Revolution* published in London.

1795 John Keats born. MW and Fanny follow Imlay to London. MW suspects Imlay's infidelity and attempts suicide. MW travels to Scandinavia on business, on Imlay's behalf, taking Fanny and her maid with her. They return to London. Discovering that Imlay is living with another woman, MW attempts suicide by jumping off Putney Bridge.

1796 *Letters Written During a Short Residence in Sweden, Norway, and Denmark* is published. MW begins relationship with the radical philosopher and novelist William Godwin.

1797 *29 March*: MW marries William Godwin in London.

30 August: She gives birth to a daughter, Mary Godwin (referred to throughout Chronology as MS).

10 September: MW dies of septicaemia. Godwin is left to look after both Fanny and baby Mary.

1798 Godwin publishes *Memoirs of the Author of a Vindication of the Rights of Woman* and MW's *Posthumous Works* including *Maria* and MW's love letters to Imlay.

1799 Godwin publishes his novel *St Leon*, which contains a portrait of Wollstonecraft.

November: Napoleon Bonaparte becomes first consul of France.

1801 *21 December*: Godwin marries Mary Jane Clairmont.

Her seven-year-old son Charles and four-year-old daughter Jane (Claire) come to live with MS and Fanny Imlay.

1803 Godwin's son William born.

1804 *May*: Napoleon proclaimed emperor of France.

1805 *21 October*: British navy under Admiral Horatio Nelson defeat combined French and Spanish fleet at Trafalgar.

1807 Family moves to Skinner Street, Holborn. There they continue their unprofitable bookselling business.

1811 *5 February*: Prince of Wales becomes Regent following George III's insanity.

1812 Percy Bysshe Shelley (PBS), an admirer of Godwin's ideas, becomes a frequent visitor at Skinner Street house. MS is at first absent on visit to Scotland, but possibly meets PBS and his wife, Harriet, briefly in November.

1814 MS begins relationship with PBS.

11 April: Napoleon abdicates and is exiled to Elba.

July: MS and PBS elope to France, taking Claire Clairmont with them, and return to England in September.

November: Harriet Shelley gives birth to second child.

1815 *February*: MS gives birth to daughter; the premature baby dies a few days later.

MS and PBS settle in Windsor.

20 March: Napoleon's 'Hundred Day' rule begins.

18 June: Wellington's armies defeat Napoleon at Waterloo.

1816 *January*: MS gives birth to son, William.

Claire meets and has affair with poet Byron.

May: The Shelley party – along with Claire – goes to Geneva. They take up residence near Byron at Montalègre, near Cologny.

June: MS starts to write *Frankenstein*.

September: MS and PBS accompany a pregnant Claire back to Bath, England.

9 October: Fanny Imlay commits suicide with overdose.

December: Harriet Shelley drowns herself.

30 December MS and PBS marry.

1817 *January*: Claire gives birth to daughter, Allegra.

The Shelleys, along with Claire and Allegra, move to Albion House in Marlow, Buckinghamshire.

May: MS completes *Frankenstein*.

September: MS gives birth to daughter, Clara.

November: MS's *History of a Six Weeks' Tour* published.

1818 *January*: *Frankenstein* published.

March: The Shelley family, along with Claire and Allegra, travel to Italy, where they visit Byron.

September: MS and PBS's daughter Clara dies.

1819 *June*: Their son William dies and MS sinks into depression.

She writes *Matilda*, not published until long after her death.

November: MS gives birth to son, Percy Florence.

1820 *January*: George III dies.

MS begins work on novel, *Castruccio* (later re-titled *Valperga*).

October: Claire leaves the Shelley household.

1821 Keats dies. MS sends *Castruccio* to London for publication.

1822 The Shelleys settle at Casa Magni, in Lerici, Italy, with Claire, and Edward and Jane Williams.

April: Claire's daughter Allegra dies.

June: MS has miscarriage and for a while is dangerously ill.

July: Shelley and Edward Williams sail to Leghorn to meet Leigh Hunt; they are drowned on return journey.

MS joins Byron and the Hunts in Genoa.

1823 *February*: *Valperga* published.

    August: MS returns to London.

1824 MS begins work on *The Last Man*. Byron dies in Greece.

1826 *February*: *The Last Man* published.

1830 *The Fortunes of Perkin Warbeck* published.

1834 Coleridge dies.

1836 *7 April*: William Godwin dies.

1837 MS's final novel, *Falkner*, published.

1839 MS publishes a four-volume edition of PBS's *Poetical Works* and a volume of his *Essays, Letters and Translations*. She becomes ill, and never fully recovers her health.

1840 MS tours Europe with her son, Percy Florence, and his friends.

1844 *Rambles in Germany and Italy*, based on MS's travels with Percy Florence, is published.

1850 Wordsworth dies.

1851 *1 February*: MS dies.